Horizontal Living

Also by Ray Green
Buyout – A Roy Groves Thriller (1)

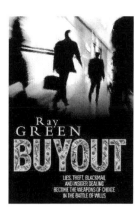

For five ordinary guys and one rather extraordinary woman, the only escape from the corporate rat-race is to buy the company they're working for: take it all to a new level, save hundreds of jobs and make some serious money.

But it quickly becomes clear that nothing is as easy as it seems. The bid is quickly undercut as twisted corporate politics and personal vendettas take over.

When the buyout becomes *all or nothing* for the management buyout team, it all spins out of control: marriages fall apart, lurid secrets are discovered, life savings are spent on the stock market, illegal insider dealing becomes a matter of fact and blackmail, theft, betrayal and manipulation are the new rules of the game.

A once-in-a-life-time opportunity turns into a lurid nightmare.

BUYOUT is a gripping and compulsive page-turner about the power of money to unveil the deepest in human nature. It's also a story about chasing one extraordinary dream. At an extraordinary price.

Also by Ray Green
Payback – A Roy Groves Thriller (2)

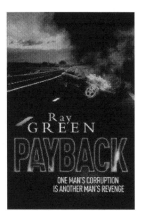

Roy Groves is Operations Director of a successful company manufacturing dashboard instruments for luxury cars.

A fatal motorway fire is traced back to a fault in the product supplied by Roy's company. Was it a tragic accident or something more sinister? As Roy and his colleagues battle to establish the cause of the fire, and save the company from bankruptcy, they discover that they have been the victims of sabotage.

Eventually, it emerges that an old enemy of Roy and the rest of the team has reappeared and is intent on destroying the company and every member of its management team. Once just a business adversary, their nemesis is now so consumed with hatred that he is on the edge of insanity; he resorts to blackmail and even murder in the pursuit of his goal.

PAYBACK is a chilling tale of how hatred can twist and corrupt the human soul.

Also by Ray Green
Chinese Whispers – A Roy Groves Thriller (3)

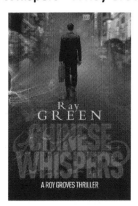

Chuck Kabel is on a business trip to China, visiting the factory to which his UK-based company subcontracts the manufacture of its products. He unexpectedly collapses and dies at the airport before he is able to report on his visit. When the Chinese authorities are evasive about the exact cause of death, the suspicions of his boss, Roy Groves, are raised.

Roy decides to investigate further; it soon becomes clear that there are serious financial irregularities within the Chinese company, and that dark forces are in play, intent on ensuring that these do not come to light. When Roy edges closer to uncovering the truth, he is warned off but refuses to back down, unaware that he is about to confront the Chinese Mafia, who will stop at nothing to achieve their objectives.

When his own family are targeted by his opponents, Roy embarks on a desperate battle to protect them, now well aware that if he should turn to the police their lives will be in even greater danger.

CHINESE WHISPERS is a frightening tale of organised crime and the way in which it uses and abuses legitimate business for its own illegal purposes, relentlessly destroying the lives of anyone who stands in the way.

Horizontal Living

A Tale of Expats Abroad

By Ray Green

Published in Great Britain by Mainsail Books in 2016
First Edition
Copyright @ Ray Green, 2016

ISBN 978-0-9575138-0-8

www.mainsailbooks.co.uk

Chapter 1

The room was packed solid: around thirty people crammed into a space perhaps fifteen feet by twenty, sitting shoulder-to-shoulder on rows of cheap-looking, white, moulded-plastic garden chairs. We were all facing towards a row of tables at the end of the room, behind which those officiating at the meeting would eventually take their seats. The various pockets of conversation in the room blended to make a noisy, but unintelligible buzz. As I looked around, I could see many of those present fanning themselves with copies of the agenda in an effort to alleviate the oppressive heat.

'Why on earth are they holding the meeting in this tiny room?' said Donna, cupping her hand around my ear and speaking directly into it in order to cut through the cacophony.

Donna is my wife. The meeting coincided with her fifty-second birthday, but she looked much younger, with her hardly-lined face, still-trim figure, and dark-blonde hair. This wasn't actually her preferred way to spend her birthday, but I'd promised to take her out for a nice romantic dinner that evening as compensation.

'Beats me,' I declared. 'I gather they normally hold them at a local hotel. No doubt we'll be told when this wretched meeting actually gets started.'

I looked at my watch: 10.25 a.m. We had already been sitting there for thirty minutes, having been under the mistaken understanding that the meeting was due to start at 10.00 a.m. The guy sitting to my right, who had only just arrived, cheerfully informed me that 10.00 a.m. was only the 'first call'.

'These meetings never start until the second call,' he said, 'because there are never enough people for a quorum at the time of the first call.'

Shame that no-one had told us that before we wasted half an hour getting increasingly hot and irritated.

1

Before going any further, I should probably explain who I am, and what I was doing on that Friday morning waiting for this godforsaken meeting to start.

My name is Roy Groves. My former career was in business, and it was one hell of a rollercoaster ride: over the years I had had to battle corporate politics and deception, fierce personal rivalries, and even vicious criminals. Fortunately, though, I was able to retire early, having made a bit of money floating my last company on the London Stock Exchange.

Having found myself in the enviable situation of having money in the bank and time on my hands, I bought an apartment in Spain, on the Costa del Sol. It's one of seventy-five in a pretty upmarket development, rather grandly named *Las Hermosas Vistas,* in the area known as Nueva Andalucía, near Marbella. Donna and I were now spending most of our time there, especially in the winter months when the weather in the UK is so awful.

So what does this have to do with our being crammed shoulder-to-shoulder with a lot of other sweaty, disgruntled people in that tiny room? Well, we were waiting for an extraordinary general meeting of the community of owners to start. For some reason, they had chosen to hold it in the woefully inadequate setting of the security guards' office near the front gate of the development.

We had never previously attended one of these owners' meetings, but had been persuaded by our neighbour, Neil, that we should attend this one, which had been convened specifically to discuss the community's financial situation. The community, Neil had told us, was in deep financial difficulties and as we, like other owners, were paying a considerable amount of money in fees every quarter, we really should find out where our money had gone. So there we sat, impatiently waiting for something to happen.

At precisely 10.30 a.m. there was a sound of scuffling and scraping behind me as some people entered the room and endeavoured to fight their way through the tightly packed chairs. After a considerable amount of pushing and shoving, the newly-arrived delegation made their way to the front of the room and took their seats at the top table.

I only recognised one of them. Jim Watkins was president of the community. Apparently every community like ours has to elect one of the owners as president – to represent all the other owners, look after their interests, and chair meetings like this one. Jim was a rather short man, probably in his seventies, with wayward white hair which curled over his collar. He was smartly dressed in a navy blue suit, white shirt, and grey tie, his black shoes polished to a glistening sheen. The whole ensemble looked strangely incongruous when most of us were clad in shorts and T-shirts.

Jim sat in the centre chair and the other two men who had come with him sat either side of him. Finally, a rather attractive olive-skinned girl sat down on the end chair, completing the line-up at the top table. There followed a few seconds of paper-shuffling and throat-clearing before Jim opened the meeting. He introduced the man on his right as administrator of the community, and the man on his left as official translator. Gema, the girl on the end seat, would take minutes; she smiled and nodded in acknowledgement of the introduction.

Just as I was expecting the meeting finally to get underway, the translator guy cleared his throat and repeated all the introductions in Spanish. Now this, to me, seemed a particularly pointless exercise since, to the best of my knowledge, there wasn't a single Spaniard in the audience. We were mostly Brits, with some Germans, a few Dutch, some Belgians, and a couple of French. The common denominator language was English. Anyway, as a newcomer to such meetings, I kept my mouth shut.

Once the lengthy introductions had been completed, Jim finally got to the meat of the matter.

'I have called this meeting in response to certain owners having expressed concern about the community's financial status.' He donned his spectacles, which had been hanging suspended from a cord around his neck. 'If you look at the agenda, you will see that item one is "Current financial situation and ideas to improve it". I think most of you are aware that our financial situation is not too healthy and I have already taken certain steps aimed at saving money.' He looked up and peered over the top of his reading glasses. 'For example, by holding this meeting here, rather than at the *Estrella de Andalucía* hotel, we have saved three hundred euros. I have used some of that saving to invest in these white chairs on which you are all seated. At just six euros each they represent outstanding value for money and a sound investment. They can be stacked for storage, ready to be used again and again for future meetings, saving much more money going forward.'

He nodded to the translator who went through the painful process of repeating everything in Spanish. When the other man had finished, Jim removed his spectacles; placed both elbows on the table; and interlinked his fingers, forming a bridge.

'Now,' he said, panning his gaze around the room, 'having started the ball rolling I'd like to—'

'AARGH!' The anguished scream was accompanied by what sounded like a gunshot, and someone in the front row abruptly disappeared from my view, dropping like a stone. There was a loud, collective gasp as everyone instinctively ducked, and then several seconds of dead silence, before heads were raised and people craned their necks to see what had happened. There was no obvious sign of a crazed gunman running amok.

Two or three people in the front row bent down; when they stood up a couple of seconds later they were helping an elderly gentleman to his feet. I recognised him as Klaus Schmidt – an amiable German guy who could often be seen taking a slow walk around the urbanisation with the aid of his trusty walking stick. One of his helpers passed him his stick, upon which he leaned heavily as he tried to catch his breath. There was no sign of blood that I could see. Next, one of the others alongside him held aloft a white, plastic chair with just three legs; the other had snapped clean off. Evidently this was the source of the pistol-crack sound. There was an audible sigh of relief which rippled around the room as someone rushed to get Klaus another chair.

By now, Jim Watkins had recovered from his shock and surprise. 'Mr Schmidt, are you OK?'

'Ja, ja ... just a little shaken. No need for fuss ... please carry on.'

Jim cleared his throat. 'Well, I'm sure we are all most relieved that you are not hurt. Now then, where was I? Ah yes ... now, I've mentioned a few cost-saving measures which I have already initiated, but in the interests of a truly collaborative approach I'd like to invite suggestions from the floor.'

An immaculately-groomed, middle-aged, blonde lady put up her hand.

'Yes, Clare.'

She spoke with a soft Irish accent. 'I think we should clamp down on the security guards' use of the community telephone for making private calls. I'm sure they're making calls home to Nigeria or Zambia or wherever it is.'

'Very good suggestion, Clare.' He nodded to the minute-taker. 'Please make a note, Gema.'

Another hand went up. 'Let's cut down on the amount we spend on the gardens. We can live with them being a bit more untidy.'

'No we can't,' protested someone else. 'They're already a disgrace.'

A forest of hands went up, but already any pretence of an orderly discussion had disappeared, as the meeting rapidly descended into a multilingual shouting match. Jim had, however, come prepared: he grabbed the auctioneer's gavel which lay on the table in front of him, banging it down repeatedly until an uneasy silence was restored.

'Please, please ... ladies and gentleman ... we must conduct this meeting in a manner which—'

'EUURGH!' The scream from behind me was accompanied by a pistol-crack noise, followed by a loud clattering sound. I swivelled around to see a middle-aged lady in the row behind sprawled on the floor, her feet pointing skyward, her lacy knickers and dimpled thighs on show for all to see. *Hmm, some bargain these cheap chairs turned out to be,* I thought.

I stood up and stepped towards her, helping her to her feet. 'Oh dear, Mrs Denby ... I didn't quite recognise you from that angle. Are you OK?'

She glared at me, shaking her arm free from my helping hand. 'Yes, I'm fine thank you very much,' she snapped – rather ungratefully I felt. To be fair, I suppose I could have phrased my remark a little more tactfully.

She retreated to the back row, muttering under her breath. I turned around and lowered myself – now rather warily – back into my chair, trying to ease my weight downward as gently as possible.

'Is everything OK at the back there?' enquired the chairman.

'Yes,' replied Mrs Denby, somewhat huffily, 'no thanks to you and your crappy bargain chairs.'

Jim coloured up. 'Well ... er ... glad no harm has been done. Now then, perhaps we can continue to take suggestions from the floor.' Several hands went up.

Jim pointed towards the owner of one of the raised hands. 'Yes, John ... go ahead.'

'Let's get rid of one of the cleaners – it's no big deal if the place doesn't get cleaned quite as often, and—'

'What?' interrupted another man. 'Have you seen the amount of dog shit which has accumulated down by the swimming pool? It's disgusting.'

'And another thing—' weighed in a very large lady seated in the front row, before she was cut off by the furious hammering of Jim's gavel. The bemused translator glanced nervously at Jim, evidently unsure whether he should make some attempt to untangle this unseemly wrangle. Jim shook his head.

'Ladies and Gentlemen ... please can we have just one person at a time speaking?' he pleaded. A subdued murmur went round the disgruntled audience before silence descended once more. Jim nodded slowly, sweeping his gaze around the room, ready to pounce on anyone else who stepped out of line.

I'd had enough of this nonsense – I decided to raise my hand. Jim pointed in my direction.

'Yes, Mr ... er ... '

'Roy Groves, 14E.'

'Yes, of course. Please go ahead.'

'Well, it seems to me that if we are to make any headway here, we need a clear idea of the scale of the problem so that we can come up with appropriate suggestions for increasing income or saving on expenditure.'

'Quite so,' nodded Jim, sagely. I waited for him to elaborate, but he didn't.

'So, what is it?' I prompted.

'What's what?'

'The scale of the problem.'

'Er ... substantial,' he replied.

'So do you have some papers we could look at? Perhaps a profit and loss account ... and a balance sheet?'

Jim looked aghast at such a radical suggestion. 'Well, not here ... but I'm sure we could send you something after the meeting.'

'Can you at least tell us how much money we have in the bank?'

'You can't expect me to go around with that kind of detail in my head,' he replied, rather grumpily.

This wasn't going well; I decided to try another tack. 'Is it true that our own staff – the maintenance guy, the security guards, and the cleaners – haven't been paid for the last two months?'

'It's not that they aren't *going* to be paid,' he responded, 'it's just that they haven't been paid *yet.*'

'Why not?'

'Because we don't have enough money in the bank.'

I sighed, despairing at this circular discussion.

'But you just said you didn't know how much we had in the bank.'

'Well, not the exact amount … but, well ... not enough. Look, they'll be paid just as soon as we get through this temporary dip in our cash flow.'

It was clear that this conversation was going nowhere; I decided to leave it for now and explore one of the other disturbing things which I had heard recently – not that I was terribly optimistic of getting a clear explanation.

'I've been told that our contract with the gardening company has been terminated. Is that true?'

'Yes,' replied Jim, tersely.

'And why is that?' I asked, with a sinking feeling in my gut.

'They were being unreasonable about payment terms.'

That looked like all the answer I was going to get.

'I guess they haven't been paid for the same reason as our own staff then?' I prompted.

'I merely asked them to bear with us for a few months, but they became unreasonable and aggressive.'

'So you cancelled their contract?'

'No, they cancelled it,' Jim snapped back at me. I got the distinct impression that he wasn't entirely happy with my line of questioning.

'So do we still owe them money?'

The pencil with which Jim had been fiddling snapped in half as he inadvertently applied too much bending force. He slammed the broken pieces down on the table and swept them to one side.

'I've told them that they'll be paid in due course.'

Oh, Christ, this situation was even worse than I had imagined. I paused for a moment, gathering my thoughts as I tried to think of a way to move things forward without pissing Jim off any more than I already had. The pause was enough to encourage a torrent of questions from others at the meeting.

'Well what are we going to do about the gardens then?'

'So where's all our money gone?'

'What about that bitch in 5A … Houdini or Ruwadi or whatever her bloody name is? I've heard she hasn't paid her fees in the last—'

'EEEK!' The scream was accompanied by the now-familiar pistol-crack of a collapsing chair, instantly silencing the baying mob. Jesus, you couldn't make this stuff up.

As several people rushed to the aid of the latest hapless victim, I glanced across at Donna, who was clearly trying desperately to avoid collapsing into an unseemly and inappropriate fit of laughter. Her hands were clamped over her mouth and tears sprang from the corners of her eyes, which she had screwed tightly shut.

'That's it!' yelled a sturdily-built guy with dyed-blonde hair, a bull neck, and heavily-muscled, tattooed arms which threatened to burst the sleeves of his T-shirt. 'I'm outta here before I land on me arse and break me fookin' back!'

It was a sentiment which, although rather crudely expressed, was apparently shared by many of the others present. All around the room people began scrambling noisily to their feet, pushing and shoving each other in their efforts to reach the door. Donna and I stood to one side to let the human torrent stream past, amid a buzz of angry muttering. Within a minute or two the room was empty apart from me, Donna, and the bemused-looking contingent sitting at the top table. I walked up to have a word with Jim.

Before I could open my mouth, Jim gave his assessment of the meeting. 'That was a lively discussion wasn't it?'

'Er … well, yes …'

'I always like to get as many owners as possible involved in community matters.'

'Well, yes… that's a very good idea, but …'

'Shame about those chairs though. I'm going to have words with the manager at Hypermercado.'

'Hypermercado?'

'The supermarket where we bought them … I'm going to demand a full refund.'

'Yes, quite so. Look, Jim, when can you get me copies of the financial statements I requested?'

His eyes narrowed. 'Why do you want them?'

I grabbed one of the plastic chairs from the front row, pulled it towards me and, with some trepidation, lowered myself very gently into it so as to sit opposite Jim.

'Well,' I said, in my most reasonable tone, 'I'd like to better understand our financial situation. Maybe I can help.'

'Help? Are you going to donate some money then?' he asked, his eyes widening as he leaned forward.

'No, not that sort of help. I mean maybe I can help with some suggestions for a plan to improve the situation.'

The hopeful expression on Jim's face evaporated in an instant, to be replaced by a barely-disguised scowl. 'Very kind I'm sure, but I am well capable of managing our finances, ably assisted by our administrator here.' He nodded towards the man on his right, who in turn gave a little nod, but said nothing.

By now, I could feel my hackles rising; I took a moment to breathe deeply before replying. 'I'm sure that's the case, but I'd still like to see copies of the financial statements.'

'Hmm,' he grumbled.

'So are you going to let me have them, or not?'

He shifted position in his chair so as to sit as upright as possible, clearing his throat before proclaiming, 'Naturally, any owner has the right to see the financial statements.'

I relaxed a little. 'OK, thank you.' I reached for a pen and pad of paper which were lying on the table. 'Perhaps you can email them to me … here's my email address.'

I slid the slip of paper across the table before levering myself – as carefully as possible – out of the chair and rising to my feet.

Jim extended his hand. 'Well, very nice to meet you … er, Roy, is it?' I nodded as I shook his hand. 'It's always nice to get new people along to these meetings … I do like a truly inclusive discussion.'

Apparently, even if said inclusive discussion achieves precisely nothing, I thought. Lost for a suitable reply which would not cause offence I just nodded, before turning to face Donna, who was now rising to her feet from a front-row chair.

When we had left the room and walked a few yards away, Donna turned to me, her expression bemused. 'I'm really not sure whether to laugh or cry,' she said.

'I'm tending towards the latter,' I replied, but chuckled in spite of myself.

'Well, perhaps things will be clearer once you've seen the accounts,' she suggested.

'Hmm … perhaps,' I said. Somehow I wasn't too convinced.

Chapter 2

A couple of days had passed since the ill-fated community meeting. We had been invited to a dinner party with our neighbours and good friends, Neil and Marion. Normally, at this time of year, we would have sat outside on the terrace to enjoy a warm, early-summer evening, but tonight we were experiencing one of those torrential downpours which can hit the Costa del Sol occasionally. The wind and rain battered the glass patio doors, causing them to flex and rattle alarmingly. Marion got up to close the curtains, even though it was still quite light outside.

'Would anyone like some more dessert?' she enquired when she returned to the table.

'Not for me,' I replied, running my hands across my stomach, which had undeniably expanded somewhat since I had retired.

'Me neither,' said Donna, smiling.

'Paul ... Kate?'

Paul MacPhearson and his wife Kate were the other two guests. They, too, were close neighbours, but for whatever reason, Donna and I had never socialised with them before. It turned out that in spite of his surname – clearly he had some Scottish ancestry – there was no trace of an accent in Paul's deep, commanding voice. It turned out that he, like me, was a retired businessman, and we had much in common. Donna really seemed to hit it off with Kate too.

Paul and Kate also declined further helpings of the – admittedly delicious – trifle which Marion had made. Marion went off to make some coffee.

So far, the subject of the community meeting had not been discussed, but I knew it was coming. Neil had been the one to alert us to the perilous state of the community's finances and had persuaded us to attend the meeting. He had also expressed a lack of confidence in Jim Watkins's ability as president, and the competence of the administration company. I somehow knew that tonight wasn't just a social occasion. It was a pound to a penny – or, I suppose, a euro to a cent – that the wily old devil had something else up his sleeve.

'So,' said Neil, placing his elbows on the table, leaning his head forward, and running his fingers back through the thin strips of grey hair either side of his shining, bald pate – *ah, here it comes,* I thought, 'did you get that copy of the community accounts which you asked for?'

'Yes,' I sighed, 'but it's almost incomprehensible. The administrators don't do a profit and loss account separately from a balance sheet in the way that I'm used to. Instead they jumble together income, expenditure, assets, and liabilities all on one document. I have, in the past, run a two-hundred-million-pound company, whose accounts I could understand perfectly, but I can't make head nor tail of this nonsense, even though the entire budget is only about half a million euros.' Neil nodded.

At this point, Marion returned with the coffee, so we put the conversation about the accounts on hold for a few moments while she poured. Once everyone was settled with their coffee, Neil continued.

'What about cash flow then? Did you manage to get any useful insight on that?'

I shook my head. 'No, not really. Look Neil, you're an accountant—'

'*Retired* accountant,' he said.

'Well, OK ... but you know better than most how to interpret financial statements; why don't you take a look and see if you can fathom it?'

Neil smiled that enigmatic smile of his. 'I already have.'

'You've already seen the accounts?'

He nodded. 'Yes, I persuaded Jim to get me a copy a couple of weeks ago. You're right – they are rather opaque.'

'Well you might have said ...'

'I wanted you to see for yourself.'

Why, the cunning old dog.

'Well, now I have,' I said, 'so where do we go from here?'

'Well,' said Neil, 'although the accounts aren't terribly clear, it's pretty obvious that we're in a dire financial situation.' I nodded miserably. 'And to be honest I don't think Jim has much of a clue what to do about it. He means well, but he just doesn't have the skills to deal with this situation.'

'The administrator guy didn't seem much help either, did he?' observed Kate. 'He hardly said a word throughout the entire meeting.'

Paul, who had said little so far, summarised. 'So we're out of cash, we haven't paid our staff or suppliers for the last couple of months, we don't have a comprehensible set of financial accounts, and neither the president nor the administrator appear to be able to get a hold of the situation.'

Everyone fell silent for a few seconds as they digested this rather depressing assessment.

Donna broke the silence with the question which begged to be answered. 'So what's the solution?'

It was Marion who enunciated the inescapable conclusion which, by now, I think we were all reaching. 'I can't see us digging ourselves out of the hole we're in without a new president and a new administrator – people with the business, management, and financial skills to understand what's going on and figure out what to do.'

I now felt a creeping, sinking feeling in my stomach; I knew exactly where this conversation was going. *Oh well, might as well get to the nub of the issue, I suppose.*

'Did you have someone in mind?'

'Neil and I have talked it over,' replied Marion, 'and with your business background, Roy, we can't think of anyone better-qualified to take over as president.'

'Well, what about Paul here? He's just as well-qualified as me.'

As I turned to make eye contact with Paul, he gave a rueful half-smile. 'Actually, Neil's already sounded me out, but with my commitments back in the UK I can't really spend more than about twenty percent of my time out here. Neil tells me you're here most of the time these days.'

'But—' I protested.

'And,' added Paul, 'I gather your Spanish is coming along pretty well; I can't speak a word.'

Pretty well? I thought. *I can just about order a bottle of wine and a gambas pil-pil, but that's about it.*

'But—' I spluttered, once more.

Paul held up his hand in a conciliatory gesture. 'Look Roy, Neil's already filled me in on the problems we are facing, and explained why he thinks that you and I are the most suitable people in the urbanisation to sort them out. I really don't think I can take on the role of president, but if you'd be prepared do it, I'd be happy to act as vice president to back you up and act as a sounding board to bounce ideas off.'

He sounded so damned reasonable that it would have seemed churlish to reject the idea out of hand.

As I struggled to frame a response, Marion added her two pennyworth. 'No need to decide right now, Roy – take a little time to think it over and discuss it with Donna.'

I turned to Donna and looked at her enquiringly; she gave a little nod.

'OK,' I said, somewhat doubtfully, 'I'll think about it.'

Neil made his final bid to seal the deal. 'That's great Roy, because I really can't think of anyone else who'd be able to do it.'

So there it was: I'd been cajoled, flattered, outmanoeuvred, and finally trussed up like a chicken – all in the nicest possible way, of course.

Chapter 3

I was sitting on the terrace, nursing a glass of chilled white *Rioja* as I turned over in my mind the previous evening's conversation. Donna and I had discussed it over breakfast, and she seemed relaxed about it either way, so it was pretty much up to me to decide whether to take on this task. Now she had gone out shopping, so I was left to my own devices for a few hours.

I chuckled inwardly as I reflected on how Neil had engineered the whole situation to inveigle me into his little plan. I couldn't feel any ill-will towards him though – Neil was such a nice guy, and I knew he had the best interests of the community at heart.

I considered the likely magnitude of the task. Although things were clearly in a bit of a mess, it was hardly on the scale of problems I had dealt with in my business career. It was also true, as Paul had mentioned the previous day, that Donna and I were now spending most of our time in Spain. We had two daughters, Beatrice and Raquel, back in the UK, but they were both married, with children of their own. They had their own busy lives to lead, and didn't need us hanging around all the time. We would take a trip back to England a few times a year, to see them and the grandchildren, but otherwise we spent most of our time in Spain.

If I were to take on this task, though, there were some practical issues to consider, which we hadn't discussed at all the previous evening. For example, how does one actually go about replacing an incumbent president, particularly if he is not keen to be replaced? Then again, Jim might be happy to relinquish control if he felt he was sinking in the mire of the problems surrounding him. Who knows? And what about the administrator? We had all agreed that he, too, needed to be replaced, so how would we find a better one, and what was the mechanism for replacing the existing one?

I took a sip of my wine, swirling it around my mouth, savouring the flavour before letting it slip down my throat.

Clearly some further discussion with Neil and Paul was going to be necessary to air these issues but, on balance, I was leaning towards taking this thing on – after all it couldn't be *that* difficult, could it?

I picked up my glass, stood up, and made my way over to the low wall which edged the terrace, leaning both elbows on it as I took in the view. Ah yes – the view: it was one of the main things that had sold us on this particular apartment. The urbanisation was situated in an elevated position in the foothills of the mountains which line the Costa del Sol just a few miles inland. The seventy-five apartments were arranged into fifteen separate blocks of five. Each block had two apartments on the ground floor; two on the first floor; and finally a larger, two-story penthouse, occupying the second and third floors.

Our apartment was one of these penthouses which, from the upper terrace, enjoyed almost three-hundred-and-sixty-degree views. From where I was currently standing I could look down upon the communal swimming pool and gardens. It was pretty quiet that morning: just two bathers describing leisurely circuits around the kidney-shaped pool and a couple stretched out on sunbeds, reading, while their toddler played happily in the nearby sand-pit. As I looked beyond the gardens I could see over the top of an extensive vista of trees – punctuated by the terracotta tiled roofs of numerous villas and apartment complexes – to the sparkling blue waters of the Mediterranean some three miles distant. I never tired of gazing out over this varied and captivating view.

It was only just past midday, but already the temperature was climbing rapidly; I felt a prickle of perspiration at my temples. It was clearly going to be scorching hot by mid-afternoon. I took another sip of my wine and ambled round to the adjacent side wall of the terrace where the view was totally different. Far below, in the valley alongside, was a large lake, its waters lapping the dam which had formed it. I could hear the steady, gentle sound of rushing water emanating from the overflow channels at either side of the dam. Beyond the lake rose a steep, densely-wooded hillside which, at the higher levels gave way to a rocky mountainside which rose inexorably to a distinctively-shaped summit resembling the head of a sleeping bear. There was a subdued sploshing sound which drew my gaze back down to the lake, where a lone angler had just cast his lead weight and was busy tightening his line and settling his rod into its rest.

I turned to face towards the third aspect of the panoramic view, one hundred and eighty degrees opposed to the sea view, when ... whoa! My gaze never got as far as the green hillside which lay in this direction.

Now, at this point, I should explain that, due to the slope upon which the urbanisation is built, the height of each apartment block is staggered in relation to the one adjoining it. As a result, our upper terrace – we lived in block fourteen – overlooked the upper terrace of the penthouse of block fifteen next door. At the time, this penthouse was not owner-occupied like ours, but was rented to various tenants. We had seen four or five tenants come and go in the time during which we had owned our apartment but, for the last few weeks, the apartment had appeared to be unoccupied.

So what was it that had stopped me in my tracks? It was the sight of two magnificent breasts, glistening with a light sheen of sun-tan oil, nipples proudly protruding. Their owner was lounging on a sunbed engrossed in a book. Her long, dark hair was pulled back in a ponytail beneath a wide-brimmed, floppy hat. The huge black-framed sunglasses which covered her eyes could not disguise her striking beauty: finely-defined cheekbones; delicately-shaped nose; and full, sensuous lips. My gaze wandered – seemingly without any conscious control on my part – back to those perfect breasts and then over a washboard-flat stomach to the tiny triangular scrap of shiny purple fabric which adorned her pubic area. My eyes roamed down her long, slim, shapely legs to the tips of her toes, nails painted in a shade similar to that of the glossy fabric of her bikini briefs. *Crikey – what a stunner!*

As my gaze finally made its way back to her face, I was mortified to find that she was looking straight at me.

'Oh ... I, uh, sorry,' I stammered, 'I ...' It then occurred to me that she probably wasn't English – certainly the dark, sultry complexion looked more Mediterranean than Manchester. 'Uh ... *habla Inglés?*'

Her face broke into a broad smile, displaying a perfect set of dazzling white teeth. When she spoke, the honeyed tones were unmistakeably French. 'No problem, Monsieur. You can speak to me in English.'

'I'm sorry ... I didn't realise you were there. I was just looking over towards ... I mean I wouldn't have ...'

'Of course ... how could you know zat I had moved in?'

She laid down her book and swung her long, slim legs over to one side of the sunbed, rising gracefully to her feet. *Heavens, when did such a slim body come equipped with a pair of boobs like that?* I guessed that it probably didn't, originally.

She moved unhurriedly towards a patio chair and took from it a thin robe into which she slipped effortlessly, tying the cord around her waist before walking towards me. She moved with the kind of feline walk adopted by catwalk models: feet placed one directly in front of the other and hips swaying conspicuously from side to side.

'I am Angelique, your new neighbour. Pleased to meet you.'

'Er, Roy ... pleased to meet you, too.' And I really was ... very.

The robe was short – about mid-thigh length – and semi-transparent. My attempts to control where my eyes roamed were becoming less and less effective.

'I just move in on Saturday. It is very nice here I zink.'

'Yes, it is. Look, I really didn't mean to disturb your privacy.'

'Oh, really it is nothing. Anyway, you can see ze same zing every day down by ze pool.'

I laughed. 'I suppose so.'

It wasn't true though – you really didn't see anyone quite like *her* down by the pool every day. Well, never, in fact.

'Whew, I am very 'ot,' she said.

You can say that again, I thought.

She removed her hat and reached behind her head to loosen the band which secured her ponytail. As she shook her head, long dark tresses of slightly wavy, jet-black hair tumbled down over her shoulders. She removed her sunglasses and wiped her brow with the back of her hand. Oh my God – those eyes! Their vibrant blue colour and startling intensity lent them a totally arresting quality. There was no doubt about it – this girl must have been at the front of the queue when the Almighty was handing out female attributes. Although, as I already mentioned, I suspected that the boobs may have been provided by a less than divine entity.

Conscious that I was spending too much time ogling her and not enough making small talk, I ventured, 'So are you here with your family?'

'Just me and my little girl, Miriam. She is at school just now – she is eight years old. My 'usband leave me six months ago, so we come to make new life down 'ere in Marbella.'

It was very hard to imagine any man walking out on a woman like *that*. Maybe she had some intolerable personality trait which made her impossible to live with. Who knows? For my part, I couldn't see much beyond her obvious physical attributes.

'Well, perhaps when you have properly settled in, you and Miriam would like to come round for dinner one evening and meet my wife.' As soon as I said it I sort of wished I hadn't – how would Donna react to a *femme fatale* like this in our home? Still, the words once uttered, could not be withdrawn.

She flashed that dazzling smile again. 'Yes zat would be very nice. I look forward to it.' She ran her hand down the front of her finely-toned stomach wiping away the perspiration which was trickling down it. 'I zink I need to go in and take a shower now – it is getting too 'ot.'

'Yes ... well speak to you again soon.'

As she turned to walk towards her apartment, my eyes were drawn inexorably to her backside. Her semi-transparent robe did little to disguise the enticing rise and fall of her buttocks as she walked towards the patio door. In a few fleeting moments, she was gone.

By now all thoughts of the community and its financial problems had evaporated from my mind.

***

An hour or so later, the sound of the chime from the elevator signalled Donna's return from her shopping trip. I opened the front door to see Donna emerge from the elevator, laden with shopping bags.

'Need some help with the shopping?' I enquired.

'Thanks. I'll put this stuff away if you can get the rest out of the car.'

Once all the shopping had been put away I poured Donna a glass of wine and we moved out onto the lower terrace, where we had an awning to provide some shade from the now-intense sun.

'Hey,' said Donna, 'have you seen our new neighbour?'

'New neighbour?' I said, in the most innocent tone I could muster.

'Yes, in block 15. She was just leaving as I was coming in.'

'Oh, block 15 penthouse? Well, yes actually ... I did see her for a moment earlier on, out on her terrace.'

'Isn't she a stunning-looking girl?'

What to say? Probably not what I actually did say. 'Well, I only saw her for a moment ... just long enough to say hello. She had a big hat and sunglasses on so, to be honest, I didn't really notice what she looked like.'

Why do we use phrases like 'to be honest' when we are about to lie through our teeth?

Donna's eyebrows rose and she tilted her head to one side in amusement. 'Oh, really?'

I could feel my nose grow a couple of inches right there and then.

Chapter 4

'More coffee, Roy?'

I nodded, and pushed my cup across the table for a top-up. 'Thanks, Neil.'

Having already told both Neil and Paul that I was, in principle, prepared to take on the presidency, I had suggested that the three of us should get together to discuss the logistics of the changeover. We had therefore decided to have an informal breakfast meeting at *La Mariposa*, a little bar/restaurant in the *Centro Plaza*.

It was 10 a.m. and the square was just starting to come to life as some of the shops began opening their doors. A smattering of early shoppers, mostly female, dressed in brightly coloured shorts and strappy tops – lime green and orange seemed to be particularly popular shades that year – drifted back and forth. The bright green parakeets bustling in the palm trees in the centre of the square had finally quietened down a little after a furious bout of screeching and squawking; perhaps they had settled whatever avian dispute they had been contesting. The morning sun warmed the back of my neck as I took a sip of my coffee.

'So,' I said, 'how do we go about making this happen?'

Neil delved into the bag which lay on the seat alongside him and withdrew a substantial-looking document which he placed in the centre of the table. 'This,' he declared, 'is the key to everything.' He cast a meaningful glance across the table. 'It's called the "Horizontal Property Act".'

I glanced sideways at Paul, who appeared to be just as bemused as I was.

'What's horizontal about it?' I enquired.

'Yes, I know ... stupid name. It's the legal document which governs how all shared or communal aspects of a community like ours must be managed. Among a host of other things it sets out the procedure for appointing presidents, vice presidents, and administrators.'

Paul picked up the document and thumbed swiftly through its pages. 'Well, I'm guessing that you've already read the relevant sections, so what do we have to do?'

'We have to hold an extraordinary general meeting of owners and take a vote. If a majority of those present at the EGM approve the appointments, then it's done.'

'So who calls the meeting?' asked Paul.

'Well normally, the existing president.'

'OK,' I said, 'so we should talk to Jim Watkins. It's best in any case, if we can secure his co-operation. You never know, he might actually be pleased to get the monkey off his back.'

Neil sighed. 'Unfortunately not ... I've already spoken to him and he is in no way willing to co-operate.'

Already spoken to him? Why do I get the feeling that I'm being led by the nose here?

'Well, that was perhaps a tad premature,' I ventured, 'but given that you have, what's plan B?'

'OK,' said Neil, leaning forward, 'there is another mechanism for calling an EGM.'

'Go on,' I encouraged.

'If at least twenty-five per cent of owners request a meeting then we have to have one, whether the president likes it or not.'

'Well, I guess we'll have to try to persuade that twenty-five percent then,' I said, somewhat dubiously.

Neil waved his hand as if to dismiss my doubts. 'Oh, I've already spoken to quite a few owners and I'm sure we'll get the necessary support.'

You really aren't leaving much to chance are you, you cunning old devil?

'Sounds good,' said Paul. 'Now then, what about finding a new administrator? We need to have someone ready to propose before we call an EGM.'

What's the betting that Neil has already done some groundwork on this too?

'Well,' began Neil – *here it comes* – 'actually I've been asking around at the golf club, and my friend Tim Stone just happens to be president of the community at *Los Cerezos* urbanisation. They use an outfit called *Financiero, Adminstración y Gestión* – FAG for short.'

'Bit of an unfortunate acronym,' I observed.

'I don't think it has the same connotations in Spanish,' replied Neil, chuckling. 'Anyway, the point is that he says they're pretty good. It's really difficult to assess the quality and competence of these administration companies by just talking to them, so a personal recommendation is probably as good a way as any to judge them.'

'OK,' I said, 'but we should at least meet them and form our own opinions before recommending them to the rest of the owners. We need to see what they charge, too – given our perilous financial state we can't afford to overspend on this.'

Paul chipped in. 'I've been thinking ... do we really *need* to employ an administration company at all?'

Neil inclined his head slightly and sucked air through his teeth. 'Well, I don't think there is actually any legal requirement for us to have one, but I think you two would have a hell of a job on your hands managing staff wages, social security, collecting owners' fees, paying suppliers, negotiating the Spanish legal system, administering the—'

'Stop!' interjected Paul. 'I wish I'd never asked the question!'

I laughed. 'OK Neil, can you set up a meeting with FAG? Christ, if we do take them on I'm going to have to learn to say that name without sniggering!'

Neil was laughing too now. 'OK I'll set it up.'

'And I'll draft a letter to owners,' said Paul, 'explaining what we have in mind and asking for their signatures on a request for an EGM.'

'When you've done so,' said Neil, 'I'd be happy to hawk it round the urbanisation, starting with the owners to whom I've already spoken.'

'Sounds like a plan,' I concluded.

***

The day gave way to a beautiful evening, so I offered to give Donna a break from cooking, and do a barbeque on the terrace.

'So does that include cutting up and marinating the meat, preparing the vegetables and peeling the potatoes?' she said – a little ungraciously I thought, considering my generous offer.

'Alright, point taken,' I conceded. 'Tell you what ... I'll mix you a gin and tonic which you can sip while doing those little bits of preparation before I start on the main job of doing the actual cooking.'

'W...ell,' she began.

'And I'll clear up and load the dishwasher after the meal.'

'Hmm ...'

'... and clean the barbeque.'

'Smooth-talking devil,' she chided, laughing.

Two and a half hours later, we had finished our meal and I had fulfilled my part of the bargain, having cleared away all the detritus which inevitably results from a barbeque. The sun had now slipped below the top of the mountains behind us, suffusing the sky with a beautiful orangey-pink glow, punctuated by a few streaks of wispy cloud which now stood out in dark relief. From the densely-packed trees which carpeted the lower reaches of the mountains emanated a tuneful and eclectic chorus of birdsong. Perfect end to a perfect evening.

As we relaxed on the sofa, Donna laid her head on my shoulder. 'Mmm, it doesn't get much better than this does it?'

'I nuzzled her and kissed her gently on the temple. 'No ... got to admit, this takes some beating.'

She lifted her head from my shoulder to lean forward and reach for her wine glass. After taking a sip and setting down the glass, she asked, 'So you've definitely decide to do this president thing, have you?'

'Well, yes, as long as ... oh heck, let's not spoil a beautiful evening by talking about that just now.'

She laughed. 'OK, let's just enjoy the sunset.'

So we sat in companionable silence, drinking in the beauty of the ever-changing hues and patterns in the sky whilst savouring the cheerful melodies conjured by the myriad species of birds occupying the trees.

Crash! The mood was shattered by the sound of a door slamming followed a second later by the sound of breaking glass.

'What the ...?'

Before I could complete the sentence, the air was rent by a harsh, screaming female voice uttering what I can only imagine was a stream of expletives, delivered in some unidentifiable Eastern European tongue. Actually, I didn't have to imagine for very long in order to determine the general gist of the diatribe as, somewhat incongruously, there were a few words of English interspersed in the otherwise seamless flow. 'You fucking BASTARD!' screamed at ear-splitting volume, sort of set the tone.

'Julia,' said Donna, her voice a piteous blend of despair and resignation. She sighed heavily, shoulders slumping.

Ah, yes – Julia; I don't believe I've mentioned her before, have I? Well Julia lived directly below our very alluring new neighbour, Angelique. Like Angelique, Julia rented her apartment rather than owned it. The owner of her apartment was, in fact, the developer who had originally built the whole urbanisation. Having sold seventy-two apartments out of the total seventy-five, he had chosen to retain the last three as rental investments, and one of these was occupied by Julia.

Anyway, the fact that both Angelique and Julia rented, rather than owned their apartments was just about the only thing which they had in common. In every other respect they were polar opposites – hard to imagine, in fact, two more dissimilar examples of, ostensibly, the same species.

While Angelique was slim and shapely, Julia was built like a Sumo wrestler.

While Angelique's face was the epitome of sultry, Mediterranean beauty, Julia's furrowed visage bore more than a passing resemblance to that of a bulldog.

While Angelique moved with a sensuous, feline elegance, Julia moved with all the grace of a wounded hippopotamus.

While Angelique's smoothly flowing French accent could turn your knees to jelly, Julia's harsh, jagged tones could shatter glass at fifty paces.

From our lower terrace, we overlook Julia's terrace. She would often sit out there to have her first few cigarettes of the day, still in her nightwear and still wearing curlers in her hair. I loved gazing out over the lake towards the mountain, but had long since learned not to do so when Julia's familiar hacking cough could be heard below, lest I should catch, in my peripheral vision, the frankly hideous sight of Julia bursting out of her sheer nightdress.

Right now though, the assault on the senses was aural rather than visual and there was no way to escape it, even though we were some distance away on our upper terrace. As she continued to rant below us, I deduced, from the fact that there was no answering voice, that the argument was being conducted via telephone. Although, to be fair, unless her opponent was possessed of extremely powerful vocal cords, it was entirely possible that even if he or she was present in person, their voice would still be inaudible in the face of Julia's onslaught.

'I suppose I'd better take a look,' I grumbled, levering myself wearily to my feet.

With some trepidation, I made my way down the stairs to our lower terrace and took a tentative peek over the wall. Julia was clad in a pink dressing gown, her head swaddled in a towel worn turban-style. Her mobile phone was clamped to her ear as she paced back and forth, yelling ever more loudly as her free hand flailed wildly in the air.

Suddenly she burst into English once more. 'I fucking KILL you ... you CUNT!'

Now it was not unusual for Julia to behave in a somewhat antisocial manner, but I really felt this was a bit much, so I tried to catch her attention. 'Er, Julia ...' No response. 'Excuse me but could you keep the noise down?' Still nothing. I tried again, much louder now. 'PLEASE if you must shout like that, can you go inside?' I might as well have been pissing into a hurricane – the torrent of invective continued unabated. OK, that was enough. 'SHUT THE FUCK UP!' I screamed, at the top of my voice.

Success! She paused for a moment, looking around as if unsure whether she had heard something or not. She didn't think to look upwards so I took advantage of the lull in the noise to press home my advantage.

'Up here!' She finally registered where my voice was coming from and turned her face upwards. 'Please can you keep the noise down, and perhaps moderate the language a bit?'

I guess the latter request was perhaps a tad hypocritical given my own previous admonition, but ... well, she started it.

The puzzled expression on her face slowly gave way to one of realisation, before her features – none too attractive in the first place – twisted into an ugly scowl, as she gave me the middle finger. She then promptly renewed her offensive against the poor bastard on the other end of the line with renewed vigour. She did, however, move inside her apartment which just took the edge off the volume.

I trudged back up the stairs and slumped down on the sofa beside Donna. 'Nice lady isn't she?' she sniggered.

I wasn't in such light-hearted mood. 'Christ, I'll swing for that bitch one of these days.'

'Calm down and have a drink,' she soothed, topping up my glass.

I gulped down a hearty swig of wine before exhaling heavily and attempting to do as Donna had suggested.

The argument below continued, albeit at slightly reduced volume and then, quite abruptly, ceased.

Donna and I looked at each other, hopefully.

'At last,' I breathed.

Ten seconds later our ears were assaulted by a tuneless, thumping bass rhythm overlaid with the mindless chanting of some damned rapper. The volume then suddenly increased as the lovely Julia turned her stereo up to maximum.

Such is the joy of horizontal living.

Chapter 5

Things moved pretty quickly over the next few weeks. We met with the owners of the proposed new administration company, and they seemed like the sort of people we could work with; we agreed to recommend them to the owners. Neil did a sterling job of canvassing the owners, and before long we had signatures of forty-one percent calling for an EGM. Although Jim Watkins would still be president until such time as a vote by owners changed that situation, he declined to chair the meeting – reasonably so, I suppose, as its purpose was to replace him. We agreed that I would chair the meeting, supported by Paul.

The meeting itself was a fairly brief affair during which Paul and I introduced ourselves and said a little about why we deemed that a change of management was required – not that many of those present needed much convincing. We successfully headed off a headlong plummet into chaos similar to that which had wrecked the previous meeting – you know, the 'collapsing chairs' fiasco – by promising that if elected, we would hold a further meeting once we had properly established the nature and scale of the problems which we faced.

When it came to a vote, almost everyone present supported our appointments, with just one vote against (Jim Watkins) and one abstention (a very tall and somewhat masculine-looking lady of Middle Eastern appearance).

'I must protest,' announced Jim.

'Protest at what?' I said. 'You're the only one voting against the motion so you can hardly—'

He didn't let me finish. 'Dr Ramani is not allowed to vote – she hasn't paid her community fees up to date.'

Personally, I couldn't really see how it mattered one way or the other given that her abstention made not the slightest bit of difference to the outcome.

Dr Ramani, however, wasn't about to accept Jim's assertion; she swivelled around in her seat to face towards him. 'What fuck you talking about you son of jackal? I not voting, I just abstaining.'

I had to admit that she had a point. I did, however, feel that the way she had addressed Jim was a little uncalled for.

'Abstaining *is* voting,' insisted Jim.

She began jabbing the air with her forefinger. 'How can I be voting when I'm abstaining, which is saying I not want to vote?'

'Madam,' declared Jim, 'I assure you that I am completely familiar with the provisions of the Horizontal Property Act, and I'm telling you ... abstaining *is* voting.'

I glanced across at Paul, who was frantically thumbing through his copy of the Horizontal Property Act, evidently trying to find some definitive ruling on this ridiculous dispute.

Ramani wasn't ready to concede Jim's point. 'You talking bollocks as usual, you bastard – if I abstain, I not voting,' she spat.

'Look here, my good lady', said Jim – *a pretty charitable description if you ask me* – 'if you don't want to vote, then just don't raise your hand. If you abstain, then you're voting to ... well, not to vote ... and you're not entitled to do that. And, by the way, I must insist that you stop using such disrespectful language. Remember I am still president until this vote is settled, and I have served you well over the years.'

'Served me well? Ha! That big laugh – you done nothing but poke nose in my business all time, you—'

I was, by now, thoroughly pissed off with both the pointless and circular argument about the abstention, and the unseemly wrangling between the two combatants. 'PLEASE!' I yelled, slamming my hand down hard on the table. That seemed to do the trick – both warring parties sunk into an uneasy silence.

I glanced across at Paul, who shrugged, helplessly; he had evidently failed to find any clarification of this technical point in the brief moments he had had to peruse the Horizontal Property Act.

'Look,' I said, trying to sound calm and conciliatory, 'we will check this point after the meeting, but does everyone accept that whether or not Dr Ramani is entitled to register an abstention actually makes no difference to the outcome of the vote?'

'Suppose so,' grumbled the doctor.

'Jim?' I prompted.

'Well yes,' muttered Jim, 'but it's a matter of principle.'

'Quite right,' I said, trying to placate him, 'and I will ensure that the minutes reflect correctly whether Dr Ramani's abstention is valid.'

'Just make sure you do,' he grumbled.

Paul and I were thus duly elected, and the new administrator appointed.

After the meeting Dr Ramani came up to talk to us.

Her first words were, 'I hope you do better job than that bastard Watkins.' Clearly she was not a lady to waste words on preliminaries.

'Er, Dr Ramani ... pleased to meet you properly,' I ventured, extending my hand. She declined to grasp it, looking down her long hooked nose as though I were offering her something which I had scraped off the bottom of my shoe.

Ignoring my attempt at conventional pleasantries she raised her eyes to meet mine. 'We have shit-load of problems in community ... what you going to do about it?' Her eyes gleamed with a somewhat disconcerting fervour.

'We do indeed have a considerable number of problems,' I said, adopting my most conciliatory tone, 'but as I said earlier, it's not until we can establish a clearer picture of—'

She cut me off mid-sentence.

'What you do about all those brazen tarts flaunting their tits down by swimming pool?'

Right, this really wasn't the sort of question I was expecting.

'I ... er, well, I don't think there is actually any rule against—'

'And, when you going to pay me compensation for that piece of camel dung, Watkins, ripping down my fence?'

'Your fence? I'm afraid I don't know anything about—'

'He never do nothing about my complaints. You know, I got people living above me who do noisy fucking at any time of day or night.' *You do?* 'You should hear that shameless harlot ... she go, "Aah, oooh, yes, yes ... give it to me ... do it ... harder ... harder ... yeah ... yeah ... yeeeaah".'

There was something deeply disturbing about being confronted with this Amazonian figure's impression of her neighbours' coupling. I glanced at Paul, who appeared to be equally disquieted.

'And bed go bang, bang, bang,' she added, completing the picture.

I took a second or two to recover from being subjected to her performance before replying. 'Well, I'm sure that must be very upsetting for you, but—'

'That scorpion's arse, Watkins, never do nothing about it. I tell him, but he do nothing ... NOTHING!'

I really wasn't at all sure quite how to deal with this barrage, but fortunately Paul came to my aid. 'These are, indeed, serious issues Dr Ramani, and I can assure you they will be dealt with.' She eyed him, suspiciously, but at least she stopped ranting for a moment. Paul pressed home his advantage. 'I'm sure you will appreciate that Roy and I are quite unfamiliar with the background to all these problems, so would you mind summarising them in writing for us so that we can take some time to investigate them?'

Oh, well played, sir! That should kick it into the long grass for a while.

Her face broke into a maniacal smile, exposing a rather crooked, yellowing row of tombstones. She delved into her handbag and withdrew a thick sheaf of papers, secured with a stout elastic band.

'I got it all here: letters, emails ... everything.'

My heart sank as quickly as it had risen. *Damn!* I accepted her offering without, it has to be said, much enthusiasm.

'Don't you lose nothing,' she ordered, but then added, 'in any case I got copies of everything.'

'Thank you. I can assure you that I won't lose your papers.'

She regarded both of us through narrowed eyes as though trying to assess our sincerity. Finally she muttered, 'Well alright then ... you just make sure you sort all this out.'

'Leave it with us,' said Paul, in his most reassuring tone.

He's pretty good at this diplomacy thing, I thought – *good man to have on board.*

She turned to leave, but was evidently struck by an afterthought. She whirled around and wagged her finger at me.

'And another thing: that slimy snake, Watkins ... he trim my bush much too close.'

Eeeuw ... too much information!

Chapter 6

The following day, I arranged to meet with Jim Watkins to see if he could help with the handover. I suggested he come up to my apartment but he, somewhat frostily, said he preferred to meet on neutral ground. Fair enough, I supposed. We chose the security guards' office by the front gate of the urbanisation; memories of the 'collapsing chairs' meeting came flooding back. The guards themselves were off duty on weekday mornings. We sat on opposite sides of the well-worn oak desk.

Jim placed both elbows on the desk and interlinked his fingers, forming a bridge. He straightened his back and raised himself to the maximum height which he could achieve whilst sitting – which actually wasn't very high at all. This felt rather like two military commanders conducting an initial parley before battle commenced. Only later did I realise just how apposite that analogy was.

'Well, what can I do for you then?' he began, the hostility in his eyes plain to see.

I decided to try to be as non-confrontational as possible. 'Well, it's very kind of you to agree to help with the handover, Jim. I know you've served the community well for several years, and I'll do my best to carry on the good work.'

'So what do you want?' he growled.

OK, so that bit of bullshit and flattery didn't work, did it?

'Well, I was hoping you'd be able to brief me on the main issues you are working on at the moment, and perhaps pass over all the relevant papers.' He sat stony-faced and silent. 'Anything you can do to help me hit the ground running, really,' I continued, in an effort to evoke a response.

'Well,' he said, 'the number of issues is vast and varied.' He emphasised the point with a wide sweep of his arm. 'If I was to try and brief you on everything, we'd be here for days.'

Oh, dear, I have a feeling we're not going to get far here.

'Well, perhaps just the main things then.'

'Oh, I'd hardly know where to begin,' he declared, waving a dismissive hand. 'I think the best thing is for you to just get your feet under the table, so to speak, and then as and when you come up against anything where you need a bit of background information, come and see me. My door will always be open.'

Now why do I have a mental image of a brick wall rather than an open door?

'OK, great. Er … well perhaps you can just pass over the files then we'll leave it at that until I need a bit of help.'

Jim spread his hands and rolled his eyes skyward. 'Oh really, I'd just be burying you in paper if I did that. I'm a shocking hoarder, you know, and I've got papers dating back for years. *I* know my way round them, but I'm afraid *you* probably wouldn't know where to start.'

'Well why don't you give them to me anyway, and I'll call you if I get stuck?'

'Oh, well I don't really have actual files – just bits of paper stowed away all over the house. You really wouldn't be able to make head nor tail of it all.'

I could see from the expression in his eyes and the slight upward curl of his mouth that he was thoroughly enjoying this little exchange. I wasn't going to give him the satisfaction of prolonging it any further.

'OK, well as and when I find I need something I'll give you a call then.'

'Of course,' he replied, smiling. 'Always happy to help.'

Guess I'm on my own then.

***

The next thing which Paul and I wanted to get underway was the transition from old to new administration companies, so we invited the owners of the latter over to the urbanisation for a meeting.

The bosses were a husband-and-wife team. Sergio was a distinguished-looking man, probably aged around fifty, with swept back hair, dark in the main, but greying at the temples. He wore a smart, dark blue suit, white shirt, and pale yellow silk tie. He moved and spoke – his English was very good – with the easy confidence of a politician, and indeed it emerged during the discussion that he was actively involved in local politics. Still, I decided not to automatically assume that he was therefore a lying, self-serving bastard like most politicians. Actually, I rather liked him; he seemed intelligent and very knowledgeable on community matters.

His wife, Marysa, was Dutch. The first thing I noticed about her was her rather unconventional dress sense. She wore a pair of very short and very tight-fitting orange shorts over multi-coloured tights of a thick woolly material which clung closely to her sturdy legs. Her bright blue, sleeveless T-shirt left one in no doubt that she was not wearing a bra. A tall lady, her compact features and small, upturned nose were framed by dark, straggly, curly hair. This lent her a passing resemblance to Olive Oyl, the girlfriend of the cartoon sailor, Popeye, of many years ago.

They seemed an oddly-matched couple, but like Sergio, Marysa appeared to be very bright, and knowledgeable on matters of community administration. I was doubly impressed to learn that, in addition to her native Dutch, she also spoke perfect English – and Spanish – and French – and German.

We talked for around thirty minutes, sitting in the security guards' office, during which time Sergio assured us that they would take care of the handover of all the records from the old administrator. In his experience, he said, such handovers were normally effected with a good deal of reluctance and bad grace, but there *was* a legal requirement that the outgoing administrator surrender the records within thirty days. He was confident that this could be achieved.

We then embarked on a walkabout, so that Sergio and Marysa could become familiar with the urbanisation and share with us any observations which they might make.

'It's a really nice layout,' opined Marysa, as we walked towards the pool area, 'but the gardens look pretty untidy.'

'Yes,' I replied, 'I understand that the gardening contractors have downed tools because they haven't been paid recently.'

'Don't worry,' said Sergio, 'once we have full copies of the financial accounts we'll be able to advise you of the exact scale of the financial problems.'

Good luck with that, I thought. *I certainly can't make much sense of them.*

'Very good,' I agreed, 'I'll look forward to that.'

Marysa wrote something on the notepad and clipboard which she was carrying, and we continued towards the pool. As we arrived at the pool, we were greeted by a most unwelcome sight: Julia – remember the Eastern European lady with the loud telephone manner? She had decided to sun herself by the pool – topless for Christ's sake! She lay on her back on one of the sunbeds, her bloated belly rising and falling with the rhythm of her breathing, and rolls of fat around her upper thighs bulging over the sides of the straining sunbed. Her enormous breasts drooped either side of her.

Hmm ... maybe Dr Ramani did have a point about topless sunbathing down by the pool.

I exchanged a brief glance with Paul, who made a *moue*, but said nothing. As we made our way past the basking Julia, she heard our voices and lifted herself onto one elbow, causing everything to wobble alarmingly. She stared a volley of daggers in my direction and muttered some unintelligible curse under her breath; I ignored her. We walked around to the far side of the pool where, for some reason, no-one was sitting. It didn't take long to figure out why: the air was permeated with a distinctly unpleasant aroma.

Now I think I mentioned earlier that *Las Hermosas Vistas* had been built on a steeply sloping plot. In order to create a large enough horizontal area in which to build the swimming pool, a large slice had been cut from the hillside and a staggered set of terraced, stone-block retaining walls built to stabilise the cut face. Sergio pointed up towards the wall behind the second level terrace, where a wet, algae-coated, green streak emerged from a gap in the stones, continuing over the lower wall and extending right down to poolside level.

'That,' he said, holding his nose somewhat theatrically, 'is leaking sewage. It's probably coming from up there.' He pointed towards the apartment block perched on the very top of the terraced slope, around forty feet above us. Marysa duly scribbled on her notepad.

As we continued our walkabout, Marysa made a list of around a dozen items where repairs or maintenance were urgently needed. We stopped for a minute or two while Marysa and Sergio pored over the list and conducted a conversation in Spanish.

At length, Sergio turned to us and summarised.

'At a conservative estimate, fixing the most urgent issues will cost at least thirty thousand euros.'

I was getting more and more depressed by the minute.

Sergio then added to my gloom. 'Apart from the really urgent jobs, we couldn't help noticing that the exterior walls of the entire urbanisation are not in very good condition. They will need refurbishment and repainting within the next year or two.'

I should explain that, as was common practice in Spain, the exterior walls of all the buildings comprising our urbanisation were rendered with cement and then painted. I guess it allows cheaper materials and construction methods to be used than the bricks-and-mortar approach typical in the UK. Basically, you build a concrete frame, fill in the gaps with some pretty scruffy blockwork and then cover it with a nice smooth layer of cement and some nicely-coloured paint – in our case a pale cream. This looks great when it's new but after a few years, cracks tend to appear in the render and the paint starts to peel.

'Well, yes, I had noticed that myself, but it's not a big deal is it?'

'Well it's not as urgent as some of the other jobs,' said Sergio, 'but this type of work is very labour-intensive. Raking out and filling the cracks, fixing any structural problems, painting ... it could be a very expensive job when the time comes.'

Terrific – and here was I thinking a lick of paint was all that would be needed.

'How expensive?' I enquired, with some trepidation.

His forehead puckered as he stroked his chin. 'A place this size, with fifteen separate blocks ... I'd say well over a hundred thousand euros.'

'A hundred *thousand*? Where on earth are we going to find that kind of money? As far as I understand it there's practically no money in the bank.'

Sergio held up his hand, palm-outward, in a calming gesture. 'It's always one of the most expensive jobs that communities have to contend with, and it crops up about once every five or six years, so there is a standard mechanism for accumulating the money to pay for it.'

'What's that?' I asked, desperately hoping that he would reveal some hidden pot of gold.

'It's called the painting fund. Each year, when the budget is set, you include a contribution to the painting fund. This money is ring-fenced from general community funds and after, say, five years, there should be enough to pay for the big refurbishment and repainting job.'

'So, we should have some money tucked away in a painting fund somewhere?'

'Indeed you should,' he replied in a reassuring tone of voice. 'Of course we'll have to study the accounts before we can find out how much is in the painting fund, but I'd be very surprised if you don't have a substantial sum deposited.'

I wasn't so bloody confident. Having already studied the accounts myself, I had seen no sign of a separate bank account with even pocket money in it, never mind tens of thousands of euros. I filed it away in my mental list of issues to be addressed after we'd stopped the metaphorical boat from actually sinking.

Finally, we made our way around to the highest point of the urbanisation where a long stretch – perhaps three hundred feet – had been cut from the hillside and faced with a near-vertical concrete wall some twenty to twenty-five feet high. As we walked along its length, we passed by a point where the concrete wall was obscured by an irregular heap of earth and small rocks. I had noticed it before but never really given it a second thought. Sergio, however, was immediately on the alert. In spite of his snappy suit and highly-polished shoes, he clambered over the first few feet of earth and began sifting through it with his bare hands.

'The cement has given way here, allowing a minor landslide to occur,' he declared.

'Cement?' I said. 'Surely this is a reinforced concrete retaining wall?'

He shook his head, gravely. 'What you have here is a very light wire mesh' – he pointed at a fragment protruding from the earth and stones – 'spread over the cut face of the hillside, and then sprayed with a thin layer of cement.' He picked up a broken fragment of said cement layer, holding it up between thumb and forefinger. It was less than one inch thick.

'Not suitable as a retaining wall then?'

He gave a derisive snort. 'This wouldn't retain a *paella*, let alone a hillside.'

'Shit,' I gasped.

'Oh, fuck,' concurred Paul.

Chapter 7

Following the disturbing revelations arising from the previous day's walkabout, Paul and I needed to speak to Jim Watkins again. There were some important questions to which we needed answers. Donna, however, had a different priority: that morning we were due to take delivery of a new bed.

When we had originally bought the apartment, we had also purchased from the previous owners all of the furniture which it contained. For the most part we were very happy with the furniture, but Donna had never liked the bed. For a start it was only about four feet wide; Donna insisted that a proper double mattress had to be at least six feet. Actually, I didn't mind the smaller mattress: it meant we had to snuggle up quite closely.

The second thing which Donna didn't like was that it was a divan-style bed; she preferred the type with a solid base which was much wider and longer than the mattress itself, so as to create a sort of shelf all the way round the bed. 'It's somewhere to sit while doing up the buckles on your shoes,' she had commented. Finally, she insisted that the mattress was way too hard and uncomfortable. It seemed fine to me.

Anyway, although I was happy enough with the bed we had, I eventually succumbed to Donna's insistent entreaties that we needed a new one. And what a magnificent beast of a bed she had chosen! The mattress was a full two metres – around six feet six inches – in width. The base – a beautifully grained rosewood affair – was around nine feet wide, creating an impressive polished-wood surround. The headboard – also in polished rosewood – was designed to fix directly to the wall; it stood around seven feet tall. The whole thing cost about the same as a small family car. It was worth it, though, finally to assuage Donna's constant niggling about the existing bed.

Although I doubted that I would actually sleep any better in this magnificent creation than I did in the old bed, there was no way on earth that I was going to be absent when the damned thing was delivered. For a start, Donna absolutely *hated* having to deal with delivery men on her own, and also, I had a nagging doubt about just how easy it would be to get this enormous piece of furniture up the stairs, which featured an awkward little turn with a low ceiling. If there was a problem there, and I wasn't around to help deal with it, I could imagine the recriminations which would follow. My next meeting with Jim Watkins would have to wait for another day.

When the delivery men arrived – around twelve noon – their first task was to inspect the access route. As soon as they saw the narrow stairwell there was much sucking in of breath and shaking of heads.

'*No es posible,*' declared one of the men. My Spanish wasn't great but I got the gist of that comment.

'*¿Qué vamos a hacer?*' I said, hoping desperately that I hadn't just suggested the man's mother was a goat or something.

Fortunately, the other man spoke very good English. 'It is most unlikely that the mattress will go up those stairs, and there is absolutely no way for the base to fit, even though it comes in two pieces.'

Donna's face fell; she looked as though a much-loved relative had just died a violent death. It had definitely been a good decision not to abandon her to deal with this situation alone. 'So what can we do?' I pleaded.

The man stroked his chin, his brow deeply furrowed, as he considered my question. He exchanged a few words in Spanish with his colleague – far too fast for me to stand any hope of following.

Eventually he turned to me with their conclusion. 'I think we can carry everything up to your front terrace OK. It is possible – *just* possible – that we could then haul the pieces up the front of the building onto your top terrace with ropes. It should then be possible to take them into the bedroom through the large patio door up there.'

OK, I thought, *QED*. 'Right, well let's give it a try.'

The man looked down at his shoes, shaking his head slightly. 'Unfortunately our health and safety rules prohibit us from undertaking such a hazardous manoeuvre.'

I had, by now, been in Spain long enough to understand the hidden message behind the spoken words. I reached into my pocket, found my wallet, and withdrew a hundred-euro note.

'Would this help with the health and safety rules?' I asked.

The man's face broke into a broad smile as he snatched the banknote from my hand. 'We will try,' he said.

Right ... now I had visions of Donna's beautiful polished rosewood bed whacking against the side of the building, sustaining all manner of damage. I delved into my wallet once more and withdrew another hundred-euro note, waving it aloft.

'And this is the reward if there is not one single scratch on it after you get it upstairs.'

Both men's eyes lit up. 'It will be in perfect condition,' asserted the English-speaker.

'*No hay ningún problema,*' declared his friend, nodding vigorously.

Forty minutes later, and two hundred euros lighter, I was gazing at our new bed, successfully installed in its proper place; the delivery men had gone. Donna climbed onto the bed and stretched out full length; she looked tiny against the background of this vast piece of furniture.

'Oh Roy, it's *wonderful.*'

'Should be, after all the trouble it's caused,' I grumbled.

'You'll love it,' she insisted, jumping off the bed. 'Now then, I should unwrap the new bed linen and get the bed made up properly.'

I tutted as I picked up the rope from the bedroom floor which the men had neglected to take with them. I guess the two hundred euros had sort of displaced from their minds all thoughts of tidying up and taking their things with them.

'Oh, well,' I muttered, coiling up the rope, 'I suppose this might come in useful sometime. I'll put it in the utility room.'

Bloody expensive piece of rope, I thought.

***

The next morning, Paul and I met with Jim Watkins in the security guards' office once again.

'Settling into things OK, then?' chirped Jim.

I ignored his irritatingly cheery manner. 'Well, we've certainly discovered a few things that need attention, but we won't trouble you with most of them. There are, though, a couple of things which we would like to talk to you about.'

'Oh, and what would they be?'

'Well, firstly, the painting fund.'

'Painting fund?' said Jim, tilting his head to one side and looking disturbingly blank.

A leaden boulder descended in my gut.

'I understand that we should be putting money aside in a painting fund to pay for the exterior refurbishment and repainting when it becomes necessary.'

'Oh, that ... no, I'm afraid we haven't been able to do that.'

'So there's no painting fund?'

'Good heavens no. Haven't you seen how many expenses we are already facing?'

At this point I felt an overwhelming urge to poke him in the eye but, with a considerable effort, resisted it. 'I understand that, but surely we should still be saving up for the big expense which we know is coming.'

He shook his head. 'It's a question of priorities,' he declared, leaning forward and raising a forefinger as though about to deliver an economics lecture to a backward student. 'You see, we only have very limited funds' – *yes, I get that* – 'so we have to use them for the most urgent jobs, not something which is still years in the future.'

He sat back in his chair, evidently satisfied that he had been able to explain to me the error in my thought processes.

'But it's going to need doing within the next two years at most,' I protested.

'Oh, we can cross that bridge when we come to it,' he said, waving his hand, dismissively.

I hung my head, exhaling heavily as I sought to supress my desire to jump up and grab him by the throat. There was clearly no point in pursuing this debate any further, so I brought the conversation about the non-existent painting fund to a close. 'So the bottom line is: no painting fund, no money put aside anywhere for painting?'

'I'm afraid not,' he confirmed, smiling.

'In that case,' I said, 'can we move on to another subject?'

'Of course.'

'It's about the main retaining wall at the top end of the urbanisation,' I said.

'Ah yes,' Jim replied, nodding sagely.

'Some of it has started to collapse,' I continued.

'Indeed it has,' he agreed.

'And it's allowing some earth and rocks to slip down.'

Jim raised a forefinger and wagged it at me. 'You're quite right ... it is.'

It was clear that this gentle prompting was unlikely to elicit much information so I decided to try a more direct approach.

'Well, we've been advised that the construction of the wall is completely inadequate and that the whole lot could come down at any moment, triggering a landslide, which could cause damage to the apartments in blocks ten to fifteen.' *Which, by the way, includes my apartment*, I thought, but didn't say.

'Yes, quite a concern,' agreed Jim.

I took a couple of deep breaths and clenched my teeth, taking a few seconds to gain control of my simmering anger, not wishing to let the words which were forming in my brain come spilling out of my mouth. Paul seemed to sense my mood and took over the conversation.

'Jim, you are clearly aware of this problem, so can you tell us when it started, and more importantly, what is being done about it?'

'Well,' said Jim, resting his elbows on the table and clasping his hands together, 'the first cracks started appearing about four years ago.'

'Four years?' gasped Paul.

Jim nodded. 'Then, about six months later, a small section broke away, and it's basically been gradually crumbling ever since.'

'What's happened to the earth and rocks which have been slipping down?' said Paul.

'Well, we've been clearing them away as soon as they come down so that the internal roadway alongside blocks ten to fifteen remains passable.'

By now I had just about composed myself enough to speak in a reasonably civil manner. 'But Jim, what about fixing the root cause of the problem: i.e. the faulty retaining wall?'

'Oh, that would cost a great deal of money: a hundred and twenty thousand euros according to a structural engineer we had look at it three years ago.'

A hundred and twenty thousand euros? And you've spent your time pissing about buying six euro plastic chairs – which, by the way were six euros more than they were actually worth – and saving a few more euros by holding meetings in this shitty little office rather than hiring a room in a hotel? My fragile hold on my temper threatened to fracture.

As I opened my mouth to speak, Paul laid a gentle restraining hand on my sleeve. 'So what was your plan to deal with the problem?'

'Well, the urbanisation is still covered by its ten-year warranty, so the developer is responsible for fixing the wall.'

'So why hasn't he?' said Paul.

'Oh, he's been asked alright, but he just refuses to do anything about it.'

'Well, can't we force him to do something about it?' continued Paul, his tone of voice betraying the fact that he, too, was starting to get frustrated at the way each snippet of information had to be dragged out of Jim's mouth.

'Only the courts can do that,' Jim replied, 'which is why, three years ago, we launched a legal action against both him and the architect who designed the wall. We're claiming the hundred and twenty thousand euros plus all legal costs.'

Well why didn't you say so to begin with? I thought.

My anger began to subside as I realised that, in spite of making us work for the revelation, Jim *had* actually taken appropriate action on the problem.

'But Jim,' I asked, puzzled, 'if you started the legal action three years ago, why hasn't anything happened yet?'

He inclined his head and shook it slowly, in the manner of a teacher trying to explain something to a small child. 'This is Spain – the case hasn't come to court yet.'

'So when will it come to court?' I pressed.

He spread his hands and shrugged. 'Who knows? Could be next month, could be next year ... could be several years.'

And meanwhile the whole fucking thing could collapse, triggering a landslide – oh shit, shit, shit!

I exhaled heavily. 'OK, well at least you've got the ball rolling; I guess we'll pick it up from here. Can you pass over all the papers relating to this matter?'

'Oh, the administrator has all that stuff; you'll have to get your new people to collect it from him.'

By now I was feeling pretty drained as the enormity of the situation sunk in. There seemed little point in prolonging the conversation right there and then.

I stood up and extended my hand. 'Well, thanks for the background info. Jim, we'll—'

Instead of grasping my hand Jim reached for a folder which he had placed on the table earlier. 'There is one more thing you ought to be aware of ...' – he passed me the folder – 'the electricity to the urbanisation is due to be cut off on Monday, and the water at the end of the month.

'What?' exclaimed Paul and I, simultaneously.

'We're a bit behind in paying the bills, you see.'

At that moment, the gradual thawing in my feelings towards Jim Watkins went rapidly into reverse.

Chapter 8

Two days had elapsed since the meeting with Jim Watkins, and by now the scale of the financial problems we faced was becoming clear. I wandered out onto the top terrace and took up my 'thinking position' – forearms resting on the terrace wall, gazing out across the lake and towards the mountain beyond – as I considered the situation.

We owed around forty thousand euros to various suppliers including the gardening company, who had already downed tools; the electricity company, who were due to cut off our supply in three days' time; and the water company, who were due to do likewise a couple of weeks after that.

Our own staff – the maintenance engineer, the two security guards, and the two cleaners – had not been paid for the last couple of months. They were in a state of despair about how to feed their families and pay their bills.

We had identified urgent maintenance and repair tasks which, at a conservative estimate, would cost around thirty thousand euros. Then there was the matter of the hundred and twenty thousand euros which would be needed to fix the retaining wall, not to mention the hundred-thousand-plus which would be needed for refurbishment and repainting of the buildings. It didn't help that over twenty percent of owners were persistently failing to pay their community charges; in some cases the debts stretched back for years.

And the funds in the community's bank account, available to deal with this litany of problems? Precisely three hundred and seventy-two euros. This, I gloomily concluded, was not going to go far.

We needed to secure an urgent cash injection of perhaps eighty thousand euros just to stave off imminent disaster, quite apart from taking action to balance the books for the longer term.

Paul had had to return to the UK, but he had agreed to start a telephone/email campaign chasing the debtors to try to get as many as possible to pay up. His plan was first to explain to the offenders the calamitous situation we were in, and appeal to their sense of guilt and/or community spirit, if indeed they appeared to be possessed of either attribute. Where he judged it to be appropriate, he would offer to write off a small percentage of the accumulated debt for those who were willing to settle right up to date immediately. Where the 'carrot' approach failed he would resort to the 'stick', threatening dire consequences including legal action against them. Mind you, if they had any idea of the excruciating sloth of the Spanish legal system this would probably not have them quaking in their boots. Still, it was worth a try.

Meanwhile I was left with the task of finding a way to rustle up eighty grand or so in double-quick time.

'Monsieur Roy, Monsieur Roy, can you 'elp me?' I hadn't even realised that Angelique was outside until her silken voice interrupted my introspective musing.

I turned towards the voice drifting up from her terrace; Angelique was, once again, clad in the skimpiest of bikinis – this time in a bright yellow colour which contrasted beautifully with her deep tan. Sadly, the bikini consisted of two pieces this time, rather than one. An arresting sight, nevertheless.

'Oh, hello again,' I called out, 'what can I do for you?'

'I 'ave some trouble wiz ze pussy and I wondered if you could 'elp me.'

Right, I'm your man, I thought. The community's financial problems would have to wait while I dealt with this urgent request.

'Er, what is the trouble exactly?'

'I leave my door open while sunbathing out 'ere and ze pussy go in my 'ouse' – she pointed to the open patio door – 'and now 'e won't go.'

'Ze pussy' in question was, no doubt, one of the numerous feral cats which loitered around the urbanisation, wailing during the night and crapping all over the place during the day. Unfortunately, some of the residents exacerbated the situation by feeding the damned things. Anyway, at least it was an opportunity to get to know our lovely new neighbour a little better.

'OK, I'll come round,' I said.

'Oh, zank you.'

'What are you looking for?' enquired Donna, as I rummaged in the cupboard under the sink in our utility room.

'My leather gardening gloves.' I replied.

'But you already trimmed and weeded all the plants on the terrace at the weekend.'

'Ah, here they are ... er, no, I don't need them for actual gardening – I'm just popping next door to help our new neighbour.'

'What ... the glamour-puss in 15E?'

'Well, yes' – I had, by now, abandoned any pretence of not noticing what a stunner Angelique was – 'but it's another puss which is the problem: one of those damned wild cats has taken up residence in her apartment and refuses to leave. I thought I'd better take these' – I held up the gloves – 'in case it gets a bit aggressive.'

'Well take care,' she said, 'I don't want you to be eaten alive.'

'Well, I know these moggies can be a bit vicious when cornered but they're not *that* dangerous.'

'I wasn't referring to the cat,' she said, deadpan.

I tutted and rolled my eyes, before setting off on my rescue mission.

When Angelique opened her front door, still clad in her yellow bikini, I was momentarily taken aback; at close quarters she was even more beautiful than I had previously appreciated. The first thing that struck you was the eyes: a deep azure blue colour with impossibly long, dark, elegantly-curled lashes. Finely-sculpted cheekbones gave way to a wide, sensuous mouth which broke into a luminous smile as she beckoned me to enter.

'Oh, zank you so much. I don't like ze pussies ... zey scare me.'

'Don't worry,' I said, trying to sound as masterful as possible, 'I'm sure we can get it out. So ... where is it?'

'In ze lounge.'

The cat was on Angelique's sofa. Predominantly black, it had one white sock and one white eyepatch which gave it a somewhat pirate-like appearance. It seemed unconcerned by our arrival in the room, as it casually plucked tufts of fibre from the velvety turquoise fabric with alternate clenches of its claws.

'Oh, my lovely sofa,' wailed Angelique.

I donned my gloves and began slowly to advance towards the feline intruder. Evidently sensing that my intentions were contrary to its best interests, it turned towards me, arched its back, and hissed loudly, its ears stiffening and laying backwards.

I hesitated for a moment, eyes locked in combat with this formidable creature. *I'll stare you out*, I thought, but the cat didn't flinch; it just stared back. After ten seconds or so, it became clear that the battle of wills was a stalemate so I decided to try a different approach. I took a couple of tentative steps towards the cat, which steadfastly refused to budge. Angelique followed, cautiously crouching behind me. As I slowly extended my hands towards the creature it arched its back again, spitting spitefully, and took a swipe at me with its right paw. Fortunately my reactions were good and the cat's aim was bad. As I swiftly stepped back, the animal's outstretched claws missed me by a couple of inches, grasping at nothing more than thin air.

At this point, the cat decided to make its move: it leapt from the sofa and darted through the gap between my legs, evoking a piercing scream from Angelique as it swerved smartly into the kitchen, paws scrabbling for grip on the polished marble floor. We stood there looking at each other for a few seconds, both somewhat startled by the sudden burst of activity. Angelique's breath came in short, ragged bursts, her delicious bosom heaving so much that it threatened to escape from the straining scrap of yellow fabric which constrained it. Sadly, it didn't.

Having regrouped, we set about tracking the beast through to the kitchen where it had somehow managed to insert itself into the narrow gap between the washing machine and the adjacent cupboard. Now having seen the creature's reaction to my previous attempt to pick it up, I wasn't keen to attempt to grab it and hold on to it, even if I could actually reach it in its new hiding place.

'Do you have a box, or something I could use to try to trap it?' I asked.

'Ah, yes ... I 'ave some cardboard boxes which I used for moving in. Zey are in ze spare bedroom.'

While Angelique went to find a suitable box, I locked eyes with my adversary, which regarded me with a definite air of hostility, occasionally drawing back its lips in a menacing hiss.

'Will zis do?' said Angelique upon her return.

'Yes fine,' I said. 'Now, if you hold the box right here' – I placed the box in position with its open side facing towards the cat – 'I'll reach in and try to push it inside.' She nodded, nervously.

As I cautiously extended my gloved hand towards the cat, it backed further into the gap, hissing and spitting furiously. Angelique craned her neck in order to see over my shoulder, in doing so lightly pressing her breast against my back and allowing her hair to brush my cheek. This I found somewhat distracting in spite of the ferocious creature which I was facing.

I leaned further forward, attempting to reach over and behind the cat in order to try to scoop it into the box. It tried to back away further, but found itself pressed against the back wall. This was my opportunity – I reached right over the creature and inserted my hand between its backside and the wall ready to pull it forward into the box.

This, the cat had evidently decided, was a step too far. It emitted a piercing yowl, and raked its claws down my forearm.

'Aaargh!' I yelled, ruining all my previous attempts to look manly and unflappable in front of Angelique.

She responded with a shrill scream and let go of the box, stepping back smartly as the cat swerved skilfully around it and bolted towards the open patio door.

'Oh, your poor arm!' she exclaimed. She grabbed a roll of paper kitchen towel and tore off a generous length with which I wrapped my forearm to staunch the flow of blood. 'Does it hurt terribly?'

'Oh, it's nothing,' I lied, gritting my teeth against the pain. 'Where has that wretched animal gone now?'

'Out on ze terrace, I zink.'

'OK, do you have anything I could use to cover my arms?'

She pressed a forefinger to the side of her chin, looking thoughtful. 'Ah yes,' she said, raising an elegant eyebrow as an idea evidently registered. She went to the under stairs cupboard and emerged a few seconds later holding a black leather jacket. 'It was my 'usband's,' she explained.

He must have been a big guy, I thought, as I shrugged myself into the garment, which hung off me like a tent. Never mind, it would serve its purpose.

'You need to cover up too,' I said.

She delved back into the cupboard and withdrew a full-length raincoat, swiftly shrugging herself into it.

'Do you have some gloves?'

She nodded and pulled a pair from the pocket of her raincoat.

'OK, bring the box,' I commanded, trying once again to look and sound as though I was in control of the situation.

We stepped out onto the terrace where the cat had taken up a defensive position in the corner nearest to the building itself. We advanced, step by step, crouching, ready for action; I led the way, with Angelique just behind, holding the box. I was feeling distinctly nervous – and bloody hot in that heavy jacket – as we closed in on our quarry.

Closer, closer ... one more step and—

The cat uttered a fearsome howl and leapt onto the terrace wall. As it whirled around to face us, it lost its footing and quite abruptly disappeared over the edge. The plaintive scream, sounding almost like a human baby, lasted for about two seconds and then ... dead silence. We looked at each other aghast, frozen and silent for several seconds, until the spell was broken and we rushed to look over the wall.

There, some forty feet below, lay the cat's body, silent and unmoving, limbs akimbo.

Chapter 9

'Oh no!' cried Angelique, clasping a hand to her mouth. 'Ze poor pussy.'

But you said you didn't like cats, I thought. I had to admit, though, that although the wretched creature had maimed me, I did feel a pang of remorse that it should have lost its life like this. All we had wanted was for it to vacate the apartment; if we had just closed the patio door after it bolted out onto the terrace it would probably have found its own way down to the ground eventually.

'We should go and collect the body,' I said.

She nodded, a tear escaping the corner of her eye.

We shed the sweltering garments which we had donned for protection and made our way down to where the unfortunate creature had met its end. I took the cardboard box with me. *What the hell do we do with the body of a deceased moggy?* I wondered.

It wasn't dead.

As I bent down to pick up the body, I could see that it was still breathing: weak shallow breaths, but breaths nevertheless.

Angelique had spotted it too. 'Oh, look 'e is still alive ... we 'ave to save 'im.'

In spite of my previous enmity towards the creature I had to agree. 'Right,' I said, 'let's get him into the box and take him to the vet.'

It was with some trepidation that I approached the prone body – I was still a little fearful that the cat might suddenly spring to life and lunge for my jugular. When I picked up the limp, lifeless body, however, it was clear that there was no fight left in the unfortunate animal; it was barely alive. In spite of myself I felt a lump form in my throat as I laid it gently in the box.

'I'll just pop upstairs to get my car keys and let Donna know what's happening, and then I'll take him to the vet.'

'I come wiz you too,' she said, 'but I should put some clothes on.'

Good idea, I thought, eying her bronzed, shapely figure – now glistening with a sheen of perspiration – *you'd cause quite a stir walking into the vet looking like that.*

The prognosis for the cat was not good, and having established that this was not a family pet, but a feral cat, the vet suggested that perhaps the best course of action was to have the animal put down. Angelique, however, was horrified at this suggestion and, rather than see her further distressed, I agreed that we should leave the cat with the vet for various tests and X-rays.

***

Two hours later, Donna and I were sitting on the terrace, under the sunshade, enjoying a late lunch of *bocadillos*, cheese, and red wine. Donna had washed and dressed my wounds which, it has to be said, didn't actually look all that bad once cleaned up. They were still throbbing fiercely, though.

'That'll teach you not to go rushing off to help the first sexy siren who beckons,' said Donna, her eyes sparkling with amusement.

'I suppose so,' I grumbled, not yet ready to see the funny side of this incident.

'Anyway what's she like?'

Well, you can see what she's like ... she's absolutely stunning.

Donna seemed to read my thoughts. 'I mean *apart* from having the looks and figure of a supermodel.'

'Well, she seems very nice.'

'Nice?' repeated Donna, raising an eyebrow and inclining her head.

'Well yes ... nice ... I mean I hardly know her, so I couldn't really say.'

'Apart from her being devastatingly glamorous,' she prompted.

'Well, yes ... apart from that,' I admitted.

'Tell you what ...'

'What?'

'Why don't you invite her round for dinner one evening? Then I can see what I'm up against,' she said.

That's a bit of luck, I thought, *now, at least I don't have to suggest it.*

'OK ... why not? She wanted me to let her know what happens with the cat, so I'll pop round when I have some news on that front, and I'll invite her then.'

That seemed to draw a line – for now, at least – under Donna's gentle probing about our new neighbour so I stood up to clear away the lunch things while Donna settled down to read a book.

Once I'd finished clearing up, I turned my attention back to the community's financial crisis, which needed urgent attention.

I spent the next couple of hours on the phone: to Paul in the UK, to Marysa at the new administration company, and to the community's bank. The latter confirmed what Marysa had already told me: that they would not, as a matter of policy, allow any community to overdraw its bank account, and in our case, given the perilous state of our finances, they wouldn't consider a loan either.

In the end, Marysa offered that FAG would extend the community a loan of forty thousand euros, provided I commit to immediately restructuring the community's finances to eliminate the ongoing deficit and start running a balanced budget. Then, in the medium term, I would have to start running a surplus on the budget in order to pay off the debt. That would clearly mean a combination of cuts in spending and an increase in owners' fees, which would have to be agreed by a majority of owners at a general meeting. It wasn't likely to be terribly popular but, I reasoned, surely the majority would vote in favour once the full gravity of the situation was laid bare. What Marysa was asking for was nothing more than sound financial common sense. I agreed to her terms.

This was a good start, but I figured we actually needed around twice what Marysa had offered in order to pay staff and suppliers, head off the threatened suspension of electricity and water supply, and deal with the most urgent repair tasks. The only solution I could see was to ask each of the seventy-five owners to put their hands in their pockets and cough up an extraordinary one-off payment sufficient to raise the other forty thousand. This would, of course be over and above their regular fees, which – for the reasons I just outlined – would themselves have to increase substantially. Oh, I really was going to be Mr. Popular!

Of course, none of this even began to address the much larger issue of the collapsing retaining wall and the repainting project, which together would cost well over two hundred and twenty thousand euros.

By now, I really was starting to wonder why on earth I had allowed myself to be talked into taking on this wretched job!

Chapter 10

Five days later, I was sitting in a large conference room in the *Estrella de Andalucía* hotel. To my right sat Marysa, today clad in a lime green micro-skirt, thick black tights, and brown suede Ugg boots – weird, given the hot weather – teamed with a sky blue strappy top. She sat, hunched over her laptop, ready to take the minutes and to undertake translation duties if necessary. To my left sat Paul, who had kindly managed to juggle his commitments in the UK in order to be in Spain for the emergency EGM. In front of us were around forty expectant faces, their owners no doubt anxious to know what we had in mind for the community.

Having dispensed with the introductions and other opening formalities I got straight to the nub of the matter.

'Paul, Marysa, and I have spent the last couple of weeks carrying out an in-depth analysis of the financial status of the community. I'm afraid this has revealed that we have some serious problems.'

Dr Ramani put up her hand. 'Yes ... what you going to do about them? I give you all my papers but you do nothing.'

'I can assure you, Dr Ramani,' I replied, 'that your complaints are under serious investigation, and I'll get back to you on these in due course, but today I have some other issues to bring to everyone's attention.'

She scowled and tutted, but lowered her arm and settled back in her chair.

I continued. 'If you take a look at the information pack you were given as you came in' – much noisy shuffling of papers – 'you will see a page headed "Balance Sheet".'

I paused for a moment to allow everyone to locate the relevant document. After a few seconds, most people had the sheet in front of them and were looking up, ready for some elucidation of the figures thereon – all except one man sitting in the second row that is. He was glued to his smartphone which he held in both hands tapping away furiously with his thumbs. He was about forty-five, I guessed, of muscular build, with tattooed arms and peroxide-blonde hair gelled into a forest of vertical spikes. A heavy gold-link chain hung around his neck, framing the mass of dark chest hair spilling from his extravagantly unbuttoned shirt. I recognised him as the man who had first stood up and triggered the mass exodus from the 'collapsing chairs' meeting. Given that I seemed to have everyone else's attention I decided not to provoke any confrontation with this guy and left him to his own devices.

I continued with my address to the rest of those present. 'There is quite a lot of detail there, which you can study at your leisure, but let me draw your attention to the most important points.'

I painstakingly explained the whole ghastly situation, eliciting various gasps from the audience as each fresh catastrophe was revealed. I'm not sure that too many of those present really understood the significance of the fact that many of our supposed assets were, in fact, monies owed to us, and which might never be collected, or that our total net assets were negative. Most, however, seemed to get the message when I revealed that we had, by the skin of our teeth, only just avoided having the water and electricity cut off.

Just in case there was any lingering doubt as to the gravity of our situation I summarised. 'In other words we are bankrupt. If we were a private company we would have gone bust and closed down.'

That seemed to do it: the room fell silent for several long seconds. Eventually, a hand went up, followed by another, and then another. Within seconds, about a dozen hands were raised.

'OK,' I said, raising my own hand palm-outward, in a calming gesture, 'we'll try to answer everyone's questions in due course, but let me first explain the action plan; that may answer many of the questions anyway.'

One by one, all the hands were lowered.

'To deal with the most immediate and urgent issues,' I explained, 'we need a cash injection of around eighty thousand euros.' A collective gasp rippled across the room. 'Thankfully though, our administrator' – I gestured towards Marysa, who responded with a nod – 'has kindly agreed to provide an emergency loan of forty thousand euros. And that' I said, 'is the only reason we still have water and electricity available today.'

The room fell silent as the seriousness of our situation began to sink in. I paused for a few moments before continuing.

'Now I'm sure I speak for everyone in thanking Marysa for authorising this loan' – murmurs of appreciation – 'but, unfortunately, that still only covers about half of our immediate needs.' I paused for a few moments to let everyone absorb this statement. 'As we need the money very urgently,' I continued, 'I see no alternative but for each of us, as owners, to contribute to an emergency, one-off extraordinary fee payment to raise the other forty thousand.'

There was a further short silence of perhaps one or two seconds, before someone called out, 'How much?'

Now, I don't believe I have yet explained about 'assessment coefficients'. Each apartment is assigned an assessment coefficient, determined according to the number of square metres which it occupies. This coefficient is used to calculate how community charges – be they regular fees or, as in this situation, extraordinary fees – are allocated across individual apartments. In *Las Hermosas Vistas*, the assessment coefficient for the penthouse apartments was roughly twice that of the regular apartments.

'Well,' I explained, 'assuming that all seventy-five owners pay' – *admittedly, by no means certain,* I thought – 'it amounts to about four hundred and fifty euros for a standard apartment, or just under nine hundred euros for a penthouse.'

'Fookin' 'ell ... that's daylight fookin' robbery, that is.'

The attention of the spiky-haired man in the front row had finally been captured when the prospect of his having to put his hand in his pocket had been raised.

'Well,' I ventured, 'I am just reporting the situation we are in, and suggesting the best ...'

'Fook that – we already pay an arm and a fookin' leg, and now you expect us to cough up four fookin' hundred more. Bollocks to that.'

I was momentarily at a loss as how to respond to this incisive financial analysis of the situation. Before I could compose an adequate reply, Jim Watkins, our erstwhile president, spoke up.

'This is surely an exaggeration of our financial problems. With a little careful management and belt-tightening I am confident that we can avoid imposing this unreasonable burden on owners' already hard-pressed finances.'

Why, you interfering bastard – it was you who got us into this mess in the first place! I bit my lip to head off the words which threatened to erupt from my mouth.

'Look,' I said, adopting my most forceful tone. 'You all elected Paul and me with a mandate to ascertain the state of our finances and recommend an appropriate course of action. Now you can shoot the messenger if you like, in which case we'll happily stand down and you can elect someone else to sort out the mess, but if you want us to do it, then I'd suggest you listen to what I'm saying.'

That seemed to shut the dissenters up.

'Hear, hear,' came a commanding voice from the back of the room.

A tall, imposing-looking man stood up: it was Joe Haven from apartment 11E. I vaguely knew him, and understood that like me, he was a retired businessman. *Come to think of it, how come we hadn't thought of trying to inveigle him into taking on the presidency? Oh, well ... water under the bridge now, I suppose.*

'We should listen to what Roy is telling us,' he said. 'With all due respect to Jim, these problems have been building up for years; we should all be grateful that someone is finally trying to get to grips with them. As for the amount of the cash-call ... well, almost every one of us here has bought their apartment as a second or even third home. If we can afford that, then I think we can afford a few hundred euros to help resolve this situation.'

I nearly fell off my chair – incidentally, a far more substantial affair than any of those at the previous meeting – at this unsolicited show of support. I nodded appreciatively towards my new-found ally.

Jim Watkins stood up to remonstrate, but Joe hadn't finished. 'And as for my foul-mouthed friend in the second row, I'd suggest you pay attention to the information which we are being provided with, and consider what is in all our best interests, rather than shooting your mouth off in a knee-jerk reaction.'

'Who the fook are you calling foul-mouthed, ya stuck-up bastard?' responded spiky-hair, rising to his feet. 'Ya want to coom outside? I'll punch yer fookin' lights out.'

'PLEASE, PLEASE,' I shouted, 'there's no point in arguments and recriminations. I suggest we take a ten-minute break to let everyone cool down and then we can take a vote on my proposal.

The situation was thus – temporarily at least – defused.

***

When we reconvened, I was somewhat relieved to see that spiky-hair had not re-joined the meeting and also that Joe Haven's face had not been rearranged during the break.

The cash-call was approved by a majority, with five votes against and two abstentions.

I moved on to the next part of the meeting.

'OK, with the combination of the loan from the administrator and the cash-call, we can stave off the most urgent crises, but we have a longer term issue to contend with. The reason we got into this hole in the first place is that for years, our income from community fees has fallen well short of our regular outgoings. There are two principal reasons for this: firstly, we have been consistently overspending the budget; and secondly, there are more than twenty per cent of owners who have been defaulting on payment of their community fees – in some cases for years.'

The blonde, Irish lady, who had previously spoken up at the 'collapsing chairs' meeting, raised her hand.

'Yes, Clare.'

'I'm very pleased that someone is finally digging in to all this, but I think it's disgraceful that so many owners are not paying their fair share. What are we going to do about it?'

'Well, the first thing is that Paul' – I gestured towards him, sitting alongside me – 'has been chasing the offenders. Can you give us an update, Paul?'

He cleared his throat before replying. 'When we went through the accounts we found that sixteen owners owed money. The total accumulated debt was ninety-seven thousand euros.'

'Ninety-seven thousand?' gasped Clare. 'How can that have been allowed to happen?'

'Well,' said Paul, 'I can't really comment on that, but the important thing is what we actually do about it. I've been in contact with most of the debtors now, and I'm pleased to say that five of them have agreed to pay some or all of their debt ... that should bring in about nineteen thousand euros. The rest, I'm afraid, are, so far, refusing to co-operate.'

Dr Ramani – who was, in fact, the worst offender of all, spoke up. 'I not pay a penny until you sort out all dreadful problems I tell you about.'

Technically I suppose, she should have been talking about cents rather than pennies, but it would probably not have been helpful, at this juncture, to raise the point. Paul had already related to me his several bizarre telephone conversations with the eccentric doctor. In her mind, withholding her fees for years on end was a legitimate protest against her being subjected to topless sunbathers by the pool, the sounds of enthusiastic lovemaking from the apartment above, and Jim Watkins 'trimming her bush'.

Oh yes, I don't believe I have yet explained about the bush-trimming incident. Thankfully, it bore no resemblance to the somewhat disturbing image which had popped into my head when Dr Ramani had first mentioned it. Apparently, Jim Watkins and the doctor had been engaged in a long running dispute about the way her garden – 5A was a ground floor apartment on the front row adjacent to the public road – had been allowed to get rather overgrown, with one very large bush, in particular, spilling out onto the road. After numerous attempts to get her to cut back the offending bush, Jim had taken matters into his own hands and arranged for the community gardeners to do it. This, it seems, had absolutely incensed her.

'Dr Ramani,' replied Paul, smoothly, 'we *will* take a look at the various issues you have raised, but they are not on the agenda for this meeting, so could we please deal with them separately?'

'OK, but I not pay nothing 'til you sort them out.' She sat back in her chair, stony-faced.

'Thank you,' said Paul. 'Now, in order to address the problem of persistent debtors I have two proposals: first I would like authorisation from the meeting to start immediate legal proceedings against the offenders.'

'Yeah, lock the fookers up!'

Oh dear – spiky-hair had not, in fact, gone home, but had taken up a different seat at the back of the room, partially obscured from my view by a pillar.

'Sssh!' hissed a number of those present.

Paul did not respond to the interjection but continued, 'Given the notoriously slow speed of the Spanish legal system, it could take quite a while to bring those concerned to court but we have to start somewhere, and who knows? Maybe the threat of impending legal action may induce some to pay up before they actually end up in court.'

Murmurs of approval rippled around the room.

'My second proposal is to introduce financial inducements to all owners to pay promptly. Apparently, under Spanish law we can't actually charge a penalty for late payment but we can introduce a discount for prompt payment.'

Joe Haven raised his hand; Paul invited him, with a nod, to speak.

'Paul, given the community's dire financial state, surely we can't afford to go giving discounts?'

Paul smiled and extended a hand towards Marysa. 'Perhaps Marysa can explain?'

She nodded. 'What we can do is increase everyone's fees by one quarter—'

'Fook that!' interjected spiky-hair.

'Please,' said Paul, 'let Marysa finish explaining.'

She resumed her explanation. 'As I was saying, we can increase everyone's fees by one quarter and then, if they pay on time, give the same amount back to them as a prompt payment discount. That way they pay the same as before. Those who do not pay on time, however, will not get the discount so they end up having to pay twenty-five per cent more than the rest.'

Joe looked puzzled. 'But how is that any different from just charging a twenty-five per cent penalty for late payment?'

'Mathematically,' explained Marysa, 'it isn't ... but in the eyes of the law, it is.' Joe's brow was still wrinkled in puzzlement. 'It's Spain,' declared Marysa, as if this explained everything.

Joe shook his head in bewilderment; he shrugged, but didn't pursue the matter any further.

Paul's proposals for tackling the debt problem were carried by majority vote, with the same handful of dissenters as before. I took over the meeting once more, to tackle the final contentious proposal.

'I am confident that the actions which have just been approved will, eventually, reduce the problem of debtors to manageable proportions. However, we have a substantial deficit between income and expenditure right now, so I am proposing an immediate revision to the budget. If you take a look at your sheet headed 'Budget and Fee Structure' I'll try to explain.'

I paused for a few seconds to allow everyone to find the sheet in question before continuing.

'There is a very definite system, set out by law, for determining the level of community fees which owners have to pay.

'You compile a budget for what you expect to spend during a given year and then you have to set the community fees at a level just sufficient to cover that expenditure. Now that's fine if every owner pays up and expenditure remains within budget, but if either of those things doesn't happen then you end up with a deficit. In our case, the premise fails on both counts: we have owners who don't pay *and* expenditure which exceeds the budget.'

'So what's the solution?' enquired Joe Haven.

'Well to start with, we need to increase the budget to reflect the amount we are actually spending. If you look at the proposed new budget compared to the existing one, you will see that many budget lines have been increased accordingly.'

'But that still leaves us with the problem of owners who are defaulting on their fees,' said Joe. 'You already explained that bringing them into line is going to take some time.'

'True,' I said, 'and until we can do so, we are going to have to increase fees even further. Given the constraints of the system, the only way to do this is to set a budget which is actually higher than the amount we really expect to spend. If you look again at the proposed budget you will see there is a new line headed "Reserve Fund", with fifty thousand euros allocated. The law allows us to include such an element in the budget as contingency for unexpected expenses or shortfall in income.'

'OK – makes sense,' said Joe.

Judging by the puzzled expressions on the faces of some of the others present, I guessed that it didn't make sense to everyone. I decided to press on with my explanation and handle the inevitable questions at the end.

'You will also see that there is another new line headed "Painting Fund", with twenty thousand euros allocated. This is money which will be put to one side in a separate bank account to start accumulating a fund to help pay for the refurbishment and repainting of the exterior walls as and when it becomes necessary.'

Actually, twenty thousand was a pitifully inadequate amount to put into the painting fund given the likely cost of repainting, and the fact that we were starting from zero, but I felt that suggesting any more than this really would be a step too far at this point.

I paused and looked around the room to try to gauge how well my words had been received. Apart from Joe, there were a handful of others who were nodding: islands of understanding punctuating a sea of blank faces.

Everyone seemed to grasp the next bit OK, though.

'The net result of all this is that the proposed budget totals five hundred and ninety thousand euros: an increase of sixteen per cent on the existing budget. That means, unfortunately, a sixteen per cent increase in everyone's community fees.'

There was a stunned silence for a moment or two and then ...

'Fook that! Sixteen bleedin' per cent ... you must be fookin' joking.' Spiky-hair was on his feet now.

Before I could respond, a stout, middle-aged lady in the front row – I hadn't met her before – added, 'That really is too much. We already pay very high fees, and besides, I'm saving up to have my kitchen refitted. It'll be lovely when it's done; I'm having those swanky De Dietrich appliances ... brushed stainless steel. And those cool blue LED lights in glass-fronted cabinets ... you know the sort? It really is going to look wonderful when it's done. But, if I have to pay extra fees, I'll have to postpone my lovely new kitchen for at least a few months.'

'Well,' I suggested, 'we'll all have to make some sacrifices if we want to sort out the community's finances.'

Jim Watkins added his two pennyworth. 'This really is unacceptable. For years I have sought to keep the fees as affordable as possible – in fact they haven't increased at all over the last three years. And now you want to increase them by sixteen per cent ... outrageous!'

And while doing all this noble work on behalf of owners, you have driven the community into bankruptcy. My patience was now exhausted.

'ENOUGH!' I shouted, raising my hand in a reasonable facsimile of a Nazi salute. This succeeded in silencing the baying mob. I took advantage of the lull to make my final point. 'Look, as I said earlier, you elected Paul and me to investigate the finances, figure out what's going on, and recommend an action plan. That's what we've done. Now if you don't like what you are hearing, I'm afraid that's hard luck, because that's the situation in which we find ourselves. I don't like it any more than you do.' Subdued grumbles slunk around the sullen crowd. 'You can choose to support our plan or reject it. I have to advise you, though, that if we don't take appropriate action now, it's just a matter of time – and not much time, actually – before we find ourselves living in an overgrown jungle, with no electricity or water, and crumbling infrastructure.'

I paused for a reaction.

Joe Haven once again came to my aid. 'Roy is right. We are in a hole at the moment and it seems to me that the plan just proposed is, indeed, the best way in which to start digging ourselves out of that hole.'

My neighbour Neil – the one who had talked me into taking on this Godforsaken task in the first place – weighed in as well. 'Hear, hear! We are fortunate to have Roy and Paul finally tackling these problems on our behalf. We should give them our full support.'

Thanks, Neil.

A surly silence followed, eventually broken by the astonishingly persistent Dr Ramani. 'But this don't do nothing to sort out my—'

I cut her off, jabbing my hand forward, palm-outward, in a 'stop' gesture. 'OK, I don't intend to take any further questions on this matter. You have all heard what we propose so I suggest we take a vote on it.'

When the hands went up, it was much closer this time, but when the votes were counted, our proposals were carried by majority, with sixty-seven per cent voting in favour.

Paul and I had discussed, before the meeting, whether to raise the subject of the collapsing retaining wall and the hundred and twenty thousand euros which would be needed to fix it. We had agreed to wait and see how the meeting went and judge whether the time was right.

I judged that the time *wasn't* right. This was a bombshell for another day.

***

After the meeting I made a phone call. A couple of days earlier I had received a text message from the vet to whom I had taken the injured cat, asking me to call back. I figured that the cat was probably dead by now anyway, so with everything else going on, it wasn't exactly high on my list of priorities.

'Ah yes, Mr Groves,' came the reply on the phone, in perfect English, with only a trace of an accent. I recognised it as belonging to the very helpful female receptionist. 'I am pleased to say that the cat is fine.'

'He is?'

'Well, "he" is actually a "she", and remarkably, she has suffered no injuries other than a sprain in her left hind leg. The X-rays show no broken bones and all the other tests are also negative. She is in near-perfect health.'

'I'm amazed,' I said, feeling genuinely pleased that I hadn't driven the poor creature to its death.

'Oh,' added the receptionist, 'one more thing ... she is pregnant. We counted four kittens, and as far as we can ascertain they are all fine too.'

'Pregnant? I ... well, that's certainly a surprise.'

'Now, before you come to collect your cat' – *my* cat? I hadn't thought it through this far, but I suppose no-one else was going to take responsibility for it – 'would you like me to run through your bill?'

'My bill? Oh ... well, yes, I suppose so.'

'Right, well the tests and clinical care amount to five hundred and seventy euros. Then, there's five nights bed and board, including tonight, at forty euros each ... that's another two hundred ... and then you will need us to supply a proper cat carrier, at ninety-four euros—'

'Whoa ... forget the cat carrier: I'll use a cardboard box.'

'I'm afraid we can't allow that, Mr. Groves: health and safety regulations, you see.'

'Of course,' I sighed, defeated.

'So that's eight hundred and sixty-four euros in total ... unless, of course you want us to look after her for a little longer, in which case—'

'I'll collect her tomorrow,' I interjected. The following morning was out because I was due to meet with the developer responsible for building the defective retaining wall, but I was damned if I was going to pay for yet another night's five star accommodation for the wretched creature. 'Would around 2 p.m. be OK?'

'Yes, that's fine. We'll see you then,' she said, bright as a button.

Eight hundred and sixty-four bloody euros to save a wild cat that I have no idea what to do with!

Chapter 11

Alfredo González was head of *Hermanos González Promociónes,* the property development company which had built our urbanisation, and in whose offices we now sat. González was a swarthy-looking character, probably in his mid-fifties, with improbably black hair slicked back from a receding hairline and terminating in a tangle of greasy curls at the nape of his neck. His olive complexion was punctuated by numerous pits and creases either side of his disproportionately large nose. If ever someone could look untrustworthy on the basis of physical appearance alone, then this was surely that person. Nevertheless I resolved to put such irrational prejudice aside and approach the meeting in a positive and constructive manner.

Accompanying me, from our administrators, were Marysa – typically, inappropriately attired in very tight-fitting yellow shorts and her trademark Ugg boots – and Sergio, who was, as usual, immaculately turned out, in a navy blue business suit. Alongside González sat his brother, José, a little younger and rather less rough-looking, but unmistakeably sharing the same genes. Apparently, he was a partner in the business.

After the preliminary introductions, handshaking, coffee-pouring, and insincere small talk, we got down to business.

'So,' said González, in heavily-accented English, 'how can I help you gentlemen? ... and of course, lady,' he added, stealing a salacious glance at Marysa's sturdy thighs through the glass-topped table. Her eyes flashed with irritation, but she said nothing. Instead she hunched over her laptop, ready to record the content of the meeting.

'Well,' I replied, trying to sound as conciliatory as possible, 'firstly, may I thank you for agreeing to see us at such short notice.'

'My pleasure,' he oozed, his thin lips curling into what passed for a smile, but was actually quite disconcerting. He waited for me to continue.

'We wanted to talk to you about the retaining wall which, as you know, is collapsing in some sections.'

'Well, I will need to correct you on a matter of fact there, but that can wait for a moment. For now, please continue.'

Oh great – I've barely opened my mouth and already he's quibbling. Smartarse.

'Since taking over as president, I have become aware that our community has been in dispute with your company for some years over this issue, to the extent that there is now a legal action in process.'

'Yes ... most regrettable,' replied González, ruefully shaking his head.

'Well,' I continued, 'to pursue such legal action to its conclusion will clearly take a very long time and cost a great deal of money, so I wanted to explore whether we could come to some sort of agreement to settle the matter outside of the courts.'

González smiled his somewhat disturbing smile once more. 'That would indeed be the best outcome for all concerned,' he agreed. He glanced sideways at his brother, who gave an almost-imperceptible nod. 'So what sort of settlement did you have in mind?'

At this point, I invited Sergio to outline our position, given that he had far more experience than me of the Spanish legal system and how such a negotiation might proceed.

'As you are aware,' he began, 'we have been advised that the likely cost of repairs is one hundred and twenty thousand euros. This is the basis of our legal claim. Now in order to avoid—'

Sergio's exposition was cut short as both González brothers began simultaneously laughing and vigorously shaking their heads.

'I fail to see any cause for laughter,' said Sergio, visibly irritated.

'This figure,' declared Alfredo, jabbing his forefinger firmly down onto the table top, 'is based on a complete misunderstanding of the situation ... something which I have made abundantly clear to the previous representatives of your community.'

'What do you mean?' I interjected.

'The cement coating which we are discussing is not a retaining wall. There is no need for a retaining wall, as the main constituent of the hill itself is quartzite: a very durable type of rock similar to marble ... only harder.'

'So what does that mean?' I asked, puzzled.

'It means that no retaining wall is necessary; the cement coating is merely a cosmetic feature intended to tidy up the cut face of the hillside.'

'But why then,' I asked, 'would the expert, previously employed by the community, have advised that a full retaining wall was necessary?'

González spread his hands and raised his shoulders. 'Who knows? Perhaps he had a brother or a cousin in the building trade whom he intended to recommend as the contactor to construct such a wall.'

This remark clearly raised Sergio's hackles. 'That,' he snapped, 'is a wholly unjustified slur on a professional architect.'

González shrugged. 'Well, I don't know why such a preposterous recommendation was made. Had your predecessors come to talk to us in a civilized manner rather than rushing into an ill-advised legal action, then perhaps everything could have been amicably settled years ago.'

Our previous game plan for the meeting was now well and truly shot to pieces. If there was any truth in what González was telling us then the whole dispute was based on a colossal misunderstanding. *Bloody Watkins again,* I thought – rather uncharitably, I suppose, given that, at this stage we only had González's own word for his assertion.

Sergio appeared now to have gained control of the anger which had threatened to burst forth. 'So what do you propose?' he asked.

'José here can answer that. He is a technical architect.'

Actually, we already knew that Alfredo's brother was an architect, since he had been named in the legal papers as the architect who had presided over the original building of the urbanisation. He was hardly neutral then, but we were at least willing to hear what he had to say.

He cleared his throat and began to speak. 'To make good those sections of the cement facing which have come adrift would cost in the region of eight thousand euros. We would be prepared to share that cost fifty-fifty with the community.'

Right, so we have sued for a hundred and twenty thousand euros and you're offering four thousand. It seemed like an absurd offer, but there seemed little point in continuing with the meeting until we had investigated González's claims. I glanced at Sergio, who had evidently come to a similar conclusion.

'I suggest,' he said, 'that we adjourn this meeting to allow time for us to complete our own investigation into the new information which you have supplied.'

'Of course,' replied González, rising to his feet, smiling. 'Let us hope that we can now resolve this unfortunate matter amicably.'

Once outside the building we held a brief post-mortem on the meeting, standing in the street.

'So what do you think?' I asked.

'What I think,' replied Marysa, 'is that he's lying through his teeth.'

'I agree,' said Sergio, 'but we should check out his claims for ourselves. If he *is* telling the truth, it could save a great deal of time, money, and aggravation.'

'What I would suggest,' said Marysa, 'is that we have a geotechnical survey carried out.'

'A geo what?' I asked.

'A geotechnical survey,' she repeated. 'It involves drilling down into the ground and extracting samples of material for analysis. That will tell us for sure what materials the hillside contains.'

'Sounds like a good suggestion,' I said. 'Any idea what it would cost?'

Marysa looked enquiringly at Sergio. 'My guess is about three thousand euros,' he said.

'Three thousand that we can ill afford,' I grumbled.

'On the other hand,' said Sergio, 'if it could save a hundred and twenty thousand ...'

'Point taken,' I conceded. 'OK, can you go ahead and arrange the survey? Once we know the results, we'll be in a better position to decide on our next steps.'

With that agreed, our impromptu meeting broke up and we all headed for home. As I opened the door of my car – unfortunately, parked in full sunshine – the wall of hot air which escaped was somewhat akin to that felt when opening an oven door. I opened the other three doors and stepped back a few paces into the shade cast by a nearby Jacaranda tree, resplendent with vibrant blue blooms. As I stood there for a minute or two, waiting for the car to cool down a little, I wondered whether another discussion with Jim Watkins might help cast more light on previous dealings with Alfredo González. I quickly dismissed the idea: it was becoming clear that Jim had no intention of helping us; indeed, he seemed to positively delight in throwing a spanner into the proverbial works at every opportunity. No, I would just wait for the results of the survey and take things from there. At least now there was a glimmer of hope that the situation might not be as dire as I had previously assumed. I certainly hoped that this would turn out to be the case, because I wasn't relishing the prospect of going back to the owners again with the news that we might have to rustle up another hundred and twenty thousand euros, on top of what they had already agreed to cough up.

***

As I drove back from the vet's I considered what to do with the cat which was ensconced within the ninety-bloody-four-bloody-euro plastic case which sat on the front passenger seat alongside me. My previously murderous thoughts towards the animal had softened considerably since learning that it – she – was a mother-to-be. I figured the best thing was just to release her back into the wild, preferably some distance away from *Las Hermosas Vistas*, which was already home to far too many stray and feral cats. First though, I was going to take her round to Angelique's; she had insisted that she'd like to see the animal to 'make sure ze pussy is OK'. Well, I was hardly going to turn down an opportunity to go and see the lovely Angelique again, was I?

As I pulled up alongside Angelique's apartment block, a plaintive meow emanated from the box alongside me. I decided to open the door, just a little, to steal a peek inside. I was greeted with a venomous glare, made all the more menacing by the white eyepatch.

'I hope you appreciate the time, effort, and expense I've been to on your behalf,' I said, locking eyes with the creature, willing it to back down.

The cat's response was to curl back its lips and bare its teeth, spitting spitefully at me before launching a well-aimed swipe with outstretched claws. This time, however, I was ready for it – I swiftly pulled my face back and slammed the plastic door shut just in time to avoid the razor-sharp claws. The cat hissed at me furiously, evidently not at all happy that its strike had been frustrated.

'Ha!' I cried. 'You're not as fast as you thought you were, eh?'

The cat merely continued hissing at me through the grille in the door.

'Come on then, let's go and show Angelique what my eight hundred and sixty-four euros has bought.'

When she opened the door, my jaw dropped anew. Clad in a very short, figure-hugging, bright orange dress, she looked spectacular. The deep 'V' neckline displayed a generous depth of cleavage which exerted a magnetic pull on my eyes, in spite of the dazzling smile with which she greeted me. This woman would probably look good in a dustbin liner, but dressed like this ... well. Was she actually dolling herself up like this for my benefit?

Don't be silly, Roy. Why on earth should she be remotely interested in dressing up for you? But then again, look at her makeup and hair: she looks as if she's just emerged from a beauty salon. Surely she wouldn't bother going to so much trouble just to stay in the house?

'Oh, 'alo Roy,' she said, standing to one side to allow me in, ''Ow is ze pussy?'

'Er ... fighting fit, I would say.' I set the plastic box down on the floor.

'Oooh, let me look at 'er.'

'OK, but be careful ... she's still pretty vicious.'

I opened the door, just a couple of inches, to allow Angelique to look inside. I was tensed to slam it shut quickly should the psychotic beast decide to launch another attack.

It didn't. Amazingly, as Angelique bent down and began cooing at it, the cat responded by slinking cautiously forward, pushing its nose through the narrow gap at the edge of the door and purring softly.

'Look,' said Angelique, 'she likes me.' And with that, she extended a tentative hand towards the cat.

'Be careful!' I cried, in alarm. 'She'll go for you.'

But she didn't. Angelique edged closer and closer: six inches ... three ... one ... and then she was touching the top of the animal's head, gently stroking the fur as it tried to push its head forward through the narrow gap which I was defending.

'It's alright,' she soothed, 'I won't 'urt you.'

The cat nuzzled its head into her hand, purring loudly now, as I relented and let it push its head right through the gap.

Abso-bloody-lutely incredible! When I go near it, it tries to rip out my jugular, but when she offers the hand of friendship the feral beast becomes, quite literally, a pussycat.

I was nevertheless concerned. I'd seen – and felt – what this cat could do and I'd have been mortified if it took a chunk out of Angelique's gorgeous face.

'Please, Angelique, don't take any chances. Let's get her back into her box.'

The look on her upturned face was almost one of pleading, but eventually she complied, easing the creature back into its box, allowing me to close and latch the door, relieved that Angelique's exquisite features remained intact.

As I stood up, she remained kneeling on the floor, gazing at the cat though the grille.

'What are we going to do with 'er?' she said, turning her face upward to look at me.

I offered her my hand and helped her to her feet. We moved over to her sofa and sat down.

'So what are we going to do with 'er?' she repeated.

As I began to outline my plan to release the cat into the countryside, somewhere away from the urbanisation, Angelique's brow furrowed and her luxuriously full lips formed into a pucker.

'But, will she be alright out there in the wild?'

'Well,' I suggested, somewhat bemused by Angelique's protectiveness towards the animal, 'she was obviously managing OK before she wandered into your apartment.'

'But she 'as 'ad a terrible fright, and she won't know where she is.'

'Well, that's true, I suppose, but—'

'And what about 'er new babies? 'Ow will she look after zem wizout zeir papa?'

This was getting silly: I was quite sure that 'Papa' was, by now, long gone – probably busy screwing the next feline temptress that flashed her butt at him.

'Er, Angelique ... I thought you told me you didn't like cats.'

She pouted prettily, and shrugged in that typically Gallic way. 'I don't really, but ... well zis cat is so pretty wiz 'er white eyepatch and 'er little white sock.'

Looks positively sinister if you ask me.

'And I'm worried about 'er kitties.'

I sighed, utterly perplexed by Angelique's one-hundred-and-eighty-degree turnaround in her attitude towards the animal. 'OK, well what do you suggest then?'

'Could I keep 'er 'ere wiz me ... just for a few days until I am sure she is alright?'

Her beautiful blue eyes widened and her eyelashes fluttered as she fixed me with a pleading expression. It wasn't easy to say no to such a persuasive entreaty; my resistance crumbled in the face of her feminine charms. In any case, I reasoned, it wasn't really for me to say whether she could or could not keep the cat for a while, was it?

'Well ... if you're sure.'

Her face broke into a luminous smile. 'Oh, zank you.'

'But, be careful ... you've seen how vicious she can be.'

'Oh, I zink she likes me. I don't zink she would 'urt me.'

I shrugged. 'Well take care then, and let me know if you need any more help.'

As I stood up, ready to leave, she followed suit, smoothing down her dress which had ridden up progressively further with each minute we had been sitting there. I suddenly remembered something.

'Oh, I ... that is we ... Donna and I ... wondered if you would like to join us for dinner one evening?'

She smiled. 'Zat would be lovely.'

'And bring your daughter too ... Miriam isn't it?'

'Yes, Miriam. Zank you so much. When shall we come?'

'Would next Saturday be OK ... about eight?'

'Perfect. I will look forward to meeting your wife.'

'OK ... well I should go now.'

'Zank you for everyzing, Roy; you are a very kind man.'

With that, she leaned forward and kissed me on the cheek, and then on the other cheek, and then on the first one again. *Well, this is not so bad*, I thought. *Maybe it was actually worth the money to save the cat* – to which I was now warming a little – *after all*.

Chapter 12

It was 1.30 a.m. and Donna had long since gone to bed. I took a sip from the glass of malt whisky in front of me, swirling it in my mouth and savouring the smoky, peaty flavour before allowing the fiery liquid to course down my throat. I gave a deep sigh of satisfaction as I gazed at the three sheets of paper laid out on the table in front of me, illuminated by the puddle of light cast by the desktop lamp alongside my laptop. The floor around me was carpeted with numerous screwed up balls of paper, the products of my many failed attempts to arrive at those three documents which I had now constructed.

That afternoon, FAG had sent me the first set of financial accounts presented in their own standard format. They were, to me, barely more comprehensible than those provided by the previous administrator. I had spent the last four hours trying to untangle them and now, finally, I had succeeded.

Now I know that, to many – if not most – people, financial accounts are about as interesting as a party political broadcast, but if you're trying to manage any sort of organisation which runs on money – and that means just about any sort of organisation – you really need to understand them. And I didn't.

There's no point in false modesty. I'm probably better than most at finding my way round a set of accounts; I had to be in order to do my previous job. The fact that I couldn't understand the accounts of a small organisation with a budget of barely over half a million euros really irked me. As soon as I realised that the new accounts sent by FAG also defeated me, I resolved to deconstruct them and then reconstruct them in a way which made sense.

And now I had. Those three sheets, painfully extracted from a massive wad of documents provided by FAG were: a profit and loss account, a balance sheet, and a cash flow statement. These three documents basically told me everything I needed to know about the financial health of the community – which, as you will have already gathered, was pretty dire.

I took another sip of my whisky and set about composing a brief email to Paul, whose accounting skills were probably on a par with my own, and Neil, who was an accountant by profession. I attached my newly-formatted accounts and hit 'send'. If there was anything wrong with my analysis, I was pretty sure one or other of them would pick it up.

I looked at the clock: 1.51 a.m. I yawned – definitely time for bed now. As I powered down the laptop and began gathering up all the rubbish from the floor, I picked up the distinctive, rattly, whining sound of a golf buggy making its way up the steeply sloping internal roadway outside. There was nothing unusual in hearing this sound during the day as the maintenance engineer, the gardeners, the cleaners, and the security guards all used these vehicles to get around the urbanisation, but at this time of night the only staff member on duty would be one of the security guards, and they had instructions to make their regular patrols on foot to avoid disturbing residents. So who could it be?

The sound abruptly stopped; the buggy had evidently pulled up right outside our block. Around one minute later the doorbell rang.

Really? At this time of night? There had better be a good reason for this.

When I opened the door I was confronted with the sight of a man who appeared to be in the grip of some sort of panic attack. His eyes were bulging, their bloodshot whites contrasting starkly with the darkness of his gaunt, sweat-streaked face. It took me a few moments to recognise him, so terrified did he look.

'Mr Groves, Mr Groves, come quick … quick. We have emergency!'

It was Calvin, one of our two security guards. He was an amiable guy who hailed from West Africa somewhere – Morocco I believe. As usual, the all-pervasive aroma of tobacco smoke clung to his clothes. He always looked rather sickly, with his sunken cheeks and stooped posture, but tonight he looked as though he was just about to have a heart attack.

'What is it, Calvin? What's happening?'

'Block 5 … the lady, she hear screams … I go, and … and …'

He was hyperventilating.

'Slow down … take some deep breaths.' He did. 'That's it … that's better.'

Once he had regained control of his breathing I tried again. 'So tell me what's happening in block 5.'

'The lady in 5B, she call me to say she hear screams from apartment above her. She think someone being attacked.'

'What … was she sure about this?'

'Yes, so I go round there to check and I hear it too … screams coming from 5C. It sound terrible … I think someone being murdered.'

'Murdered?'

He nodded vigorously.

Oh shit. I really, really don't need this.

'What we do, Mr Groves?'

To be honest I wasn't too sure.

'OK, let's get down there right now.' I would try to formulate a plan in the couple of minutes it would take us to get there.

'Roy … what's going on … who's that at the door?' Donna's sleepy-sounding voice wafted down the stairs from our bedroom.

'It's nothing … go back to sleep. I'll explain later.'

'OK, let's go,' I said to Calvin, grabbing the torch which always hung from a hook alongside the front door.

Calvin, who now seemed to have entered some sort of catatonic trance, snapped out of it, spun around and bounded towards the lift, with me close behind.

The buggy skidded to a halt outside block 5. All was quiet, and everything was in darkness, apart from one window in apartment 5C, which was illuminated with a soft light, diffused by what looked like voile curtains.

We watched and we waited. Nothing for around thirty seconds or so, but then a figure – a large male figure, visible only in silhouette – approached the window and pulled back the curtain a little. Perhaps he had heard the approaching buggy and decided to investigate. I instinctively shrank back in my seat, as though making myself as small as possible would somehow make me invisible. I needn't have worried, though: the buggy was in complete darkness – I doubted that he could see us. After a few seconds he had evidently concluded that there was nothing to see, and closed the curtains. As he did so, I could see that he was holding something in his right hand.

'Look, Mr Groves,' whispered Calvin, his voice thin and tremulous, 'he got a gun.'

A gun? Was it a gun? I wasn't sure, but I wasn't taking any chances. 'Right, Calvin, go down to your office, call the police, and wait there until they arrive. I'll stay here and make sure no-one enters or leaves.' How exactly I was going to prevent a gun-toting murderer from leaving, however, armed only with a torch, I wasn't entirely sure.

Calvin nodded, his Adam's apple bobbing up and down furiously. He stepped silently out of the buggy and set off on foot, adopting a stealthy cartoon-burglar-style creeping action. I settled down to wait.

I didn't have to wait long. It was less than ten minutes later that Calvin came striding up the path flanked by two police officers, one male and one female. He looked a lot bolder now.

The three of them approached stealthily as I stepped out of the buggy to meet them.

'¿Ha ocurrido algo desde que llegó?' asked the policeman.

I looked at Calvin, helplessly; the limits of my meagre grasp of Spanish had already been breached.

'He ask if anything happen since you arrive.' I shook my head.

The two officers exchanged a brief glance before both drawing their guns. 'Quédense allí,' ordered the female officer, gesturing with palm turned outwards that we should stay put. Well, I certainly wasn't about to lead the way.

The two of them strode up to the front door and rang the bell. No answer. They waited around fifteen seconds before ringing it again. Still no answer. After another ten seconds or so, the policeman tried the door handle. The door wasn't locked; it swung open easily. A big, muscular figure could be seen, framed in the hallway. Both police officers dropped to a crouching posture, levelling their guns in double-handed grips.

'What the fook ...?' exclaimed the man.

I recognised the voice immediately.

'Levante las manos,' commanded the male officer.

I'm not sure whether spiky-hair understood the Spanish but he certainly got the message: he immediately raised both hands. In his right hand, silhouetted against the light behind him, could be clearly seen what looked like a gun.

'Deje caer la arma!' shouted the policeman.

'What the fook you talking about?'

Calvin, who had, by now jumped out of the buggy and moved up behind the police officers quickly translated. 'He say drop your weapon.'

'What ... this?' said spiky-hair, lowering his right hand which was holding the weapon in question and extending it towards the two police officers.

The two of them tensed in their crouching postures and pointed their guns more forcefully. '*Deje caerla!*' yelled the female officer.

'You drop gun, now!' added Calvin, helpfully. He appeared to actually be enjoying the situation now that he had two armed police officers between him and the villain of the piece.

'I can't fookin' believe this,' muttered spiky-hair. 'You gotta be fookin' joking.' Nevertheless, he did as he was ordered.

The policeman rushed up and forced spiky-hair's hands behind his back and handcuffed him, all the time covered by the female officer, who kept her gun trained on him.

'What the fook's goin' on here?' demanded the prisoner.

No-one replied to his question, but the policeman bent down and picked up the weapon. He studied it for several seconds before turning and offering it to his colleague for inspection. After a couple more seconds both of them burst out laughing.

With the suspected assailant constrained, and both police officers apparently now pretty relaxed about the situation, I decided to move forward and see what all the hilarity was about. The policewoman turned and held out the offending object. It wasn't a gun: it was plastic, about nine inches long, bright purple in colour, with a jutting protuberance near one end.

A Rampant Rabbit. In case I was in any doubt as to as to its intended use, the policewoman pointed it down towards her crotch and jerked it back and forth a few times, making a face which was a parody of sexual bliss. She collapsed into fits of giggles, as her colleague un-cuffed spiky-hair.

'Well, thanks for that,' said spiky-hair, his voice heavy with sarcasm, adding – rather inadvisedly, I thought – 'you bastard fookers.'

Fortunately for him, it seemed that the police officers' grasp of colloquial English was not quite up to interpreting this remark.

'What the fook are you lot doing barging into my home and bringing the filth with you?'

I thought it best if I – as the only native English speaker in our little party – now stepped in. 'We had a report of a woman screaming and we thought there might be some sort of assault taking place.'

'Oh, that'll be my Tracy. She screams like crazy when I'm givin' her one. She's always gaggin' for it you see ... can't get enough of it.' He turned his head and yelled over his shoulder, 'Trace ... Trace, babe ... can you come out here?'

A few moments later, a very curvaceous young lady, clad in a silky red bathrobe, stepped out from the bedroom, wearing very heavy eye makeup and bright red lipstick. Her long, harshly-blonde hair spilled in a dishevelled tangle over her shoulders.

'Tell 'em babe ... tell 'em how you just can't keep quiet when I'm stokin' the old fire down below.' He turned back towards us to elaborate. 'When you got a dick the size of mine, you see, the ladies just can't help a bit of screaming.'

'Oh, Bruce,' she giggled, 'doooont ... you'll embarrass me.' Her cheeks flushed red enough to show through even the generous layer of blusher which adorned them.

'Honestly, though,' said Bruce – as I now knew he was called – 'she just can't get enough. Even outlasts me sometimes, and that's not easy 'cos I'm the man, if you know what I mean.'

'Er, yes ... I think so,' I murmured, somewhat disoriented by this whole bizarre exchange.

'That's when I give her a taste of the old Rabbit,' he said, gesturing towards the purple object which the policewoman still held in her hand. She passed it to him, her face a picture of amused bewilderment.

Tracey giggled again, putting her hand to her mouth. 'Oh, I *am* awful, aren't I?'

Bruce placed a reassuring arm around her shoulders. 'No you ain't babe – you just got a healthy appetite, that's all.'

The male police officer was now looking distinctly less amused than he had earlier, perhaps feeling that police time was being wasted. He gabbled something in Spanish which I didn't follow at all.

Calvin translated. 'They want to know if anyone press charges.'

'Er ... well no, I don't think so.' Could you just explain that it's all been a bit of a misunderstanding, and we're sorry to have wasted their time?'

Calvin spoke for about a minute, after which the policeman – rather grudgingly, I thought – nodded, his expression still dark and stern. The female officer, who looked as though she was still stifling a giggle, turned to Bruce, put her hands on her hips and gave a couple of pelvic thrusts.

'You want a bit of the old horizontal tango, darlin'?' responded Bruce, leering salaciously. 'Well, I'm your man … any time.'

She blew him a kiss, before being dragged away by her increasingly grumpy colleague.

'Can you open the gate and let them out please, Calvin?' I said.

He nodded and set off down the path with the two officers.

'I'm really sorry about the misunderstanding Mr … er …'

'Lee … Bruce Lee.' My face must have been a picture because he immediately continued, 'Yeah, I know … thing is my parents' name was Lee and they just loved the old martial arts movies so they thought it'd be a fookin' great idea to name me Bruce. Anyway,' he said, winking conspiratorially, 'I do a bit of the old Karate myself' – he crouched into a combat pose, fixing me with an icy stare for a second or two, before relaxing and laughing – 'so it's actually quite a laugh having this name.'

'I see. Well, sorry again, and to you … er … Tracy.'

'Tracy Charms,' she replied, nodding absently as she fussed with her hair, gazing into a handheld mirror.

Yes, I'll bet she does, I thought.

'I'm Roy Groves.'

'Yeah I know,' replied Bruce. 'President of the residents' committee thing, right?'

'That's right.'

'Well, make sure you deal with them fookers who won't pay their fees. If you need a bit of help persuading them, I'm your man.' He emphasised the point by slamming a fist into his cupped palm.

'Well, I'm sure that won't be necessary, but thanks for the offer, anyway.'

'Oh, and by the way,' he added, 'I think you're doing a right good job. Glad someone's actually trying to sort things out at last.'

You could have knocked me over with the proverbial feather.

Chapter 13

It was Saturday evening, 8.10 p.m. when the distinctive chimes of the doorbell sounded.

'Ah, that'll be her,' said Donna.

When I went to the door, I was greeted by Angelique's dazzling smile. I was relieved to see that, for this evening, she had dressed rather more conservatively than usual. She wore a floral print, knee-length dress with a high neckline. The closely fitted cut of the dress did little to disguise her superb figure, but at least she wasn't showing acres of thigh or flaunting her décolletage, which is exactly where the emerald pendant she was wearing would have nestled. She had also, I noticed, toned down the makeup a little: her eye liner subtler than usual and her lipstick a pale shade of pink.

She stepped forward and kissed me on the cheek ... once ... twice ... three times. I was, by now, quite used to the practice, in Spain, of a kiss on each cheek as a standard greeting between men and women or between two women, but not the three-kiss routine. Maybe it was a French thing, or maybe it was because Angelique especially liked me; I preferred to think the latter.

''Alo Roy ... I am sorry we are a little late.'

'Not at all ... come in.'

''Zis is Miriam,' she said, moving to one side, to allow her daughter to step forward.

Miriam was a mini-Angelique: the same olive complexion; the same long, jet black hair; and a face whose childlike good looks, bereft of any makeup, would soon mirror her mother's beauty. Her slim frame was clad in pink leggings and a black T-shirt with a sparkly gold logo on the front bearing the words 'Von Swiss'.

'Pleased to meet you, Mr Groves.' Amazing: barely a trace of an accent; you could almost have taken her for a native English speaker.

I wasn't entirely sure about the correct protocol for a middle-aged man greeting an eight-year-old girl. *Do you do the three-kiss thing? No ... might make you look like some sort of paedophile. Maybe just shake her hand? Hmm ... a bit formal.* I settled for bending down and taking her hand, kissing it lightly. Even as I did so, I thought this just made me look like a pretentious prat. *Oh well ... too late now.* 'Pleased to meet you too, Miriam,' I said.

Anyway, whatever she might have thought, she accepted my gallant gesture with good grace, dipping her head and performing a little curtsy.

I stepped aside and ushered them into the hallway where Donna had now appeared. She had chosen a long, black, velvet dress that evening, which made the most of her trim figure and contrasted nicely with her dark-blonde hair. Though she hadn't previously said anything, I sensed she might be a little concerned about being outshone by the new glamour-puss on the block. She needn't have worried: in spite of the age difference between the two women, they both looked great.

Angelique swept up to Donna and greeted her with the three-kiss routine. 'It is lovely to meet you at last, Mrs Groves.'

'Oh, please ... call me Donna.'

'Zank you ... and I am Angelique.'

Donna nodded. 'And this must be Miriam.'

Evidently suffering none of my inhibitions, she bent down and enveloped the little girl in a warm hug. 'You look just like your mother!' she exclaimed.

'Thank you,' said Miriam, in her perfect, barely-accented English, 'because my mother is very pretty.' Angelique tutted, raising her eyes, but smiling anyway.

'Yes, she is,' said Donna, laughing.

'Well, shall we go through to the lounge and sit down?' I ventured. 'And can I get you both a drink?'

'Do you 'ave any sparkling wine?'

'Yes, in fact we've just opened a bottle of Cava.'

'Zat would be perfect.'

'What about you, Miriam.'

'I like Cava, too,' she said, looking enquiringly at her mother.

Angelique smiled. 'Well, as we are out, just a little, but only if you 'ave some orange juice mixed wiz' it.'

'OK,' said Miriam. She turned to me and informed me, earnestly, 'That's called "Buck's Fizz" you know.'

'Is it indeed?' I replied, chuckling under my breath. 'I'll try to remember that.'

'So,' I said, once everyone was seated, 'how is the cat?'

'Oh, she is fine,' replied Angelique, 'and ze other news is that she 'as 'ad ze kittens – four of zem.'

'What … well, where are they?'

'Zey are still in my apartment. Zey are so cute; zey all have ze white eyepatch and ze little white sock like zeir mama.'

'So what are we going to do with them?'

'I 'ave decided to keep ze mama.'

'What?' I exclaimed. 'But she's dangerously wild.'

'Oh, no,' said Angelique, 'she is quite friendly now.'

I glanced involuntarily at the still-visible scratch marks on my arm. 'Friendly?'

Angelique nodded. 'Really … I zink she knows we are 'er friends.'

I shook my head in disbelief.

Miriam, who had been nodding excitedly throughout this exchange could contain herself no longer. 'And I am going to keep one of the kittens. It is a girl, and I am going to call her "Nicole".'

'And we 'ave named ze mama "Brigitte",' added Angelique.

I was, by now, completely lost for words; Donna took over.

'What about the other three kittens?'

A shadow flitted across Angelique's face. 'I can't keep zem all … I 'ave to find good 'omes for zem.' Her face brightened a little. 'Would you like to 'ave one?'

Judging by the expression on Donna's face when she glanced in my direction, I think I must have been gawping like a goldfish. I was still trying to form the words to express 'not in a million fucking years' in a more polite fashion, when she rescued me.

'That's very kind, but we really can't keep a pet here: we return to England quite often and it really wouldn't be fair on the cat.'

Oh, well done Donna … quick thinking.

Angelique's face fell once more.

'I'll tell you what,' said Donna, placing a comforting hand on Angelique's arm, 'I'll ask around some of my friends here in the urbanisation. Maybe one or two of them might want to take a kitten.'

'Oh, zank you,' cooed Angelique, flinging her arms around Donna and hugging her.

'Hey,' added Miriam, 'wouldn't that be cool? I mean if they lived around here I could still see them, and take Nicole to play with her brothers.'

Un-bloody-believable! Far from ridding the urbanisation of one of its troublesome feral cats, I had contributed to, potentially, increasing the moggy population by four!

***

Two hours later, we were on the dessert. So far, apart from the startling revelation about the cat – no, make that cats – the evening had gone better than I could possibly have wished for. There was none of the undercurrent of wariness between Angelique and Donna which I had feared might exist; on the contrary, they seemed really to have hit it off well, and had already planned a shopping trip together. Donna had also invited Angelique to a 'ladies' lunch' with some of the other women who lived in the urbanisation. Apparently, a local artisan was to speak on the subject of handmade jewellery using local materials, followed by an auction of some of her wares. Sounded expensive, I thought, but it was nice to see the two of them getting on so well.

As for Miriam, she was such a charming little girl: polite and well-mannered, yet brimming with confidence. And so pretty – definitely destined to break a few hearts in the future.

'Donna, that was delicious,' she declared. 'You are a very good cook.'

'Why, thank you,' said Donna. 'And your English is so good, I can hardly believe it. Where did you learn?'

'I went to an international school in Madrid,' she replied. 'They spoke English all the time there.'

Angelique expounded further. 'We move to Madrid before Miriam was even born. My 'usband, Jean-Claude, work for ze fashion chain, Von Swiss. 'E open up zeir first shop in Spain … in Madrid. I 'elp in ze shop, too. One year later my lovely Miriam was born.' She leant over and stroked Miriam's glossy black hair.

Miriam shook herself away, tutting loudly. 'Mama … please … I am not a little girl anymore.'

Angelique smiled. 'I know … sorry. Anyway, we send Miriam to an international school where zey speak English all ze time.'

'So she's grown up in an English-speaking environment,' said Donna.

'At school, yes … but at 'ome we always speak French.'

Miriam interjected, 'But a lot of my friends were Spanish, so at break times I learned to speak Spanish.'

Donna smiled at Miriam. 'So you can speak French, English *and* Spanish?'

Miriam nodded, beaming, 'And a little Russian.'

'Russian?' said Donna, her eyebrows rising in surprise. 'How's that?'

'Oh, some of my friends were Russian … and so are quite a few of my new friends at my school here in Marbella.'

'I send 'er to international school here too,' confirmed Angelique.

'So what happened?' asked Donna. 'I mean, well … Roy told me that you separated from your husband, but why did you decide to move away from Madrid?'

'I just didn't want to live zere anymore after …' She paused for a few moments, her eyes clouding over. And then it just all came tumbling out. 'Jean-Claude, he meet zis English woman who keep coming into ze shop. She was much older zan me … and she wasn't zat pretty, but anyway 'e falls for 'er. Eventually 'e tell me 'e wants to be wiz 'er, and zen, just like zat, 'e goes off to England wiz 'er … to Dartford.'

Dartford? He's got a good job in Spain's vibrant capital city, and an absolutely stunning wife, yet he leaves her for an older woman to live in Dartford. The man must be unhinged. I mean, no offence to anyone who lives in Dartford, but if you had experienced the buzz of Madrid, and if you could have seen the woman sitting opposite, whom he had abandoned – not to mention his delightful daughter – you would surely be asking the same question.

Miriam interrupted my pondering. 'I hate him.'

'Miriam,' chided her mother, 'you shouldn't speak like zat.'

'I do,' she reiterated. Then, pointing at the sparkly logo emblazoned across her chest, explained, 'I mean I do hate him, but I still like the Von Swiss clothes … they're really cool.' Donna nodded, indulgently. 'I mean the fact that I still wear the clothes from the shop doesn't mean I don't hate him.'

'Miriam,' snapped Angelique, a small tear escaping the corner of her eye, 'whatever 'appened, 'e is still your father.'

'I *do* hate him, Mama. He left us all alone.'

'Miriam ...' Angelique was clearly struggling to hold it together now, but Miriam hadn't finished yet. Her jaw took on a determined set, her lower lip jutting fiercely.

'He's a lying, cheating piece of SHIT!'

That was it: Angelique broke down into floods of tears.

Clearly, talk of her father's infidelity was quite sufficient to completely break down this otherwise delightful young girl's normal demeanour. I suppose she did have a point though, and I had to admit that, while her comment might not have been entirely appropriate, her grasp of colloquial English was impressive for an eight-year-old.

Donna placed a comforting arm around Angelique's shoulders, and offered her a tissue with which to dab her eyes.

'We should go 'ome now,' sniffed Angelique.

'I'll walk round with you,' offered Donna.

When they had all left, I poured myself a large malt whisky and sank back into the sofa. It had been a strange and distressing conclusion to an otherwise lovely evening.

Chapter 14

The following morning, Donna went round to see Angelique again. She had seemed so upset the previous evening that Donna felt the need to see if she was OK, and offer a bit of support and comfort. I elected to stay at home while she did so. Now you'll already have gathered that I would normally seize any excuse to go and see the delectable Angelique, but I'm afraid I'm just useless at handling women who are upset or tearful. I can't ever seem to think of the right things to say, and if I adopt the touchy-feely approach – hugs and stuff – I'm always afraid that my motives might be misinterpreted. No, this was a job for Donna, who had an uncanny ability to bond quickly with other women – even complete strangers.

For my part, I was determined that Sunday would be a day free of community business. I really hadn't appreciated that this stuff would take up so much of my time – in exchange for no monetary reward, constant sniping from Jim Watkins, and liberal helpings of abuse from various other residents. Anyway, the plan for today was to get stuck into a good book, have a nice snack lunch at home with Donna, and then, tonight, dinner with Paul, Kate, Neil, and Marion at *Il Giardino*, the new Italian restaurant which had just opened up nearby. I settled back onto my sunbed, pulled my hat forward to shade my face, and began to read. Before long, the warm sun and the distant buzz of some garden machinery had blended to make a soporific cocktail which began to make my eyelids heavy.

Where was I? Had I already read that page? I backtracked … ah, yes, that was it … I picked up the story once more.

I started, as my book drooped from my hands. *Oh, damn it … lost track again.* I went back a few pages … *no, I already read that bit, I'll just …*

Somewhere in the distance, muffled by the blanket of semi-consciousness I heard the sound of a door closing. I was too comfortable in my own little cocoon to investigate.

Moments later, I heard a familiar voice penetrate the warm, cosy place which I inhabited. 'Come on sleepy-head ... wakey wakey.'

With a considerable effort, I forced my eyes open. Donna was standing over me holding two glasses of white wine.

I blinked a few times and shuffled into a slightly more upright position. 'Thanks,' I said, propping myself up on one elbow, while accepting the drink with my other hand.

'How's the book?'

'I think I only read about thirty pages. Guess I'm a bit over-tired. Never mind, today's a day off from community crap.' I took a grateful sip of the chilled wine. 'So how's Angelique?'

'Oh, I think she's OK now. It's obvious that when Jean-Claude left her it was a hell of a blow, but she's gradually getting over it and settling into her new life without him. It's all still a bit raw though, and when Miriam had her ... episode ... last night, I think it all came flooding back and sort of overwhelmed her.'

'Must admit, I was pretty shocked to hear little miss perfect come out with *that* outburst.'

'She's really sorry now; she spent almost all the time I was there apologising to her mother.'

'Hmm ... it did seem out of character ... or at least out of the character which she portrayed for the first few hours.'

'No, I'm sure Miriam would never normally react like that, but she's just eight years old. When her father, who she really looked up to, just abandoned them both, it really hit her hard. I think she's still trying to rationalise it in her young mind.'

'Poor kid. Anyway, she strikes me as having some steel in her; I think she'll get through it OK.'

Donna nodded, absently. 'You know with Angelique, I think part of what has hit her so hard is shock and surprise ... any woman who looks like that will be used to men falling at her feet.' I felt a slight flush of blood rise unbidden to my cheeks. 'She's probably always been fighting them off, and to actually be rejected like that must have been a real shock.

'I mean, I'm not saying she didn't love her husband – in fact I'm convinced that she did – but for him to go off with an older woman who, by all accounts, wasn't exactly a stunner – Miriam described her as a "wrinkled old crone" – must have been a hell of a blow to her self-esteem.'

Amazing: in a couple of hours, Donna had learned more about Angelique than I had gleaned in several previous encounters. Maybe I had spent too much time ogling her and not enough time listening … I don't know.

Donna rounded off the subject on a more upbeat note. 'Anyway we're going shopping together tomorrow. A bit of retail therapy works wonders for a broken heart.'

***

After a light lunch of *bocadillos* and cheese, we spent a pleasant afternoon reading and chatting. It was now just after 6 p.m. but still pretty hot. Donna decided to go in for a cool shower before getting ready for dinner; we were due to meet the others at 8 p.m. I settled down to read another couple of chapters before I would go for a shower myself.

I heard the tell-tale rattly whine of a golf buggy making its way up the internal roadway. Where was it going this time? As I heard it approaching our block, I felt a nagging sense of unease. When the noise stopped, the sense of unease morphed into a resigned certainty. I waited, breath bated … twenty seconds … thirty seconds … nothing. I began to relax; it was probably nothing to do with me at all.

Ding, dong … ding dong. *Bugger it!* Wearily, I dragged myself to my feet and made my way to the front door.

Calvin was hopping animatedly from one foot to the other. 'Mr Groves, Mr Groves, come quick … there is emergency in swimming pool!'

I sighed. 'What emergency?'

'Electric wiring fall in pool. I think lady electrocuted.'

Oh Christ! I *had* heard some screaming, but I thought it was just kids playing by the pool.

'Come quick,' he repeated, his bloodshot eyes bulging alarmingly.

'OK, OK … let's go.' I gasped. We hot-footed it down the stairs and made for the pool area at a trot. I was still clad in just my board shorts.

When we arrived at the pool. There was no-one – alive or dead – in the pool. There was, however, one rather large lady shouting excitedly and urging the handful of other bathers to back away from the water's edge. They were all talking over each other, creating a disjointed hubbub.

'Excuse me,' I called out. No response, so I tried again, louder this time. 'Please can we have some quiet?' Still no response, so I resorted to yelling at the top of my voice, 'QUIET PLEASE!'

That did the trick – everyone stopped chattering and turned toward me.

'OK, what's happened ... who's been electrocuted?'

The large lady who had been at the centre of the ruckus stepped forward. She wore only tiny black bikini briefs which strained worryingly with the force of trying to contain her substantial backside. Her huge, pendulous breasts swayed back and forth alarmingly as she amplified her explanation with wild hand gestures. Calvin's eyes were just about popping out of his head.

'Look,' she said, grabbing my hand and pulling me towards the edge of the pool, 'see that? The light has come right out from the edge and it's floating in the water.'

Sure enough, one of the submerged lights which were installed at intervals around the edge of the pool, in order to provide agreeable mood lighting after dark, had come adrift and was floating in the water, still illuminated and still tethered by its cable to its mounting recess.

'Yes, I can see that,' I said, puzzled, 'but who's been electrocuted?'

'Well, no-one ... yet,' she said, 'but that pool's a death trap now; anyone who steps into it will be fried in an instant.'

My first reaction was a wave of relief that no-one had actually been hurt. That emotion was very quickly replaced by an intense irritation with Calvin, who, if the water had indeed been live, I would have happily thrown into the pool there and then.

I am no swimming pool expert, but even I know that submerged lighting in swimming pools is designed to work ... well ... submerged. Each lamp would be sealed against water ingress, and it would, in any case, most likely be a low-voltage system. Even if it wasn't, it would be quite safe because in the event that the seal failed, allowing water into one of the lamps, there would be a safety trip somewhere which would cut the power to the whole system. In this case, however, the offending light was still shining merrily, along with all its neighbours, so whatever kind of system it was, there was absolutely no chance of any danger.

A though struck me. *Must get Ernesto – he was the maintenance guy – to adjust the timer so we don't waste electricity by having the lights on during the daytime.* Not exactly germane to the matter in hand, I know, but I still had the community's financial catastrophe lurking at the back of my mind, and well … every little helps.

I turned to the lady with the enormous boobs. 'Please, don't worry … it's perfectly safe because—'

She became agitated, waving her arms wildly. 'How can it be safe? You should cordon off the whole area and inform the authorities.'

The little gaggle of onlookers were murmuring amongst themselves, some scratching their heads in puzzlement.

'Look, really, I can assure you—'

'Don't you go assuring me … just get the fire brigade or—'

Oh fuck this, I thought. I just jumped into the pool, evoking a piercing scream from the big lady, and gasps of astonishment from the others present.

'See,' I said, as I bobbed to the surface, 'it's perfectly safe.'

'Oooh,' she gasped, 'aren't you brave?'

'Not really – I knew it was OK. Now let me see what's happened here.'

First I examined the lamp unit which had a smooth flexible rubber perimeter ring. It looked as though it was simply a push fit into some sort of receptacle. Reaching down as far as I could without actually ducking under the surface, I was able to confirm, by feel, that there was indeed a matching receptacle set into the side of the pool, from which the cable emanated.

I explained my findings to the lady. 'Looks like it's just a push fit into its socket. I can probably fix this right now.'

She nodded, her face a mask of wonderment – perhaps at my bravery or perhaps at my evident technical skills. Who knows? Anyway, all the animosity had evaporated and she appeared rapt by my performance.

I took a deep breath and ducked down under the surface clutching the lamp unit. I could see, through blurred vision, exactly how the unit was supposed to engage, but it was rather a tight fit, and after struggling for about twenty seconds to insert it, without success, I was forced to pop up for air.

'Did you do it?' she asked, leaning forward for a better view over the edge of the pool.

'Not yet,' I gasped, wiping the water from my eyes. 'I'll have another go.'

Down I went once more. Still the blasted thing resisted my efforts to get it into its socket properly. I must have been under the water for around thirty seconds, and about to give up, when suddenly the unit slid home, with a satisfying squishy sound. *At last!*

I swiftly made for the surface, but instead of being greeted with a welcome rush of cool, fresh air coursing into my lungs I found myself enveloped in blackness and unable to breathe, as my ears, nose, and mouth were enclosed by a clammy, fleshy, yielding mass.

It was as terrifying as it was brief; the big lady pulled backwards, releasing me from the smothering embrace of her breasts. She had evidently decided to kneel down and hang over the edge of the pool in her efforts to observe what I was doing, allowing her pendulous breasts to hang right above me, unwittingly setting the trap which had ensnared me. I gratefully sucked in a great lungful of air.

'Oh, sorry about that,' she giggled. 'These tits of mine are always getting in the way ... they seem to have a mind of their own.'

'Er ... that's OK,' I gasped, still struggling for breath. 'Easily done.'

'It is with these babies,' she declared, emphasising the point by cupping a hand under each breast and alternately jiggling them up and down. 'Anyway,' she continued, with a conspiratorial wink, 'there are a lot of guys who'd pay good money for what you got for free!'

Eeeuw!

Well, at least I would have plenty to talk about at dinner that evening ...

Chapter 15

I gazed in dismay at the email from Sergio, having read it for a third time ...

To: Roy Groves, Paul MacPhearson
From: Sergio Ortega
Subject: Geotechnical survey

We have the results of the geotechnical survey. It is, of course in Spanish, but I have translated for you the two most important passages ...

1 The material of which the slope is composed consists mainly of shale, soil, and gravel. It is very friable and unstable and it is therefore essential that any vertical or near-vertical face cut from the hillside be supported by a properly designed and constructed retaining wall.

2 Clearly, the current facing of wire mesh and cement is totally inadequate. We also have some concern about the proposed new design specified in the architect's report which you kindly let us have sight of. We note that there appears to have been no geotechnical survey carried out at the time, so it is likely that the architect who designed the proposed new retaining wall was unaware of the very unstable nature of the ground.

We should make it clear that we are not technical architects ourselves and not qualified to give an expert opinion as to the suitability of the proposed design, but given our geological findings, we would strongly advise that you seek a further technical architect's opinion, formed with full knowledge of our report.

A lead weight settled in the pit of my stomach as the implications of this revelation sunk in. Alfredo González and his slimy brother had offered to pay four thousand euros towards a repair consisting of bit of chicken wire and a quick squirt of cement, whereas the wall designed by the architect would cost at least one hundred and twenty thousand euros, and now it seemed that even that might not be enough. *Oh crap!*

***

I sat next to Paul, opposite Sergio and Marysa at a hastily-convened lunch meeting at *Las Brisas del Mar,* a pleasant little restaurant on the *paseo marítimo* in Marbella. A constant stream of passers-by flowed back and forth along the seafront walkway: some on roller blades; some on bikes; and some simply ambling along on foot, chatting happily. Beyond the restless human stream, the azure sea sparkled with a million starbursts as the afternoon sun glinted off the wave tops. Further out, a luxury motor yacht cut a white swathe through the waves as its powerful engines thrust it forward. It was an agreeable vista, but I wasn't in the mood to sit back and admire the view; we were here to discuss the alarming news about the retaining wall.

'So, the González brothers weren't exactly being honest with us were they?' said Paul.

'Well, that's not a huge surprise,' I suggested, 'but what's really scary is the possibility, raised by the report, that even the hundred-and-twenty-thousand-euro design – which, by the way, could have gone up in cost anyway over the last three years – may not be adequate.'

'So what do we do now?' said Paul, spreading his hands and elevating his shoulders. We all looked at each other, as if waiting for the answer to this question to drop magically into our laps.

Sergio was first to proffer an opinion. 'I would suggest that we should immediately commission another technical architect to give a second opinion on the proposed design of the wall, taking into account the results of the geotechnical survey.'

'Wouldn't it be better to get the original architect back to review his design in the light of the survey report?' suggested Paul.

Sergio's face broke into a slow, wry smile. 'You have to understand the culture here in Spain.' Paul and I looked at him blankly. 'For a professional architect to admit that he is wrong on something like this is virtually unheard of - the loss of face would be totally unacceptable.'

'But,' I replied, 'if he wasn't in possession of all the relevant information at the time then surely—'

Sergio raised his hand, gently cutting me off, 'But that's the point: he *should* have been in possession of all the facts; he should have insisted on a geotechnical survey before coming up with his design.'

I exchanged a glance with Paul. His almost-imperceptible nod and raised eyebrows told me that his conclusion was the same as mine: Sergio was probably right.

I exhaled heavily. 'So how much will it cost to get another architect in?'

'As it happens, I have a friend who is an excellent technical architect. I am sure he would do it for the most favourable possible price.'

For some reason, I felt a little alarm bell ring in my head. While I had no reason to suspect that Sergio's motives were anything other than entirely honourable, I had, by now, had enough experience of the way things work in Spain to feel slightly uneasy about the potential for dodgy deals where 'friends' are involved in business dealings.

'Forgive me for asking, but do you, or your company have any business relationship with this friend?'

Sergio's face fell; he looked positively wounded. 'I can assure you, that Alejandro Cuadrado is a professional, possessed of the highest ethics. I recommend him simply because I know that he will do an excellent job for a fair price.'

Hmm, I didn't handle that too well, did I? I tried to make amends.

'Of course. I wasn't suggesting anything improper; I just wanted to be assured of his complete impartiality.' Sergio's face flushed red; this really wasn't going too well. I tried to steer the conversation away from what was obviously a sensitive area. 'Anyway, are you able to give me any indication of the likely cost?'

'You will have to wait for Alejandro's quotation ... that is *if* you want me to contact him.' He fixed me with a challenging stare.

I glanced across at Paul. 'What do you think?'

He shrugged and nodded.

I turned back to Sergio. 'Yes ... we'd appreciate that.'

Sergio, who had been leaning forward with fingertips pressed onto the table top, sank back into his chair and the florid tone in his cheeks began to subside. 'I will arrange it then,' he said, stiffly.

Marysa – whose straggly curls had been piled up on top of her head today, and bore a striking resemblance to a bird's nest – took over the conversation. 'Meanwhile, I will look into our legal position.'

'Our legal position?' repeated Paul.

'Well, the existing claim is for one hundred and twenty thousand euros, and we now understand that the eventual cost of building a proper retaining wall may be higher. I want to see if we can amend the amount of the claim if we can show that the original claim was insufficient.'

'Yes,' I said, 'good idea.'

She continued, 'And, if that is not possible, I'll look into whether it would be possible to claim against the original architect on the grounds of negligence.'

'OK, very good,' I replied, 'but one thing bothers me ...' She raised one eyebrow – somehow, quite independently of the other – and inclined her head. 'Even if we *can* follow up on some of this legal action, how long is it all likely to take?'

Marysa spread her hands and shrugged. 'It's Spain,' she reminded me.

***

Later that afternoon I sat, nursing a coffee, out on the terrace as I reflected on our meeting. Donna was busy in the kitchen making a huge batch of cakes for a function which she and Angelique had arranged with a few of the other women in the urbanisation.

In addition to the disturbing possibility that fixing the wall might cost even more than originally estimated, the question of timescales was really bothering me now. Winter was fast approaching, and anyone who has spent a few winters on the Costa del Sol will know that the weather can be incredibly variable. The afternoons can be sunny and warm – warm enough to sunbathe – but equally, there can be horrendous storms with gale-force winds and torrential rain, persisting relentlessly for several days at a time. Given that the existing wall – if you could call it that – had already begun to collapse, I was worried that a sustained downpour could precipitate further, more serious deterioration. It was likely that decisive action would be required sooner rather than later.

There was no telling when the legal case would actually come to court, nor whether we could increase the amount of our original claim, nor whether we would win – even though our case was surely very strong – nor whether, even if we did, we would receive the full amount claimed, nor whether we could sue the original architect ...

I drained the remains of my coffee and stood up, pacing back and forth across the terrace as I wrestled with the intractability of the whole ghastly situation. I wandered over to the edge of the terrace, propped my elbows on the wall, and gazed out over the lake towards the mountain beyond. There was some sort of very large bird – possibly an eagle – soaring on the thermals rising between the lake and the mountain. It circled lazily, with barely a movement of those vast wings, just angling the tips to change direction as it sought the rising columns of air. If only *my* life was as serene.

My thoughts were interrupted by the onset of a regular rasping sound, which repeated every few seconds – it sounded like someone snoring. I glanced down; the sight which greeted me evoked a swift double-take.

Julia, our somewhat antisocial neighbour, was stark naked, stretched out like a beached whale, her huge breasts drooping to the sides and *what?* There, propped in the triangular nook between the rolls of fat on her belly and the those adorning her vast thighs, was a mobile phone, snuggled into a nest of coarse, black, curly hair. Well, I suppose it was a convenient place to keep it – unlikely to fall to the ground and handily available should a call come in. I stifled a laugh.

Donna just had to see this. I backed away silently from the wall and made my way into the apartment and through to the kitchen.

'Come quickly,' I whispered, taking Donna's hand and pulling her gently towards me, 'there's something you have to see.'

'Why are you whispering?' she said, her brow creased in a puzzled frown. Good point, I suppose – there was no way the slumbering Julia would hear us talking in there.

'Never mind,' I said – still, for some reason, whispering – 'just come and look at this.'

She shook her head in puzzlement and followed me as I led her towards the wall, adopting a stealthy tiptoe, which she replicated.

When she looked over the wall, Donna took a second or so to register what she was seeing and then her eyes widened as she clamped a hand over her mouth in an effort to stifle the laugh which threatened to betray us. Her shoulders began to shake with barely-suppressed mirth. The hilarity was infectious and I, too, struggled to contain myself. We both stepped back from the wall, taking a few seconds to compose ourselves before sneaking forward for another peek.

We stood there in dead silence for several long seconds, aware that we were unfairly intruding on Julia's privacy, but somehow mesmerised, unable to tear our eyes away. Suddenly a faint buzzing sound penetrated the silence. Julia woke abruptly.

'Oooh!' she cooed, sitting up and clutching the vibrating phone closely to her crotch, working it against herself, evidently in no hurry to answer the call.

That was it: there was no way we could contain ourselves any longer. We sprang back from the wall and rushed into the apartment before dissolving into fits of laughter onto the sofa.

I'd forgotten all about the collapsing wall.

Chapter 16

Four thousand two hundred euros. That was what Sergio's architect friend, Alejandro Cuadrado, wanted to design a new retaining wall. A few phone calls had confirmed that this was pretty much par for the course, and we saw no reason to go with another architect of whom we would have no knowledge, when we at least had Sergio's recommendation for this one. We hired him, with a commitment that we would have a new design, together with estimated costings, within two weeks.

Meanwhile, we needed to catch up on the other points which we had previously discussed relating to the collapsing wall. That was why Paul and I were huddled around my speakerphone that morning on a conference call with Sergio and Marysa.

Sergio related his latest discussion with the developer, Alfredo González. 'I have sent him a copy of the geotechnical survey. I told him that this makes his existing offer of compensation totally unacceptable, and invited him to improve his offer in the interests of avoiding a long and costly legal battle.'

'And ...' I prompted, 'what was his response?'

'Well the colloquial Spanish doesn't translate exactly into English, but the gist of it was that I should perform an act on myself which is actually physically impossible.'

'Bastard!' hissed Paul. 'I knew from the moment we clapped eyes on him that he was a lying, conniving sonofabitch.'

I wasn't entirely surprised that González wasn't going to play ball – I had formed much the same impression, myself.

'OK,' I said, 'so I guess we need to press ahead with legal action. Is there anything we can do to speed it up?'

Sergio's reply was delivered in that patient, somewhat patronising tone which one reserves for explaining something very simple to someone who is nevertheless too dense to understand.

'Sadly, no: the Spanish legal system proceeds at its own pace and is completely impervious to all external representations ... that is of course unless they come from someone who has a personal connection or is able to offer some ... inducement.'

'Inducement?' I said, 'You mean a bribe?'

'Well, I couldn't possibly suggest that, but ... well, there are certain administrative costs associated with prioritising one particular case over others. Now if you'd like me to look into the possibilities ...'

I glanced at Paul, who looked as uncomfortable as I felt with the way this conversation was going. This was not a path I wanted to go down. While I knew full well that bribery, corruption, and nepotism formed the lubricant routinely used to oil the painfully sluggish wheels of the Spanish legal and administrative systems, there was no way *I* was going to get tangled up in a game whose rules I did not understand and which might ultimately land me in prison. Christ, I wasn't even getting paid to do this damned job! There was also a more prosaic and practical reason for declining Sergio's offer: we didn't actually have any money to pay bribes.

'No, Sergio,' I said, 'we'll play by the rules.'

'Of, course,' he replied, 'I wouldn't suggest otherwise.'

But you just did, didn't you? I was becoming increasingly unsure about Sergio.

Paul moved the conversation on. 'Marysa, you were going to look into whether we could increase our claim if necessary in the light of new information.'

'Yes,' she replied, 'and I'm afraid the only way it can be done is to withdraw the existing claim and launch a completely new action supported by the latest reports.'

'What ... start from scratch?' I gasped, dismayed.

'I'm afraid so.'

'But we are already more than three years down the line and have spent thousands of euros on legal costs. Wouldn't we end up writing all that off?'

'Yes, I'm afraid we would.'

My heart sank. 'Not really worth doing then,' I opined.

'That would be my view too,' she replied, her voice devoid of emotion.

We lapsed into an uneasy silence, broken by Paul a few seconds later. 'What about your idea, Marysa, of taking legal action against the architect who came up with the first design – for negligence in not commissioning a geotechnical survey?'

Marysa sounded a little brighter. 'Yes … our lawyer advises that this stands a reasonable chance of success.' She then put the inevitable damper on this glimmer of good news. 'It could take many years to come to court though, and would incur significant additional legal costs.'

I let out a long, weary sigh.

Paul voiced his conclusion. 'I guess we probably need to wait and see what cost estimate the new architect comes up with before deciding what, if any, additional legal challenges we should launch.'

'I guess you're right,' I agreed, gloomily.

With little more to discuss at this point, we closed the conference call, agreeing to reconvene when we had the new design and cost estimate in front of us. It had been a pretty unsatisfactory discussion, really, but there wasn't a great deal more we could do until we had the architect's report.

I decided that a brief walk might help to clear my head. As soon as Paul had left, I took a leisurely stroll around the urbanisation, making my way down to the front entrance where the mailboxes for all the apartments were located. I opened mine and withdrew the contents: mostly utility bills by the look of it. There was, however, one envelope marked up in spidery handwriting, 'To the president, from Dr Ramani – list of most urgent and important problems.' *Seriously? Right now?* I exhaled heavily, stuffing the envelope into my pocket.

***

I really wasn't expecting the sight which greeted me when I returned to my apartment. There, sitting on my sofa, was spiky-hair. *Whoa! What's going on here?* Donna sat in the armchair alongside, arranged at a right angle to the sofa.

As he registered my approach he stood up and faced me. He really was an intimidating figure, with heavily muscled arms, completely covered in tattoos, and thighs like tree trunks, rippling beneath his lycra shorts as he stood up. I tensed, preparing for the forthcoming confrontation. I was grateful for the sturdy coffee table interposed between us. Best try to defuse the situation, I reasoned, rather than provoke him.

'Look,' I said, 'I'm really sorry about the other night … I didn't realise … well we thought it was …'

He cut me off with a dismissive wave of his hand, his face cracking into a broad grin, revealing a perfect set of pearly-white tombstones which seemed quite at odds with his rugged features.

'Oh, don't worry about that. Me and Tracy had a right good laugh about it afterwards. And those coppers seemed to see the funny side of it too … especially the chick; she was pretty hot too, wasn't she?' And then turning to Donna, 'Oops sorry about that … but you know what they say about a woman in uniform.' He winked sideways at her.

'Oh, really, don't mind me,' she said putting a hand to her mouth as she stifled a giggle.

I was pretty much gobsmacked … just what the heck *was* this all about?

Donna enlightened me. 'Mr Lee here came up hoping to have a word with you.'

'I'd have phoned first, but I didn't have your number,' he interjected.

'I told him you'd be back soon,' continued Donna, 'so I thought he might as well just wait for you.'

'Your lovely wife made me a nice cup of coffee while I was waiting.'

'Oh,' I murmured, a wave of relief coursing through my body as understanding finally dawned. I motioned for him to sit back down and took my own seat in the other armchair, opposite Donna. 'Well, what can I do for you?'

Donna interrupted. 'I'll get you a coffee shall I?' I nodded, dumbly. 'And what about you, Mr Lee … would you like another?'

'I'd love one … great coffee' – he held out his empty cup –'and it's Bruce; we don't want to stand on ceremony, do we?'

Donna smiled as she took his cup.

'So, how can I help you?' I said.

'Well, it's like this: from all that stuff you was talking about at the meeting, I reckon you're a bit of a whiz with figures … you know, accounting like.'

'Well, I do know my way round a set of accounts – that was a big part of my previous job.'

'Yeah,' he said leaning forward and clapping me on the shoulder, 'that's what I figured. Well that's what I wanted to talk to you about. I could do with a bit of help sorting out my company accounts.'

'Your company ... what company is that?'

'I own three tattoo parlours in London.'

'Oh, I see.'

'We don't just do tattoos ... body piercing as well, you know.'

I nodded, eying the gold ring which adorned his right earlobe.

'I don't have much to do with actually running them,' he continued, 'I've got a manager for each shop, and an accountant who does the bookkeeping for all three.'

Donna arrived with the coffees and set them down on the table. 'I'll leave you boys to chat then.'

'Thanks darlin',' he said, flashing his gleaming gnashers once more. *A bit familiar*, I thought, but Donna seemed OK with it, smiling back at him as he took the cup.

Donna disappeared into the bedroom, and spiky-hair – *I really should call him Bruce* – continued. 'The thing is, I don't really understand the accounts properly. I mean the money keeps rolling in OK, and as far as I know, me accountant, Mickey, is a straight enough guy, but I'd really like to understand what's actually going on a bit better.'

'Well, wouldn't it be best to talk to your own accountant about it?'

He shook his head, a rueful smile crossing his face. 'Trouble is, Mickey's been doing me accounts for years, and I keep acting as though I actually know what the fook he's talking about. I'd feel a bit ... well, stupid, having to admit that I've never had a fookin' clue all these years.'

There was something strangely poignant about seeing this huge muscle-bound man admitting to me – after all, a virtual stranger – his own perceived inadequacies. In spite of the hard time he'd given me in some of our earlier encounters I felt disposed to help him.

'Well, I could certainly take a look at your accounts with you and see if I can help.'

'You'd do that for me?' he said, his rugged countenance lighting up in an expression which was almost childlike.

'You must understand though, that I can't give you any official financial advice ... it would just be a bit of help to enable you to interpret your own accounts.'

'That'd be great,' he said, slapping my shoulder, a little too forcefully.

'And I can't advise you on any decisions you might wish to make as a result of what you see in the accounts,' I added, anxious to make sure he understood the ground rules.

'No ... got it,' he confirmed. 'Er ... well, when could we get together?'

Well, as it happened I had no particular plans for that day, and I knew that Donna was going out to lunch with Angelique and a couple of the other women in the complex, so why not? 'Well, I'm fairly free today, actually.'

'You are? That's great ... could you come over to my place right now then? All me papers and stuff are over there.'

'I'm not going to bump into Tracy in a state of undress am I?'

He let out a hearty guffaw. 'Ha ... nice one! No, she's not there at the moment.'

'Right, well let's go then.' I called out to let Donna know we were going over to Bruce's.

She emerged from the bedroom, having already changed into a bright pink, summery dress for her lunch date. 'Nice to meet you at last,' she said.

Bruce ignored her outstretched hand and instead bent down to kiss her on alternate cheeks. Donna is actually quite tall, but she looked tiny as this giant of a man enveloped her.

'You look great in that dress,' he said, standing back and eying her up and down, appraisingly.

'Why, thank you,' she simpered, dipping her head, coyly.

***

Three hours later, I was feeling a little tipsy. Bruce had insisted on plying us both with cans of beer as we worked through his accounts.

As far as I could see, his accountant had done a good job in preparing a clear and professional set of documents and there was no obvious sign that anything untoward was going on – well, at least as far as the finances were concerned. Heaven knew what went on in the shops themselves.

As for Bruce, he was a willing student. Contrary to what his physical appearance and somewhat coarse manner might suggest, he was bright and attentive and had, by now, pretty much grasped the fundamentals of a profit and loss account. He too, was now starting to feel the effects of the alcohol. We decided it call it a day and reconvene at a later date to tackle the balance sheet.

'You're a good bloke, Roy,' said Bruce, as he sank back into his sofa, popping the ring-pull on yet another can of beer. 'I've been wondering what I can do to pay you back for helping me.'

'Oh, that's OK,' I said, for the first time noticing the slight slur in my own voice.

'What about them fookers who aren't paying their fees? I could have a word with some of them for you.'

Now Paul had already had some success with persuading a number of the defaulters to pay up. The debtors total had come down from almost a hundred thousand euros to just over sixty thousand, but progress had stalled; we were now down to the hard core who refused all inducements to pay. We had initiated legal action against these owners, but I knew full well that it could be years before this approach bore fruit.

In my alcohol-befuddled state, Bruce's offer suddenly sounded quite appealing. Maybe had I been completely sober I would have been more reticent, given the sort of tactics which I suspected he might employ.

'That's a bloody good idea,' I heard myself say out loud, before a little voice in the back of my head – evidently more sober than I was – urged caution. 'You'd have to make it clear though, that you weren't acting officially for the community ... just one concerned owner speaking to another.'

'Yeah, I get it,' he said, 'appeal to their better nature, like' – I nodded – '... and their sense of self-preservation.' He collapsed into a fit of drunken laughter.

Oh well, I suppose what I don't actually sanction, or even know about, won't bother me.

***

When I got home, Donna had just returned.

'So how was lunch?' I enquired.

Angelique had offered to drive on that occasion, and Donna had evidently taken full advantage of the opportunity to have a few glasses of wine. She was unusually giggly and her voice ever so slightly slurred when she replied.

'It was brilliant … Angelique told me all about her ex. It seems he was your typical Mediterranean lothario type … all seductive eyes, black chest hair and gold medallion … and really good in bed apparently. Oops! Shouldn't have spilt the beans on that should I? That's confidential girl-talk.' She began giggling uncontrollably for some seconds before a shadow flitted across her face and she suddenly became much more subdued. 'She really did love him though, even if he was a bit of a bastard.'

'Did she know what he was like before she married him?'

'Uh, huh … but she really fell for him and she thought she could change him. And to be fair, she did manage to tie him down for almost ten years.'

Tie him down? Most men would kill to be 'tied down' – figuratively or literally – by a woman like Angelique.

Donna hiccupped. 'I need a glass of water.'

I went into the kitchen and poured a glass for each of us.

'The thing is,' she continued, jabbing her glass in my direction and causing some of the contents to slop over the edge, 'men like that never really change.'

'I guess not,' I replied, weakly.

Something inside stabbed me as I wondered whether there was an oblique reference to me in there somewhere. Some years earlier, during my business life, I had had a brief, but intense, affair with a woman who had worked for me. Racked with a sense of guilt, I had ended it before – so I thought – Donna knew about it. I was forced, however, to come clean sometime after the affair had ended, when a business enemy threatened to blackmail me with photographs and other evidence he had collected. It turned out that Donna had known all along but had decided not to confront me, hoping that things would run their course and come to an end anyway – which is exactly what happened. But the episode made a deep wound in our relationship.

Now though, we had long since moved on from that unhappy period in our lives, and mostly it seemed, our partnership was stronger than ever, but sometimes I still wondered whether Donna had completely forgiven me. You know … just an odd word here or there, such as 'men like that never really change', would suddenly jar.

On this occasion, at least, it seems my fears were unfounded, for Donna came over, wrapped her arms around me – still holding her glass of water, some of which spilled down my back – and pressed her lips to mine.

'I'm glad I have you,' she said, hanging onto me, as much to retain her balance as anything else, I thought.

'Do you need to lie down for a bit?' I suggested.

'Only if you come and lie down with me.' She slid her hand down my back and gently squeezed my left buttock.

I knew this scenario well. Donna would quite often come over all amorous after a few drinks, but then fall fast asleep as soon as her head hit the pillow. Nevertheless, the thought of a couple of hours snooze with Donna in my arms was indeed very appealing, even if the buttock-squeezing was destined to come to nought … after all, I wasn't exactly stone-cold sober myself.

'OK, let's go,' I said, leaning forward to nibble her ear.

She pushed me away, giggling. 'Anyway, how did you get on with Bruce?'

'Pretty well, actually. He's not such a brute as he appears at first glance. I'm really sorry I wasn't here when he first came over here to our apartment though … it must have been a bit disconcerting to have a huge guy like that just show up out of the blue, not knowing what he actually wanted.'

'As a matter of fact,' she said, tilting her head and smiling coquettishly, 'I thought he was quite charming … in a rough and ready sort of way.'

No doubt about it, I thought, *a bit of roguish flattery clearly goes a very long way.*

Chapter 17

Donna had gone out shopping, and I had no special plans for the day, so I decided to sit down and read Dr Ramani's letter. Considering she was apparently a practising doctor in the UK when she wasn't in Spain, her English left quite a bit to be desired.

> I very disappoynted that you do nothing about all problms I tell you abat. That jackal's arse Watkins do nothing and now you do nothing niethur.

Now I thought this was rather unreasonable since I had, less than a week earlier, sat down with the wretched woman and done my best to deal with her complaints, even offering her some monetary compensation for some of the perceived injustices she had suffered, and a substantial discount on her overdue fees if she settled immediately. It seemed that my diplomatic efforts had been in vain. I read on ...

> For start, that pice of camul dung Watkins pull down my luvely bambu screene ...

Ah yes, the bamboo screen: she had, according to Jim Watkins, erected a ten-foot-high screen along the front of her garden which faced onto the road. This was against community rules and Jim had had the thing removed while she was in the UK. This did not please the good doctor, who insisted that the screen was just five feet tall and aesthetically beautiful. I didn't know who to bloody well believe, but in the interests of trying to resolve the long-running dispute, I had offered her five hundred euros compensation *and* to pay the full cost of installing a one-point-five-metre-high screen, which was the maximum allowed under community rules. She had haughtily refused my offer.

> ... and he cut back my butyful bush so much that it die. And anuther thing is that those brazen hoars down by swimming poole keep flashing there tits for all to see ... its disgustin. And if I want to get mine out in privicy of my own gardin, I cant becos my screen and my butifol bush gone. I got no privicy from pepul in road.

I tried swiftly to banish the disturbing image which had flashed, unbidden, into my brain.

> And those sex maneacs upstairs keep going at it like rabits. That woman squeel like stuck pig, and bed bangs agenst wall. And you seen the way she dress? She look like one of thos hukers who hang abowt down back street in Porto Banus.

I had, in fact, some time ago, deduced that the amorous couple causing Dr Ramani such distress were none other than Bruce and Tracy. I had already had a quiet word with Bruce, and in response he had promised to fit some foam pads behind the headboard of his bed. As for the enthusiastic noises, he said he would ask Tracy to try to tone it down a bit, although as he had reasonably pointed out, 'When you got a dick the size of mine, and I'm really giving it the full works, it'd be hard for any woman to keep quiet'. Ah well, I'd done my best.

As for Tracy's dress sense, well she did tend to wear very short skirts, skyscraper heels, and thin, stretchy tops, which did little to disguise her ample bust. To be honest, though, she did have the legs and the figure to pull off the look pretty successfully. I'd certainly seen plenty of less agreeable sights, as women – and men – who really should cover themselves up, sought to embrace the young, carefree look of the Costa del Sol.

> Then there's thos wild cats that make awfool noises in night. Wot you doing abat them?

Well, I had at least contributed to the domestication of one of them, but how the hell was I supposed to stop rest of the damned things from roaming around the place and noisily shagging in the middle of the night?

And wot abat my SKY TV? Every so often my box seize up and I hav to turn it off and on again – it always happen when I wont to watch East Enders which is my favurit show.

Oh, right ... so now I'm responsible for the performance of her bloody satellite TV box! I was, by now suffering a serious sense of humour failure.

To be honist you no betur than that son of a scorpion Watkins. I not paying nothing until you sort everything owt.

Your's Faythfully , Dr S. Ramani

OK that was it: I'd had enough of this wretched woman. There was clearly no reasoning with her, and I resolved to waste no more time trying to do so.

I picked up the phone and called Sergio.

'Hello, Roy. How can I help you today?'

'I want to talk to you about one of our debtors ... Sadira Ramani, 5A.'

'Ah, yes, I remember her from the meeting ... rather outspoken lady, I recall.'

'Quite. Anyway, can you tell me what her debt to the community currently stands at?'

'Let me see ...' – tap, tap, tap ... a few seconds silence ... tap, tap – 'yes, it's just over sixteen thousand euros.'

Her debt had increased by another two thousand euros since I'd last checked; this did nothing to make me feel any better disposed towards her. And no doubt the debt would continue to increase until she was forced to pay.

'Right, can I just confirm that we have a live legal action against her underway?'

'Of course,' replied Sergio, 'as agreed at the meeting.'

'OK, now assuming we win the case, what actually happens?'

'Well, the court will order her to pay the outstanding debt, and most probably legal costs as well – both hers and ours.'

'How much will those legal costs be?'

'We...ell,' mused Sergio, 'by the time we actually get to a court judgment I'd imagine they'd be higher than the actual debt itself ... maybe twenty thousand euros.'

'Twenty thousand?' I gasped.

'Well, it's only a guess ... but an informed and educated one.'

My God, this guy certainly doesn't suffer from an excess of false modesty.

'What happens if she refuses to pay, even after the court has ordered her to do so?'

'Well, she would very foolish to do so, because the court has the power to seize any of her assets, such as cash, car, jewellery, and so on, sufficient to cover the amount outstanding.'

'And if she doesn't have a sufficient amount of such assets here in Spain?'

'Then they would seize her main asset: her property. But no-one in their right mind would allow things to get to that point.'

'But if *did* come to that,' I insisted, 'what would happen next?'

'Well, then they would sell her apartment at auction, deduct from the proceeds whatever she owes to her creditors – including your community – and give her back whatever's left.'

'What if she has a large amount owing on a mortgage?'

'Roy, surely this is a rather pointless discussion – she's never going to allow her apartment to be seized rather than pay what she owes.'

'Just humour me, will you?'

He exhaled loudly before replying. 'OK ... well, an outstanding mortgage debt would take precedence over ours ... hold on a moment ... let me check.' I heard him lay the handset down and all went quiet for a couple of minutes. 'Right,' he said, when he came back on the line, 'according to our records there is no mortgage – she owns her property outright.'

'So we would get paid in full?'

'Well, yes, unless she owes a *very* large amount of money to other creditors, so that her total debts and legal costs actually exceed the value of her property, which seems highly unlikely.'

At last we had got to the bottom line. *Good!*

I changed tack. 'When we were discussing the wall the other day, you mentioned that there might be ways and means of speeding up the legal processes if one was willing to ... er ... assist with administrative costs.'

'Ah ... I see,' he said, his tone betraying his dawning understanding of where I was going with this.

'What would it cost to "assist with administrative expenses" in a case like this?'

'Oh, a minor case such as this could probably be expedited for a few thousand euros … as long as one knows the right people.'

'And you do … right?'

'Well, modesty prevents me from—'

I interrupted his preening. 'Well, do it then. I want this bitch up before the court at the earliest possible opportunity.'

'Well, I'll have to make a few calls, but I'm sure we will be able to move things along a little. Now regarding the actual amount you would be willing to—'

I cut in. 'Five thousand. If that's not enough, come back to me and we'll see where we go from there.'

'Of course,' he replied, smoothly, 'I'm sure we can make some significant progress with that budget.'

Maybe I had over-cooked my offer. If so, I wanted to make sure I got full value for money. 'I want her up before the court within three months.'

'Three months?' he spluttered. 'That is impossible … you must realise that these things normally take years.'

'Yes, I do realise – that's why I'm offering five thousand euros.'

'Even so, what you are asking simply cannot be—'

'Six months then – not a day longer.'

'It might take a little more money.'

I was beginning to get a bit pissed off now. 'Look, I already said we could talk again if five thousand wasn't enough, so will you just get on with it?'

'Of course … I'll see what I can do. If anyone can achieve such an ambitious result, it would be me.'

Oh, please – spare me any more of this bullshit.

'Thank you,' I said, tersely, and hung up.

Now I'm not normally a vindictive sort of person, but this bloody Dr Ramani had really rubbed me up the wrong way – figuratively, I hasten to add. Why the fuck should she think she could pick and choose whether to pay her fees, according to her own warped views of what should or shouldn't be allowed in the community, and leave the rest of us to make up the shortfall?

Authorising Sergio to use community funds for what amounted to a bribe was probably stepping over a line that shouldn't be crossed, but if we could spend five thousand to recover well over sixteen thousand, then I figured that would be money well spent. And to be honest, I had come to realise by now, that this was just the way things were done around here. It was a case of 'When in Rome ...', or, more pertinently, 'When in Marbella ...'.

The doorbell rang. *Oh, what now? If it's bloody Calvin again, I'll ...'*

It wasn't Calvin, it was Angelique. She wore a short, clingy, bright yellow dress which contrasted beautifully with the bronzed tone of her skin. Her jet black tresses tumbled carelessly over her shoulders. My eyes defied my instructions to the contrary and swiftly roamed all the way down her body and legs to her Louboutins and back to her beautiful face.

All, of a sudden, Dr Ramani was a distant memory.

'Oh,' I said, hoping that she hadn't noticed my involuntary assessment of her body, but knowing that she almost certainly had. Anyway, she didn't appear to be bothered by it: she flashed that dazzling smile and fluttered her long black lashes.

'I am very sorry to disturb you, Roy, but I 'ave a problem wiz ze electricity.'

'Oh,' I repeated, 'well, what exactly is the problem?'

'I 'ave no power. It was all working OK earlier but all of a sudden everyzing just went off.'

'I see.'

'I was wondering if you could possible 'ave a look and see if it is somezing you could fix ... before I call ze electricity people.'

I was, of course, willing and eager to seize another opportunity to demonstrate what a heroic fellow I was ... and this time I wouldn't be facing a ferocious feline adversary. Electricity was something I understood and didn't fear; wild cats however were a different matter.

'Of course,' I said, trying to sound commanding and masterful. 'I'll come round right now.'

'Oh, zank you so much.'

When we entered her apartment, the first thing I did was to check the distribution board. The problem was immediately obvious: two of the over-current trips had tripped out; one was the master trip for the whole apartment, the other controlled an individual circuit whose function was not immediately identifiable. I clicked both back to their normal positions; immediately the hum of the fridge started up and the lights in the kitchen flickered into life.

'Oh, you 'ave fixed it already. Can you show me what you did?'

As I pointed to the over-current trips and explained their purpose, Angelique craned over my shoulder, her hair brushing my cheek and her perfume filling my nostrils.

Having strung out the explanation for as long as I reasonably could, I stepped aside. She hooked long tresses of hair behind her ears as she studied the rows of switches.

'So all of zese little switches should point upwards?' she said, her azure blue eyes wide and enquiring. I nodded. 'And if any of zem don't, I just push zem back up?'

'Well, yes ... to start with at least. If they keep tripping though, it means there's a fault somewhere which will need to be fixed. It's always worth trying just pushing the switch up first, because they sometimes trip when there's a current surge but no actual fault.'

'Oh, you are very clever to know all zis stuff.'

'Not really,' I replied, shrugging in a matter-of-fact manner, but actually feeling rather pleased that she thought so.

'Would you like some coffee?' she said, 'I was just about to make some when ze power went off.'

'That would be lovely,' I said, more than happy for an excuse to linger.

She walked over to switch on the coffee machine. Suddenly, a loud 'click' sounded behind me and the lights went out.

'It 'as 'appened again,' she commented, somewhat superfluously.

'It was when you switched the coffee machine on,' I observed. 'Was that what happened the first time?'

'Yes, I zink it was exactly when I switched ze machine on zat ze lights went out.'

'Right, then I think that's the problem.'

I switched the coffee machine off, went back to the distribution board to reset the trips and then came and turned the coffee machine on once more. 'Click' – off went the lights again.

'That's the problem,' I confirmed. 'Your coffee machine is faulty: every time you switch it on it's drawing too much current and triggering the trips.'

'Oh, so do I need to get a new coffee machine?'

'Yes … it wouldn't be worth the cost and hassle to try to get it repaired.'

I unplugged the faulty appliance and reset the trips once more. 'Everything should be OK now as long as you don't try to use the coffee machine again.'

'Zank you so much, Roy.' Her face fell as she appeared to realise something. 'But now I cannot offer you zat coffee.'

'Oh, that's OK, I should probably be getting back anyway.'

'Oh surely not so soon.' She looked around, seemingly searching for some sort of inspiration. 'Do you like Bucks Fizz?'

Well, Donna probably wouldn't be back for at least another hour or so, and if it was a choice between spending an hour on community problems or spending an hour sipping Buck's Fizz with Angelique … well, no contest really. 'Yes I do … that would be lovely.'

'I'm afraid I don't 'ave any proper champagne … I will 'ave to make it wiz Spanish Cava.'

'Perfect,' I said. She clapped her hands together and giggled.

'You take zese,' she said, extracting the Cava and a carton of orange juice from the fridge, 'and I'll bring ze glasses.'

My old adversary, the cat, was curled up on the sofa. As soon as she saw me approach, her ears lay back against her head and she drew back her lips, baring her fangs and spitting spitefully. I hesitated, unwilling to confront the fearsome creature on what was now its home territory.

'Oh, Brigitte,' chided Angelique, 'don't be so unsociable.'

She set down the glasses on the glass-topped coffee table in front of the sofa and, in one fluid movement, scooped up the cat in her arms. I was ready – well, at least willing – to leap to Angelique's defence should the beast try to savage her, but the cat passively accepted being evicted from its place on the sofa, even purring when Angelique ruffled the fur on its neck.

'Now go to your little bed,' said Angelique, lowering the animal to the floor and giving it an encouraging shove in the direction of the kitchen. It dutifully sloped off.

It was an hour and a half later that I drained what was, I think, my fourth glass of the tangy cocktail. Angelique leaned over to top up my glass, placing her hand on my thigh to steady herself as she tipped up the bottle. Just three drops trickled into my glass. She picked up the bottle with both hands and raised it to her eye, looking into the mouth as though it were a telescope.

'Zere is none left,' she announced, solemnly. 'Shall I open anozer bottle?'

Now there is very little I would have liked more than to spend another hour with Angelique – who was becoming increasingly tactile with each glass of cocktail – getting totally plastered, but Donna would surely be home soon, and I wasn't sure she'd be entirely happy about me rolling in half-cut before midday, particularly when she knew the identity of my drinking partner.

'Thanks,' I said, levering myself from the sofa, 'but I really should be getting back now.'

'Oh, zat's a shame,' she said, rising unsteadily to her feet. 'We should do zat again sometime ... it was fun.'

Angelique hung onto my arm as I made my way to the front door, seemingly a little unsteady on her feet, in spite of having long since kicked off her skyscraper heels.

'Zank you so much for fixing my electricity,' she said, and after the customary three-pecks-on-the-cheek routine, she folded her arms around me and hugged me, pulling me to her, breasts pressing gently against me. I felt an involuntary tingle in my groin.

What was going on here? I found it difficult to reconcile her increasingly familiar approach to me with her growing friendship with Donna. Maybe she was just naturally a touchy-feely sort of person, or maybe, on this occasion, it was the alcohol talking. Anyway, I enjoyed the embrace for several long seconds, savouring the feel of her shapely body, before disentangling myself and saying goodbye.

'Goodbye, Roy ... see you again soon ...' She hiccupped, putting a hand to her mouth and giggling, before blowing me a farewell kiss.

The cat appeared at her feet, baring its teeth and hissing malevolently at me.

'I don't zink she likes you,' observed Angelique.

I didn't think so either.

Chapter 18

It was Friday afternoon. I had enjoyed a morning mercifully free of community business, and had actually managed to get stuck into a good book – a rare pleasure of late. Donna and I had been out for a long, leisurely lunch and I was feeling pleasantly sleepy.

Donna had declared her intention to watch a TV show we had recorded, called 'Marbs Forever': one of those dreadful so-called 'reality' shows, in this case, set in Marbella. It featured a bunch of vacuous, over made-up young girls with massive breasts and immobile, Botox-filled faces, and boorish young men with gelled hair and abundant tattoos. All of them spoke with contrived Essex accents so extreme as to be barely intelligible. It didn't help that the words 'was' and 'were' were invariably interchanged, or that every sentence was peppered with superfluous and meaningless insertions of the word 'like' (*Me and Chardonnay was going down the port like, when we saw these two really fit guys like checking us out. They was both like really ripped.*). I'd watched fifteen minutes of a previous episode and it seemed that all any of the 'stars' of the show ever did was get drunk, get laid, or have rows with their supposed friends about who *they* were getting laid by. I'd vowed never to watch the wretched show again, but Donna was, inexplicably, hooked by it. She claimed it was because she enjoyed spotting the local landmarks. Hmm ...

I thought that I'd resume reading my book, out on the terrace, although it was more than likely that I'd only manage a few pages before drifting off into a pleasant afternoon snooze. First though, I decided to check my emails: I wanted to make sure there were no burning community issues which might interfere with what I hoped would be a nice, leisurely weekend.

FAG had sent the latest set of community accounts. I couldn't face ploughing through them at that moment, but I did just check the state of the bank account: the balance was just over twenty thousand euros; this was rather better than I had expected. I also checked trade creditors: the amount of money we owed to various suppliers. This was also about twenty thousand euros – the lowest it had been since I'd been involved. We were in the unprecedented position of actually having enough money in the bank, to pay all of our creditors if it came to the crunch!

I was intrigued to understand how this unexpected improvement in our cash position had come about. As I scanned the document – with whose somewhat opaque and unconventional format I was now becoming more familiar – for an answer. I found it when my eyes settled on the debtors list: owners who were behind on payment of their community fees. The total owed was just twenty-eight thousand euros – down from almost a hundred thousand when I took over as president. Of the sixteen owners who were in default at that time, only four remained. Dr Ramani now owed around seventeen thousand euros, and the other three made up the remaining eleven thousand.

How had this turnaround come about? Paul's efforts, which had yielded some pretty good results to start with, appeared to have stalled recently, so how ...? Bruce ... it had to be Bruce. It seemed that his tactics – details of which I had not enquired about – had been most effective in persuading many of the offenders to pay up. I definitely owed him a drink for his efforts.

As I further examined the document I noted that all four of the remaining debtors were women – strange, considering that of the original sixteen, only five had been women. Then the penny dropped: Bruce, for all his belligerence with men, was as gentle as a lamb when it came to women; there was no way that he'd employ any sort of threats with the fairer sex. I couldn't help but smile.

Buoyed by the good news on debtors, I resolved to go through the rest of the accounts the following morning, even though it would take a couple of hours out of my 'weekend off'. For now though, I had a date with my sunbed and my book.

***

Something, someone, had hold of my shoulder, gently but insistently shaking it. I tried to shrug it off, but the intruder would not be deterred. *Why won't they leave me alone? I like it here.*

'Wake up … Roy … wake up.' As my eyes reluctantly opened and began to focus, the first thing I saw was Donna's face. 'You have some visitors.'

'Visitors?' I repeated, rubbing my eyes and attempting to lever myself into a sitting position.

My book tumbled to the ground from where it had evidently been lying on my chest; inevitably the pages sprang shut. *Damn it!* This would doubtless necessitate another frustrating session of trying to find where I was up to – inevitably, in the process, rereading a chunk of what I'd already read. For the umpteenth time I resolved to join the twenty-first century and get a Kindle.

'In the lounge,' Donna said.

I struggled sleepily to my feet and went inside. The sight which greeted me was definitely not what I wanted to see at 6 p.m. on a Friday afternoon.

The diminutive figure of Jim Watkins was dressed in khaki shorts, a black T-shirt, bearing the printed inscription 'Boss', and inevitably, his trademark baseball cap, from beneath which escaped copious, straggly strands of white hair. Alongside Jim stood a very tall, sturdy-looking chap, probably aged around fifty, with blonde hair which contrasted starkly with his deeply-tanned face. They made a rather comical, mismatched pair, with Jim's head not even reaching the other man's shoulder.

Jim was first to speak. 'Sorry to disturb you on a Friday afternoon, Roy' – although the smug expression on his face suggested that he was, in fact delighted to have an opportunity to do so – 'but something very important has come up, and I didn't think it could wait.'

'I'll leave you boys to it then,' said Donna, beating a hasty retreat out onto the terrace.

'I'm not sure if you've met Robert,' said Jim, gesturing, with upturned palm, towards the taller man.

I did, in fact, vaguely recognise him; he had been at the previous community meeting and I'd seen him around the urbanisation once or twice.

'Robert Hultmann, 6B,' he said, stepping forward and extending his hand.

His accent sounded as though it might be German, though heavily overlaid with an American-sounding pronunciation; his handshake was crushingly firm.

'Pleased to meet you,' I said. Actually I wasn't – I had an overwhelming sense that this visit spelled trouble. 'So how can I help you?'

Jim Watkins stepped forward, elbowing himself into a position slightly in front of the newcomer.

'Robert has reported to me a most serious matter.'

I waited for him to elaborate, but he was evidently intent on prolonging the pregnant pause for maximum dramatic effect.

'Yes ...?' I prompted.

'There is a ... young lady ... who has moved into 6D, directly above Robert.' Another long pause; I could cheerfully have throttled him.

'So what is the significance of that?' I said, struggling to keep my tone as level as possible.

'She has been engaging in somewhat ... antisocial ... activities.'

What activities? Loud parties ... littering ... allowing her dog to shit in the gardens ... breathing the same fucking air as you do? What?

'Sorry Jim, you're going to have to be a bit more specific.'

Robert Hultmann was evidently getting as frustrated as I was with this obtuse conversation. He decided to interject.

'She's a hooker ... a bloody Russian I think.'

OK, well that at least clarified the issue.

'Naturally,' jumped in Jim, evidently intent on regaining the lead in the discussion, 'I explained that if I were still president I would deal with the situation immediately. However, as *you* have now taken over that responsibility I felt I should introduce him to you and let *you* resolve the problem.'

Having delivered this little broadside, he just couldn't suppress the smirk which crept across his features.

I was somewhat at a loss as to how to respond, eventually managing, 'Er ... so how do you know that this woman is what you say she is?'

'For a start,' said Hultmann, elbowing Jim Watkins aside, while I took a step backward to maintain my personal space, 'she has men visiting at all hours of the day and night. She lets them in through the garage, leaving the door wide open for hours on end by sticking duct tape over the sensor.'

Now, I should explain that *Las Hermosas Vistas* is a gated community, and we do our best to make sure that only residents and authorised persons can gain access. The garage beneath my block, and many of the others, are only accessible from an internal roadway – you know, the one threatened by a landslide – so you have to already be inside the community gates before you can enter one of these garages. However, some of the garages, including the one beneath block six, open directly onto a public road, so if these are left open, anyone can enter the community, defeating the object of having a fenced and gated community. For this reason the doors to these garages close automatically a short time after they have been opened to allow access or egress. That is until someone sticks duct tape over the sensors. I could understand Hultmann's concern about this behaviour.

'Are you sure it's her who's doing this?' I asked.

'Well, who else would it be?' he retorted.

'Well, I don't know, but it would be best to be sure before—'

'And another thing,' he continued, getting into his stride now, 'she's always flinging used condoms out of her bathroom window onto the grass outside. It's disgusting.'

'Well, I have to agree that really is— '

'And she clacks about on the marble floor in high heels at four and five in the morning. The only time that noise stops is when she gets down to business and then she starts screaming and squealing as if every one of her punters is giving her the best fucking orgasm of her entire life. You know ... like the way the women in those internet porn movies ham it up.'

Well, I didn't actually – not being an aficionado of the genre – but I understood the gist of what he was telling me. I had to admit, that if all this were true, he had good reason to be a bit pissed off.

He paused in his account of his new neighbour's litany of transgressions. His ruddy complexion had grown ruddier, and I could distinctly see a vein pulsing in his temple. He looked as though he needed to take a few moments to calm down. Jim took advantage of Robert's pause to ensure that there was no ambiguity about whose shoulders the monkey was now perched upon.

'So you can see why I felt it was so important that we come and see you at once.' I nodded, dumbly. 'I've assured Robert that you're the man to sort this unfortunate situation out.'

'OK,' I sighed. 'I'll look into it and see what can be done.'

122

'You won't take too long about it, though, will you?' said Jim.

'I said …' now on the point of losing my cool, 'that I'd look into it. Right?'

Obviously, I couldn't see the expression on my own face, but from the reaction it evoked in Jim Watkins, I deduced that it must have telegraphed how I was feeling with some degree of clarity. He visibly recoiled.

'Er, well …' he said, turning to his new best friend, 'I think we should leave it with Roy now, don't you?'

The other man nodded, sullenly. I took advantage of the moment to step smartly towards the front door and open it, ushering the two of them towards it.

As I closed the door and turned around, I could see Donna coming in through the patio door opposite.

'A prossie in block six … oooh, how exciting!'

'I thought you had decided to "leave us boys to it",' I protested.

'Well, I couldn't help but overhear, could I?'

'I guess not, especially when you leave the door open and strain to hear every word.'

She laughed. 'You've got to admit that it's rather exciting, though.'

'I could do without that sort of excitement, thanks.'

'I guess it does need sorting out though,' she opined.

'Yes,' I sighed, 'it does. I'll get onto the administrators on Monday to see what we can do.'

'I'll tell you what though …' she said.

'What?'

'That Jim Watkins is a vindictive so-and-so, isn't he?'

'Yes, he certainly is,' I responded, with a wry smile.

'He was positively *revelling* in the opportunity to dump yet another problem on your back.'

And so he was, but it didn't alter the fact that this was an issue which needed to be tackled. I resolved to try to put it out of my mind until Monday.

***

I was unsuccessful in my effort to avoid dwelling on the hooker issue over the weekend.

As planned, I had spent the first couple of hours of Saturday morning going through the community accounts. As I'd already noted during my brief glance through the accounts the previous afternoon, there had been a continuing improvement in the community's finances, aided in no small part by Bruce's unofficial assistance with debt collection.

I could not, however get the subject of Robert Hultmann and his new neighbour out of my mind. On Saturday afternoon I had phoned Paul – who was now back in England – to inform him about the latest addition to our list of unresolved problems. He had been unable to come up with any immediate ideas, but agreed that we should take advice from FAG as to how to approach the issue. I'd emailed Marysa on Sunday, and she'd responded on Monday saying that she needed a few hours to look into the possibilities.

It was now Tuesday morning, and I sat opposite Marysa at FAG's office in Marbella, an anonymous building nestling among several others in a drab industrial estate. The main office was open plan, with perhaps twenty staff whose desks were crammed together in a space barely adequate for half that number. Marysa, however, had her own office, as befitted her status as top dog – or, I suppose, bitch. Sergio, it transpired, didn't even reside in the office, but worked from home, popping into the office occasionally as required. I guessed that he had his eye on greater things in the world of Andalucían politics.

'OK,' said Marysa, 'the woman in question is Svetlana Petrov. She is renting apartment 6D from the owner, Mario Bellini, whose previous long term tenant moved out six weeks ago.'

Neither name meant anything to me, so I got straight to the nub of the matter. 'So what can we actually do about this situation?'

'Well, the first thing to say is that you don't appear to have any evidence that this woman is actually a prostitute.'

'No ...' I admitted.

'Secondly, I have checked the Horizontal Property Act, the Articles of Association, and the community rules; it seems there is no actual rule anywhere against her plying that particular trade in her apartment.'

'But she's making her neighbours' lives a misery,' I protested. 'I've told you about all the things that she's doing.'

'Where's your evidence?' she said.

I was beginning to get just a little irritated with Marysa's rather unhelpful attitude.

I ignored her question. 'So what *can* we do?' I asked.

'Well, you could start by contacting Mr Bellini, explaining the problems that his tenant is causing, and appealing to his sense of community spirit to see if you can persuade him to put her on notice.'

'Hmm … does this Bellini guy actually spend any time here or is he an absentee landlord?'

'As far as I can tell,' replied Marysa, 'he lives full time in Milan. His apartment here is purely an investment and a source of rental income.'

Right, so he's hardly likely to evict a paying tenant whose behaviour is of absolutely no consequence to him, is he?

'I'll tell you what,' I said, 'why don't *you* write to him, as the community's authorised representative?' I had no intention of wasting my time on that particular strategy.

Marysa looked aghast at such a suggestion but, eventually, grudgingly agreed.

'Now,' I continued, 'if, as seems quite likely, Mr Bellini declines to take any action against his tenant, what else can we do?'

'Well, as I already explained, you can't really go after her on the grounds of her alleged profession. You have to concentrate on any of her behaviours which contravene community rules or break the law.'

'Like overriding the sensors on the garage door, making excessive noise all through the night, and littering the gardens with used condoms?'

'Exactly … but you'll need to gather evidence of such behaviours in order to take legal action against her.'

'OK, I'll set up some CCTV cameras and microphones to capture the evidence.'

Marysa shook her head, causing her straggly fronds of hair to flap wildly to and fro. 'You can't do that.'

'Why not?'

'Infringement of her civil liberties.'

'Oh, give me a break. If I set up some cameras, how can she prove they are specifically directed at her? And if I set up microphones in her neighbour's apartment, she won't even know that they're there.'

Marysa shook her head again, hair flailing like a bunch of rat's tails. 'Don't even think about it ... the courts take these matters very seriously. You could easily end up in prison if you go down that route.'

So the courts take it very seriously if I try to gather evidence of antisocial behaviour, but they apparently don't give a toss about a crooked developer who builds a substandard retaining wall which threatens life and property with a potential landslide? They also seem to be indifferent to community members who persistently refuse to pay their fees. I was beginning to lose my cool now.

'How can she prove that any of these measures are directed at her?' I insisted.

Marysa shrugged. 'It doesn't matter. Even if she decides not to claim infringement of civil liberties – and if she has a half-decent lawyer, as most of the hookers around here do, she definitely will – the moment you try to use any of the data collected as evidence, it will be self-evident that you've been stalking her.'

Stalking her? Christ ... I can't believe I'm hearing this!

'So what can I do?'

'I'd suggest you set up a complaints book in the security guards' office. Get her neighbour downstairs – and anyone else who is affected by her behaviour – to go and record the date, time, and details of every incident in the book. Then, over time you can build up a dossier of evidence that would be acceptable in court.'

Oh, great! So now I should suggest to Robert Hultmann that if he gets disturbed at 5 a.m. by clacking of high heels or sounds of energetic humping, he should get up, get dressed, and make his way down to the office to fill in a complaints book.

I was, by now, losing the will to live, but it seemed unlikely that, for the moment at least, I was going to get any further help from Marysa.

'OK,' I conceded, wearily, 'if we do all that and eventually collect enough evidence to take her to court, how long is it likely to take to get a result?'

Marysa spread her hands and raised her shoulders, her mouth turning down at the corners. 'Who knows? Three years ... four ... impossible to say.'

'Three or four *years*?' I repeated, dismally.

'It's Spain,' she reminded me.

Chapter 19

Paul had just returned from his trip to England. We sat in my lounge, gazing in disbelief at the report lying on the coffee table in front of us. Two hundred and twenty thousand euros: that was the estimated cost of building a new retaining wall to the specification drawn up by the architect, Alejandro Cuadrado. Where the fuck were we going to find two hundred and twenty thousand euros?

'Where the fuck are we going to find two hundred and twenty thousand euros?' said Paul, in a bizarre echo of my own unspoken question. Paul wasn't normally prone to swearing, but under the circumstances, I thought this uncharacteristic lapse was entirely justified.

'Well, I don't think we can rely on the court action,' I replied. 'Even if we win, the very best we can hope for is a hundred and twenty thousand, and heaven knows when the damned case will ever actually be heard anyway.'

We sat in silence for some seconds, each waiting for the other to voice the inevitable conclusion. Paul said it first.

'We're just going to have to go back to the owners and ask them to put their hands in their pockets again.'

'I guess so,' I agreed. In my head, a preview of the meeting in which I would break this unwelcome news to the troops began to play as vividly as if I were watching an HD movie. My heart sank. 'They won't like it,' I suggested – probably something of an understatement.

'No, they won't,' echoed Paul, but we have to bite the bullet sooner or later, and I'd prefer sooner. Judging by last night's downpour, it looks as though the winter rains are starting earlier than usual this year.'

'I know,' I said. 'I was looking out of my window yesterday evening and the water was absolutely gushing out of the cracks in the cement. God knows the extent to which it must be scouring away the soil behind. It's only a matter of time before we suffer a major collapse if we don't do something soon.'

Paul nodded, sagely. 'I guess we need to set up another EGM as soon as possible then.'

'Hmm ... but before we do so, I want to get some competitive quotes from construction companies based on Cuadrado's spec. So far we only have his estimate, and as he said himself, we shouldn't take that as gospel. Who knows? The actual cost may be even higher.'

'Or lower,' Paul suggested, perhaps trying to raise my spirits.

'With our luck?' I said.

'Well, OK ... probably not. In any event, you're right: we should get some quotes before we go to the owners.'

'And whatever the quoted price is,' I said, 'I'd suggest we add, say, twenty per cent contingency. You know how it is with construction projects: there are always cost overruns.'

'Agreed,' said Paul.

'I'll get onto Marysa and Sergio later on today, but for now, shall we attend to the other little matter which we had planned to tackle today, before Cuadrado's report intervened?'

'Hmm ... OK, Let's get it over with,' said Paul, sounding distinctly unenthusiastic.

***

We stood outside Svetlana Petrov's apartment, each waiting for the other to ring the doorbell.

Having previously discussed Marysa's somewhat unhelpful advice as to how to tackle the question of the Russian prostitute, we had decided to try a different approach, at least to start with: we would just talk to her face-to-face and see if we could make some progress that way. After all, the fact that she chose to make her living in that particular way did not automatically make her wilfully antisocial towards her neighbours. Maybe we could reason with her.

We did agree, though, that we should avoid directly referring to her alleged profession, and also that we should approach her together, so that there was a witness should she turn nasty and try to accuse one or other of us of some inappropriate behaviour. You see, we hadn't entirely succeeded in banishing our preconceptions about how a stereotypical prostitute might behave under these circumstances.

Anyway, it had all seemed perfectly reasonable and logical when we had previously discussed it, but now, confronted with that doorbell, we were both rooted to the spot, seemingly incapable of action, even though I had spoken to her on the phone earlier to arrange an appointment – no, that sounds wrong doesn't it? What I mean is that I'd asked her if she wouldn't mind our coming over for a chat. Then again, it was more than likely that some of her clients would start off by saying they just wanted to chat ...

I snapped out of the trance I was in and rang the bell.

I'm not sure exactly what I was expecting, but it certainly wasn't the sight that greeted me. The young woman who opened the door was very, very attractive. Her makeup was sufficient to enhance her natural beauty but stopped well short of the severe war paint worn by the hookers who frequented the back line in Puerto Banús. Her jade green, almond-shaped eyes slanted upwards slightly above pronounced cheekbones, giving her a kind of feline appearance. Her shoulder-length hair was of a rich, deep chestnut colour, full and lustrous. Her clothing was as tasteful as her makeup. There was no sign of the micro-skirts and fishnet stockings favoured by the aforementioned streetwalkers. Instead, she wore a knee-length cotton print dress which could almost have been described as modest, apart from the deep V neckline and closely-tailored cut, which displayed her superb figure most effectively.

'Mr Groves and Mr MacPhearson?' she said, flashing a welcoming smile.

I nodded, 'Yes, I'm Roy Groves, and this' – I turned towards Paul, whose jaw had, quite literally, dropped – 'is Paul MacPhearson.' Paul was staring like a love-struck schoolboy, and apparently lost for words at that moment, so I continued, 'And you must be Svetlana.'

'Yes ... I am pleased to meet you both. Won't you come in?'

Her accent was quite subtle, but unmistakeably Russian ... I have to admit I found her lilting tones rather engaging. My preconceptions had already been comprehensively shattered.

She stood to one side and ushered us inside with a sweep of her arm.

Paul appeared still to be rooted to the spot so I stepped forward, which appeared to break the trance. He followed me inside. Svetlana led us through to her lounge.

I surveyed the surroundings: neat, tidy, tastefully-decorated, furnished in a contemporary style with plenty of glass and chrome in evidence. No sign of whips or bondage accessories that I could see – mind you, the bedroom might be a different matter entirely, but I didn't feel that it would be entirely appropriate to ask to inspect that particular room.

'Would you like some coffee?' she said, in that attractive accent.

'Thank you ... white, no sugar,' I replied.

Paul had finally found his voice. 'Er ... yes ... same for me, thank you,' he stammered.

'Please,' she said, 'do sit down.'

She went into the kitchen to make the coffee.

Paul turned to me and whispered, 'God, she's absolutely stunning, isn't she?'

'Not exactly what I was expecting, I must admit,' I said. 'However, that doesn't change what we're here for, so let's stick to the plan, eh?'

'Right,' he said, with less conviction than I might have hoped for.

A few minutes later she returned with the coffees and sat down opposite the sofa on which Paul and I were seated. She crossed her shapely legs, smoothing her dress down so as not to display too much thigh. Glancing sideways at Paul, I noticed his Adam's apple bobbing up and down as he struggled to tear his eyes away. *For God's sake man! You're fifty-six years old – stop behaving like an adolescent teenager, will you? She's a hooker for Christ's sake.* The latter point, I reminded myself, wasn't actually proven.

'So how can I help you, gentlemen.'

'Well,' I began, 'as I already mentioned on the phone, one of your neighbours has made some complaints, and we wanted to discuss these with you.'

'Complaints?' Her eyes took on a wounded expression and her generous lips formed into a pout. 'But I always try to be a good neighbour.'

'I'm sure it's just a little misunderstanding,' interjected Paul. I glared at him; he got the message and shut up.

'I'll bet it's that Hultmann downstairs,' continued Svetlana. 'He's not a very nice man.'

I didn't respond to her comment but said, 'Can I just go through some of the things we've been told?'

She placed one hand on top of the other in her lap and nodded, still maintaining the expression of an innocent victim wronged. 'Of course.'

'We have been told that you have a lot of ... visitors' – I had just stopped myself saying 'men' – 'coming and going at rather unsocial hours.'

She shrugged. 'I have a lot of friends.'

'But the noise they make, arriving or leaving in the middle of the night, is apparently causing a lot of disturbance to your neighbours.'

'Oh, I see. Well, I will make sure that in future, I ask my friends to be as quiet as possible.'

'Thank you,' I said. 'However, there is a more serious aspect to this: we have been told that you have been overriding the automatic closing mechanism on the garage door in order to allow access to your friends.'

'Oh no, I have never done that,' she said, looking me unflinchingly in the eye.

'But Mr Hultmann has told us ...' *Dammit! I'd intended to avoid actually mentioning him by name.*

'I knew it was him,' she said. Her tone was level and calm, but her eyes betrayed the animosity which she felt towards her neighbour.

'Well,' I continued, 'he insists that he has, on several occasions had to peel off adhesive tape which has been placed over the sensor.'

'In that case it must be someone else who has been sticking this tape on.' Her face was a picture of wide-eyed innocence.

Paul stepped in. 'Well, it's true that we cannot be sure who—'

I cut him off smartly, 'You do appreciate that leaving the garage door open for long periods is a security risk? Anyone could walk right in off the street ... burglars, thieves, muggers ... anyone.'

'Yes,' she said, 'that is very frightening. I will make sure I keep my eyes open to see if I can find out who is doing this bad thing.'

Clearly I was not going to get much further on this particular tack, so I decided to move on. 'We have also been told that you, or perhaps your friends, have been walking about the apartment in high-heeled shoes in the small hours of the morning.'

'Oh,' she said, 'well, yes, I do like to wear nice shoes when entertaining. A nice pair of heels looks so much stylish than flat shoes, don't you think?' She extended a beautifully-toned calf, turning her ankle to display an elegant, mock-snakeskin court shoe with perhaps a four-inch heel.

'Oh, yes,' said Paul, 'those look very nice indeed on you.'

Christ, Paul ... can you please stick with the program? I had to admit, though, that they did.

'Thank you,' she said, treating him to an alluring smile.

'They may look nice,' I said, my patience with both of them now wearing a little thin, 'but the noise they make clacking on these marble floors carries right through to the apartments below. Could I suggest that you avoid wearing them indoors after midnight?' Her pretty features puckered in a frown. 'Or, alternatively, perhaps you could put down some carpets.'

Her face immediately brightened. 'Oh, yes ... that's a better idea.'

Ah! Some progress at last. I decided to seize the moment to press home my advantage.

'That way you can still wear your heels at night without disturbing your neighbours ... everyone's happy.'

She stroked her chin, small vertical creases appearing above the bridge of her nose, as she considered my suggestion.

She maintained that thoughtful expression for a few seconds before responding, 'I don't suppose the community would pay for them?'

Well, you had to admire the woman's nerve.

'I'm sorry, but I'm afraid that really isn't possible.'

'Oh ... well, as you have asked so nicely, I will do it anyway and pay for them myself. I have always thought these marble floors were a bit cold and impersonal.'

'Thank you,' I said, relieved to have won at least one concession.

'So is that everything you wanted to talk to me about?' she said.

'Not quite. We have also been told that you have been throwing certain items of a ... er ... well, a personal nature out of your bathroom window, littering the garden outside.'

Her brow furrowed in puzzlement. 'Personal items? I'm not sure I ...' Her eyes suddenly widened and her hand flew to her mouth. 'Oh, you mean ... oh, no ... that's not me. I've seen those disgusting things on the grass, but they're nothing to do with me.' Her eyes flashed with what looked like barely-suppressed anger. 'Do I look like the sort of person who would do such a thing?'

I heard the slight inhalation of breath alongside me signalling that Paul was about to speak. I swivelled my head and shot him a barbed glance. His mouth froze for a moment, half-open, and then closed without any word being uttered.

'We are just bringing to your attention what we have been told, and it does seem that the items in question are always found just below your window.'

She folded her arms and the corners of her mouth turned sullenly downward. 'Well, maybe some disgusting people are actually *doing it* ... right there in the garden, underneath my window.'

This seemed to me to be a pretty improbable scenario, given that the grounds were regularly patrolled – or at least they were meant to be, although I sometimes had my doubts – by the security guards. In any event, I couldn't imagine that a couple regularly bonking on the lawn in plain view would go unnoticed by the entire population of the urbanisation.

'Have you seen or heard anything of that sort?'

'No,' she admitted, pressing her folded arms more firmly against herself beneath her impressive bosom, which had the effect of pushing it up and making it even more prominent.

There seemed little point in labouring the issue further; hopefully I had said enough to discourage her from persisting with this behaviour.

'OK, well, if you should see anything that would help us identify the culprit, would you please let us know?'

Her sullen stance dispersed as quickly as it had appeared. 'Of course,' she said, unfolding her arms and placing her hands demurely in her lap once more. 'So is there anything else I can help you with?'

This was the bit I'd been dreading. My throat was suddenly dry as sand, and the words I had rehearsed now deserted me. I glanced at Paul, who simply gave an almost-imperceptible nod. *Right, so now you've got nothing to say, huh? Oh well, here goes ...*

'Well, there was one other ... er ... noise-related issue.'

'What's that?' she said, her green, catlike eyes looking directly into mine.

I felt the blood surge to my cheeks in a burning rush. 'Your neighbours have reported sounds of ... well ... er ... enthusiastic lovemaking at very unsocial hours.' There, I'd said it.

She didn't flinch; she just held my gaze for several seconds before replying, 'So is it now against the law to make love?'

Now I really wanted the ground to open up and swallow me. 'Well, no ... of course not. It's just that any sort of noise loud enough to cause disturbance to neighbours during the middle of the night is not really acceptable.' *Help! Someone get me out of here.*

'Mr Groves ... I am a very sensual person.' As if to emphasise the point she leant forward, crossing her legs, revealing a little more thigh, before placing her elbow on her knee and her chin in the crook between thumb and elegantly-manicured forefinger. *Now I want to die ... really, right now.* 'My boyfriend and I enjoy a very physical relationship, and I cannot help but express my passion out loud.'

I could maintain eye contact no longer; I glanced sideways at Paul in a desperate bid for some help. There was none forthcoming: Paul sat transfixed, eyes wide and jaw suspended loosely.

'Er, Svetlana ...'

'Miss Petrov,' she corrected me.

'Yes, of course ... Miss Petrov ... I'm really sorry to have had to bring this up, but if you could possibly do anything to ... well ... to minimise—'

'You want me to keep quiet when I'm fucking.'

Well yes, that's exactly what I want you to do.

'No of course not, but it would be helpful if you could ... well ... sort of tone it down a bit during the ...' She continued to gaze, unblinkingly, into my eyes, saying nothing. I had to look away. 'Maybe the carpets will help,' I suggested, weakly.

Chapter 20

'That went well didn't it?' I suggested, as we trudged up the slope towards our own apartments.

Paul appeared completely oblivious to my heavy sarcasm. 'She actually seems very nice … not what I expected at all.'

'By "nice", I assume you mean "sexy"?'

'Well, she *is* very attractive,' he agreed, 'but you have to admit she was pretty helpful in responding to our concerns.'

'Until I brought up the subject of her screaming her head off while entertaining her clients.'

'Now that's hardly fair. It's by no means proven that she's actually a hooker … in fact I find it hard to believe that such a nice girl could make her living like that.'

I can't believe this! How can such a normally level-headed guy be reduced to jelly the moment this – admittedly, very attractive – hooker flashes him a smile? But then again, I had to admit that I wasn't much different when Angelique was around, so I couldn't judge him too harshly.

'Look Paul, I know nothing's absolutely proven but I'll bet you a pound to a penny that she is exactly what Hultmann says she is. After all, he's living right below her and he sees and hears what goes on day-to-day. All we have to judge her by is a brief meeting when she was on her best behaviour … and to be honest I didn't even find that performance very convincing.'

'Even so—' began Paul before I cut him off.

'I can see that you fancy the pants off her, but that shouldn't affect how we treat her.'

'I only said that she's very attractive,' he protested, 'I never said—'

'Oh, come on, man. Your tongue was practically hanging out all the time we were in there.'

We had reached the point just outside the entrance to Paul's block. As we stopped walking, he folded his arms and fixed me with a stony stare. 'I'm just saying we should treat her with a bit of respect and not do anything too hasty.'

'So how do *you* suggest we handle her?' I said, immediately regretting the unintentional *double entendre* – which Paul either didn't notice, or chose to ignore.

'Let's give it a little time. Maybe our chat will have had the desired effect. If she gets the carpets fitted and takes on board the various other things we discussed, then perhaps the problem will just go away. After all, even if she *is* a hooker – and I remain unconvinced – you said yourself, that in itself isn't breaking community rules. As long as she doesn't behave in a manner which is damaging to the community or antisocial to her neighbours there is nothing we can or should do.'

Well, I had to admit that what Paul had said was quite logical and correct, but deep inside I knew that this wasn't a problem which would just go away.

'Hmm …' I said, scratching my head as I sought – without success – a reason not to go along with Paul's suggestion.

'After all,' said Paul, 'if the problems continue, I don't doubt that Robert Hultmann will let us know.'

My heart sank. 'Yes, and I'm damned sure his new best friend, Jim Watkins, will be right behind him.'

I added Svetlana Petrov to my ever-growing list of community problems which seemed to have no solution in sight.

***

The next morning dawned clear and bright. As I slid open the patio door I was greeted by the sight and sound of a huge flock of swallows and swifts, swooping and swirling against a cloudless, azure blue sky. They chattered incessantly as they danced this way and that, plucking from the air the countless insects which swarmed there.

The air was cool against my skin, in spite of the fact that the sun was now fully above the horizon. I looked at my watch: just after 10.00 a.m. The approach of winter was unmistakeable. Nevertheless, it was clearly going to be a beautiful day.

I felt a pair of arms close around my waist from behind and silky hair brush against my neck.

'What a beautiful morning,' sighed Donna.

I tilted my head back and nuzzled her. 'Yes it is – why don't we have breakfast outside on the terrace this morning? It's still a little chilly but give it another half an hour or so and it should be warm enough.'

'Good idea,' she said, kissing me lightly on the neck. 'By the time we're showered and dressed it should be lovely.'

Over breakfast, I described the previous day's meeting with Svetlana. Donna dissolved into a fit of giggles as I described Paul's rapid transition from sensible businessman to lovelorn schoolboy in the face of Svetlana's charms. When I'd finished relating the whole episode, Donna gave her opinion on the uneasy conclusion that Paul and I had reached about the way forward.

'Well, I do tend to agree that it's pretty unlikely your little chat yesterday will have been enough to resolve all the issues, but on the other hand, I think you do have to give her a chance.'

'I guess so,' I grumbled, popping the last piece of croissant into my mouth and chewing on it, thoughtfully.

'As you say, if things don't improve I'm sure you'll have that German guy over here again soon enough.'

'And his new buddy, Jim Watkins,' I added.

She laughed. 'Well if the problems *do* continue, I suppose you'll have to start doing all that stuff that Marysa spoke to you about. You know, the complaints book and so on.'

I nodded, feeling distinctly pessimistic that any of this was actually going to do any good. 'I just wish Paul would back me up more on all this. He's normally such a rational and determined individual, but he just went completely gooey in front of Svetlana. Heavens above, he's old enough to be her father.'

Donna leant forward and placed her elbow on the table, propping her chin in the crook between thumb and forefinger as a ghost of a smile traversed her face. 'Now who else do I know who goes to pieces in the presence of a young and glamorous woman who lives nearby?'

'I don't know what you're talking about,' I protested, feeling the blood rush to my cheeks.

'You do so!' she exclaimed, eyes wide with amusement.

'If you're referring to Angelique,' I said, adopting my most indignant tone, 'that's entirely different.'

'Oh, so how is it different?' she spluttered, now laughing out loud.

I couldn't see what was so bloody hilarious; I sought to rescue the situation. 'I'm just trying to be a good neighbour.' This did nothing to stem Donna's mirth; if anything it seemed to do the opposite. 'She doesn't have a man about the house so it's the least I can do to help out occasionally.' Even as I uttered the words, I realised what a pathetically lame excuse this was.

'If you say so,' she said, taking a napkin from the table and dabbing her eyes as she tried to compose herself.

Clearly, I hadn't entirely convinced her that I was immune to Angelique's feminine charms, but I decided that any further protest on my part would be counter-productive. I picked up my napkin, dabbed my mouth and pushed my chair back to stand up.

'I'm going to take a walk down to the front office and check the mailbox,' I announced.

'Off you go then,' said Donna, waving me away with her napkin, still struggling to stop laughing.

As I trudged down the hill towards the main entrance, where the mailboxes were located, I was still smarting a bit at how effortlessly Donna had seen through my feigned indifference to Angelique's charms. *Oh heck, why am I trying to hide it? I'm a man; we're biologically programmed to react in the presence of an attractive woman. The fact that I find Angelique so attractive doesn't mean I love Donna any less, does it?* For a second or two, that seemed a perfectly rational analysis … but only for a second or two. I resolved to try even harder in future to appear disinterested.

As usual, the contents of the mailbox consisted mostly of junk mail and utility bills. I dumped the former in the nearby waste bin and slipped the latter into my pocket. As I turned to walk back up to the apartment I happened to glance through the vertical bars of the main gate where there was a small parking bay at the side of the road. It was used by visitors to the urbanisation who did not have access to bring their vehicles inside.

It was still there. For over two weeks now, a large, battered old trailer had been parked there, taking up two parking spaces. Its cream paintwork was streaked with rust stains, bird droppings, and greenish algae. The trailer was quite tall and fully enclosed; the double doors at the back were secured with a sturdy padlock and chain, which looked considerably newer and more substantial then the trailer itself. There was no licence plate.

I wasn't in the best of moods to start with, and the sight of this eyesore right outside our main entrance irritated me to an extent which was quite disproportionate to the offence itself. I rapped on the door of the security guards' office – as it was Saturday, one of them should be on duty even during daytime. After a couple of seconds Calvin opened the door, preceded by an overpowering smell of stale tobacco smoke. His startled expression swiftly gave way to a crooked smile, displaying an uneven row of yellow, tobacco-stained teeth.

'Mr Groves, what can I do for you?' he said, with a subservient dip of his head.

'What's that old heap of a trailer doing out there?'

His eyes followed my pointing finger and his expression immediately became fearful, eyes darting back and forth as he appeared to search for the words to reply. 'It ... it nothing to do with me, Mr Groves,' he stammered.

'Well, whose is it then?' I said.

He jumped back as though stung, and began hopping from one foot to the other, his eyes bulging and beads of perspiration suddenly appearing on his forehead. 'I ... I not know.'

'Well, what *do* you know about it?' I insisted.

'Nothing ... I know nothing ...' he was wringing his hands desperately now. 'Maybe Sam know something.'

Ah, Sam ... now we're getting somewhere. Sam was the other security guard, with whom Calvin alternated shifts. Although they apparently both hailed from the same part of Africa, they were about as different as two people could be. In terms of physical appearance, Calvin was a tall, gangly figure who looked permanently sickly and was invariably unkempt. By contrast Sam, whose skin tone was rather lighter and whose features looked more Middle-Eastern than African, was a small, neat, dapper fellow who always looked well-groomed and clearly cared about his appearance. But it was in their characters, rather than their physical appearances that the two men differed most starkly. Calvin was a simple soul who couldn't do enough to help anyone who asked but, as you may recall from some of the incidents which I've already related, was very easily panicked. Sam, on the other hand, I had never entirely trusted – he was way too smooth and assured. I had often suspected him of involvement in some less-than-entirely-legal activities. Nothing had ever been proven, but I could easily imagine that Sam might be conducting some sort of clandestine business from a trailer right under our noses.

'OK,' I said, 'this is what I want you to do: you talk to Sam when you swap shifts this evening.' Calvin nodded. 'If he knows anything about the trailer he's to come and see me at once.'

'Yes, yes, Mr Groves … I tell him.'

'If he doesn't know anything about it, then first thing tomorrow, you phone the police and tell them that there's an abandoned trailer on the public road outside our urbanisation, and ask them if they can have it removed.' More nods. 'One way or another I want the damned thing gone by the end of the week.'

'Yes, Mr Groves … you can count on me. I sort everything out.'

I looked into his frightened eyes for a few seconds before turning on my heel and stomping off up the hill.

As I trudged up the slope, muttering darkly to myself about Sam, Calvin, and the bloody trailer, a dog rounded the corner in front of me, coming down the hill. It was a strict community rule that dogs be kept on a lead at all times within the grounds, but this one – an overweight, ugly black pug – was plodding down the hill, apparently unaccompanied. It stopped, staring at me confrontationally.

It always annoyed me, at the best of times, to see community rules flouted, but this was not the best of times, and to make matters worse, I knew who the owner was. I looked up, and there she was, rounding the corner.

She wore a pink, quilted dressing gown, carelessly tied at the waist, and a pair of faded purple bedroom slippers. Her hair was in curlers and a cigarette dangled from the corner of her mouth.

'Good morning Julia,' I said glancing at my watch to note that it was actually very nearly midday. By Spanish standards, that wasn't exceptionally late to still be in one's nightwear, but most people did at least get dressed before going out. Not Julia though.

'What's good about it?' she grunted.

This was not the best start to the discussion we were about to have.

'You know that it's against community rules to allow dogs to be off their leads in the grounds, don't you?'

They say that dogs often grow to look like their owners, or owners grow to look like their dogs – something like that. Anyway, as Julia scowled back at me, I was struck by the thought that, in this case, the dog was actually better looking than the owner.

'What fucking business is it of yours?' she replied, making her way towards me in that lumbering gait which was her trademark mode of perambulation.

I knew it was pointless to mention that I was president, with a nominal responsibility for helping to maintain some sort of order, for in truth, I had no actual authority. It was a case of 'government by consent' and if someone chose to thumb their nose at the rules there was very little I could do about it, short of embarking on the tortuous progress of collecting evidence in preparation for an excruciatingly protracted legal action. I decided to bite my lip and appeal to her sense of community – if indeed she had one. She was, by now, facing me directly, just a few feet away.

'Julia, living in a community like this, we all have to share space and get along with each other. Having a set of rules is just one way to help facilitate that process.'

'Well the rules are fucking stupid ... what harm does it do for little dog to be running around in grounds?'

That dog, I thought, *could no more run than fly; it's so fat that it can barely walk.*

I sighed. 'Well you may not agree with all the rules but they have been drawn up and agreed by a majority of owners and approved at an owners' meeting. So really, we all just have to go along with them ... even the ones we don't agree with.'

She completely ignored my – well-argued and extremely restrained, I thought – entreaty. 'And why the fuck you always up my arse about noise I make? You want to live in fucking church or library or something?'

'Up her arse?' Eeeuw! I sought swiftly to banish the disturbing image. 'Look, if we are to live in a community like this we really have to—'

But she was in full flow now. 'If you don't want bit of noise from time to time or see little dogs running free you should go and buy big house up in mountains or somewhere where there are no other people. Rest of us got to live our lives without nosey bastard like you interfering.'

Having made her point she placed her hands on her hips and stuck out her jaw defiantly. The dog did likewise – well the jutting jaw bit, anyway.

Now I could quite reasonably have responded that if she wanted to do exactly as she wanted, ignoring rules and pissing off her neighbours then *she* should be the one to go and live by herself up in the mountains, but somehow I didn't think this would be a fruitful line of argument.

As I struggled in vain to think of a way to reason with the wretched woman, the dog squatted and deposited a huge pile of excrement on the path. It took a step forward and then turned to look at the steaming pile of poo. Evidently satisfied with its handiwork, it turned to face me once more, taking another step forward and sitting down, rubbing its bottom back and forth on the path to remove any remaining residues before settling down and glaring malevolently at me.

I waited for Julia to produce the obligatory poo-bag and clear up her dog's waste. She made no attempt to do so.

Don't lose it now – keep calm. 'Are you going to pick that up?' I asked, striving to keep my tone level and composed.

'Pick up that filthy mess? What you think I am?' she blustered, wagging her finger at me.

Oh please ...don't tempt me.

Her vigorous gesticulation caused the towelling belt securing her dressing gown to loosen, revealing her sheer black nightdress which was fighting a losing battle to constrain the alarming swaying motion of her huge, pendulous breasts.

She must have detected the momentary – and, I hasten to add, involuntary – flicker of my eyes down towards the gap in her clothing. 'You staring at my tits, you pervert?'

She wrapped her dressing gown around her almost-escaped breasts, and retied the belt, adopting the indignant pout of an innocent maiden, brutally harassed.

'You want it picked up? Then you do it, you fucking sex maniac.' I swear the damned dog actually nodded to reinforce what she had said.

She stuck her nose in the air and set off down the hill in her familiar lumbering gait. The dog struggled awkwardly to its feet and followed suit, leaving me alone with the steaming pile of dog shit.

I stood there in a daze, trying to rationalise how I had managed to make such a monumental fuckup of the whole encounter. How come *I* had apparently emerged as the villain of the piece?

I looked down at the cooling, congealing pile of poo – surprisingly large, considering the size of the animal from whose arse it had emanated. My stupor dispersed, to be immediately replaced by anger.

I looked around me and swiftly located the nearest waste bin. When I went over and checked, I was gratified to discover that it contained a fresh plastic liner with, as yet, no actual rubbish inside. I removed the bin liner and went back to the scene of the crime. I placed my hand inside the bin liner and turned it inside out, wrapping the rim back over my wrist. Turning my head a little to one side to mitigate the ripe aroma, I grabbed the offending pile of poo and swiftly pulled the rim of the bag back down, neatly encapsulating my prize without actually getting any of it on my hands. Satisfied with the manoeuvre, I held the mouth of the bag closed and set off back up the slope.

Before returning to my apartment, however, I had an intermediate stop to make. I approached Julia's front door and, pausing to steal a furtive glance to left and right, inverted the plastic bag, depositing its contents onto her doorstep.

Childish? Yes. Petulant? Certainly. Unprofessional? Most definitely. But did it feel good? Hell, yes!

Chapter 21

After the irritating events of the previous day, I was determined that today I would put Calvin, Sam, Julia, the trailer, and the wretched dog out of my mind. We were due to go out for dinner with Paul and Kate that evening, and prior to that I was determined that we would enjoy a 'normal' day doing things that folk who retire to the Costa del Sol normally do.

We decided that we would take a boat ride from Puerto Banús to Marbella, just a few miles along the coast. A gentle stroll around the narrow streets of Marbella's old town and a light lunch in the *Plaza de Los Naranjos* – the 'Orange Tree Square' – seemed like the perfect way to spend what was forecast to be the last clear, sunny day before the first really bad storm of the winter swept in.

We parked our car in the underground car park beneath the *Plaza Antonio Banderas* and walked down to the marina, swiftly crossing the distinctly down-at-heel second line street – after dark, home to all-night bars and clubs, hen and stag parties, and hookers, but during the day, merely dirty, crumbling, and deserted. We soon arrived at the front line street bordering the marina; the contrast between the two streets, separated by only a few yards, could hardly have been more marked. On the front line, exclusive designer shops rubbed shoulders with a host of attractive restaurants, whose customers could look out across a vista of luxury yachts, gleaming white hulls glinting in the morning sunlight. Parked alongside the boats was an equally impressive array of top-end cars: Ferraris, Lamborghinis, Aston Martins, and many more.

It was only about two hundred and fifty yards from the point where we had entered the front line street to the embarkation point for the ferry but it took us almost twenty minutes to cover that distance, as Donna insisted on stopping to window-shop at every one of the designer stores. Actually, Donna always chose her clothes carefully, favouring good quality, stylish, but reasonably priced items. She would never dream of paying the inflated prices charged by these designer stores, but all the same she loved to look.

We were in no particular hurry, so I didn't try to chivvy her along. Instead, while Donna was browsing, I amused myself by watching the many tourists posing in front of the supercars to be photographed by their friends. As something of a car enthusiast myself, I winced as kids pressed their noses against windows and sticky fingers against gleaming paintwork, while girls in very short shorts and strappy tops posed for photographs, draping themselves across the bonnets of the cars attempting to emulate the models that, no doubt, many aspired to be.

If I had spent a small fortune on a car like those arrayed along the waterfront, there was no way on earth that I would park it down there. Actually, these low-slung sports cars were desperately impractical for anyone living in the area, anyway. The underground car parks nearly all featured wickedly steep entry ramps, seemingly specifically designed to wreck the front skirts and splitters of such cars, and most of the roads, other than the highways, were infested with viciously severe speed bumps, which appeared to have been designed with equally malicious intent. No, the only reason to own such a car in this area was to pose, and that was exactly what the owners did. When they weren't parked in front of a superyacht, many of the cars could be seen repeatedly circulating around the marina at walking pace, edging their way through the sea of pedestrians who dutifully stood aside and ogled as these status symbols crept past.

Eventually we made it to the ferry. Fifteen minutes later we were rounding the exit point from the marina and heading towards Marbella. To be honest, the short voyage along the coast wasn't blessed with spectacular scenery – other than the impressive mountains set back a few miles inland – but there was something so intoxicating about just being out on the water, with the wind in your hair and the sun on your face.

Donna laid her head on my shoulder and squeezed my hand. 'Nice to just get out and relax, isn't it?'

I put my arm around her shoulder and gently pulled her closer. 'Makes a bit of a change, doesn't it? We haven't done anything like this since I took on this wretched president thing, have we?' She chuckled.

Suddenly she sat bolt upright and pointed out to sea. 'Look! Out there!'

I followed her pointing finger, shading my eyes from the sun. Then I saw it, or rather, them.

'Flying fish!' I exclaimed, turning for a moment to catch the delight dancing in Donna's eyes.

I had only ever previously seen these creatures when we had been to Hawaii a few years earlier, and had no idea that they were present in these waters. There were perhaps six or seven of them performing their incredible display, emerging from the waves and gliding for astonishing distances just a foot or so above the surface before re-entering the water. The display lasted only for a minute or two, but it was the highlight of our short boat-trip, and our main topic of conversation during the further ten minutes it took us to reach the marina in Marbella – a rather less affluent-looking affair than that in Puerto Banús, with a far more modest array of craft moored there. Nevertheless, it was a pleasant stroll around the perimeter of the marina to reach the *paseo marítimo* with its restless stream of walkers, cyclists, and skateboarders flowing in both directions.

We made our way up through the large open square, heading towards Marbella's old town centre, stopping occasionally to admire the statues of weird and mystical creatures – reproductions of works by Salvador Dali – which punctuated the square. Crossing the main road we were quickly immersed in the maze of narrow streets which made up Marbella's old town. With no cars allowed, it was a delight to just wander and soak up the atmosphere. While I did not share Donna's fascination with the pretentious designer stores of Puerto Banús, I just loved perusing the eclectic mix of tiny shops which lined these streets and alleyways. Tourist souvenir shops alternated with genuine craft shops and some fascinating local food outlets. It was a truly delightful place.

'Feeling hungry?' said Donna, after we had wandered for perhaps an hour or so.

'Well we shouldn't eat too much, as we're going out for dinner this evening, but I could certainly manage a couple of glasses of wine and some *tapas*.'

We made our way to the *Plaza de los Naranjos*, bordered by bars and restaurants on all sides and sporting a sea of colourful sunshades, suspended over the numerous tables interspersed among the orange trees which gave the square its name. The perfect venue for a relaxed, leisurely lunch.

It was an hour and a half later that we paid our bill and began strolling back towards the marina, tired, happy, and a little tipsy. It was the first time in ages that we had actually spent a nice day out together, and I hadn't once thought about the community and its ever-growing list of problems.

***

Paul offered to drive that evening. As it was now getting a little too chilly to sit outside, we chose to eat at *Los Abanicos*, a local Argentinian restaurant which made the most of its agreeable interior ambience by putting on a display of Argentine Tango in a space in the centre of the restaurant. The space looked barely large enough for the young couple to perform their routine, but they managed it expertly, the man effortlessly sweeping his slender partner into the air in a series of breathtaking lifts, and she somehow managing to avoid knocking wine glasses from the nearest tables with her feet, or injuring one of the diners with a misplaced stiletto, while performing her airborne gymnastics. Their interlocking leg moves and vigorous body twirls were just as impressive as the lifts.

The steaks were, to be honest, only average, but the stunning performance of the dancers – soaked in perspiration by the time they took a bow to the enthusiastic applause of their audience – made it a memorable evening. It was the perfect conclusion to a thoroughly enjoyable day. Now though, I was very tired, once again a little drunk, and definitely ready for my bed.

As we rounded the corner by the front gate of the urbanisation I noted, with some irritation, that the dilapidated trailer was still there. But there was something different: it had been turned so that the towing bracket now faced towards the urbanisation. *Odd ... why would anyone do that?* Then as we swept up the hill, past the trailer and towards the second gate where we would take the car in, it dawned on my slightly addled brain that turning the towing bracket towards the buildings also meant that the doors at the back were now facing *away* from the buildings – any activity there would not be easily visible. I swivelled around in my seat to catch a glimpse, through the back window, of a shadowy figure in a dark, hooded top stepping out of the trailer carrying a box of some kind.

'Stop the car, Paul!' I yelled.

'What ... why?'

'Just stop, will you?' I bellowed.

He did so, turning to face me, his face a mask of puzzlement. 'What's going on?'

I already had the door open and one foot on the ground outside as I shouted, 'Look ... down there ... the trailer. Come on!' I set off at a run, with Paul a few paces behind. I could see now that there were two figures by the trailer, and also a dark coloured van, which had been obscured from our view by the trailer as we had driven towards it a few moments earlier. 'Come on!' I encouraged again. Paul was right behind me.

But they had spotted us. Both figures froze for a moment, looking directly towards us before rattling off a quick-fire exchange in a language which I couldn't quite place. One of the figures ran round and climbed into the driver's seat of the van while the other tossed the box he was holding into the back and slammed the doors shut. For a moment I thought there was something familiar about him – his posture, his body language – I couldn't quite put my finger on it. But in an instant, the moment had passed. He rushed round to the passenger door and jumped in, slamming the door as the van sped off, smoke spewing from its tortured rear tyres.

I tried to discern the registration number of the vehicle – a Mercedes of some description – but the street lighting was dim and they had sped off without turning on their own lights. All I managed to ascertain was that the font was similar to that used on UK-registered cars, and the first letter was a 'G', indicating that the vehicle was registered in Gibraltar.

'Dammit!' I hissed, slowing to a halt and slamming a fist into my open palm in frustration.

Paul drew up alongside me, panting for breath. 'What the hell do you think you were doing?' he chided. 'They could have been armed, or at least beaten the living shit out of us.'

Strangely the thought had never crossed my mind; I just wanted to find out what, and who, this damned trailer was all about. I didn't respond to Paul's comment, but just walked towards the trailer whose rear doors were still swinging slightly back and forth in the stiff breeze.

The trailer was empty, save for two unopened bulk packs of Marlboro brand cigarettes and one similarly untouched box containing six bottles of Johnnie Walker whisky. Paul and I looked at each other; it was clear what was going on here.

'So,' said Paul, his breathing still ragged and uneven, 'it seems we have interrupted a smuggling operation.'

The evidence left in the trailer, and the fact that the van used to unload the trailer was registered in Gibraltar, meant that it could hardly be anything else. Gibraltar was well known as one of the main conduits for illegal smuggling of goods into Europe. Someone had evidently parked a whole trailer-load of illegal contraband right outside our main gate.

'But why suddenly decide to move the goods tonight?' I mused. 'The trailer's been sitting here for weeks, apparently untouched.'

Paul's eyes narrowed. 'Didn't you say that you challenged Calvin about it yesterday?'

'Yes, and I also told him to talk to Sam about it.'

'Bit of a coincidence then,' said Paul, 'that the booty gets cleared out the following day.'

'And talking of Sam,' I said, 'where the hell is he? He's meant to be on duty tonight.'

As if in answer to my question, the main gate swung open and a uniformed figure appeared, but it wasn't Sam, it was Calvin. He came loping towards us, torch in hand.

'What is happening?' he asked, apparently totally bemused as the three of us gazed into the almost-empty trailer.

'I might ask you the same question,' I replied, irritably. 'Didn't you see what was going on?'

'I just got back from doing my patrol around urbanisation. I been away from my station for the last half hour or so.'

'So you didn't see anything?' He shook his head. 'Anyway, how come you are on duty tonight? I thought it was Sam's shift.'

'We swap shifts. Sam call to tell me that he got some problem with water leak in his house, and can I cover for him tonight. I got no problem with that so we swap shifts.'

I looked directly into his eyes, trying to assess whether he was lying to me. I could detect only fear.

'So he'll be on duty tomorrow night then?'

'Yes, Mr Groves … he be here then.'

'OK, I'll talk to him then. Meanwhile, I want you to call the police and tell them that we have found a vehicle which we suspect to have been involved in smuggling. I'll come and see you first thing in the morning to check what happened with the police.'

'Yes, I call them right away.'

By now Kate had reversed the car back down the hill to where we were standing. Both women stepped out of the car.

'What was that all about?' said Donna.

With the adrenaline rush now subsiding, the effects of the copious amount of alcohol I had consumed that evening reasserted themselves. I really, really needed my bed now.

'Long story,' I said. 'It'll keep 'til the morning.'

Chapter 22

The following morning, I woke to the sound of a steady drizzle hammering against the windows. My throat was dry, and my head throbbed with a dull ache. I propped myself up on one elbow, and, with fumbling fingers, located the glass of water on my bedside table. I took a deep, grateful swallow, relishing the feel of the cooling liquid caressing my parched throat. It was still very dark outside as I checked my bedside clock: 6.47 a.m. All I wanted to do was crawl under the covers and go back to sleep, but I needed to catch up with Calvin before he finished his shift at 8 a.m. so, reluctantly, I hauled myself out of bed. Thirty minutes later I was on my way down to the front gate, rain drumming out a steady beat against the large golf umbrella under which I sheltered.

As I stepped under the covered area by the mailboxes, just inside the front gate I collapsed the umbrella and shook off the excess water before peering out into the gloomy greyness of the morning light.

The trailer had gone. I was astonished: the local police weren't exactly renowned for their rapidity of action, so for them to have removed the trailer so promptly was nothing short of incredible. I rapped on the door of the office and within seconds was assailed by the familiar fug of cigarette smoke through which Calvin's pallid face appeared. His forehead was furrowed by a deep frown and his thin lips were clamped together in a straight line.

'G … Good morning, Mr Groves,' he stammered.

I wasted little time on pleasantries. 'Good morning Calvin. What's happened to the trailer?'

'It's gone.'

Calvin was a master of stating the bloody obvious. Telling myself that it surely wasn't through any intent to be deliberately obtuse, I did my best to remain calm and patient.

'Yes, I see that … but what's happened to it?'

He raised his shoulders and pursed his lips, his eyes widened within their sunken sockets. 'Someone take it away.'

My patience was quickly wearing thin.

'What do you mean, "someone" … the police?'

He shook his head, recoiling slightly before my withering gaze. 'No … trailer already gone by the time police arrive.'

'Well who took it?'

He shrugged and spread his hands. 'I don't know.'

'OK … but surely if you were right here, in the office, you must have been able to see the trailer being taken?'

He shook his head again, eyes bulging now. 'No … I go on patrol as usual and when I get back, trailer gone.'

I took a deep breath and held it for two or three seconds – losing it with Calvin wasn't going to help the situation.

'So let me get this straight,' I said, struggling to keep my voice calm and level. 'After I left you last night you phoned the police, but instead of keeping an eye on the trailer until they arrived, you went off on another patrol, and when you got back the trailer was gone.'

'Yes Boss,' he affirmed, 'I always do my regular patrols whatever happen … like you always tell me to.'

Now in fairness to Calvin, I *had* previously impressed on both security guards that they were expected to carry out regular patrols rather than spend the whole shift every night sitting in the office – probably either asleep or on the phone to Morocco. But surely on this occasion he could have applied a bit of initiative and kept an eye on the evidence until the police arrived? No, I realised as soon as the thought flitted through my mind – Calvin and initiative simply did not go together.

I let out a deep sigh. 'So what did the police say?'

'They not really interested. With no trailer and no evidence they say they can't do nothing.'

Then a thought struck me. 'But what about the whisky and cigarettes?'

Almost as soon as I uttered the words I knew what Calvin's answer was going to be.

'They gone too.'

'You left them in the trailer.' It was more of a statement than a question.

'Yes Boss.'

So that was it: we – no *I* – had monumentally fucked up the whole episode. I knew that Calvin could never handle anything out of the ordinary without utterly precise instructions, and it was stupid of me to assume otherwise.

Suddenly, a thought struck me. 'What about the CCTV? Can't we check the recording to see what happened?'

Calvin shook his head, ruefully. 'That parking bay not covered by any of our cameras.'

Of course it's not – with my luck, why should I have ever imagined it would be?

My headache had returned with a vengeance, pounding against the inside of my skull like a jackhammer. I decided to abandon any further questioning of Calvin and go back to my apartment to lie down for a bit.

***

By that evening, my hangover had finally subsided, but the steadily intensifying rain, combined with the stiffening wind, had done little to improve my mood. I decided to go and have a word with Sam, the other security guard. As I approached the covered porch area by the main gate I could see, through the curtain of water streaming from the rim of my umbrella, his familiar, slight figure standing there hands-on-hips, relaxed and confident as ever. In spite of the appalling weather conditions he wore his trademark Aviator sunglasses which, combined with his neatly-trimmed moustache and olive skin, always reminded me of a young Omar Sharif. He clearly had no intention of getting wet, waiting for me to reach the cover of the porch area before extending his hand.

'Hello, Mr Groves. How are you?' His accent was a blend of African and American, his command of English near-perfect.

I collapsed my umbrella, shaking off the water, causing Sam to back up a pace as a few errant drops besmirched his immaculately-pressed uniform trousers.

'I'm fine, thank you,' I replied, a tad tetchily. 'Did you sort out your plumbing problem?' A shadow of puzzlement flitted across his eyes and he appeared lost for an immediate response. 'The water leak ... did you get it fixed?'

Had he been wrong-footed by my question, or merely confused by the way I'd initially phrased it? I wasn't sure, but in any event his

153

recovery was swift and confident. 'Ah, yes … thank you for asking. There was a faulty seal in my water heater, but I managed to find an emergency plumber prepared to come out in the evening. Everything is fine now. It was very kind of Calvin to swap shifts with me at short notice.'

As I looked into his eyes, all I could detect was a smooth confidence.

'So what do you know about the trailer?'

He spread his hands and tilted his head to one side, raising his eyebrows and pursing his lips. 'Well, only what Calvin has told me, really.'

'So you wouldn't have any idea who owned it or what it had been used for?'

'Well,' he replied, raising a forefinger as if about to instruct me on something I didn't already know, 'from what Calvin has told me, I would suspect that it was used for illegal smuggling.'

'By whom?' I prompted.

'Well, that's the question, isn't it?'

I was, by now, about ready to poke him in the eye. 'And what is the answer to that question?'

'Sadly,' he replied, his face a picture of regret, 'I have no idea.'

Since I had absolutely no evidence which might link him with the trailer, and he wasn't about to fold in the face of my interrogation, I decided to abandon this line of questioning.

'How long were you aware of the trailer being parked there?'

'Now let me see,' he said, stroking his chin and casting his eyes skyward, 'I would say probably two or three weeks.'

'And you didn't think to do anything about it?'

'Well, it's a public road you know.' *Of course I know, you smug bastard.* 'Although it's mainly our people and their guests who use that parking area, there's no actual law against someone else using it, is there?'

This was going nowhere. Much as it irked me to be outmanoeuvred and outsmarted by this smooth-talking little weasel, I knew that there was no mileage in dragging this out any longer.

'Well,' I concluded, 'if you find out any more, you are to let me know immediately.'

'Of course,' he said, dipping his head deferentially.

'And if you see any sign whatsoever that something similar is happening in the future, once again, let me know immediately.'

'Most certainly.'

I couldn't afford to spend any more time on this issue right now; I needed to concentrate on preparing for the EGM – now only two days away – when I would be asking every owner to stump up several thousand euros in order to build a retaining wall to avert a potential landslide.

Why the fuck did I ever let Neil talk me into taking on this bloody job?

Chapter 23

The rain continued unabated for the next two days, now accompanied by gale-force winds and occasional bouts of thunder and lightning. It seemed sensible for Donna and I to share a car with Paul and Kate rather than each make our way independently to the EGM, so I had offered to drive. The road which I was cautiously negotiating resembled a fast-flowing river, and I was seriously beginning to doubt whether my car had enough ground clearance to make it to the *Estrella de Andalucía* hotel. I was beginning to see why many of the long-term residents in the area chose massive four-by-four SUVs – vehicles which I had previously regarded as a ridiculous irrelevance for people who never venture off road. Right now, though, such vehicles seemed an eminently sensible choice - far more so than the numerous Ferraris and Lamborghinis which prowled the locality.

I wondered just how many owners would actually make it to the EGM, given the atrocious weather conditions. Well, to be honest, the fewer the better as far as I was concerned, given the less-than-entirely-cheerful news which I had for them.

My hopes were unfounded. There were probably around fifty people in the room when I opened the meeting. It seemed that the word was out that significant money was on the agenda, and this was always guaranteed to pique people's interest. I was glad to have Paul at my elbow, ready to step in with a bit of support if things got rocky.

After the initial welcome and formalities, I got straight to the meat of the matter. 'As you can see, there is just one item on the agenda today: the approval of an extraordinary budget to cover the cost of constructing a retaining wall for the cut face of the hillside opposite blocks 10 to 15.'

Silence. I should have just pressed on but, slightly unsettled by the absolute quiet, I was foolish enough to seek some sort of response.

'Does everyone understand what we are here to discuss?'

A dark-haired guy in the back row – I'd seen him around but didn't know his name – raised his hand. I invited him to speak.

'Yes … er, hello … Tom Wilkins 2A.'

As no further words seemed to be forthcoming I offered him some encouragement. 'Yes, Tom… what is your question?'

'Well …' he said, haltingly, 'I've heard all about this retaining wall and it sounds like an absolute nightmare.' He didn't immediately elaborate.

Good point, well made. And your question is …? I nodded in what I hoped was an encouraging manner.

'Well, the thing is, I've heard that it's going to cost a small fortune to fix it, so … well, if the wall is causing such a big problem, wouldn't it be better to just not have a wall at all? I mean that would save loads of money, wouldn't it?'

I had prepared myself for most of the questions which I had expected to face, but certainly not this one. As I struggled to even comprehend the mental processes which lay behind the question, I hoped against hope that my face didn't betray what I was feeling. I honestly just couldn't find the words to reply. Thankfully, Paul, apparently sensing my dilemma, stepped in.

'Well, you see, Tom, when they built the development in the first place, they had to cut away a lot of the existing hillside in order to create a space flat enough to build on.' Tom Wilkins nodded, his face intent and engaged by Paul's explanation. 'Now, when you cut away a big chunk from a natural slope like that, you have to put something in place to stop the part above the cut face from collapsing.' A light bulb illuminated somewhere behind the man's eyes. 'But the developer didn't do that job properly; he just put a thin layer of cement over the cut face, whereas what was need was a strong retaining wall.'

'Ah,' he said, evidently now grasping the situation, 'so that's why the earth and mud have been slipping down?'

'Indeed it is,' confirmed Paul.

He appeared satisfied with Paul's explanation so I made ready to continue. 'So, if everyone is clear on the—'

I was interrupted by a rather portly, grey-haired man in the second row. He, too, looked familiar, although I didn't know his name. 'So where is this wall, anyway?'

Didn't I just tell everyone ten minutes ago?

'And you are, sir?' I asked, anxious to know the identity of this cloth-eared prat.

'Charlie Simmons, 3B.'

'Thank you. Well, Charlie, the wall, as I just explained, is opposite blocks 10 to 15.'

'Oh, right ... well, that doesn't affect me: I live down on the front row.'

Yes, I do know where block 3 is. 'Well, although a collapse of the wall wouldn't affect you directly, my proposal to raise a supplementary budget affects all owners.'

'How's that then?' he enquired.

'Well, because every owner would have to contribute toward the new wall.'

'But I already told you, it doesn't affect me.'

'Well, it does, Charlie, because you will have to pay a contribution just like every other owner.'

'Why?' he persisted.

'Because, according to the Horizontal Property Act—'

'But my property's not horizontal,' he interjected.

I sighed in exasperation. 'Let me rephrase that,' I said. 'There is a legal requirement that all owners contribute to repairs to communal elements of the community ... whether or not said repairs affect them individually.'

'Seems bloody unfair, if you ask me.'

Well I wasn't asking you, dickhead.

'Sorry, but that's the law. Now if I may continue, I'd like to outline—'

Charlie Simmons wasn't done yet. 'We...ll ... if we have to have a wall ... and we're all going to have to put our hands in our pockets' – *yes, I just told you that, didn't I?* – 'then we need to keep the cost as low as possible.'

I waited a few seconds for him to develop his argument further, but he didn't say anything; he just sat with his forefinger against the side of his chin and his brow furrowed.

I prompted him. 'Well yes, clearly we want to get the job done at the most advantageous price, but well ... did you have some idea that you wanted to put forward?'

His face broke into a smile. 'My brother's pretty good at bricklaying. I mean he's not actually a bricklayer by trade, but he's very good at it. He just did a really nice job building a low wall around my front garden back in England.'

'I ... er ... so how exactly does that have a bearing on the subject we are discussing?'

'He could build the new wall ... I'm sure he'd do it for a really good price.'

Give me strength!

'Er, Charlie, have you *seen* the wall which has to be replaced?'

'No ... I never go up there. I live down on the front row you see.'

Yes, I think we already established that.

I took a deep breath in order to ensure that I kept my reply level and civil. 'The wall we are talking about building will have to be a very much more substantial structure than the one which your brother built around your garden.'

'You haven't seen it,' persisted Charlie Simmons, 'he's done a really nice job.'

I exhaled slowly, trying hard to maintain my composure. 'I'm sure he has, but we really are dealing with a very different scale of project here. Look, if I can be allowed to continue with presenting my proposals, it should all become a bit clearer.'

He folded his arms and sat back sullenly. 'OK ... well, go on then.'

'Right,' I sighed, relieved to have finally circumnavigated this particular line of discussion, 'now, as I was saying earlier—'

'That's all very well,' piped up an irritatingly familiar voice, 'but it should be the developer who pays for building a proper retaining wall. It's outrageous to ask owners to put their hands in their pockets to pay for his shortcuts.' The new contributor was none other than Jim Watkins, today no longer feeling the need to come attired in full business suit, but instead wearing jeans and sweatshirt, and sporting his trademark baseball cap.

OK ... more deep breaths now.

'Jim, as you well know, we have a legal case running against the developer, but there is absolutely no telling when, or whether, we will actually get any money as a result of that action.'

'Even so—' he began, but I cut him off.

'Look,' I said, waving a hand towards the window, 'you can see what this weather is like.'

Now, I'm not a religious person, but I swear that, at that moment, there must have been some sort of divine intervention on my behalf because, right on cue, a particularly violent gust of wind caused a large, potted palm just outside the window to topple over, its terracotta tub shattering with a loud crash.

'See what I mean?' I added, rhetorically.

With a silent acknowledgement to whatever heavenly entity had leapt to my support, I continued. 'It is my opinion, and that of experts who we have consulted, that we cannot afford to wait an indeterminate time for a court judgement. Unless we take immediate action to retain the hillside we may experience a catastrophic collapse which could cause serious damage to property, and injury or death to our residents or their visitors.'

That seemed to shut him up for the moment, so I pressed on.

'In any case, even if we do win the court case, the very best we can hope for is a pay-out of a hundred and twenty thousand euros, and as you will learn in a moment, if I can be allowed to present my proposal, that is not going to be enough.'

He didn't respond, so I seized the opportunity to move things forward. 'So ... if there are no more immediate questions perhaps I can move on to—'

'What about my fence?' My heart sank as I registered the strident tones of Dr Ramani. 'You cut down my fence, cut down my bush, and now you threatening to take me to court, you camel's prick. I got rights you know.'

I paused for a moment, trying to frame my response in a manner appropriate to the occasion. In the event, it wasn't necessary, for Bruce spoke up on my behalf.

'What the fook are you going on about, you stupid bitch? We ain't here to talk about your fookin' fence or your fookin' bush – we're here to talk about the fookin' retaining wall. And as you never pay a fookin' penny of what you owe, I can't see that you've got any fookin' say in what we do anyway. So I'd suggest you shut the fook up and listen to what Roy has to say.'

Well, I wouldn't have put it in those exact words, but I had to admit that Bruce had pretty much captured the essence of what I would have said had he not got there first. Anyway, it worked, because she stopped ranting and pressed herself back into her seat, arms folded tightly and face set in an angry scowl.

Taking advantage of the lull which then ensued, I pressed on. 'My proposal is that we take action as soon as possible to build a proper retaining wall. As we have no resolution, as yet, to the court case, that means paying for it ourselves – for now at least. If, and when, we get some money back as a result of the court action we can decide then what to do with it – either reimburse everyone here some of what they have paid, or, alternatively, use it to strengthen the community's balances. That will be a subject for an EGM as and when we get the money.'

'Hear, hear,' came Neil's voice from the back row.

'Yes ... good plan,' agreed Joe Haven, seated in the second row. 'Let's hear the full proposal.'

Thank heavens for Neil and Joe. Encouraged by their support, I continued.

'If you take a look at the sheet you were all handed when you arrived' – I paused for a few seconds amid much rustling of paper – 'you will see that we have received five quotations for the work. They range from two hundred and twenty thousand to three hundred thousand euros.'

A flurry of gasps – a sound like a swirling wind whipping up – filled the room. I waited a few seconds for the sound to subside and the news to sink in before continuing.

'Now obviously we want to get the job done at the lowest possible cost, but our technical architect has recommended that we don't take the cheapest quotation here. The company in question apparently has a bit of a reputation for cutting corners.'

I was expecting some reaction to this remark, but it seemed everyone had been stunned into silence. I pressed on.

'By contrast, the company which has submitted the second cheapest quotation, *Hermanos Montoya*, is well known to the architect, and has in fact worked with him before. Montoya's quotation, at two hundred and thirty-three thousand euros, is only thirteen thousand more than the cheapest. It is the architect's opinion – and mine too – that this is the quotation we should accept.'

Joe Haven raised his hand.

'Yes, Joe.'

'That's all very well, and I understand the rationale for not taking the cheapest quote, but how can you be sure that there won't be some additional hidden costs which crop up once the project is underway? I've never, in my own business career, known a construction project which didn't end up costing more than originally estimated.'

It was almost as if I'd set him up to ask that exact question – I hadn't by the way – for it was the perfect segue into introducing my next bombshell.

'A very good point indeed. You are, of course, quite correct, and that is the reason why, in proposing a budget for the project, I have added twenty percent contingency, making a total of two hundred and eighty thousand euros.'

This was enough to break through the collective stupor which had, until that moment, gripped the audience. All of a sudden there were a dozen voices clamouring for attention. Within the space of just a few seconds, the meeting was on the point of descending into chaos.

'Please … please …' I implored the howling crowd, raising my voice as much as I could without it becoming a desperate and unseemly scream. I might as well have been spitting into the wind for all the effect it had.

Paul was less restrained. He slammed his weighty English-Spanish dictionary onto the table with frightening force. 'QUIET!' he commanded, at a decibel level which cut through the hubbub and immediately quelled the revolt. An uneasy silence ensued.

'Thank you,' I said. 'Now I'll be happy to take questions, but one at a time please, so please raise your hand if you wish to speak.'

Bizarrely, no hand was raised and no-one spoke for several seconds. It was, however too good to last. Jim Watkins didn't just raise his hand – he rose to his feet, panning his gaze to left and right to make sure he had everyone's full attention before speaking.

'On behalf of everyone here,' he began, 'I have to object in the strongest possible terms to this outrageous proposal. This is a preposterous amount of money to ask owners to come up with. Two hundred and eighty thousand euros? Why that's … well with seventy-five owners … and fifteen of those being penthouse owners … it would amount to …' His brow furrowed and he placed the forefinger of his right hand against the inside of his left pinkie as though counting out the numbers. The mental arithmetic had clearly defeated him. I was in no hurry to rescue him.

I let him stew for several further seconds before stepping in. 'Perhaps I can answer that question for you?' He didn't reply. 'The emergency budget which I am proposing amounts to just over three thousand one hundred euros from each owner of a standard apartment, or six thousand two hundred euros from a penthouse owner.' More gasps from the audience. 'I appreciate that is a considerable sum of money, and I do have some proposals to soften the blow a little by spreading the cost.'

'Nevertheless—' began Jim, but this time I cut him off.

'Before you continue, Jim, *I* have a question for *you.*' This seemed to unsettle him: his eyes widened and he pulled his head back sharply. 'What is it that gives you the right to speak on behalf of everyone here?'

'Well, I … I know perfectly well how … well, how people feel about this matter.'

'No you fookin' don't,' interjected Bruce, helpfully.

'And you certainly don't speak on *my* behalf,' added Joe Haven.

Seizing the moment, while the tide had turned – however briefly – in my favour, I pressed home my advantage. 'As you can see, Jim, you *don't* speak for everyone. When you have heard the proposals in full, you'll have the opportunity to vote on them … just like everyone else.' Jim's face was, by now, creased in a furious scowl, his cheeks flushed a startlingly bright shade of red. 'So perhaps you would now like to sit down, and give others an opportunity to speak?'

He looked around, evidently searching for support, but as none seemed to be immediately forthcoming, he sank back into his chair.

The debate – in which Jim took no further part – raged for almost an hour, with opinion seemingly equally divided as to whether to cough up the money or take our chances on a landslide.

I was getting very weary and just about ready to draw the discussion to a close and take a vote, when a stout middle-aged lady in the back row raised her hand. By the time I recognised her I had, unfortunately, already invited her to speak. *Damn!*

'I've already postponed my lovely new kitchen once; if I have to pay three thousand euros towards this wall I'll *never* get it done.'

My patience was now just about exhausted and my response really wasn't terribly professional. 'And just how much is your new kitchen going to cost, Mrs … I'm sorry I don't know your name.'

'Mrs Bucket … Rosemary Bucket.'

'Thank you, Mrs Bucket … and the cost of your kitchen?'

'Well it's twenty-six thousand euros … but it'll be really lovely when it's done. I've gone for the most beautiful, dark, sparkly granite worktops and top-class appliances.'

I really shouldn't have gone down this path but I was sort of committed now, and in any case I couldn't resist pressing home my point.

'I'm sure it will be beautiful, but wouldn't it be possible to get very nearly as beautiful a kitchen for twenty-three thousand euros?' Not that I imagined anyone prepared to spend twenty-six thousand on a kitchen couldn't find another three grand from somewhere.

Her eyes widened in astonishment at what she clearly considered a preposterous suggestion. 'But I've already chosen exactly what I want. If I have to cut the cost by three thousand euros I would have to change something.'

Indeed you would madam – well spotted.

'Look,' I said, now feeling a little churlish at the way I had handled this, 'it's not for me to say how you, or anyone else here, should prioritise your own finances. I am merely acquainting you with the facts about the crisis which we face and presenting a proposal for dealing with it. You will all have to make your own judgement about whether to support that proposal.'

Mrs Bucket did not respond; she just sat there in silence, her face a picture of desperate confusion. Miraculously, everyone else had fallen silent too. Maybe most of the audience were feeling as fatigued by the whole affair as I was. Paul swiftly stepped in to move things along.

'I think Roy has now answered everyone's questions as fully as possible, so I suggest we now put his proposal to a vote.' Before anyone had a chance to object he said, 'Those in favour?'

Around half of those present raised their hands. Paul and I both counted the raised hands.

'Twenty-six?' I said, turning to Paul.

'Twenty-six,' he confirmed. 'And those against?'

It looked about the same number. It was with some trepidation that I turned to Paul, after counting, for confirmation. 'Twenty-five?'

'Twenty-five,' he agreed. The relief which flooded through my body was almost overwhelming.

'Then I declare—'

'What about abstentions?' interjected Marysa, who had, up until now refrained from participating in the debate. I looked at her, uncomprehending. 'You need an overall majority to carry the motion.'

Of course ... dammit!

My heart was in my mouth as I continued. 'Yes, of course. Abstentions?'

A solitary hand went up. It was Rosemary Bucket. *Shit!* I was crestfallen, but this, I supposed, was democracy in action. I couldn't let the moment pass, however, without saying something to her.

'Mrs Bucket, it is, of course, your decision to abstain, but you do realise that by so doing you have prevented this very important proposal from being carried.'

'I object!' cried Jim Watkins, jumping to his feet. 'This is a blatant attempt to pressurise the good lady into changing her mind after a legitimate vote has been taken.'

'No, no ... wait ...' wailed Mrs Bucket. 'I wasn't putting my hand up to abstain ... I have already voted in favour of the proposal. I was just putting my hand up to explain why. You see, what I can do is delay buying my new car for six months. That way, I can afford to pay the three thousand cash-call *and* get my lovely new kitchen.'

I was utterly lost for words, but Marysa stepped in. 'Yes, I can confirm that Mrs Bucket was, indeed, one of those who voted in favour. The motion is therefore carried by twenty-six votes to twenty-five with no abstentions.'

A noisy buzz of conversation broke out, eventually silenced by Paul slamming his dictionary down on the table once more. I seized the opportunity.

'I will write to everyone shortly to detail the way that the payments can be spread over the coming months. Thank you all for coming. I declare the meeting closed.'

As we drove home, the rain was still lashing down furiously; even with the windscreen wipers on their highest speed setting it was very difficult to see clearly.

'That was an edgy moment ... when the Bucket woman stuck her hand up,' declared Paul, as we rounded the corner at the bottom of the road which led to the gate at the top of the hill.

'It certainly was,' I replied, laughing.

'You know, I think we should all go and see this wonderful kitchen when it's done,' said Paul.

'Oooh ... good idea,' chipped in Donna, from the back seat. 'Maybe we could get some ideas for *our* kitchen.' I assumed she had her tongue firmly in her cheek, but you could never be sure with Donna. Anyway, a quick glance in the rear-view mirror was sufficient to show both of the ladies' eyes sparkling with mirth.

'Nice try,' I said, as we drew to a halt by the double gates.

As Paul pressed the button on his remote control, the gates began describing their customary juddering arc. Something didn't look quite right though – in the momentary glimpses which I could steal between each sweep of the wipers I could discern something very big and very dark ahead. As the gates reached their fully-open position I selected first gear and carefully engaged the clutch, struggling to avoid the wheels spinning on the wet, slippery concrete slope. As the tyres achieved some purchase and we moved slowly forward, the sight which gradually emerged through the gloom caused my stomach to clench, sickeningly.

'Oh Christ!' I exclaimed.

'Oh, fuck, no!' said Paul.

The internal roadway was blocked by a massive mound of earth and rocks. As I edged forward as far as I could go, I could discern, protruding from the rubble, the back of a white Mercedes, the roof crushed inwards and the rear window shattered.

Chapter 24

Paul and I jumped out of the car and, ignoring the torrential downpour, rushed towards the stricken Mercedes. Was there anyone trapped inside? Pulling my sleeve down over my hand to protect it, I tried to pull away the remaining fragments of glass which clung to the rim of the narrow, irregularly shaped aperture which was once the rear window. Peering through the tiny gap I could see nothing; it was as black as pitch in there.

'Here, try this,' yelled Paul, fumbling with the button on the tiny torch attached to his keyring.

The beam was barely sufficient to reveal any details inside the car, but, as far as I could see, there was no-one in the back seat. What about the front though? It was impossible to tell: the roof had caved in so badly as to almost totally obstruct the view, and the feeble beam of light was completely inadequate to explore what little visibility there might be.

With the rain still pummelling our faces and the fierce wind whipping away our voices, any sort of meaningful communication was all but impossible.

'Let's get back in the car,' I shouted. Paul nodded.

'Is there anyone in there?' said Donna as we sunk into our seats and slammed the doors.

'Can't tell,' I gasped, blinking to clear my eyes of water. 'Paul, I have a larger torch in the boot. I'll get it and go back for another look. Can you phone Marysa or Sergio to get the emergency services here urgently while I do that?' He was already reaching for his phone as I stepped out once more into the swirling deluge.

I flipped open the boot and grabbed the torch before making my way back to the wrecked vehicle. In my haste, I slipped on the treacherous layer of mud which oozed down the concrete roadway, smacking my head painfully against the tow bar fitted to the Mercedes. Struggling to my feet, I gingerly felt the side of my head;

I couldn't tell whether the slick sensation beneath my fingertips was due to mud or blood. There was no time for self-pity, so I scrambled up onto the boot lid, hauling myself forward by gripping the rim of the shattered window, wincing as a fragment of glass stabbed my index finger. I switched on the torch and poked it right through the narrow aperture, moving my face as close as possible in an effort to see more clearly. It was impossible – the inside of the roof was pushed right down onto the headrests of the front seats. I abandoned my effort and rushed back to my own car.

'What happened to your head?' gasped Donna as I sank into my seat.

'Fell over,' I panted.

She fumbled in her bag, withdrawing a wad of tissues which I pressed against my temple.

Paul was still on the phone; he paused and turned to me. 'What's the verdict?'

'Still can't tell,' I said.

He resumed his call. 'OK, but tell them to hurry ... there could be people trapped inside the car.' He hung up.

'So what now?' I said, turning the wad of tissues – now soaked with blood – and dabbing my temple.

'The emergency services should be here soon,' said Paul. 'We can't get the car past here, so why don't you take it back down and park near the front gate? Then you can get the girls back to your apartment, where they can patch up that head wound. I'll wait here for the fire brigade and police ... I can shelter over there in the entrance to block 10.'

'OK,' I said.

Paul stepped outside, rushing over to the covered entrance area of the nearest building while I put the car in reverse and backed down towards the gate through which we had just come.

***

An hour and a half later, the four of us had changed into dry clothes and were sitting in my apartment, sipping hot coffee as we waited anxiously for news from the emergency services. My head was throbbing like hell but Donna had done a creditable job of cleaning and dressing the wound, and the bleeding had almost stopped. The cut to my finger was pretty superficial, requiring nothing more than some antiseptic and a Band Aid. The rain had finally eased and the ferocious wind had moderated somewhat.

'Does anyone know whose car—' began Kate, but she was interrupted by the doorbell.

As I opened the door I was confronted by one very wet and bedraggled fireman, and the immaculately dressed figure of Sergio, as usual clad in suit and tie. How the hell had *he* managed to stay dry? It would have been almost comical were it not for the gravity of the situation.

'Come in,' I said, standing aside, and gesturing for them to enter.

'*Creo que no,*' said the fireman, indicating the muddy water streaming from his clothing. *Considerate guy*, I thought, considering the shitty job he'd just been engaged in.

'I won't come in either,' said Sergio. 'I just wanted to let you know the situation.'

'Go on,' I urged him.

'They've cleared away enough debris to get to the car and cut the roof right off it.'

'And?' I said.

'There's no-one inside.'

'Thank God,' I breathed. 'Do they know whose car it is?'

'They are just about to check. Obviously the first priority was to get into the car to see if there were any casualties, but now they'll ascertain who the owner is.'

I nodded. 'OK, so what happens now?'

'Well, the emergency services will be leaving shortly, but I have arranged for a specialist company to be here first thing in the morning to clear the roadway and fit some sort of temporary retaining structure to shore up the freshly exposed face of the hillside to try to prevent a further landslide. Luckily, the volume of material which collapsed wasn't sufficient to cause damage to any of your buildings. Apart from the car, a fence, and a lamppost, you have got away unscathed. If any more material comes away, however, I fear it could affect the stability of the buildings further up the slope in the neighbouring urbanisation, quite apart from any damage to life or property in your own development.'

Oh, Christ, I thought, *that's all we need – one of next door's apartments crashing down on us from about forty feet up the hillside.*

'OK,' I sighed, 'thanks for your help. I guess we'll talk again tomorrow. Oh, and' – to the fireman – '*gracias a usted, también.*' He nodded in acknowledgement of my remark.

As the two of them walked away, I noted, before closing the door, that the rain had now stopped completely and, as if to mock us, there was even a glimpse of the sun peeping through a gap in the clouds. The bitter irony was that I now had the mandate – and hopefully soon, the money – to fix the wall. Why the hell couldn't the wretched thing have held for just a few more months?

I trudged back into the lounge, not really sure what to say or do next. There was no need to decide, because before I had even sat down, the phone rang.

'Hello ... Robert Hultmann here.'

I really, really didn't feel in the mood for a conversation with the scratchy German.

'Yes, Robert,' I sighed, 'what can I do for you?'

'That bitch upstairs is still up to all her old tricks. She had three clients in last night. The noise was absolutely unbelievable; they must all think they've given her the best fuck of her entire life. She deserves a bloody Oscar for a performance like that.'

'Robert, I have spoken to her and she's assured me that—'

But he was ranting again. 'She's been jamming the garage door open again, so much so that the damned thing has now broken completely and wouldn't open at all this morning. I couldn't even get my *own* car into the garage.'

'OK, I'll talk to her again, and—'

'I'm not leaving my car outside in the road, so until you get the garage door fixed, I'm parking my car on the top roadway inside the urbanisation. I don't give a shit about whether I'm supposed to park up there. That's where my car is parked, and that's where it's staying until I can get back into the garage.'

'Look, I've got a bit of a crisis on my hands just now, so would you mind if we could leave it for a day or two to talk about ...' My words tailed off as an awful suspicion struck me. 'Wait a minute ... what sort of car do you own?'

'It's a white Mercedes ... not that I see how that's relevant.'

I was, quite literally, dumbstruck. It took me several seconds to find the words to reply. 'Er Robert, I may have some bad news for you ...'

Chapter 25

As I stood, cradling my cup of coffee in both hands, elbows propped on the wall, I gazed out over the lake, where a heron was lazily wafting along just a few feet above the surface, with slow, seemingly-effortless strokes of its vast wings. I followed its progress to the point where it touched down on the water, splashing noisily as it made for a gap in the reeds lining the bank.

Two weeks had elapsed since that fateful day when a large section of the wall had collapsed. A great deal had happened since then.

The company that Sergio had brought in to take care of emergency repairs had done a good job. Within two days they had cleared all the rubble and removed Robert Hultmann's wrecked car. They had erected wooden boards against the newly exposed face of the hillside along the twenty-yard-long stretch which had given way. These were supported by metal poles set at an angle to resist a further collapse. The poles protruded some way out into the roadway but there was still just sufficient width left for cars to pass. They had warned us, though, that this was nothing more than a temporary measure and they could give no guarantees that a further collapse would be prevented. Clearly we needed to get on with the construction of the permanent retaining wall as soon as possible. But by now we were well into winter and the weather was unlikely to permit work to start until the spring. *Let's hope the temporary fix holds up until then.* Another unfortunate aspect of this episode was that the road clearance and temporary supporting structure had eaten up ten thousand euros of the budget before we had even started on the main construction project.

The building contractors *Hermanos Montoya* had warned that once work did finally start, the internal roadway would be impassable to residents' cars for a period of around three months. I had therefore had to arrange the temporary hire of a nearby car park for the use of all of us who lived in apartments along the top row. That was going to consume another four thousand euros.

Robert Hultmann wasn't best pleased about his car. He had threatened to take legal action against the community, claiming for the cost of a new car as well as temporary car hire until such a replacement could be sourced. He was also claiming for loss of earnings, although as he seemed to spend most of his days playing golf, I was somewhat suspicious of that claim. Anyway, on Marysa's advice, I had placed Hultmann's claim in the hands of the community's insurance company. I had enough to worry about without getting involved in that issue.

Incredibly, some seven months had now elapsed since Paul and I had been elected to sort out the community's problems and yet, somehow, we had managed to preside over an escalation, rather than a reduction in those problems. And now we faced a decision. The community's regular Annual General Meeting, or AGM, was due to be held in less than one week's time. One of the agenda items – dictated by the Horizontal Property Act – would be election of the president and vice president for the following twelve months. We could, quite legitimately, stand down and not put ourselves forward for re-election, but who the hell else was likely to volunteer to take on this thankless task? In any case we both felt that we could not abandon a task half-done – well in all honesty, not even anywhere near half-done. We had therefore agreed that at the forthcoming Annual General Meeting we would offer to stand for re-election but invite anyone else who felt so inclined, to stand also. Then it would be up to the owners to decide: if they wanted to chastise us for rank incompetence and appoint someone else, then so be it.

My introspective musing was interrupted by the sound of a familiar hacking cough from below. I glanced down to see that Julia was, as usual, clad in her dressing gown, hair in curlers, puffing furiously at her cigarette as she paced up and down her terrace. She seemed, somehow, to sense my presence, and looked upwards.

'What are you staring at?' she demanded.

I was in no mood for an argument and simply said, 'Just enjoying the view across the lake and the mountain.'

Ignoring her scowl, I turned away and walked back towards my apartment, where Donna was just emerging from the patio door.

'Bruce is here,' she said.

I'd forgotten that I'd invited Bruce over to go through with him a couple of things that were troubling him in his company accounts. As I stepped inside I was greeted by Bruce's strangely infectious smile: perfectly straight, dazzlingly white teeth incongruously punctuating his rugged countenance.

'Hi Roy, good to see you again.' He enfolded my hand in a vicelike grip, pumping it furiously.

'Good to see you too, Bruce,' I said, massaging my crushed fingers to restore some circulation.

'It's good of you to offer to take a look at these accounts with me. Thanks to you, I'm pretty confident on the normal monthly stuff, but now, at year end, Mickey – me accountant – has added a load of stuff to the balance sheet which wasn't there before.' His brow furrowed. 'We've now got "provisions" and "accruals" whatever the fook they are. Oops!' he said, turning to Donna and putting his hand to his mouth. 'Sorry darlin' ... just sort of slipped out.'

She smiled. 'No problem ... I'm starting to hear far worse from Roy since he's been doing this president thing.'

Bruce's booming, baritone laugh filled the room. 'I'll bet it's enough to make anyone swear having to deal with all these f—' He stopped himself just in time.

Donna stifled a giggle. 'Would you both like some coffee while you're going through that stuff?'

'Love one,' said Bruce. 'By the way, have you just changed your hairstyle?'

Donna touched the side of her hair, just where it turned under, and tilted her head to one side. 'Well, just had it tweaked a little bit and some highlights added.'

'It looks great,' he said, beaming appreciatively.

'Why, thank you,' she said, turning and flouncing off to the kitchen. Now why the hell hadn't *I* noticed her new hairdo?

Bruce and I sat down as I began to explain the significance of the new additions to his balance sheet.

A few minutes later, Donna returned with coffee and biscuits. As she set the tray down on the coffee table, I caught a waft of perfume. I was quite sure that she'd been wearing none earlier so she must have dabbed it on in just the last few minutes. Bruce had noticed it too.

'Mmm ... love your perfume. Chanel no. 5 isn't it?'

173

Her face broke into a broad smile. 'Why yes ... you certainly know your perfumes, Bruce.'

Hey hang on a minute – you're supposed to be here to talk about your accounts, not chat up my wife!

'Tracey wears it too,' he offered, by way of explanation. 'Anyway, thanks for the coffee.'

'You're most welcome,' she gushed. 'Well, I'll leave you boys to your high finance while I go and read a few chapters of my book.'

As she walked away, I noticed that she was wearing stockings and heels. She *never* normally bothered with such things when we were at home on our own.

As Donna left the room, we turned our attention back to Bruce's financial accounts.

Some thirty minutes later, Bruce was a happy man. He now fully understood the meaning of the new items on his balance sheet. I never ceased to be amazed at how this man's rough-and-ready appearance belied the intelligence which lay beneath.

'Thanks a million, Roy. Well I guess I should be going now, but first I must say goodbye to your lovely wife.'

'OK, I'll just call her and—'

The doorbell rang.

When I opened the door, I was stunned by the sight which greeted me. Robert Hultmann's head was swathed in bandages, and his left eye, blackened and swollen, was completely closed. His lower lip was pumped up to the point where it resembled a fat, livid slug. Just behind him stood the diminutive figure of Jim Watkins, complete with baseball cap.

'Wh ... what on earth happened?' I stammered.

'The bitch upstairs set her minders on me ... that's what happened,' he snarled.

'You'd better come in.'

'Christ man ... what the fook happened to you?' said Bruce as we moved through to the lounge.

'We have a crisis in the community,' announced Jim Watkins. 'The place is being turned into a brothel.'

'Well I ain't got no problem with brothels as such,' declared Bruce. 'Actually they offer a valuable public service, but I can't say I want to see one on my doorstep, like.'

Oh, for Christ's sake shut it, Bruce.

'Jim, Bruce, please ... I'd like to hear from Robert what happened.'

'Can I sit down?' said Robert. He looked and sounded genuinely shaken.

At that moment Donna, evidently having heard the voices, stepped into the room. As she caught sight of Robert, her hand flew to her mouth.

'Oh, my God! What on earth happened to you?'

I pre-empted Robert's reply. 'Let's all sit down and let Robert explain.'

'It was yesterday evening,' he began. 'I got in about 9 p.m. and as I got out of my car, these two goons were waiting for me in the garage. They didn't say a word before laying into me; one had some sort of knuckleduster on his hand. When I fell to the floor they both started kicking me ... the doctor says I have two cracked ribs.' He winced in pain, clutching his chest as he shifted position on the sofa.

'Were they after money, or what?' asked Donna.

He shook his head. 'Once they had decided that I'd had enough punishment they just said that this was a warning to stop harassing their "lady friend", and that if I didn't, I could expect much worse.'

'My God!' I breathed. 'Do you know who they were?'

'Well no ... not by name or by sight, but they both had what sounded like Russian accents; they are obviously the minders looking after the bitch upstairs,' he hissed.

Christ ... when Paul hears about this, I thought, *he might revise his opinion about the – admittedly very attractive, and superficially plausible – Svetlana Petrov.*

'So what are you going to do about it?' said Jim Watkins.

I ignored his question and addressed myself to Robert. 'Have you reported the incident to the police?'

'Yes ... they've been round to talk to me and to question that bitch upstairs.'

'And?' I prompted.

'The smooth-talking little cow fluttered her eyelashes and flashed her cleavage at them and managed to convince them that the whole thing had absolutely nothing to do with her.'

Hmm ... yes, I've seen that performance for myself, I thought.

'So what are they going to do?'

'They say they'll investigate, but I get the impression that they are treating it as just a one-off random mugging – even though the bastards didn't steal anything.'

Bruce, who had listened in silence up to this point, chipped in. 'They won't do fook all. The local police around here won't tangle with the Russian mafia who control the whores around here. In any case, most of the cops are taking backhanders to turn a blind eye.'

I was somewhat taken aback by Bruce's casual assessment of a situation with which, clearly, he was far more familiar than I.

'So what are you going to do about it?' demanded Jim Watkins, for a second time. With some difficulty, I resisted the temptation to smack him around the head.

'Look,' I said, 'it's clear that the warning discussion I had with this woman has had no effect, so we'll need to adopt a more forceful approach. I've already been advised that we can't do much about what she actually does in the privacy of her own home, but we can go after her for breaches of community rules: tampering with the garage door, excessive noise at night, littering the lawn with used contraceptives, and so on.'

'That's all very well—' began Jim, but I cut him off.

'Please ... let me finish. I have already spoken with the administrator about what we would need to do if Miss Petrov persists with her antisocial behaviour. The key thing is that we need to collect evidence, so I'll set up an incident diary in the security guards' office. Every time either of you sees or hears anything untoward, I'd like you to report it to the guards and record it in the incident diary. If you can provide any photographic evidence, so much the better. I'll also set up additional CCTV cameras in and around the block 6 garage' – I was past caring about Marysa's warning not to do so – 'and instruct the security guards to step up surveillance. Once we have collected sufficient evidence we can launch a legal action against her.'

Robert was listening attentively, but Jim Watkins just had to cut in again. 'However long is all that going to take?' he blustered.

'I'm well aware of how painfully slow the legal process is here in Spain, so I'll also try making contact with the owner of the property. Hopefully, if we make him aware of what's going on, he might be persuaded to evict his tenant.' I didn't mention that Marysa had already written to him, and failed even to elicit a reply.

'Well, OK ... I suppose,' murmured Robert, sounding doubtful ... but now I'm scared shitless about her bloody minders.'

Bruce cut in. 'Any idea if and when the bastards are coming back?'

The fear which flashed in Robert's eyes was plain to see. 'They said they'll be back within the next forty-eight hours to make sure that I've understood them properly and to administer a little more "persuasion" if necessary.'

The skin at the bridge of Bruce's nose puckered up and he stroked his chin, thoughtfully. 'OK,' he said, 'I'll keep an eye out for them. If they turn up in the next few days, I'll make sure they wish they hadn't. I've got a few good mates who owe me a favour or two and who I'm sure would be willing to lend a hand.'

Oh Christ no! The last thing I needed was a public brawl involving one of our residents – particularly if I was seen as being complicit in some way.

'Bruce, you can't go taking the law into—'

'Relax,' he soothed, waving his hand up and down slowly in a 'calm down' gesture, 'if the police get involved, you don't know nothing about it ... but they won't.'

'Won't what?' I said, puzzled.

'Get involved ... they leave this sort of thing to be sorted out on the streets.' I shook my head in utter bewilderment.

Bruce tore off a sheet of paper from the notepad which he had been using to record his insights from our – now forgotten – analysis of his balance sheet, and scribbled something on it, handing it to Robert. 'Here's my phone number. If you hear anything more, or get an idea of when these fookers may turn up, just call me.'

Robert grabbed the scrap of paper as though it were a lifebelt offered to a drowning man.

Jim Watkins had listened in silence for the last ten minutes or so, his jaw dropping progressively lower, but now he found his voice. He turned towards me 'I can't believe what I'm hearing,' he said. Actually, I could hardly believe it myself. 'You can't possibly sanction this sort of thing.'

Before I could frame the words to reply, Bruce smoothly interjected. 'Roy's not sanctioning nothing, are you Roy?' I shook my head, dumbly. 'I gotta tell you though, Jim, that if you were to say anything to anyone about our little chat here it would really,

really upset me.' He paused to let these words sink in, before adding, 'And you wouldn't want to upset me, now would you?'

Jim shrank back in his chair – and he was already pretty small to start with. He looked desperately from Robert to me in turn, evidently searching for support. He found none. 'I won't say anything,' he confirmed.

'Good man!' boomed Bruce, clapping Jim on the back so hard that the poor man nearly choked. 'Well I guess we're more or less done here,' he said, rising to his feet. Then, turning to Robert, 'Remember, if you hear anything more from these fookers, call me.'

Five minutes later, Donna and I were alone. I poured myself a generous brandy and her a Tia Maria.

'Hell of a day, huh?' said Donna, summarising in typically succinct manner.

'Surely, things can't actually get any worse, can they?' I suggested, more in hope than expectation, given the way events had unfolded of late.

Donna raised a quizzical eyebrow. 'You think?'

I slumped in my chair. 'And we haven't even started yet on the big wall construction project.'

'I think you're secretly loving it. After all life was getting a bit dull after leaving the corporate rat-race wasn't it?'

'Right now, "dull" would suit me just fine.'

She laughed, 'You and Paul will sort it all out eventually.'

'I hope you're right,' I said. 'I can't believe the conversation which we just had, though. Is Bruce really intending to try to warn these people off?'

'Well, it certainly seems that way.' She paused for a moment before adding, 'He's quite an enigma isn't he?'

'How do you mean?'

'Well, at first glance he looks like some sort of thug himself, yet he runs his own business, and you said yourself that he's actually far brighter than he appears.'

'Well, that's true,' I agreed.

'And look at the way he's supported you in those awful meetings.'

I smiled at the memory of Bruce's forthright defence of some of my proposals. 'Yes, that *was* a bit of a surprise,' I agreed.

'And now he's offering to help Robert Hultmann when the police are not prepared to do anything. You know,' she added, 'in his own way, he's actually one of the most community-minded people around here.'

'Well, yes ... I suppose you're right,' I admitted.

'And he's really quite charming – in a rough-and-ready sort of way,' she added, a hint of a smile flitting across her face.

Chapter 26

The following day, Marysa phoned me.

'I have some good news for you.'

'I could certainly use some,' I sighed, still preoccupied by the previous evening's events. 'So what is it?'

'Things are finally starting to move with respect to the legal action regarding the wall.'

Now she had my full attention. 'What ... do we have a date for the court hearing?'

'Well, no ... the news is not quite *that* good' – my spirits sank as quickly as they had been raised – 'but it's the next best thing. The court is sending its own independent surveyor to inspect the site tomorrow at 12 noon. That's an indication that the case will be heard quite soon now.'

I was puzzled. 'So what's the purpose of his – or her – visit?'

'It's a "he". His job is to advise the court, from a technical standpoint, as to the validity of the size of our claim. Basically, he'll give his opinion of what the cost of repairs would be. What usually happens is that the party making the claim asks for more than the job will actually cost, while the defendant tries to argue for an amount far less than the job will actually cost. The job of the surveyor appointed by the court is, in effect, to arbitrate and ensure the settlement is fair to both parties.'

'Whoa ... hold on a minute. We know that our claim is already only about *half* of the true cost. If this guy is coming along with the preconceived idea that we're *over*-claiming, won't it affect his judgement?'

'In principle, no. He's supposed to come at it from a completely impartial position. In theory, he could even decide to advise a figure which is *higher* than our claim.'

Yeah, right, I thought. 'And how likely do you think that is?'

'Well, not very likely at all,' she admitted, 'but we've been through all this before: we can't increase our claim without dropping the action completely and starting again, which would put things back years.'

I exhaled heavily. 'Yes, I know ... but it doesn't make the situation any more palatable.'

'Look, there's nothing we can do to influence the outcome of his visit so let's just wait and see what happens shall we?'

'I guess so,' I muttered. Then another thought struck me. 'Will Alfredo González – the developer – be present at the visit?'

'Well, the other side always has the right to attend such visits, so I'd be very surprised if he wasn't there.'

'Are you coming too?'

'Yes, and Sergio.'

'OK ... until tomorrow then.'

'Oh, one other thing before you hang up,' she said.

'Uh, huh ... what's that?'

'Since you are intent on installing extra CCTV cameras ... against my advice' – she sounded a little tetchy at this point – 'I've been on to the security company, and they've confirmed that our system can accommodate two additional CCTV cameras in or around block 5. The cost would be around one thousand five hundred euros including installation.'

It was another unexpected expense which we could ill afford but I really wanted to deal with the problem of Svetlana Petrov as quickly as possible, hopefully avoiding the situation escalating into an ugly confrontation.

'OK, good,' I said. 'When can they come and install them?'

'If I call them back this morning they can be there tomorrow afternoon at 2 p.m.'

I was astonished, but very pleased, that this feat could be achieved so quickly, in a country where, normally, the only things that people do quickly are talk, and drive – usually inches from the bumper of the vehicle ahead. I gratefully accepted this proposal.

After I hung up, my thoughts returned to the surveyor's visit. This was a step in the process which I had not anticipated, and I felt distinctly uneasy about it.

***

That afternoon, I decided to phone the owner of Svetlana Petrov's apartment, Mario Bellini. He hadn't replied to Marysa's letter, but I hoped that he might perhaps respond more favourably to a phone call directly from me. I had never met him in person, and as far as I knew, he very rarely even visited his apartment. He did, however, speak excellent English – which was just as well, as I spoke no Italian whatsoever. It turned out that Mr. Bellini lived in Milan but owned fifteen properties spread across several different countries, the letting of which provided his main source of income.

I spent perhaps twenty minutes on the phone explaining the problems which his tenant was causing us, but although he listened politely enough, it quickly became clear that he wasn't particularly interested.

As he reasonably pointed out, 'Look, from what you have told me, it seems you have no hard evidence to connect my tenant with any of the unfortunate occurrences which you have described.'

'But surely,' I pleaded, 'you must see that the vicious assault on one of our residents is a step too far. Something just has to be done now.'

'Of course,' he replied, 'but that is a matter for the police, and in any case, once again, you have no evidence that these unpleasant people have anything to do with my tenant.'

'But they specifically said that the attack was to dissuade your tenant's neighbour from "harassing their lady friend". Surely that makes it quite clear why they were there, doesn't it?'

I could somehow sense the Italianate shrug which I was sure was taking place on the other end of the line. 'Perhaps your resident was mistaken. After all, it must have been a very distressing incident and it wouldn't be at all surprising if, in the heat of the moment, some of the details were lost or misheard.'

It was clear that this discussion was going nowhere.

'So am I to understand that you are not prepared to take any action with respect to your tenant?' I said, trying my damndest to keep the note of irritation out of my voice.

'Mr Groves,' he replied, 'while I have every sympathy with your situation, as far as I can see, you have no evidence that Miss Petrov is involved at all. From my point of view she is a good tenant who always pays her rent on time and gives me no trouble whatsoever. I only wish that all my tenants were like that.'

His response was bloody irritating, but I had to admit that if I was in his position, hundreds of miles away from a situation which did not impinge on my life in any way whatsoever, I might take a similar view. After all, why should he evict his tenant and cut off some of his income on the say-so of someone who just phoned out of the blue with unsubstantiated allegations?

'Then I guess we have nothing more to discuss,' I sighed.

'Call me again,' he said, 'if you *do* find some evidence that my tenant is connected with some of these unfortunate incidents.'

I hung up without bothering to reply to his last remark.

'Dammit!' I hissed, pacing towards the kitchen to pour myself a glass of wine.

'I assume it didn't go too well then,' observed Donna who had been in the kitchen baking some cakes.

'He just wasn't interested,' I said, opening the fridge and grabbing a bottle of white wine.

'Well, you weren't really holding out much hope that he would be, were you?'

'No, but he still got my back up.'

'Well it was worth a try,' she said, 'but I guess you'll just have to press ahead with plan B.'

'Hmm I suppose so,' I grumbled as I held up the bottle. 'Do you want a glass?'

'Oh, go on then,' she laughed.

I had barely taken my first sip of wine when the doorbell rang.

'Oh, what now?' I moaned, stomping towards the door.

When I opened the door, my irritation melted away in an instant. Angelique was casually dressed in jeans and T-shirt, her hair tied back in a ponytail, and her face adorned with only the subtlest of makeup. She looked barely less alluring than when done up to the nines and wearing full makeup.

''Alo Roy.' She stepped forward and gave me a perfunctory kiss on the cheek.

Hey, hang on a minute ... what happened to the three kisses and a bit of a hug? I felt distinctly short-changed.

Donna, hearing Angelique's voice, stepped out of the kitchen. 'Oh, hello, Angelique ... how lovely to see you. Won't you come in?'

The two women exchanged a kiss on the cheek, which I noticed was every bit as rushed as the stingy peck to which I had been treated.

'I 'ave a bit of a problem and I wondered if you could 'elp?' She looked anxiously backwards and forwards between the two of us, as if the plea wasn't addressed to either of us in particular.

'Of course,' said Donna. 'What's the problem?'

'My car ... she won't start ... and I 'ave to collect Miriam from school in twenty minutes.'

'Well, I need to stay here to take these cakes out of the oven, but Roy can give you a lift to the school, can't you, Roy?'

My spirits immediately lifted at the prospect of, once again, having an excuse to spend a little time with Angelique. 'Of course, I'd be glad to.'

'Oh, zank you so much.' She flung her arms around my neck and hugged me. *Now that's a bit more like it.*

'I'll just grab some shoes,' I said, 'and then I guess we'd better go straightaway.'

We arrived at the school just in time, as the chattering stream of children began to emerge from the main entrance. I quickly spotted Miriam among the throng, her long black hair swaying from side to side as she skipped along, chatting to her friend. She looked to have grown perceptibly in just the few months since she had come round with Angelique for dinner. She looked puzzled as she scanned the row of parked cars, evidently searching for her mother's and probably not recognising mine.

Angelique stepped out of the car and waved, catching Miriam's eye. 'Our car is not working,' she explained as her daughter approached the car. 'Roy very kindly offered to give me a lift.'

Miriam nodded and stepped into the back of the car. 'Thank you Mr Groves,' she said, a little formally I thought.

She said very little on the way home, but when we got back to her apartment she turned to me and said, 'Mr Groves, I am very sorry for the way I behaved when you invited us in for dinner. It was very rude of me to carry on like that in your home.'

I couldn't believe it: that was months ago, and Miriam had apparently been dwelling on the incident ever since. I bent down so that our faces were on a level and looked straight into her beautiful, blue eyes, which seemed almost too big for such a petite face.

'Miriam, think nothing of it. It wasn't rude at all – you were just ... well, upset about what had happened ... and understandably so. Please let's forget the whole thing shall we?' She nodded, her whole countenance noticeably brightening. 'And I'd like us to be good friends, OK?'

Her little face lit up with a luminous smile and she leaned forward to kiss me on the cheek. 'I'd like that too. My mother really likes you as well, you know.'

'Miriam!' exclaimed Angelique, a hint of a flush appearing in her suntanned cheeks, 'zat's enough now. I zought you were going down to ze swimming pool to meet Gema and Sofía after school.'

'I am,' she said, skipping off to change into her swimming costume.

'What a lovely, polite little girl,' I said. 'She's a credit to you.'

'I am so glad she decided to apologise to you,' replied Angelique. 'She 'as been worrying about it ever since zat evening, even zough I kept telling 'er you wouldn't be concerned about it. I'm sure she will be much 'appier now.'

I smiled. 'Perhaps I'll see a bit more of her now then. Er, will she be alright down by the pool on her own?'

'Oh yes, Miriam swims like a fish ... and in any case, ze father of 'er friend Gema will be down zere to keep an eye on zem.'

'In that case, shall we take a look at that car of yours?'

The battery was flat. It turned out that Angelique had accidentally left the lights on when parking the car in the garage. I went back to my apartment to fetch my battery charger and explain to Donna that I might be a little while as I had to check that there wasn't some other problem with the car.

She rolled her eyes. 'OK, but if you're going to spend goodness knows how long sorting out your lady friend's problems—'

'She's not my "lady friend",' I protested, feeling the surge of blood to my cheeks, 'she's just a neighbour who needs a bit of help.'

'Only joking,' said Donna, laughing, 'but she *has* got you wrapped right around her little finger hasn't she?'

Well, I suppose so, I thought.

'Certainly not,' I said, 'I'm just trying to help,'

'Whatever,' she said, still stifling a laugh. 'Anyway, I don't want to start cooking until I know what time you'll be back.'

'Tell you what,' I said, desperately trying to retrieve the situation, 'why don't we go out for dinner tonight when I get back?'

'Deal!' she said, slipping off her apron, and picking up her glass of wine from the worktop. 'Meanwhile I'll top this up and watch that last recorded episode of "Marbs Forever".'

Now it was my turn to roll my eyes. I picked up the battery charger and set off to attend to Angelique's car.

Chapter 27

The following day was pretty hectic.

My first task was to check on Angelique's car. She had left me a key, so I went straight down to the garage, where the battery charger was now indicating a healthy state of charge in the battery. I disconnected the charger, slipped into the driver's seat, and when I twisted the key in the ignition the engine sprang to life immediately.

I went upstairs and rang Angelique's doorbell. When she answered the door she was wearing a short, bright pink, figure-hugging dress and black, high-heeled, strappy shoes. Her long black hair tumbled over her shoulders. It was quite a different look from that which she had adopted for the school run the previous day.

'How is ze car?' she enquired.

'It seems fine. I think the problem was just due to the lights being left on for so long yesterday. There's no sign that there's anything else wrong.' I handed her the key.

'Oh, zank you Roy.' She turned her head and called out, 'Miriam ... time to go now.'

Miriam came bounding down the stairs looking cute in the tartan skirt and white blouse of her school uniform. 'Hello Mr Groves. Have you fixed the car?'

'Yes, I think so.'

'You are very clever,' she said, earnestly. 'Thank you very much for fixing it, and for collecting me from school yesterday.'

'You're very welcome,' I replied, bending down to her level.

She responded by kissing me on the cheek; evidently all her inhibitions towards me were now well and truly forgotten.

'Come on,' said Angelique, 'we really should be going now.'

The two of them stepped outside and Angelique closed the door. We shared the lift down to the garage level where Angelique turned towards me and opened her arms to enfold me in a hug.

All too soon she pulled away. 'Zanks again, Roy. I don't know how I can repay you for all ze 'elp you 'ave given me.'

Well, a whole raft of totally inappropriate ideas sprang instantly to my mind, but I did my best to dismiss them. 'Oh, it's nothing,' I said. 'Goodbye then ... have a good day at school, Miriam.'

She waved goodbye, smiling prettily, and turned to follow her mother, who was making for their car.

As I opened the door of my own apartment, I heard Donna's voice. 'Oh, wait a minute I think that's him now.' She stepped into the hall, holding her hand over the mouthpiece of the phone. 'It's Marysa ... from the administrators.' She handed me the phone.'

'Hello, Marysa ... what's up?'

It was unusual for her to call me so early; I was immediately on the alert for bad news.

'I've had a call from Alfredo González, the developer. He wants to meet with us today before the court surveyor comes round, to see if we can perhaps reach some sort of agreement on an out-of-court settlement.'

Well, I certainly wasn't expecting *that*. Maybe my fortunes were about to improve after all.

'Why the change of heart?' I enquired.

'Who knows? Perhaps now that the court hearing is drawing closer he's worried that he'll lose, and have to pay not only a substantial settlement but also considerable legal fees.'

'OK,' I ventured, 'but the surveyor's coming at noon isn't he? That doesn't give us much time.'

'He's willing to meet us at eleven ... on-site in the urbanisation.'

'OK, let's see what he has to say.'

***

Alfredo González sat directly across the table from me, alongside his brother José, the architect. I was flanked by Sergio and Marysa,

'Thank you,' said Alfredo, running the fingers of his right hand back through his lank, greasy, black hair, 'for agreeing to meet us at short notice.' I nodded in acknowledgement of his remark but said nothing. 'We thought' – he inclined his head towards his brother – 'that as we would all be here on-site for the surveyor's visit, it would be a good opportunity to see if we could come to some sort of agreement to avoid a lengthy and costly court action.' He had been looking down at his notepad while speaking, but now he paused, raised his head, and made eye contact with me.

'We are always willing to talk,' I said, 'but I have to say that your previous offer was derisory. You will have to come up with something very much more substantial if we are to make any progress here.'

'Well, let me hand over to José to outline our position.'

The architect cleared his throat before speaking. 'In the light of recent events, and following our own technical investigation we have come to the conclusion that there is a limited section of the cut face of the hillside which is of more friable material than the quartzite which makes up the bulk of the area.'

Well, I thought, *it doesn't take much of a 'technical investigation', to work that one out when the damned thing has collapsed in a fucking great pile of earth and rubble, does it?* I decided not to respond until he had finished explaining his proposal.

'This' – he pushed an A3-sized sheet of paper towards the centre of the table – 'is a revised plan for remedial action.'

The three of us on my side of the table looked at the drawing briefly but it didn't mean much to me, and when I glanced sideways at Sergio and Marysa, it was clear they were not much wiser.

'Perhaps you can explain it for us,' I said.

'Of course,' he said. 'This' – he pointed at a feature on the drawing – 'is a reinforced concrete structure positioned along the weak section. It will be secured to the hillside behind by ground anchors.'

I had no idea what a 'ground anchor' was, but if the material behind the new structure was as crumbly as that which had collapsed onto our road then I couldn't see that there would be much point in trying to 'anchor' anything to it. Nevertheless, I kept quiet while he continued.

'Once the weak section has been stabilised in this way we can cover it with an attractive cement facing and blend it in with the rest of the existing facing. Once this had been done the whole thing will look very much as before.' He looked from Sergio, to me, and to Marysa in turn, evidently waiting for a response.

Sergio stepped in. '*If* we were to accept such a plan – and I hasten to add we would have to have our own technical experts review it – I assume your company would bear the full cost?'

Alfredo swiftly cut in; he extended his arm across in front of his brother in a gesture indicating that he should now take a back seat in negotiations. 'Gentlemen ... and lady' he added, directing a lopsided and rather unpleasant smile at Marysa, 'that would of course be an unreasonable request, but we are willing to make a generous contribution. We estimate that the total cost of such works would be twenty-two thousand euros. We are willing to pay half of that sum.'

Right, that's it: these bastards are wasting our time. I took a couple of deep breaths in order to contain the torrent of invective which threatened to spill from my lips. After a few seconds I had composed myself enough to reply.

'Thank you for outlining your proposal, but I have to tell you right now that it goes nowhere near forming the basis for any kind of agreement, because—'

'Mr Groves,' interjected González, 'please take a little time to fully consider—'

I cut him off sharply. 'There is nothing to consider ... let me tell you why. Firstly, your assertion that the hillside – or now *most* of the hillside – is made of quartzite is nonsense. We have had a geotechnical survey done which indicates it's all made of the same stuff which came crashing down, destroying a car and which, by the way, could easily have killed someone.'

'Oh, really, I think you are rather exaggerating the situation now.'

I ignored his remark and continued, 'In the light of the geotechnical survey, we now know that constructing a suitable retaining wall is going to cost well in excess of two hundred thousand euros – far more than we are currently claiming.' I fixed him with a withering glare. 'And you come along offering eleven thousand euros? You can take your pathetic offer and—'

Sergio laid a restraining hand on my arm, just succeeding in stopping me from making a very inappropriate – and probably physically impossible – suggestion.

'As you can see,' said Sergio, 'your offer is woefully inadequate. Unless you are able to make a much more serious offer then I'm afraid we have nothing more to discuss.'

Alfredo's eyes narrowed and deep furrows appeared in the skin above the bridge of his nose. He placed both hands, palm-downwards on the table, fingers spread wide, as he leaned forward, his dark eyes boring into mine like gimlets.

'So be it,' he growled, 'but I warn you ... you will regret your decision.'

His intimidating manner was distinctly unsettling but I wasn't going to back down. 'We'll let the courts decide, shall we?' I said. Without waiting for an answer, I pushed my chair back and stood up, glancing at my watch. 'The surveyor is due to arrive any time now so I suggest we make our way up to the wall to meet him.'

***

By the time we got there, the surveyor had already arrived and was well underway with his inspection. Paul had waited to meet him while we held our abortive meeting with the González brothers.

'He's early,' I observed, shaking Paul's hand.

'Yes, he arrived half an hour ago.'

'Half an *hour*?' This was nothing short of astonishing: no-one *ever* arrives early for *anything* in Spain.

Paul had evidently registered the look of surprise on my face; he shrugged. 'No, I don't get it either. Ideally, I'd like to have given him a bit of background before he got started, but he speaks practically no English and as both Sergio and Marysa were tied up in the meeting I thought it best to just let him get started.' I nodded. 'By the way, how did the meeting go?'

'Don't ask. The bastard' – I flicked my eyes sideways towards where Alfredo and his brother were lurking some thirty feet away – 'was just taking the piss.'

'Hmm,' mused Paul, 'I guess it was too much to hope for that he'd come along with a serious offer.'

We lapsed into silence and watched the surveyor going about his work. A small, dapper figure with a neatly-trimmed goatee beard, he was dressed in a grey business suit – not the most suitable attire, I thought, for a potentially grubby scramble around the site. But he wasn't actually doing any scrambling; he was just walking slowly up and down the collapsed section making notes on a clipboard. He never once touched anything or even got within six feet of the shored-up earth face.

Paul and I exchanged a puzzled glance. 'Doesn't look very thorough,' I observed.

Sergio looked equally bemused. 'I'll talk to him when he's finished,' he said.

But the first people that the surveyor spoke to, when he'd finished, were Alfredo González and his brother. Observing the casual body language of all three men, I had the uneasy feeling that this was perhaps not the first time that they had met.

'Can you hear what they're saying?' I asked, of Sergio and Marysa. To me their hushed conversation was nothing but an indistinguishable murmur.

'No ... let's move a little closer,' suggested Marysa.

We began edging our way towards them, trying not to be too obvious but, before we got into eavesdropping range, the three men shook hands and the González brothers set off down the hill towards the front gate. They did not so much as glance in our direction.

The surveyor came towards us, pausing for a moment as his eyes raked up and down Marysa's body, no doubt taking in the generous expanse of thigh revealed by her very short skirt. I swear I detected a salacious glint in his eye. She had evidently caught sight of his fleeting assessment, and glared back at him defiantly.

What is it with these Spanish men and Marysa? I had previously observed Alfredo González eying her up and down with a similarly lustful gaze. She certainly didn't do it for me, but hey, each to their own, I suppose.

'This is Pedro Barquero,' said Paul, before introducing each of us in turn.

'Encantado,' responded the Spaniard.

As Paul had already intimated, he appeared to speak no English at all, and as neither Paul nor I spoke anything beyond the most basic Spanish, we took a metaphorical back seat and handed over to Sergio and Marysa.

The conversation was conducted at such a rapid pace that I followed practically none of it. After some ten or fifteen minutes, though, it was clearly winding up.

'I think we are about finished now,' announced Sergio. 'Marysa, can you see señor Barquero down to the front gate while I summarise for Roy and Paul?'

She glared at him. 'I just need to write a few notes while it's all fresh in my mind. Why don't *you* see señor Barquero out?'

Sergio shrugged. 'Yes, if you wish.'

We all shook hands and Sergio set off down the hill with the surveyor.

'OK,' she said, as soon as they were out of earshot, 'let me summarise for you what was said.'

'Don't you want to make your notes first?' I enquired.

'Oh,' she said waving her hand dismissively, 'I don't need to make any more notes; I just couldn't bear spending a minute alone with that horrible little man.' The look on her face was one of ill-disguised disgust.

Paul and I exchanged an amused glance.

'Fair enough,' I said. 'Anyway, what about the survey? Did he give you any idea what sort of valuation he's going to come up with?'

She shook her head. 'He says he has to go away to consider that question in the light of his observations.'

'But how does he expect to come up with an informed valuation of remedial work by just looking at the bloody thing and taking a few notes?'

'Sergio asked him more or less the same question. He says that with our geotechnical survey report, plus various other reports and plans supplied by the other side, he has enough technical data to come to a considered conclusion.'

'Makes you wonder why he bothered with a site visit at all,' ventured Paul.

'Well,' said Marysa, 'the charge that the court makes for appointing a surveyor is useful extra income. They never pass up an opportunity to make extra money.'

'And who pays?' said Paul.

'That's for the court to decide,' she replied. 'Usually it's the losing party.'

'Hopefully not us,' I grumbled.

'There's another reason to send a surveyor,' she continued. When they decide on the amount of any award which they may order either party to pay, they need to be able to point to the fact that it's based on independent, expert technical advice. As I explained before, they tend to assume that the party making the claim will exaggerate the cost, and that the defending party will understate it.'

'Except that in our case, we already know that the real cost is even higher than ...' My voice tailed off, as I realised the futility of persisting with this argument which we had already done to death. 'Oh, well, I guess we now have to wait for his report. How long is that likely to take?'

She spread her hands and shrugged. 'It's Spain,' she reminded me.

When Marysa had left, Paul and I spent a further ten minutes discussing the visit before concluding that there was really nothing we could do now but wait.

'I'm afraid I have to go now,' said Paul. 'Sorry I can't be around to meet the CCTV people. Kate and I have to be in Marbella by two, to meet some friends for lunch.'

'Oh that's OK,' I said, 'I'll take care of it. Enjoy your lunch.'

As Paul returned to his apartment, I checked my watch: 1.40 p.m. The CCTV people were due to arrive in about twenty minutes. I decided to walk down to collect my mail from the mailbox by the front gate, and then wait down there to meet them.

As I leafed idly through the stack of mail, depositing the obvious junk mail straight into the already-overflowing bin alongside, I caught site of some movement in the street outside. I glanced casually across the street. It took me a few seconds to register who and what I was witnessing, but when I did, the scene suddenly had my full attention. Alfredo González was deeply engaged in conversation with the surveyor. *Hang on a minute ... I thought everyone had already left. What the hell's going on here?*

I watched as González withdrew a large brown envelope from his briefcase, glancing furtively all around before handing it to the surveyor. The two men shook hands briefly, and within a few more seconds they were each in their respective cars and heading off up the road.

Oh, shit!

Chapter 28

The AGM – held in the usual hotel – was a fairly quiet and civilised affair compared to some of the previous bunfights. This was helped, in no small measure, by the fact that Dr Ramani had chosen not to attend. Her non-attendance was no doubt linked to the news which I had received from Sergio the previous day: she was due to appear in court in less than two months' time – something of a record by Spanish standards.

Most people had now come to terms with the extra money they were having to cough up for the construction of the new wall, and even Mrs Bucket now seemed satisfied with her kitchen plans, especially since Donna had taken the trouble to go round and discuss them with her over a cup of coffee. Good for Donna – although I was getting a bit disturbed by her frequent hints that perhaps *we* needed a new kitchen, too.

When I summarised the daunting list of problems which the community still faced, the audience listened in silence, but at the end of my account I had the impression that most people were satisfied with the way we were handling the issues.

I was able to report a continuing improvement in the community's financial situation, and when I proposed a budget and fee structure for the coming year at much the same level as the current year, this was accepted, with only a smattering of grumbles from the more bothersome residents.

Finally, we came to the point in the meeting where community officers were to be elected for the following twelve months.

'So,' I said, 'are there any nominations for the posts of president and vice president?'

The silence was palpable; evidently no-one was terribly keen to take on the litany of problems which I had just outlined.

'Any nominations at all?' I prompted.

The heavy silence persisted, finally broken by Joe Haven. 'It seems to me that Roy and Paul are doing an outstanding job in tackling the various issues which confront us. I'd like to ask them to stay on for the coming year.'

A ripple of what sounded like approving murmurs suffused the room, eventually hushed by Bruce's distinctive, booming voice. 'Yeah, they're doing a right good job. Come on guys, don't quit now.'

I was somewhat surprised to observe that Bruce was sitting right next to Robert Hultmann. Robert was no longer wearing any dressing to his face and head, but the cuts and bruises inflicted during his assault were still plain to see. Rather disturbingly, I noted that Bruce also now sported an ugly purple bruise below his left eye.

Robert nodded vigorously in support of Bruce's remarks, adding, 'Yes, we really need you to stay on to continue the good work.'

Paul and I looked at each other and then back towards the audience: a sea of expectant faces, but no sign that anyone else wanted to speak.

'Well,' I said, 'if there are no nominations—'

Jim Watkins raised his hand.

I could hardly believe it: surely he wasn't seriously proposing to put himself forward? Anyway, I invited him to speak. 'Yes, Jim ... do you wish to stand for election?'

He shook his head. 'No ... I just wanted to echo some of the other owners' remarks. I have had my differences with Roy and Paul, but I have to acknowledge that they are indeed doing a good job. I, too, would like to ask them to stay on for another year.'

I could hardly believe what I was hearing. That must have been a very hard thing for Jim to say; at that moment, my animosity towards him began to evaporate.

For a second or two I was lost for words, but Paul stepped in. 'Thanks, Jim. We really appreciate your support.' I nodded to reinforce Paul's remark.

'Well,' I said, if there are no other nominations, then Paul and I are happy to present ourselves to continue in our current capacities for a further twelve months.'

Bruce and Robert were smiling and nodding to each other like old friends. *What's going on there, then?*

'All those in favour?' said Marysa. A forest of hands went up. 'All those against?' Not a single hand was raised. 'Abstensions?' Still no hands raised. 'Then Roy and Paul are duly elected,' she declared.

After the meeting, as the attendees began to disperse, I went over to Jim Watkins. 'Jim, I just wanted to say how much I appreciated your support during the meeting. I know we haven't exactly always seen eye to eye on a lot of things but, well ... that was a very generous thing to say.'

Jim looked down at his feet. 'I don't agree with everything you're doing, but I acknowledge that you're making progress on some of the issues we are facing. I've always been an advocate of "credit where credit's due".'

Well, I'd never previously seen any evidence of such advocacy, but I was more than willing to try to build bridges, particularly as Jim had made the first move.

As he slowly raised his eyes to meet mine, I extended my hand. He seemed to hesitate for a moment, but then accepted my handshake with seemingly good grace. Maybe we really were about to turn over a new page in our relationship. I hoped so.

***

After everyone else had left, Paul and I sat down with Robert Hultmann and Bruce in the hotel bar.

Bruce downed his beer in a couple of gulps – before I had even started on mine – wiping the froth from his upper lip with the back of his tattooed hand and emitting a deep sigh. 'Ah ... that hits the spot.'

'Want another?' I said, grinning.

'Mmm ... yes please. Don't know why they make these fookin' glasses so small.'

He approached his second beer with a little more decorum than the first, quaffing only about one third of the glass before setting it down.

'OK, so what's with the black eye?' I enquired, more serious now.

'Them fookers who beat Robert up' – he slapped the German heartily on the back – 'turned up again.'

My heart sank as my worst fears were confirmed. 'So what happened?'

'Well, when Robert said that the bastards had threatened to come back, I decided to ask a couple of mates to stay round at mine for a few days so we could get there quick if there were any trouble like. Terry's heavily into body-building ... and shit hot on all the martial arts stuff. Gazzer's not in quite such good shape, but he's a big fella, and you certainly wouldn't want to cross him ...'

'OK,' I said, a tad impatiently, 'I get the picture. So what happened?'

'Oh yeah, right ... well, Robert spotted these two geezers hanging about outside the garage and phoned me, so me and the lads came round into the garage from the inside. Once we were ready, Robert opened the outside garage door with his remote control and these two pricks came right on in ... like lambs to the slaughter.'

Oh, Christ! I hope the 'slaughter' bit is not too literal.

'So what happened next?'

'I told the fookers to lay off and never come back again but one of them – big guy with a shaved head ... Russian I think – decided to take a swing at me.' He indicated the ugly bruising around his eye. 'Big mistake.' I shook my head in despair as Bruce continued. 'Me and the lads had come prepared like: we brought a couple of baseball bats. We sent them fookers packing, I can tell you.'

'Stop!' I said. 'I can't be hearing this. You just can't go taking the law into your own hands like that.'

He drew his eyes together in a puzzled frown; he actually looked quite hurt by my remark. 'But you don't want them fookers around the place do you?'

'Well, no,' I admitted, 'but I can't sanction this kind of thing within the community.'

'Ah, no ... of course not,' he said, tapping the side of his nose with his forefinger. 'You don't know nothing about it.' The incongruous combination of his perfect, dazzling teeth, his rugged features and the multi-coloured bruise below his eye rendered his broad smile somehow both disturbing and amusing in equal measure.

'Well,' interjected Robert, 'I, for one, am most grateful for Bruce's intervention.'

'Hmm,' I said, doubtfully, 'well, in future let's stick to the agreed plan with the cameras and the complaints book rather than physical violence, eh?'

'Oh, I don't think them fookers will be back anytime soon,' declared Bruce.

I hope you're right, I thought.

Chapter 29

It was late February, and the weather was still too unpredictable to start work on the construction of the new retaining wall. The long range forecast suggested that we would need to wait at least another four weeks. Paul and I had decided that in the meantime we should tackle one or two of the smaller projects which were still outstanding. The most pressing of these was the leakage of foul water from the sewage system down to the corner of the swimming pool area. Now, no-one but the most foolhardy of folk would venture into the unheated pool in February but we were keen to deal with this problem before springtime when the pool area would once again become busy. The last thing either of us needed was for one of the unsuspecting bathers to contract some godawful stomach condition caused by contact with the leaking sewage.

We had already had the site inspected by a plumbing contractor recommended to us by FAG. Their rather gloomy assessment was that the leakage probably originated from underground pipework located somewhere beneath the foundations of block 13. Tracing the leak, they had informed us, would be an extremely difficult and costly task. They recommended that instead, we should block off that part of the sewage system completely and install an entirely new section of pipework from block 13 to link up with the existing system from the adjacent block 14. Apparently there was a basement below the garage of block 13, through which the pipework ran before disappearing underground. This was where they proposed to cut the pipe, block off the underground section, and run a new section of pipework through to block 14.

It was Sunday morning, and Donna and I were due to go out for lunch with Neil and Marion, but first, I planned to meet Paul and inspect the areas where the remedial work was to be carried out.

We started out down by the pool. Predictably enough, there was no-one else down there. As we approached the corner where we knew the leakage emerged, our nostrils were assaulted by the foul smell of sewage. Even though the temperature was cooler now, the intensity of the stench seemed to have increased.

'Look ... there,' said Paul, pointing to a slick, green streak of algae clinging to the rocks below the point where the foul water was clearly seeping through.

'It looks as though the amount of water escaping has increased,' I observed, extending a forefinger towards the slimy, green surface.

'I wouldn't touch that if I were you,' suggested Paul. 'It's probably teeming with just about every kind of noxious bug known to science.'

Realising the wisdom of his timely advice, I swiftly withdrew my finger. 'Hmm ... probably a few which are *not* known to science, too.'

'There's no doubt that it's getting worse,' said Paul. 'We definitely need to get this fixed as soon as possible.'

'Yes,' I sighed, 'but we could do without yet another bloody bill. What was the quote ... twelve thousand euros?'

'Twelve thousand four hundred and seventy I believe.'

'Not much option though,' I grumbled. 'Come on, let's take a look in the basement below the block up there.' I raised my gaze to where block 13 towered above us.

We moved away from the leak site, savouring the much sweeter air as we trudged up the steep path.

Due to the slope of the land, the door to the basement under block 13 was accessible directly from ground level.

'I'm not sure if there's a light in here,' I said, as I turned the handle to open the door, 'so I brought this torch in case—'

I didn't need the torch. The basement was actually very well-lit, and what I saw made my jaw drop. As we stepped through the door, eight startled faces turned towards us.

The scene was frozen in time. We stared at them; they stared at us, the whites of their eyes contrasting starkly with their very dark skin tone. There were three men, three women, and two children, all of African appearance. The only sounds which could be heard were the hum of a generator and the muted tones – I didn't recognise the language – emanating from a television in the corner, the volume turned down low. I glanced around the room; it was quite comfortably furnished with folding garden chairs, pictures on the walls and a portable gas cooker atop a large trestle table.

I have no idea how long the silent standoff continued; it felt like an eternity.

Paul eventually broke through the paralysis which had seized everyone in the room. 'Who are you people ... what are you doing here?' He had adopted that very commanding, booming tone which he could turn on at will, and which had been most effective at quelling potential revolts at previous community meetings.

From the puzzlement on their faces, I suspected that they didn't actually understand the words, but there was no doubting that they had understood the tone. As one, they jumped to their feet and began backing away, raising their hands, palm-outward in defensive gestures and then, suddenly, it seemed they were all speaking at once. At first I couldn't discern the language, spoken in harsh, guttural tones, but after a few seconds I realised that it was French: not the silky, pure French that Angelique spoke but a deep, grunting kind of dialect. Not that it made any difference what form of French they spoke, as neither Paul nor I spoke a word.

'OK, OK,' I said, making a calming gesture with my hands. 'You speak French ... er Français?'

One of the men nodded furiously.

I looked at Paul 'They'll be from North or West Africa somewhere I guess.'

'What about grabbing Calvin or Sam?' he suggested. 'Coming from Morocco I expect they'll both speak French.'

'Good idea,' I said. 'Why don't you go down and fetch whichever of them is on duty while I stay here to keep an eye on things?'

'OK.' In an instant, he was gone.

I tried to calm our unexpected guests. 'We go find someone who speak your language. We no want hurt you.'

What the fuck am I doing adopting some sort of Pidgin English? How's that going to help them understand? I smiled at my own stupidity. I'm not sure if it was my smile that did it, but the three men now seemed to be getting over their initial fear, and took a step towards me, now looking a little threatening.

'OK, OK,' I said, raising my hands, defensively, and backing away, 'I go wait outside.'

There I go again ... why am I speaking like that? I stepped smartly outside. *Come on Paul, don't take too long.*

As the minutes ticked by, I could hear a rising cacophony of voices from within the basement. What were they planning? Were they about to storm through the door and attack me? I moved away a few paces just in case. *Come on Paul, hurry up.*

Eventually, I heard the distinctive, rattly whine of a golf buggy, faint at first, but rapidly increasing in volume as the buggy approached, slewing to a halt just twenty feet or so from where I stood. Paul approached, accompanied by a very reluctant-looking Calvin, whose wild eyes betrayed his rising panic.

'Anything happened?' said Paul.

'No,' I replied, 'they're all still inside.' Then turning to Calvin, 'What do you know about this?'

His eyes darted this way and that; perspiration streamed down his sunken cheeks. 'Nothing … I don't know nothing.'

'You speak French?' He nodded. 'Right, I want you to ask them who they are and what they're doing here.' Before he could protest I had wrenched open the door and shoved him inside, following closely behind.

The babble of conversation among the occupants of the basement stopped abruptly. Calvin turned to glance back at me and Paul in turn.

'Well, go on then,' I prompted.

Calvin nodded nervously before turning towards the intruders and beginning to speak. It was less than a minute before the first interruption by one of the newcomers. Calvin had barely opened his mouth to respond to whatever question he had been asked when another of the interlopers stepped in.

And then it began. At first the conversation was somewhat staccato, but within seconds it grew to an unrelenting assault on the senses: an uninterrupted, and to me, completely unintelligible, wall of sound, accompanied by much hand-waving and finger-pointing. It didn't really look as though the dialogue was progressing to any sort of constructive conclusion.

'Enough,' yelled Paul, in his most commanding tone. It worked: everyone fell silent.

'So who are they?' I asked.

'They from Mauritania,' Calvin replied. They come to make new life in Europe.'

'But what are they doing here?'

'They say they just look for somewhere to stay until they decide where they go to settle.'

'Are they here illegally?'

Calvin visibly squirmed. 'They not got proper papers, no.'

'How did they get into the urbanisation? Did you let them in?'

'No, no, Mr Groves. Wait … I ask them.'

There was another brief exchange in that strange French dialect, during which I caught the same word repeated several times, but couldn't quite discern what it was.

'Well?' I prompted, when the exchange ceased.

Calvin's eyes now looked about fit to burst from their sockets; his mouth hung open, his lower jaw rising and falling soundlessly as he apparently sought to frame his reply.

'Well?' I repeated.

Calvin's Adam's apple performed a little dance in his neck as he stutteringly replied. 'Th … they say that one of the people who live here give them the code for the front gate, and then—'

'Who?' I demanded. 'Who gave them the code?'

'I … I ask them.'

Another unintelligible, quick-fire exchange ensued.

'Well … who was it?'

'Th … they not know his name … just someone they spoke to.'

'Are you shitting me Calvin? Because if you are—'

'No, no, Mr Groves … that's what they say. Once they got code they wait until a time when neither me nor Sam on duty and then move all their things in.'

I shook my head in frustration, taking several seconds to gain control of my rising anger before continuing. 'OK, well here's what I want you to tell them: they can stay here tonight, but if they have not gone by twelve noon tomorrow, I'm calling the police' – I withdrew my mobile phone from my pocket and held it aloft, tapping it for emphasis – 'and having them forcibly evicted. Then they can explain to the authorities what they are doing here without the proper papers. Got it?'

Calvin nodded, desperation evident in his eyes. The ensuing exchange lasted perhaps two minutes, becoming distinctly heated at several points, but eventually the three African men who had been doing most of the talking, lapsed into silence, shoulders slumping in defeat.

'Well … what did they say?' I asked.

'They be gone by midday tomorrow,' said Calvin.

'OK, make sure you are,' I commanded – rather pointlessly, I suppose, since it was clear that none of them understood English – sweeping my gaze back and forth across them, brandishing my mobile phone for additional emphasis.

We stepped outside and shut the door behind us, leaving the hapless squatters to contemplate their next move.

'I should get back to watching CCTV,' pleaded Calvin.

Not that it did any fucking good in stopping this lot from getting in and taking up residence, I thought. 'Go on then … oh, and Calvin' – I was starting to feel a little remorseful about having given him such a hard time – 'thanks for your help this morning.'

For the first time that morning, a hint of a smile brightened his gaunt features. 'No problem, Mr Groves.' He scuttled off towards his buggy before we could ask him any further questions.

Something was bothering me though. I turned to Paul to air it.

'Did you notice them repeating the same word over and over?'

He looked puzzled. 'I don't think so … my French is even worse than my Spanish.'

'Something like "sarm" or "sum" I think. Hard to tell with that heavy African pronunciation.'

Then it seemed to hit us both simultaneously. In the moment of dawning realisation, our eyes locked.

'Sam!' we said, in unison.

Chapter 30

'Well?' I demanded, 'how did they get in?'

Calvin was visibly shaking as he turned his perspiration-streaked face towards Sam.

It was now two days since our unexpected guests had left, and I wanted some answers. I strongly suspected that Sam was behind this incident, but even if this were the case, I couldn't imagine that Calvin was blissfully unaware of what had been going on. I had decided to have it out with both of them together, accompanied by Marysa.

'We...ll,' said Sam, lounging back in his chair, his fingers interlaced behind his neck, his expression thoughtful, 'obviously we can't be sure, but I guess it was probably just as they told Calvin: somehow they found out the code for the gate and slipped in when no-one was watching.'

Calvin looked towards me, nodding furiously, causing several drops of perspiration to fly from the tip of his nose, landing on the table just in front of Marysa. She said nothing, but withdrew a couple of tissues from her bag, mopping up the offending wet blotches.

'S ... sorry, Miss Marysa,' he stammered.

'Mrs,' she corrected him.

'Yes ... yes, Mrs ...' he replied, nodding feverishly. Another couple of droplets flew from his nose, one of them describing a graceful arc en route to landing on Marysa's cheek. Calvin's eyes widened in horror. 'Oh no ... for the love of Allah. I ... I ...' Further words evidently failed him.

The corners of Marysa's mouth turned down in disgust as she grabbed another tissue and dealt with the latest projectile. She said nothing, but turned towards me and indicated, with a curt nod, that I should continue.

'Have you checked the CCTV recordings?' I said, looking from Sam to Calvin in turn.

'Yes, Mr Groves,' said Calvin, this time managing to control the movement of his head, preventing the launch of another volley of sweat, 'I check everything.'

'And?'

'Nothing ... I not see nothing.'

'Nothing?' I said, spreading my hands in frustration. 'How can there be nothing?'

Calvin shrank back in his chair shaking his head from side to side – at least this meant the only person at risk of being struck by another missile was Sam. 'It's just that ... well, the recordings ... they not ... well they only—'

Sam placed a soothing hand on Calvin's arm, interjecting smoothly, 'The problem is that we only keep recordings for the last seven days ... not enough memory capacity to keep more, you see.'

'Seven days,' I repeated, dumbly. Come to think of it, I did actually know that already.

'Yes,' said Sam. 'Now if you could find the money to invest in upgrading the equipment to the latest—'

'Enough!' I commanded. 'We are not here to discuss the specification of the surveillance system.' I took a second or two to gain control of my rising anger before continuing. 'OK, so those people must have been here for at least seven days, right?' They both nodded. 'And neither of you knew anything about it?'

'No ... we were as surprised as you were,' said Sam, looking way too smug for my liking.

There was clearly no way to prove their complicity, but I wasn't going to let them get away scot-free. I had already discussed the matter with Marysa before the meeting.

'OK,' I said, panning my gaze from one to the other in turn, 'so are you telling me that you had no knowledge of, or involvement in, the admission of those people?'

Sam dipped his chin and shook his head, his lips pursed and his brow furrowed in an expression of regret. Calvin raised his shoulders, shrinking even further back in his seat, eventually muttering, 'That's right, Mr Groves.'

'Well, in the absence of any evidence to the contrary, I guess I have to accept that.'

Calvin let out a noisy sigh, visibly relaxing. Sam's face creased in a smile as he nodded slowly.

'However,' I continued, 'the fact that those people were living here, apparently undetected for *at least* seven days' – I suspected it was much longer, given their comfortably furnished surroundings – 'indicates to me that both of you have been negligent in the carrying out of your regular patrols and surveillance.'

Calvin shook his head furiously, showers of perspiration now flying from side to side, several droplets finding their mark on Sam's cheek.

Sam flinched as the missiles struck but made no move to wipe them away. His smile had now disappeared. 'Mr Groves, it is hardly fair to—'

'Be quiet and listen. You will both be issued a formal written warning for dereliction of your duties. Any further misconduct by either of you will result in your dismissal. Understand?'

Sam's eyes narrowed as he placed both hands on the table, leaning forward. 'I really must protest at this—'

'Protest all you like … you will receive your formal warnings by tomorrow. This meeting is over.'

***

By the afternoon I had largely put aside the irritation engendered by the frustrating meeting with the security guards, and was feeling much mellower. The *paella* which Donna had cooked for our lunch was truly delicious, and after sharing a nice bottle of Rioja, we were both feeling a little sleepy. Donna decided to settle down on the sofa for a nap.

I stepped out onto the terrace to find that it had turned out to be one of those beautiful, warm, sunny days which unpredictably arise in-between some truly horrendous storms in a Costa del Sol winter. Glancing at the thermometer on the wall, I noted that the temperature was 22C – not bad for the beginning of March. I decided to sit outside for a while with the two-day-old English newspaper which had lain unread on the coffee table since I had bought it. Feeling the warmth of the sun caressing my face, I soon found that my eyelids were drooping.

The newspaper slipped from my grasp as I slid into that strange state of consciousness which resides somewhere between wakefulness and sleep. A random tangle of characters began drifting through my mind: Dr Ramani, ranting with indignation; Alfredo Gonzaléz, greasy hair and greasy manner; Bruce, rugged features creased in a convivial smile; Julia, her face twisted in an expression of hatred; and Angelique, walking slowly towards me just as she had on that first day I met her ... unhurriedly wrapping her semi-transparent robe around her, hips swaying sensuously as she glided towards me ...

Dammit! Just as I was savouring that delicious vision, my mobile trilled harshly, performing a little dance as it vibrated against the surface of the table alongside me. I fumbled to grab it, succeeding in doing so just before it went into a kamikaze dive over the edge of the table.

'Yes,' I snapped, rather more irritably than I had intended.

'What's rattled your cage?' came the familiar Dutch accent. A*mazing,* I thought, *how this woman, who speaks so many different languages, can have such a command of colloquial English.*

'Sorry Marysa, I was just dozing off to sleep.'

'Well,' she said, somewhat huffily, I thought, 'some of us have to work in the afternoons.'

I resisted the temptation to bite back. 'Yeah, I get that. Anyway, what's up?'

'After this morning's meeting with your two layabout security guards, I checked my emails, and I have two items of news for you.'

'Oh, I get it,' I said, doing my best to lighten the tone of the conversation, 'it's the old "good news / bad news" thing, eh?'

'Well, both bad news, actually.'

My heart sank. 'Oh, great ... well let's have it then.'

Her tone didn't change. 'We have the report from the court surveyor.'

I sat up, sharply: this was crucial. Even though we – and he – knew that we were already committed to a cost of well over two hundred thousand euros, I knew that the surveyor was highly unlikely to recommend a figure above the one hundred and twenty thousand in our original claim.

'OK, so what's he come up with?' I braced myself for the reply. *A hundred thousand? Ninety*

'Fifty-three thousand euros.'

'Fifty-three thousand?' I repeated, incredulously. 'How the fuck – excuse my language – does he come up with that figure?'

'His report seems to accept the form of technical solution which the developer proposed to us.'

'What ... that bullshit "ground anchor" thing?'

'Yes, but he recommends that the same approach be extended along the full length of the wall rather than just the section which has already collapsed ... as a "precautionary measure". That's how the twenty-two thousand which the developer quoted has grown to fifty-three thousand.'

'Is there any possibility that this guy is right and our architect is wrong ... that we don't actually need to build such an expensive structure as he has proposed?'

'I've just come off the phone to him. He is adamant that what the court surveyor is proposing is totally inadequate.'

'So where do we go from here?'

'As far as the court case is concerned, all we can do is go ahead knowing that the best we can hope for, even if we win, is fifty-three thousand euros.'

Oh great – that will go down well with the troops, many of whom are expecting to get a fair chunk of what they have paid toward the wall reimbursed if we win the case.

'As regards who's right and who's wrong about the technical solution,' continued Marysa, 'I would trust our architect, Alejandro Cuadrado – we've done a lot of work with him in the past and he has a very high reputation in his field.'

Hmm ... that may be, but ... 'OK, I hear what you're saying, but we're talking about a lot of money here. Do me a favour will you – can you get a second opinion from another reputable technical architect who has absolutely no connection with either us or the other side?'

'Yes, if that's what you want, but it will further increase our costs and I really don't—'

'Please,' I said, 'just do it, will you?'

She took a second or two before replying. 'OK, I will do it.'

'Thank you. Now look ... assuming you are right and Cuadrado's design really is what we need, then that suggests the court surveyor is either completely incompetent or—'

'Or you were right,' interjected Marysa. 'He's been bribed by González.'

'And which do you think it's likely to be?'

'Well,' she said, pausing as though choosing her words carefully, 'the courts don't employ idiots.'

'But,' I suggested, 'they might just employ people who are not completely incorruptible.'

'Yes, they might,' she agreed.

'Shit!' I hissed. 'We've been completely outmanoeuvred by that slime ball, González.'

'It's Spain,' she said, ruefully. 'These things happen.'

I was, by now, getting seriously pissed off with this catch-all explanation for every miserable piece of lunacy or skulduggery, but there seemed little point in airing that issue at this particular point in time.

'Just get the second opinion on the design for me, will you please?'

'I already said I would,' she retorted.

Suddenly, I remembered something which had been swept from my mind by the conversation which we had just had. 'Anyway, you said you had two items of news for me.'

'Yes. The developer has mounted a legal challenge, contesting the legitimacy of the resolution passed to collect the two hundred and eighty thousand euros from owners to pay for the new wall.'

'What?' I exclaimed. 'He can't do that … it was approved by a majority of owners at the meeting.'

'It's all to do with the interpretation of the Horizontal Property Act.'

I might have known that it would have something to do with that uniquely-obtuse piece of legislation.

'OK,' I sighed, 'explain it to me.'

'Well, as you know, expenditure on repairs and maintenance essential to the upkeep of the community and the safety of its residents just needs to be approved by a majority and then everyone is obliged to pay their share.'

'So what's the problem?'

'According to the HPA, if the works are deemed to be an "enhancement" rather than a repair, and if the cost of the works exceeds three months of regular fees then those who vote against it are not obliged to pay.'

'An "enhancement"?' I spluttered. 'How can it be an "enhancement" when the bloody mountainside is about to fall on

211

someone's head? And how can it *not* be essential to residents' safety? This is bullshit.'

'It's not me you have to convince,' she said. 'Now that he's formally launched legal action, it's the court that will decide.'

I took a few seconds to compose myself and head off the stream of invective which threatened to burst forth from my lips. After all, as Marysa had reasonably pointed out, there was nothing to be gained by ranting at her. At that moment, though, I could cheerfully have strangled Alfredo González.

'He doesn't stand a chance of winning this does he?' I asked, praying that not even a legal system as totally dysfunctional as Spain's appeared to be, could possibly entertain such madness.

'Well, if you'd asked me yesterday, I'd have said no, but given the way he seems to have been able to influence the court surveyor, I really can't be sure now.'

'Fuck,' I said. 'Er, sorry, it's just ...'

'Understandable, under the circumstances,' she opined, in her never-changing, unperturbable tone.

It was no use venting further; I needed to understand the possible consequences of this development. 'OK. If by some chance he *was* to win the case, what happens?'

'Well, then those who voted against the cash-call would not have to pay.'

'But we've already collected most of the money now.'

'Then we'd have to pay it back.'

'But it could be years before we know the outcome of the case,' I grumbled. 'If we delayed the works until then we'd almost certainly face a major landslide.'

'Yes, it's quite a dilemma,' she observed, with characteristic understatement.

'What if we just go ahead anyway? Then *if* we should lose the case, the money would already have been spent.'

'Then you, personally, as the legal representative of the community, would be liable to pay it back.'

Un-fucking-believable. The very best we can hope for from our legal action against González is fifty-three thousand towards a job that's probably going to cost more like three hundred thousand. If we delay building the wall, someone's quite likely to get killed in a landslide. If we go ahead with building the wall and subsequently lose the case which González has launched, then I get stung for a bill of perhaps a hundred thousand euros to be paid out of my own pocket.

As I contemplated this unpalatable set of conclusions, Marysa delivered the *coup de grace*. 'Oh, and by the way, the building contractors called me today to say that, having checked the long range weather forecast and their own work schedule, they could start work on the wall week commencing 20th March. That's less than three weeks away.'

'Three weeks,' I repeated, torpidly.

'They'd like an answer by Monday.'

Chapter 31

I spent the next few days consulting with Sergio, Marysa, and the community lawyer, exploring the likely consequences of a decision to go ahead with the construction of the new wall. The consensus was that Alfredo González had little chance of success with his legal challenge, and that he probably knew that. He was probably either trying to delay having to pay his contribution to the cash-call or just being plain bloody-minded ... or both. However, they all stopped short of actually advising me on what to do.

As the lawyer most reassuringly put it, 'There is of course a small chance that the judgement could go against you, and I believe you are well aware of the consequences of such an outcome. The final decision has to be yours.'

I chewed the matter over, at great length, with Paul. He pointed out that the vote on the cash-call had been taken before the first serious collapse had occurred. Many owners, he reasoned, may not previously have believed just how real the risk of a major landslide was. But now they could see it with their own eyes. He expressed the view that, in the – hopefully unlikely – event of our losing the case, we might now be able to convince many of those entitled to a refund to forgo that right. *Hmm ... maybe.*

'In the end though, if we *were* to lose, you *would* most likely be landed with a substantial bill, even though it could well be less than the worst-case scenario. The final decision has to be yours.'

'Thanks,' I said, ruefully, 'that's exactly what the lawyer said.'

I had faced tougher decisions in my former business life and I wasn't afraid of this one, but the one person who I felt absolutely had to have the major say was Donna. If it all went horribly wrong we could be facing a bill which could run to perhaps a hundred thousand euros. It wouldn't bankrupt us, but it was still a hell of a lot of money to put at risk.

It was my discussion with Donna which finally helped me see a way forward.

'You don't have to do this, Roy,' she had said. 'You are doing an unpaid job on behalf of everyone who lives here, and no-one would blame you for putting the whole thing on hold until the outcome of the legal case is clear.'

'But that could take years,' I said, 'by which time it will probably be too late – the whole damned thing will probably have collapsed.'

Her brow puckered as she considered what I had said. After a few seconds she said, 'You still have a week or so before the proposed start date for the work don't you?'

'Yes.'

'Then why not call another emergency EGM, explain the situation to owners, and seek a second vote on the cash-call in the light of the latest situation? You might well be able to persuade a larger proportion of owners to vote in favour. Surely then, even if the previous vote were to be deemed illegal, it would, in any case, have been superseded by the later vote.'

Now why didn't I think of that?

'You might just have something there,' I said, brightening considerably. 'And even if the second vote were also to be judged illegal, the amount of money at risk could be less.'

'Exactly,' she said. My growing enthusiasm for this idea must have been clearly written across my face, for Donna jumped to her feet, smiling. 'So what do you think?'

I too, rose to my feet, gathering her in my arms. 'I think it's a brilliant idea.'

'You probably need to check it out with the administrator to make sure it's all legal and above board,' she cautioned.

'I will,' I said.

'Of course,' she said, 'depending on how many people you can persuade to change their minds, the amount of money at risk could still be considerable.'

'I know,' I replied, 'but it's definitely worth a try.'

'How many people do you suppose you can convince?'

'No idea,' I said. 'Let's just take it one step at a time. The first thing is to check whether the whole idea is legal. I'll call Marysa right now.'

I pulled Donna towards me and kissed her. 'You're quite something, you know.'

As I relaxed the hug, she stepped back, tutting as she smoothed down her hair which I had managed to ruffle. 'And how many years has it taken you to realise *that*?' she said. The indignant tone of voice was betrayed by the broad smile which she was unable to suppress.

***

A flurry of phone calls between Marysa, Sergio, and our lawyer resulted in a tentative conclusion that Donna's idea was, indeed, feasible. I therefore arranged an EGM to be held the following week in which I would explain the whole picture to owners in detail and hope that a significant proportion of the previous dissenters could be persuaded to change their minds.

That evening, after enjoying a delicious *Coq au Vin,* which Donna had cooked, and several glasses of a nice *Ribera del Duero,* I was feeling much more relaxed about things; now there was at least the possibility of a way through the dilemma. We sat down together to watch a late-night movie.

We were about an hour into the movie when I paused it in order to go and make us both a cup of coffee. It was just as I was spooning out the ground coffee into the filter machine that I heard it.

Years earlier, my late father had related to me stories of the Second World War and the Blitz. He talked of the German V-1 flying bomb, or 'Doodlebug'. Apparently, the engine had a very distinctive sound, which Londoners grew instantly to recognise. All the time you could hear that sound continue, he would say, you could be relatively relaxed, as the flying bomb was just passing overhead. It was when the sound abruptly stopped that you needed to worry, for that was when the engine cut out and the bomb began its deadly dive.

Well, so it was with the distinctive sound of the security guards' golf buggy approaching. As the sound suddenly ceased, right outside our block, my heart sank like a stone. I glanced at my watch: twelve minutes past midnight. Absently, I tipped the last spoonful of coffee into the machine, closed the lid and flipped the switch on, all the time, hoping against hope that there was some explanation for the buggy stopping outside which didn't involve me.

My hopes were dashed as the doorbell sounded. When I opened the door, my nostrils were immediately assaulted by the familiar aroma of stale cigarette smoke. Calvin's wild-eyed expression announced, without the need for words, that he was confronting some sort of crisis. In a way, it was handy that the expression on his sweat-streaked countenance was able to communicate the situation without words because, at that moment, he was quite incapable of forming a coherent sentence.

'Mr Groves ... come quick ... he got ... she screaming ... terrible ... I ... it's—'

'Whoa ... slow down, Calvin. Take a deep breath.' He gulped in several, his shoulders heaving with the effort. 'OK, slowly ... tell me what's happened.'

'Block 11 ... man and woman having big argument ... and now another man ... you got to come quick.'

Here we go again.

'Coffee's on,' I called out to Donna. 'I'll be back as soon as I can.'

When we arrived at block 11, I could immediately hear raised voices emanating from the vicinity of the penthouse – that was Joe Haven's apartment. I climbed the stairs, with Calvin a couple of paces behind. As I rounded the final bend in the staircase I was confronted by the sight of Joe, bare-chested, clutching the waistband of his trousers, which appeared not to be properly fastened. Opposite him was a young woman with long, crimson hair, clad in a fur coat – which seemed a little unnecessary, given the mild temperature that evening – and very high heels. Neither of them appeared to be particularly happy.

'Whassamatter with you, you bitch? I already paid the fucking money.' Joe sounded more than a little drunk.

'Well, you never pay for extras,' she retorted. 'I already told you it's extra if you want blow job.' The accent sounded Eastern European.

'This issa fuckin' joke,' declared Joe, swaying unsteadily. 'You give me back that hundred euros you stole or I'll damn well take it.'

'You just fucking try, and I take your fucking eye out,' she screamed, reaching down and taking off one of her stilettos, wielding it threateningly. In doing so, she allowed her fur coat to fly open, revealing that she was naked underneath. This was perhaps the explanation as to why she needed such a warm garment. I had to admit that, notwithstanding the strident and less-than-ladylike voice, the body was pretty damned good.

Concentrate on the matter in hand, I chided myself.

Barrp! The sound of a car horn added to the disharmony already prevalent. I glanced toward the gate at the top of the hill, some thirty yards away, where a taxi waited, driver's door open. I couldn't begin to understand the quick-fire stream of Spanish flowing from the driver's lips. I could, however discern that he was a tad impatient.

'You going to let my taxi in, or you want this?' the woman screamed, stepping forward, waving the stiletto from side to side, inducing a rather fetching wobble in her generous breasts.

'Not 'til you give me my money back.' He took an unsteady step backward, placing a hand against the wall for support, and in doing so, releasing his grasp on his waistband and allowing his trousers to fall to his ankles.

'Ha!' she cried, pointing with her shoe at his flaccid member, 'you couldn't get it up ... even with this waiting.' She ran the middle finger of her free hand down the front of her stomach and between her legs, squatting slightly as she slid it back upwards, eventually taking it up to her mouth, extending her tongue, and licking it.

I heard a sharp intake of breath behind me and detected the sour tang of stale tobacco smoke as Calvin moved alongside me for a better view.

'Well thass because you're fucking ugly,' responded Joe.

This was a little harsh, I felt. While the young lady lacked the startlingly sultry looks of our own local exponent of her trade, Svetlana Petrov, she certainly wasn't that bad, and as I said, the body was well up to scratch. I had to conclude that whatever inadequacy Joe had suffered, it was probably due more to the amount of alcohol which he had obviously consumed than to any shortfall in the quality of his purchase. *Actually*, I thought, *if you're that fussy why don't you just go across the garden to Svetlana rather than take a chance on a home delivery?* I dismissed the thought almost as soon as it had arrived: encouraging such an exchange of services within the community really wasn't going to help our situation in any way whatsoever.

Barrp! The taxi driver was now out of the car and gesticulating furiously. *Time to intervene*, I thought.

'Joe!' I called. No response. 'Joe!' I repeated, louder this time.

He turned towards me, eyes wide with surprise. As recognition dawned on his face, he cast his eyes downwards, contemplating his own nether region, evidently now feeling somewhat self-conscious about his nakedness. As he reached down to try to gather up his trousers from around his ankles, he lost his balance and staggered backwards against the wall, sliding slowly to a sitting position, knees apart, ankles pinned together and genitals on display, centre stage.

'Whoopsy ...' he said, as he contrived, with only partial success, to pull up his trousers while still sitting on the ground.

'Fucking drunken idiot!' hissed the woman.

Barrp!

'Venga ahora mismo. ¡Si no, me voy!' yelled the cab driver.

By now several of the neighbours were out on their terraces craning to see what was going on.

'See, you fucker,' screamed the woman, 'I going to lose my ride – let him in right NOW.'

Joe appeared not to hear her as he concentrated intently on the more-or-less-impossible task of pulling up and fastening his trousers while sitting on the ground.

Oh, screw this, I thought, *I really don't have time to arbitrate between a hysterical hooker and her half-comatose client.* I reached into my pocket for the remote control which operated the gate and pressed the button. After a second or two's delay the gate began to describe its squeaky, juddering arc towards the open position.

I must get Ernesto to oil that gate, I thought. Funny isn't it, how such trivial matters intrude at the most inappropriate moments?

The cab driver jumped back into his car, slammed the door, and with much theatrical revving of the engine and spinning of tyres, sped through the gate and into the complex.

'OK, now go,' I said, turning towards the woman.

'And who the fuck are you?' she demanded.

'I'm the president of this community. You have your money, so please go now.'

The change in her demeanour was as abrupt as if an invisible switch had been operated. 'Well ... happy birthday, Mr President,' she breathed, in a bizarre, Eastern-European-accented parody of that iconic moment when Marilyn Monroe sang to JFK all those years ago. She took a couple of slow steps towards me, allowing her coat to fall open at the front once more.

219

'You sure you want me to go? You pay cab driver now and I do special deal for you.' She ran her tongue back and forth across her lips.

Seriously? You had to admire the woman's front though … in a figurative sense, of course.

'Get out of here,' I ordered, jerking my thumb towards the stairs for emphasis.

She shrugged. 'Your loss. You want my card for another time?'

'I said, get out!'

With a toss of her long, crimson locks, she wrapped the coat around herself and made for the stairs.

'OK, show's over,' I called out to all those who had emerged from their apartments to rubberneck.

I turned to Calvin, whose lower jaw hung slackly, and whose eyes threatened to pop from his head. 'OK, time to get back to your post.' He nodded, blinking dazedly.

As the gate swung closed behind the taxi, Calvin stepped into the buggy and made his way down the hill. I turned my attention back to Joe Haven. Remarkably, he had succeeded in hoisting his trousers up to near enough their intended location but had passed out before managing to fasten his belt.

'Come on Joe,' I said, as I struggled to drag him to his feet and drape one of his arms over my shoulder.

With a considerable effort, I managed to get him inside the apartment and onto his sofa.

As I lifted his feet onto the sofa he mumbled, 'Whess my hundred euros? Never got my f … fucking blow job, did I? Whassamatter with the bitch … she …' He passed out once more.

All in all, quite a day.

Chapter 32

The EGM had been a rather more subdued affair than some of the previous meetings. It was clear that many owners had been severely unsettled by the collapse of a section of the wall, and the general mood had swung significantly towards the point of view that we needed to take action sooner rather than later. After a lengthy discussion, the vote was finally taken and the number voting against the cash-call was now thirteen – down from twenty-five at the previous meeting. This, I estimated, would bring my maximum personal exposure down to perhaps fifty thousand euros.

That was still not exactly a comforting figure, but the more I thought about it, the more improbable it seemed that we could actually lose the case. After all, given the fact that a physical collapse had already occurred, it surely must be obvious to everyone, including the court judge, that the existing wall was inadequate. This surely rendered absurd Alfredo's argument that the new wall was some sort of optional improvement. Donna had accepted my assessment of the risk and we had decided to press ahead. I hoped to Christ that I was right.

Just after the EGM, we got the second opinion on the proposed design for the new wall. As expected, the second architect agreed that the court surveyor's proposal was inadequate and that something along the lines of Cuadrado's design would be necessary. That confirmation cost us another three thousand euros. *Oh well, best to be sure I suppose.*

The diggers and dumper trucks had arrived, on schedule, on Monday 20th March, and now, four days later, work was well underway. They had chosen to start work at the opposite end of the wall from the section which had previously collapsed, explaining that this would minimise the chances of a further collapse occurring before the new wall had been completed. The previously-collapsed section did at least have a temporary supporting structure in place.

They had pulled down a section of the old cement coating about twenty yards long and cut back the earth behind until a near-vertical face was created. They were now digging a trench where the first of the massive stone blocks which would form the foundation of the new wall would be placed.

Strangely – to my mind at least – they had not removed the earth cut away from the hillside but instead spread it across the internal roadway to a depth of anything up to around four or five feet. This, they explained, was to protect the roadway from damage by the big diggers, which now performed their manoeuvres on top of this earth layer. I assumed that, as the experts, they knew best.

Access to the garages of blocks ten to fifteen was now completely blocked to residents' cars, so we had to park in the car park we had hired outside the complex itself and walk to and from it via the main pedestrian entrance next to the security guards' office. It was a bit of a pain, but most residents had grudgingly accepted the arrangement which, after all, was only going to be in place for about three months. All in all, I was feeling fairly happy with the way things were going.

My mood improved further still when, that afternoon, I got a call from Sergio.

'I have some good news for you,' he said.

Well, that makes a change, I thought. 'Go on.'

'The date for the court hearing regarding your Doctor Ramani's outstanding debt has now been confirmed: it's next Wednesday.'

My heart jumped. It wasn't that Dr Ramani's debt was the biggest issue on my mind just then, but as a matter of principle, and as a deterrent to others, I desperately wanted to see this woman held to account.

'That *is* good news,' I said. 'Er … I assume you had to use some of the money we discussed to expedite these proceedings?'

'Well, all of it actually, but you said yourself that it would be worth it to avoid months or years of delay.'

'Yes I did,' I admitted.

'I've just written to Dr Ramani,' continued Sergio, 'to tell her that if she pays her debts in full by the end of this week we can have the court hearing cancelled and avoid further distress and unpleasantness all round.'

'Has she replied?'

'Not yet, but if she's got any sense she'll do as I've suggested.'

Hmm ... you really don't know the lady in question, I mused. 'OK,' I said, 'I guess we wait and see. Anyway thanks for letting me know.'

As I hung up, I felt a pang of guilt about having used community funds for what was, effectively – let's call a spade a spade – a bribe, in order to nail this woman. Did this make me as bad as Alfredo González?

The feeling was short-lived. González had almost certainly paid the court surveyor to misrepresent the cost of a new retaining wall. I hadn't paid anyone to influence the outcome of Ramani's court case, but had merely sought to expedite it. As far as using community funds to do so, I was pretty sure that, by forcing Ramani to court earlier, my action would bring in more money than it had cost.

No, I convinced myself, *my conscience is clear on this one.*

***

Thump, thump, thump ... the insistent bass beat reverberated through the entire building, rousing me from what had been a deep, deep sleep. I wiped the sleep from my eyes, groggily propped myself up on one elbow, and fumbled for the clock on my bedside table, eventually locating it and pressing the button to illuminate the display: 3.47 a.m. *Give me a break.*

I switched on my bedside lamp to reveal that Donna was standing by the open patio door, leaning out, evidently trying to ascertain the source of the noise.

'It's Julia,' she declared, coming inside and sliding the door shut. 'This racket has been going on for hours.' I guess I must have been sleeping rather more heavily than I thought. 'It's just got much louder though,' she added, as if sensing my unspoken thought.

'Bloody woman,' I grumbled, stepping out of bed and pulling on my dressing gown, 'I'll go round and see if I can get her to turn it down a bit.'

'Good luck with that,' said Donna.

When I arrived at Julia's door, the noise emanating from within was almost deafening: a mindless, repetitive, pounding beat which appeared to be totally devoid of any actual melodic structure. As I prepared myself for the encounter which was about to ensue, I rather hoped that Julia might have forgotten about the dog-poo incident, for that was unlikely to have made her any more well-disposed towards me.

I rang the bell; after a minute or so there was no answer. I rang it again, with a similar lack of success. I rapped on the door with my knuckles; I might as well have been floating in the sea trying to attract the attention of a passing aircraft with one of those whistles provided with my lifejacket. I looked around me and spotted a small, decorative stone effigy of a Buddha – which bore more than a passing resemblance to Julia herself. *That should do it.*

I picked up the statuette, shifting it in my hands until I had a firm grip, and then swung it against the door with considerable force. The crash as the door bucked in its frame was even louder than I had anticipated. I stepped back, allowing the hand holding the stone ornament to hang free at my side, noting the ugly dent in the varnished wood surface which I had unintentionally inflicted. Frankly though, I couldn't summon much remorse for the damage at that particular moment.

Anyway, my action had, finally, had the desired effect. The door opened and Julia appeared; what an apparition! She wore a bulge-hugging, stretchy, bright red dress – one which was clearly made for someone a couple of sizes smaller. Her ample breasts looked about ready to pop out from the perilously-low neckline and the hemline finished about halfway up her dimpled thighs. The absurdly dense black eye makeup, heavily-rouged cheeks, scarlet lipstick, and wildly teased-out hairdo combined to create a freakishly scary appearance. In one hand, she clutched a half-empty beer bottle.

'Bit late to be joining the party issn't it?' she said, swaying a little unsteadily on her feet, and then, as she registered that I was clad only in my dressing gown, 'Iss not fancy dress you know.' She dissolved into a fit of cackling laughter.

Now I could quite reasonably have made a similar observation about her outfit, but I judged that this would not have helped the situation.

'Julia, it's four o'clock in the morning. Some of us are trying to sleep.'

'Sleep?' she said, hanging on to the door frame for support. 'Oh, you're so fucking boring. Come on in and have some fun.' Maybe she really *had* forgotten about the dog-poo.

'I'd rather not, thank you. Can you *please* turn the music down a bit?'

Her mood changed in an instant; an ugly scowl spread across her painted features. 'No I fucking won't. You're always on my fucking case you stuck-up prick. Well, this time you just go fuck yourself. Piss off!' With that she slammed the door in my face.

As I stood there on the doorstep, reeling from this verbal onslaught, I judged that further negotiation was unlikely to achieve much. I decided that a more forceful approach was required.

Donna had evidently given up on any idea of getting back to sleep – when I stepped through the door I found her sitting in the kitchen, nursing a cup of coffee.

'Any luck?' she asked, but the expression on her face told me that she knew what the answer would be.

'No,' I said shaking my head, 'and I'm now well past playing Mr Nice Guy.'

I picked up the phone and called the security guards' office. It was Calvin's shift that evening.

'Calvin, this is Roy.'

'Yes, hello Mr Groves. What can I do for you?'

'Are you not aware of the racket coming from block 15?'

'Racket?' he repeated, sounding perplexed. 'What ... you mean like ... tennis?'

I just about restrained myself from biting his head off. After all, there was no question that his command of English, while far from perfect, was a damn sight better than mine of Spanish, or French, or any other foreign language come to that. 'Noise ... I mean noise.'

'Ah yes,' he said, understanding now registering in his voice, and then, once again displaying his unique talent for stating the bloody obvious, 'lady in 15C having a party.'

'Yes, and what have you done about it?'

'W ... well I just keep the eye on things. You know ... make sure no trouble or anything.'

'Calvin, it's four thirty in the morning. You know full well that community rules prohibit excessive noise after midnight. Why haven't you done anything about it?'

Now he sounded distinctly nervous. 'I ... well ... I ... er ... the lady, she not very nice.' *Yes, I get that.* 'She get really nasty if I try to tell her what to do.'

I took a couple of deep breaths in order to restrain myself from yelling down the phone at him, and answered in the calmest tone I could muster. 'Right, here's what I want you to do: you phone the police right now, you tell them there is an unacceptable disturbance going on and ask them to send a car as soon as possible. Got it?'

'Y … yes Mr Groves. Right away.'

When I hung up, I was feeling almost as irritated with Calvin as I was with Julia. A security guard who is too frightened to ask a woman – admittedly a pretty scary one – to turn her music down is about as useful as a chocolate fireguard. I would definitely have to do something about him – and Sam, though for different reasons – but that was a matter for another day.

'Want a coffee?' said Donna.

I nodded and, as she poured my coffee, settled down to wait, all the time conscious of the pounding bass beat, which I could feel in the pit of my stomach as much as hear.

It was about fifteen minutes later that I heard furious hammering and raised voices. *'Policía. Abra la puerta!'*

Ah, they're here. Good.

Evidently their first effort to attract someone's attention had been unsuccessful, for as I stepped out of my front door to see what was happening, they hammered on the door again, even harder. *'Policía. Abra la puerta. ¡AHORA MISMO!'*

After a few seconds I heard Julia's dulcet tones. *'¿Cuál es el problema … qué quieren?'*

'La música … está demasiado fuerte.'

Up to this point, I had been able to follow the exchange: she had asked what they wanted and they had told her the music was too loud; so far so good. What followed, however, completely defeated me. Julia launched into a multilingual torrent of what I could only assume was abusive language.

By the time I made my way round to her front terrace the two policemen were shouting and gesticulating in a very animated fashion. When Julia stepped forward and started jabbing a forefinger within inches of one officer's face, he grabbed her wrist, and with what looked like a considerable effort, swung her corpulent frame around, pulling her hand behind her back. With a swift, fluid movement he pulled a pair of handcuffs from his belt and moments later she was secured with both hands behind her back. With a quick word to the other officer he grabbed her upper arm and marched her down the stairs.

The other policemen turned to me and began firing questions at me in quick-fire Spanish which I stood no hope of following.

Fortunately, at that moment, Calvin emerged from the shadows of the stairwell, evidently willing to get involved now that the worst of the drama was over.

'Calvin, come here,' I said; he did so. 'Can you ask the policeman what's happening?'

After exchanging a few words with the officer, Calvin explained, 'Lady very rude. They take her to police station and lock her up until she calm down.'

Serves her damn well right, I thought.

'OK. Can you thank the officer for his help and tell him we'll take it from here.'

Another brief exchange took place before Calvin said, 'He want us to give statement for his report.'

'OK,' I replied, 'you can go down with him and give him a statement. I'll try to get this lot out of her apartment.'

When I entered Julia's apartment, the music – if you could call it that – was still pumping at ear-splitting volume. I pushed my way through the crowd of people to the sideboard where her music system was located and flipped the switch off. After the previous din, the silence was stark, palpable. Around thirty pairs of eyes stared at me, confusedly; it occurred to me that the way I was dressed might be adding to their bewilderment.

'Party's over,' I announced. There was no response. 'The police are here.' Still no response. 'Julia's been arrested.' I wasn't actually sure whether that was technically correct but I judged that, assuming some of those present spoke English, it might add some weight to what I was saying. 'Now go home, please.'

That seemed to do the trick. A low hum of conversation broke out and the first few revellers started shuffling towards the door. Within a few minutes, they had all gone and I stepped outside onto the front terrace, taking the precaution of first pocketing the door key which protruded from the lock on the inside of the door; I really didn't want to compound the situation by leaving Julia locked out of her own apartment.

I looked over the terrace wall to see one of the policemen leaning on the roof of Calvin's buggy, taking notes as Calvin gave his account of events. At quarter past five in the morning I had no desire whatsoever to get involved in that discussion and decided to leave Calvin to it.

'Hello, Roy. Is it all over now?' The silken, French-accented tones wafted down from directly above me, soothing like a balm after the fractious exchanges which had characterised the events of the last couple of hours.

When I looked up, I was treated to the sight of Angelique leaning over her terrace wall, clad in a semi-transparent nightdress. The fact that her long, dark hair was tangled and wayward, rather than brushed into flowing waves as usual, and her face was devoid of makeup, did little to dim her allure.

'Oh, hello Angelique. Yes, the party's over, and the police have taken Julia away.

'Zey have taken her away? Why?'

'I think she was rather abusive to the police officers when they asked her to turn down the music.'

'Ah! Serves 'er right then. She is an 'orrible woman.'

'Yes,' I chuckled, 'she is.'

'Poor Miriam 'as 'ad no sleep. Thank goodness it is Friday and she 'as no school tomorrow. Anyway, we will both try to get some sleep now.'

'Me too,' I replied.

'Goodnight zen, and zank you for your 'elp.'

'More like good morning really,' I observed.

She laughed. 'Good morning zen.' She blew me a kiss and, moments later, was gone.

***

The following afternoon, about 2 p.m., Julia appeared at my door, still clad in her red party dress, but now looking extremely dishevelled after a night in police custody. Her hair exploded randomly in all directions and her heavy eye makeup was now smeared down her cheeks; she made an even more alarming apparition than she had the previous night – or rather, earlier that morning.

'Sam tell me you got my key,' she muttered.

'Look, I'm sorry it ended up like that last night,' I lied, 'but really, I had no option other than to call the police when you refused to even talk to me.'

I could see the anger flare in her eyes, but she managed to hold it in check. 'You going to give me my key?' she hissed.

I sighed; there was clearly no point in attempting to build bridges. I retrieved her key from where it lay on the kitchen worktop.

'I made sure everything was switched off before I locked up,' I said, in an attempt to at least keep things civil, as I proffered the key.

She snatched it from my hand and stomped off towards the stairs without uttering another word.

'She didn't sound too happy,' observed Donna, who had stayed tactfully out of sight in the lounge until Julia had gone.

'Well, maybe last night's experience might just make her think twice before being so bloody objectionable in the future,' I suggested.

'You think?' said Donna, raising a sceptical eyebrow, a smile dancing around her lips.

Chapter 33

A week had passed since Dr Ramani's case had been heard in court. As the defendant's Spanish was rather limited and that of the principal witness – me – even more so, the entire proceedings had to be conducted in both Spanish and English. This made the hearing a rather tortuous and drawn-out affair as every word had to be laboriously translated. It didn't help matters when Dr Ramani occasionally embarked on one of her characteristic rants, rendering the translator's job well-nigh impossible at times.

Today, we were back in court for the judgement and sentencing; Marysa sat next to me, while Dr Ramani was seated a couple of rows in front of us.

The judge – a stout, unsmiling, middle-aged lady – tipped her head forward a little, peering over the top of her reading glasses and panning her head back and forth until she was satisfied that she had everyone's full attention. She then began delivering her ruling, reading from a sheet of paper on the desk in front of her. She spoke for a minute or two before pausing to allow the translator to convey her words.

'The defendant is found guilty of the charge brought against her and is ordered to—'

'How you say I guilty?' cried Dr Ramani. 'You not listen to a word I say?' I already told you I got good reason to—'

She was silenced by the insistent hammering of the judge's gavel. The judge, clearly irritated by this interruption, barked a few terse words in Spanish, swiftly translated by the man seated at her side.

'The defendant is ordered to remain silent while the judge is speaking.'

Dr Ramani huffed and folded her arms, but said nothing further.

The judge spoke for another couple of minutes before pausing once more for the translator.

'The defendant is ordered to pay all outstanding debts to the community of *Las Hermosas Vistas*: a sum of sixteen thousand three hundred and seventy euros, plus interest of one thousand five hundred and seventy euros.'

Dr Ramani clutched the back rail of the bench in front of her; I could see her knuckles turning white, but she managed to restrain herself from delivering another outburst

The translator continued. 'The defendant is further ordered to pay legal costs for both sides, amounting to eighteen thousand euros.'

That was it: she could contain herself no longer. She jumped to her feet jabbing a forefinger towards the judge. 'This ridiculous – I told you about how those bastards in community ruin my beautiful garden and—'

'*¡Silencio!*' shouted the judge, cutting her off sharply. The bemused translator looked nervously back and forth between the stern-faced judge and the increasingly agitated Dr Ramani, seemingly unsure what to say. In the end he elected to say nothing, which seemed like a pretty sensible decision since the judge's meaning was abundantly clear to everyone present.

The judge removed her spectacles and skewered the wild-eyed doctor with a withering stare. '*Siéntese – ahora mismo,*' she commanded, extending her hand, palm-downward and gesturing with a sort of patting motion, for Dr Ramani to sit.

The two women locked eyes for several seconds before Dr Ramani eventually capitulated and sat down. The judge indicated, with a curt nod, that the translator should continue.

He cleared his throat and delivered the final part of the judgement. 'The defendant is ordered to pay all outstanding sums within ninety days. Failure to do so will—'

Dr Ramani was on her feet again. 'This not fair. I got to listen to those sex maniacs upstairs fucking all time, I can't go down to pool without seeing sluts down there flaunting their tits, I got to—'

She was cut off once more by the furious hammering of the judge's gavel. The translator's eyes widened and his head shrank between his shoulders; I imagine he wasn't relishing the prospect of translating this colourful language to the judge.

In the event he was let off the hook, as the judge turned to him and delivered a rapid stream of words of her own: two minutes of machine-gun Spanish with barely a pause for breath. When she had finished she nodded to him sharply and then inclined her head towards Dr Ramani, who was still standing up.

The translator returned the judge's nod before continuing.

'In view of the defendant's continued disrespect for the court, the judge has decided to reduce the period of grace for payment of the sums awarded from ninety days to seven days.'

'What? You can't do that. I—'

The judge slammed down her gavel once more, gesturing to the translator to continue.

'Furthermore,' he said, 'if there is one further word from the defendant, she will be held in contempt of court and face further penalties.'

The man's face was now deathly white and he was visibly shaking, but the judge just stared fixedly at Dr Ramani, who finally exhaled heavily through clenched teeth and sank back into her seat.

Dr Ramani had finally met her match.

***

Once outside the courtroom, Marysa and I crossed the street to where a small coffee bar was located. After ordering two coffees, we sat outside, on white plastic chairs – disturbingly similar in appearance to those which had sabotaged the community meeting the previous year – shaded from the warm sunshine by a faded, red parasol.

'Well, that was entertaining,' said Marysa, for once, a hint of mirth breaking through her usually-impassive manner.

'Absolutely priceless,' I replied, laughing. 'Wouldn't have missed it for the world. So, anyway, what happens now?'

'Well, if she's got any sense, she'll pay up on time.'

'And if she doesn't?'

'Then the court will seize her apartment and sell it at auction, taking all the money she owes from the proceeds of the sale.'

'Well, even *she* isn't crazy enough to let that happen,' I said, 'so hopefully, this will be the end of the saga.'

'Hopefully,' repeated Marysa, deadpan.

'While on the subject of antisocial residents,' I said, 'have you made any headway with Alfredo González regarding his obnoxious tenant, Julia, in 15C?'

'I've written to him twice about her but, as you know, we're not exactly top of his Christmas card list.'

'No,' I sighed, 'I guess not.'

'You could try talking to him yourself, I suppose,' she suggested, 'but in all honesty I don't think you'll get anywhere. The only way you're likely to get her out is to start gathering written evidence as you are doing for the hooker in 6D.'

Not that that's likely to produce a result anytime soon, I thought.

'OK,' I groaned, 'but I'll try phoning the bastard first, although I suspect that if he knows that she's really pissing me off he'll be showering her with gifts rather than evicting her.'

'You're probably right,' suggested Marysa, her tone completely neutral.

I drained my coffee – Marysa had already finished hers – and pushed my chair back, preparing to stand. 'OK, well I guess that's all for now. Speak to you again soon'

'Before you go,' she said, 'I have some news for you.'

'Good or bad?' I sighed, pulling my chair forward and placing my forearms on the table.

'Bad,' she said, flatly. 'The builders have discovered that all the main services – water, electricity, phone, satellite TV etc. – all run along underground exactly where they are digging the foundations for the new wall.'

'What do you mean, "discovered"? Surely our architect's plans and specifications would have shown them that.'

'Apparently not. He says it was impossible to know what lay underground at that point – either for him or for the builders.'

I sensed a stitch-up coming. 'So what does that mean for the works?'

'The builders say they will have to cut off all these services for a short time, while they temporarily re-route them. Then later, when the construction work is finished, they will reinstate them permanently along the base of the new wall.'

'And let me guess,' I sighed, sensing where this was going, 'they want more money to do this.'

'An additional twenty-seven thousand euros,' she confirmed.

'What? Surely we can contest this.'

'I don't think so,' she said. 'Since our own architect says that this amounts to additional, unforeseen work, we are more or less bound to accept it.'

'Then the architect is incompetent. Surely we can hold him accountable?'

'Do you really want to embark on a court case against our own architect, on top of everything else which is going on?

The answer was obvious, but now my antennae were really twitching. The architect, Alejandro Cuadrado, was supposedly a personal friend of Marysa's husband and came highly recommended. Now it seemed that the architect was only too willing to support the builder's claim that the additional work was completely unforeseen.

Were the three of them all in this together?

Chapter 34

After what had apparently been a tense and tetchy meeting – which I had been unable to attend, due to a stomach upset – with Julio Montoya, the head of the building contractor, Marysa informed me that the bill for the additional work related to dealing with the pipework and cables running along the base of the wall had been negotiated down from twenty-seven thousand to twenty-three thousand euros. This was still a sum which we could ill afford, but it was pretty clear that I had little option but to authorise them to go ahead. They assured me that the interruption to services could be kept to no more than a few hours, by which time the temporary rerouting would be in place. Knowing how things normally pan out in Spain I decided to play it safe and warn those residents who would be affected – about half of the total – that services would be down for a full day.

Oh, how optimistic that turned out to be!

For the next five days we had no electricity, no water, no phone, no television, and no internet. Predictably enough, not all the residents accepted this situation with good grace.

'What the fuck do you think you're playing at?' asked the corpulent, shaven-headed occupant of apartment 10A – I couldn't remember his name, and actually, I still can't. 'First you charge us a shit-load of extra money, then you make us park half a fucking mile away, then you spread a great pile of earth and mud over the sodding road outside our doors, and now you've cut off our water, electricity and TV. I can't even watch the England match tonight can I?'

Now in terms of factual content I couldn't really dispute much of what he had said – with the exception of the half a mile bit: I reckoned it was no more than five hundred yard. But I guess that didn't really alter the gist of his argument. I did feel, however, that he could have been a little more understanding, After all, I hadn't actually engineered this unhappy state of affairs with the express intention of pissing him off, even though I had clearly succeeded in doing so.

I received two other calls expressing similar sentiments that day, and by the time I had lit the candles that evening – no electricity, you see – and poured myself a large brandy, I had just about had enough; I was in a particularly grumpy mood.

Donna helped me put it all in perspective. 'He's just one man who doesn't take the slightest interest in what's going on as long as everything's ticking along as usual. He's just one person who likes to complain – *you're* at least trying to sort things out.'

My dark mood began to lift. 'You always know how to settle me down when I'm having a bit of a meltdown, don't you?'

She gave a mischievous smile. 'Wait there and I'll try to do even better.' She swept from the room, leaving me to slump back into my chair and sip my brandy.

Ten minutes later, when she returned, I almost choked on my brandy; she wore a black, lacy negligee over a barely-there G-string and towered over me in skyscraper heels. My God, she still had it; I immediately felt an involuntary tingle in my groin.

'There's something about candlelight,' she breathed, 'which always makes me feel a bit ... well ... horny.'

The day was definitely finishing on a better note than it had started.

***

My first thought, upon waking up the next morning, was to make a mental note to keep well stocked up on candles, just in case of future power cuts. My second thought was that I might just engineer the occasional power cut by accidentally-on-purpose switching off the electricity at the mains. What a shameful thought!

Anyway, by mid-morning the electricity was back on, and by lunchtime we had running water once again; we celebrated by taking a long, hot bath together, which was something we hadn't done for quite some time.

They say things come in threes, well so it was that day, for later, in the afternoon, the phone came back on line, too. My first call came at around eight that evening; it was Marysa.

'Ah, so they've finally got the phones working again,' she said.

'Just today,' I replied. 'We also have water and electricity now, so I guess things are looking up. Anyway, what's new?' Marysa never phoned just to see how things were going, and certainly not that late in the day, so I guessed she had some news for me, be it good or bad.

'Ramani still hasn't paid – either the money she owes us, or her legal fees. Her deadline expired yesterday so the court will be proceeding with seizure of her assets.'

'Unbelievable,' I gasped. 'What's the matter with the wretched woman?'

Marysa didn't respond to my rhetorical question, but continued, 'The only significant asset she has in Spain is her apartment, so they'll be setting a date to put it up for auction. Unless she pays before that date she'll lose her apartment.'

'My God, she's a stubborn bitch,' I sighed.

'Quite,' agreed Marysa, in typically succinct manner.

'How long will it be before the auction?' I asked.

'Usually it takes some months, but I think in this case it could be considerably quicker.'

'Why's that?'

'Well, as you are aware, Sergio made certain arrangements with the court to ensure that this case was dealt with promptly.' *Ah yes – money well spent*, I thought. 'Also, the judge was particularly irritated by Ramani's attitude in court so I think she has actually taken a bit of a personal interest in seeing this woman get her comeuppance.'

I smiled, not only at the memory of Ramani ranting at the judge in court, but also at Marysa's incredible grasp of colloquial English.

'I guess we wait and see then,' I concluded.

As I hung up, I was feeling pretty good about the way things had panned out that day. After a string of setbacks, we were finally making some progress on at least some of the issues which beset us.

'Come and take a look at this,' said Donna, passing me a glass of white wine.

She led me upstairs and out onto the upper terrace. 'Look,' she said, pointing towards the mountain range to the west.

The sun was a huge deep-red disc, hanging just above the mountains, wreathed by a wispy halo of thin cloud. The sky was graduated from deep blue above to a fiery orange along the top of the mountains, punctuated by dark, horizontal smudges of cloud, forming an intricate pattern.

'It's beautiful,' I breathed, squeezing her hand.

'And look over here, too.' She led me towards the east-facing edge of the terrace where 'our' mountain towered over the lake.

Every crevice, ridge, and peak was picked out in sharp relief by the low angle of the evening light, orange-tinted rock contrasting sharply with deep black shadows. A huge flock of swallows and swifts dived and whirled as they hunted insects above the lake.

'Let's sit and watch the sun go down,' she said, leading me towards the table in the centre of the terrace.

I set down my glass alongside hers and topped them both up from the bottle which she had already placed there.

'A perfect end to a pretty good day,' I said, as we clinked glasses and settled back to enjoy the last few minutes as the sun began to slide behind the mountains.

Chapter 35

'Red sky at night, shepherds' delight' ... or so the famous proverb goes. Well, so much for bloody proverbs! After the wondrous display of colour in the sky the previous evening, I was awoken early the next morning by the sound of torrents of water gushing from our roof and crashing noisily onto the terrace. For some reason, best known to the Spanish, the vast majority of buildings in the south of the country have no gutters. Perhaps they consider that to fit gutters in an area called the 'Costa del Sol' is unduly pessimistic even though, when it *does* decide to rain along that coastal strip, the downpour is often on a biblical scale.

'Dammit!' I muttered, as Donna, too, sat up in bed, woken by the Niagara-like racket outside. 'There's no chance of any work being done on the wall today.'

As she realised that it was still completely dark outside, she groaned, slumping face-down and pulling a pillow over her head in a vain attempt to muffle the sound.

I had hoped that, by this time, we had seen the end of the winter rains, and that we could now look forward to at least six months of uninterrupted sunshine, by which time the works would be completed.

Given my luck of late, I thought, *why should I be surprised that it wasn't to be? Oh well, hopefully, this will just be a short, sharp downpour and the work can start again soon.*

Unable to get back to sleep, I left the mound buried under the duvet and pillows that was Donna, pulled on my dressing gown, and went downstairs to make myself a coffee, before going to check my emails. Scrolling quickly through the headers, I was surprised to see one from Alfredo González, the developer. Following some of our recent exchanges I really didn't think we had much left to talk about. I clicked to open the email.

To: Mr Roy Groves
Copies: Ms Julia Petchnik, Mr Sergio Ortega, Mrs Marysa Ortega.
From: Alfredo González

Subject: Harassment of my tenant

I have received a complaint from my tenant, Ms Julia Petchnik, in apartment 15C, that you have, for some months, been waging a campaign of harassment against her. I understand that you have been rude and aggressive towards the lady, and have shown threatening behaviour towards her dog. This conduct is, of course, quite unacceptable, but what is even worse is that she has become aware of your deliberately spying on her when she has been in a state of undress in what should be the privacy of her own apartment terrace.

I must insist that this intimidating, and frankly disgusting behaviour cease at once. If not, I shall be forced to report your actions to the police.

Saludos,

Alfredo González

Un-fucking-believable! At first, I couldn't quite decide with whom I was most furious – Julia, or Alfredo. I decided that, by a narrow margin, it was Alfredo. Julia was rude, loud, anti-social, and, in this instance, downright manipulative: extremely irritating but not actually a serious danger to the community – only to my sanity. Alfredo, on the other hand, had endangered life and property with his shoddy building shortcuts and was costing each of us living in the complex a great deal of money and anxiety.

Anyway, I reflected, this email rather put paid to any hopes I had of reasoning with Alfredo about Julia's behaviour and perhaps getting her evicted. It was abundantly clear whose side he would take.

With a considerable effort of willpower, I resisted the urge to immediately write back to the bastard telling him just what I thought about him, his slob of a tenant, and his bloody attitude. In the end, I

240

didn't dignify his email with a reply. He could go to the police if he wanted to – they would have on record the incident regarding Julia's loud party, so if it came to it, I didn't think there was much chance that they'd take her word over mine.

***

The rain persisted, stubbornly. Donna and I spent the entire day indoors, watching TV and reading, although I found it difficult to devote my full attention to either activity, so irritated was I with González and his wretched tenant. My mood was certainly not improved by the phone call I received from Marysa late in the afternoon.

'Oh, hi Marysa. What's new?'

'There's been another development with Alfredo González.'

'That bastard? I assume you've seen the email he sent me regarding his loathsome tenant?'

'Yes,' she said. 'Have you replied?'

'No - I didn't think it deserved a reply.'

'Quite,' she said. 'Anyway, I think you will want to hear about his latest move.'

'Go on.'

'He's launched yet another legal action against us.'

'What ... regarding Julia?'

'No ... at least, not directly. He's claiming that, by blocking access to the garages on the back line, we have subjected his tenants to unreasonable hardship and inconvenience. He's claiming damages of four thousand euros for each of his three tenants: twelve thousand in total.'

'Why, the scheming bastard!' I raged. '*He's* the one who failed to build a proper retaining wall in the first place. *He's* the one who has refused to put things right. *He's* the one who has refused to even contribute to the cost of putting things right. And now, if we don't build a proper wall, it's quite likely to be one of *his own* apartments that gets damaged, or one of *his own* tenants that gets killed.' I paused for breath.

'Yes, it does all seem rather perverse,' said Marysa, in a breathtaking feat of understatement.

'And another thing ...' I continued, 'why does he seem to think that it's only his bloody tenants who are experiencing some inconvenience? Don't *I* have to park down the road? Don't around *forty* of us have to do so? And how the hell does he come up with a figure of four thousand euros for each of his precious tenants?'

I wasn't actually expecting Marysa to provide answers to any of these questions – I just needed to vent. When I finally dried up Marysa spoke again.

'Look, I don't know any better than you do why he's doing this. Sergio and I have discussed it with the lawyer and he considers that Alfredo has practically no chance of winning this action.'

'Unless he's got someone in the court system in his pocket,' I said, suspicious now of just about everyone and everything in the Spanish legal system.

'It's possible,' she said, 'but it would hardly be worth the cost of a bribe to win an award of just twelve thousand euros. More likely he just wants to make our lives as difficult as possible. That's why he's contesting the legality of the cash-call, and that's probably why he's sent you that stupid email about Julia Petchnik.'

'I just don't get it,' I said. 'I can understand his attempts to minimise his own financial liability in all this, but he still owns three apartments along the back line. You'd think he'd be as keen as any of us to make the hillside safe as soon as possible.'

'I don't believe he's thinking rationally about all of this anymore,' she opined. 'It seems to have become personal.'

'Well, it's starting to feel pretty personal with me too,' I said.

'Take care,' she warned, 'Alfredo González could be a formidable enemy.'

Chapter 36

It's often been said that you should never write and send a stroppy email when gripped by bad temper, and all my years in business had convinced me of the wisdom of this advice. An email sent in a knee-jerk reaction to whatever has pissed you off rarely produces a good outcome.

Well, on this occasion, I was so incensed that all such wise thoughts went straight out of the window – the moment I got off the phone to Marysa, I was straight onto the laptop.

To: Alfredo González
From: Roy Groves
Subject: Collapsed retaining wall

I have just been informed of your decision to launch legal action against the community in respect of inconvenience caused to your tenants during the construction of the new retaining wall.

I consider this action to be extremely unprofessional, particularly coming as it does after your previous decision to challenge the legality of the supplementary budget, approved at our EGM, to collect from owners funds sufficient to finance the construction of a new retaining wall to replace the wholly inadequate structure which you originally installed.

I must point out that it is only due to *your* refusal to rectify the original problem that the community has been forced to seek redress through the courts. Furthermore, due to the inordinately long time taken for the case to come to court, and the resultant danger to life and property posed by the risk of a further landslide, I have been forced to collect a supplementary budget from owners in order to allow remedial works to begin as soon as possible.

Has it not occurred to you that, as owner of three apartments yourself, your continuing actions, aimed at undermining our efforts to rectify the dangerous state of the hillside, have the potential to damage your *own* best interests, and those of your tenants?

I want you to be aware that you cannot employ such underhand tactics without incurring consequences, so let me make my position crystal clear. I have been elected to represent the community to the best of my ability, and therefore I am determined to fight you every step of the way with regard to this matter. I will do whatever is necessary to ensure that you pay what is due in respect of your corner-cutting, shoddy workmanship.

Regards,
Roy Groves – presidente, comunidad de propietarios.

I didn't for one moment suppose that my message would make the slightest bit of difference to the outcome of the dispute, but I felt better once I'd hit 'send'.

***

Four days later, there had still been no further work carried out on the wall, in spite of the fact that there had been no further rain for three of those days. According to Julio Montoya, head of the building company, the heavy rain had turned the thick layer of earth spread over the internal roadway to a slippery quagmire on which the heavy diggers and other machinery could not work. Apparently we were going to just have to wait until the mud had dried out sufficiently before work could continue.

Brilliant, I thought, *so it's come as a surprise out of the blue to this 'expert' contractor that when you spread a layer of earth several feet thick on the road, and then you experience twenty-four hours of heavy rain, you are going to get a serious amount of mud.*

To add insult to injury, Montoya had also suggested that when the permanent services were reinstated we might like to have some manholes installed, to facilitate maintenance and repairs in the future. Good idea, I had thought, but I was less than impressed when he told us that would cost another six thousand euros.

Concerned about the spiralling costs and potential time overruns on this project I had called a breakfast meeting with Marysa and the architect to discuss the situation. The venue was a small bar alongside the marina at Cabopino, located some ten miles or so along the coast from its bigger and glitzier neighbour, Puerto Banús.

'He's late,' muttered Paul, glancing at his watch.

'He's Spanish,' offered Marysa, by way of explanation.

We were waiting for Alejandro Cuadrado, the architect who had designed the new wall and was managing the project on our behalf. I was becoming increasingly uneasy about Cuadrado, who seemed way too cosy with the builder for my liking.

I didn't bother to respond to Marysa's cryptic remark; I had, by now, become used to the somewhat laid-back attitude to timekeeping which seemed to permeate the Spanish culture, and I was determined not to allow my irritation to get the better of me before the meeting had even started.

I took a sip of my coffee and gazed out across the row of boats bobbing gently at their moorings. The morning sun caught the wavelets which punctuated the sea beyond at a glancing angle, myriad points of sparkling light dancing across the surface.

Finally he turned up, thirty-five minutes late. As usual, he was immaculately dressed, his pale beige business suit teamed with a crisp, blue shirt and yellow silk tie. His pointy-toed brown shoes were polished to a dazzling lustre. His attire contrasted starkly with Marysa's typically irreverent notion of appropriate style for a business meeting: tight-fitting, purple shorts, worn over thick, orange tights, and her trademark Ugg boots.

Alejandro made no attempt to apologise for his lateness – apparently regarding thirty-five minutes as a perfectly normal margin of tolerance for the start of a meeting.

After exchanging the usual pleasantries and ordering our breakfasts, we got down to business. The first thing I wanted to tackle was the issue of unexpected extra costs.

'So how is it,' I asked, 'that we have to pay twenty-three thousand euros extra to deal with the temporary rerouting and eventual permanent reinstatement of services?'

'Well,' said Alejandro, 'it's a very involved business, rerouting all of those services. In all honesty, I don't think the cost is unreasonable.'

Was he being deliberately obtuse? I decided to give him the benefit of the doubt, for now at least.

'It's not the actual cost which I'm querying,' I replied, 'it's the fact that it wasn't included in the original quote.'

Alejandro's brow creased in a frown. 'But how could it be? It's work which was not originally foreseen.'

Already, my hackles were beginning to rise.

Paul, evidently sensing my rising irritation, stepped smoothly in. 'What Roy is asking,' he said, 'is *why* wasn't it foreseen? Surely when you drew up the specification for the invitation to tender you would have included the necessity to deal with these services?'

'But I didn't know they were there,' protested Alejandro.

I gripped the edge of the table tightly with both hands, fighting to contain an unseemly outburst which would probably get us precisely nowhere. Paul continued to pursue the point.

'You had access to all the technical drawings for the urbanisation, did you not?'

'Well, yes ... of course,' replied Alejandro, 'but they are of very poor quality and detail. It was not at all clear where the principal services ran.'

'So you had no idea that all the services would have to be lifted in order to build the new wall?' Paul persisted.

'Listen to me,' said Alejandro, puffing himself up to the maximum height achievable whilst still seated, 'I have been a professional architect for more than twenty-five years. I have vast experience of interpreting technical drawings. I can assure you that it was impossible to tell from the drawings that all the vital services ran along the bottom of the cut face of the hillside.'

Paul glanced sideways at me, silently but unmistakeably enquiring whether he should continue to press the point. I gave a slight shake of my head. Whether we had made a good choice in employing Alejandro Cuadrado was almost immaterial now; we were stuck with him for the duration of the project. There was no point in pushing things to the point of an irreconcilable breakdown in relations. As long as Cuadrado knew that we were going to ask the difficult questions when appropriate, maybe that would be enough to keep him on his toes. Anyway, I now had another difficult question for him.

'OK, so *if* we accept that the issue of the services was a problem that no-one could have foreseen' – he visibly bristled –

'why did Montoya not include the cost of the manholes in his quote to deal with this problem?'

'That,' he retorted, 'is a question you would need to put to señor Montoya.'

'Alright then ... let me ask a slightly different question: in your professional opinion, are the manholes a "nice to have" or are they, in effect, essential?'

Beads of perspiration began to spring forth from the pores on the forehead of this usually-cool character. 'I ... I am sorry ... my English ... I do not understand this "nice to have".'

Your English is bloody perfect, I thought, *unless it suits you for it not to be.* 'What I mean,' I persisted, 'is would it make any sense *not* to have the manholes?'

'Well ... no, not really,' he admitted.

'And it did not occur to you, when you saw their quotation for the additional work, to question this point?'

'I ... I assumed that the manholes were included,' he muttered.

'OK,' I replied, 'well this is what I'd like you to do: I want you to go back to Montoya and insist that he includes the manholes within the original cost of rerouting the services. Tell him we will not pay extra for a facility which, in your professional opinion' – I tried to keep the irony out of my voice – 'is an absolutely essential feature of the works.'

'But—' he spluttered. He was interrupted by the arrival of our breakfasts.

We waited in tense silence while the waitress set out the dishes. When she withdrew, Alejandro tried to continue. 'You have to understand—' he began, but I cut him off.

'I'm not discussing this subject any further,' I asserted. 'Just do as I ask, OK?' He said nothing, but merely gave a sullen nod. 'Now,' I said, 'shall we eat our breakfasts, before they get cold?'

We ate our food mostly in an atmosphere of stony silence, punctuated only by the occasional awkward comment about the weather, the charming surroundings, or the European football scene – in which I had no interest anyway, but on which subject, Paul seemed able to comment knowledgeably.

When everyone had finished eating I brought up the final point which I wanted to explore. 'Now then ... about the issue of work stopping for several days just because we've had a bit of rain—'

'You have seen the terrible mud ...' interrupted Alejandro, 'you cannot expect a twenty tonne excavator to work in such conditions: it could slither sideways and crash into one of your buildings, causing untold damage.'

'My point,' I said, as calmly as possible, 'is that this situation was completely foreseeable. Why did they spread all that earth across the working area, knowing full well that, in the event of rain, the site would be rendered unworkable?'

Perspiration streamed down Alejandro's temples; he withdrew from his pocket a monogrammed handkerchief, and mopped his brow. 'The decision to work on top of the earth was theirs, and theirs alone ... it was nothing to do with me. I believe they were trying to prevent the heavy machines from damaging the road.'

'So were there no other methods available to protect the surface of the road?'

'Well, possibly, but as I said, it wasn't my idea to—'

'And once they *had* decided to work on top of the earth layer, couldn't they have covered it with tarpaulins when the rain set in, so that it didn't become so badly soaked?'

'This is all very well,' he spluttered, 'after the event, but ... well ...' He had run out of defensive ideas.

'How long is it going to take for the mud to dry out sufficiently for work to resume?'

'I ... I don't know,' he admitted.

'So, once they *do* start work again, I want you to instruct them, at the first signs of any further rain, to cover the earth with tarpaulins.'

'Oh, we're well into April now: it's very unlikely that we'll get any further significant rain.'

I glared at him. 'But you'll instruct them what to do if it *does* rain again, OK?'

He nodded, silently.

Marysa had remained strangely silent throughout most of the meeting; I wondered why. 'Do you have anything to add, Marysa?' I prompted.

'I don't think so,' she said, without further elaboration.

'Then I suppose we're done.'

Marysa and Alejandro said their stilted goodbyes and departed.

Paul and I were about to go too, when the lurking presence of the waitress reminded us that we hadn't yet paid.

Terrific, I thought, *on top of all the other costs that he's landed us with, we now get to pay for his bloody breakfast, too.*

***

When I got home, Donna greeted me with a broad smile; she looked positively overjoyed about something or other.

'What's made you so cheerful?' I grumbled, a little ungraciously, I suppose.

'I've been on the phone to Bea.'

Well, there was nothing particularly unusual about that: Donna normally called each of our daughters at least three times a week, and their phone conversations often lasted over an hour. How they found enough to talk about to occupy so much time was a bit of a mystery to me, but these phone chats were a lifeline which, for Donna, made the long periods of separation from the girls and the grandchildren tolerable. I missed them too of course, but my phone conversations with Beatrice and Raquel tended to be much shorter. For me, a phone is a device primarily for communicating specific items of information as succinctly as possible; I've always found just chatting casually on the phone a particularly unnatural thing to do. Maybe it's a man/woman thing.

'So ... what's her news then?' I asked.

Donna was positively bursting to tell me. 'Jason is going to have a little brother or sister.'

'She's pregnant?' I said – a particularly dumb response, I suppose, since there could be no other interpretation of what Donna had just said.

'Yes,' cried Donna, beaming from ear to ear as she rushed up to me and flung her arms around my neck. 'Isn't it wonderful?'

Seeing Donna's unbridled joy chased away my previously irritable mood. 'Yes it is,' I said, hugging her to me. 'Let's have a glass of champagne to celebrate.'

'But it's not even midday yet,' she laughed, easing herself from my embrace.

'Oh, to hell with that,' I replied. 'It's not every day we get news like this, is it? Now sit down while I open the champagne and then you can tell me all about it.'

A few minutes later we were both seated beneath our sunshade on the terrace; the spring sunshine was surprisingly warm.

'So when's the baby due?' I asked.

'Around mid-November.'

'Boy or girl?'

'Oh, it's far too early to tell at this stage. In any case, she doesn't want to know; she wants it to be a surprise.'

'Well it's wonderful news,' I said, kissing Donna on the cheek and squeezing her hand.

'I told her we'd try to spend a couple of weeks in England just before the baby's born. Rick will be working right up to the birth and she's going to need all the help she can get coping with Jason in those last days.'

I smiled. Jason was an extremely exuberant two-year-old; he was a lovely little boy, but exhausting at the best of times. 'Of course we should go.'

'I know that you have a lot going on here, but—'

'Sssh ...' I said, placing my finger gently on her lips, 'family comes first. In any case, the wall should be finished by then, the Ramani issue should be wrapped up, and we might even have some resolution on the other court cases. Anyway I'm sure Paul can deal with anything else which crops up while we're away.'

'You're sure?' she said.

'I'm sure. Look, I don't even get paid for dealing with all this community crap, so I'm damned if I'm going to let it get in the way of being there for the birth of our grandchild.'

She laid her head on my shoulder and nuzzled my neck, sighing contentedly; it was a positive delight to see her so blissfully happy. I hoped I was right in my upbeat assessment of where we'd be with community issues when the time came to travel back to England.

Chapter 37

It was two full weeks after the rain had stopped before the builders deemed that the mud had dried out sufficiently for work to recommence. This delay was on top of the time which had already been lost due to the unscheduled extra work to reroute the services. We had therefore lost almost four weeks on the project, and we had barely started work on the construction proper. This did not bode well for completion of the project in the promised timescale of three months. The only saving grace was that the contract with the builders contained penalty clauses for late completion, so if it *did* overrun – almost a certainty in my estimation – we would at least claw back some of the extra costs which kept arising. Anyway, work was finally underway again, and I had left both architect and builder in no doubt that we would be enforcing penalty clauses to the hilt if they didn't find a way to get the timescale back on track.

This particular evening, however, I had another matter on my mind: Dr Ramani's apartment was to be sold by public auction at 2 p.m. the following afternoon. Astonishingly, she still hadn't paid the money ordered by the court. Now she now stood to lose a great deal more money than if she had just paid up in the first place.

As I understood it, the sole purpose of selling the property was to raise enough money to cover her debts and legal fees, which amounted to about thirty-four thousand euros. Once the property was sold they would withhold this amount and return the rest to Dr Ramani. The court therefore had no interest in achieving fair market value for the property, and would set a very low reserve price to ensure an immediate sale. It was possible, therefore, that the apartment – probably worth around five hundred thousand euros – would be sold at an absurdly low price, leaving Dr Ramani seriously out of pocket. She had to be even more deranged than I had previously taken her for.

I had even considered attending the auction and bidding for the property myself if it could be acquired for a real bargain price. Donna, however, had advised, probably wisely, that I would be laying myself open to all sorts of accusations of engineering the situation for personal gain. Furthermore, if it ever came out that I had used community money to expedite court proceedings ... well, you can imagine how that would look. Somewhat reluctantly, I had abandoned the idea.

Over dinner that evening, Donna and I spent practically the whole time discussing the subject of Dr Ramani and her astonishing obstinacy.

Donna summed it up succinctly. 'She must be absolutely stark-staring-mad.'

'Must admit,' I said, shaking my head, 'I can hardly believe it, either.'

As we were clearing away the dishes, the doorbell rang. When I opened the door, the first thing I was aware of was a waft of perfume. The sight which then met my eyes took me completely by surprise. Svetlana Petrov was barely recognisable at first glance, so different did she look from the lightly-made-up and conservatively-dressed woman whom Paul and I had previously met. No, tonight she was sporting what I can only assume was her working attire.

Her jade green eyes, vibrant beneath exaggeratedly long black lashes, were outlined in heavy black liner, extending outwards and upwards at the edges, accentuating their natural slant. The dark green eye shadow mirrored the colour of her eyes. Her cheeks were heavily rouged and her lips were painted a vivid shade of scarlet.

Arrested for a second or so by her undeniably beautiful face and startlingly extreme makeup, my eyes then decided to ignore any conscious commands which my brain might issue to the contrary and swiftly roamed down her body right to the tips of her red stilettoes and back up again. The short, red leather skirt finished about three-quarters of the way up her shapely, fishnet-clad thighs. Above it, around four inches of tanned and toned midriff were on display, giving way eventually to a black, lacy top which clung to her ample breasts like a second skin, doing very little to hide the dark outline of her nipples. I gulped as I finally managed to regain focus on her face. Her scarlet lips were set in a tight, straight line and her jaw jutted fiercely forward. I sensed that she wasn't too happy about something.

I was right. 'What the fuck is that oaf of yours up to now?' she demanded, jabbing a bright red acrylic nail within inches of my face. Her voice, so soft and pleasant when we had previously met, had taken on a distinctly strident tone.

'I'm sorry,' I said, trying to sound as conciliatory as possible, 'but I really don't know what you're talking about.'

'Don't give me that shit,' she shouted. 'I know you sent him.'

'Sent who? I really don't know what—'

'You know who I'm fucking talking about,' she screamed.

The last thing I needed was a noisy scene on my own doorstep.

'Look, you'd better come inside,' I said, taking her arm and gently pulling her towards me, hoping to get her inside before a host of nosy neighbours started appearing on their terraces to eavesdrop.

'Take your hands off me,' she yelled, shaking her arm free.

I stepped aside to let her in; she obliged, stomping right through into the lounge, her heels clacking loudly on the marble floor. As I shut the door and followed her inside she turned to face me, legs slightly apart and hands on hips. She appeared completely oblivious to Donna, who was in the kitchen, staring over the granite counter which separated it from the lounge, her mouth open and eyes wide.

'Donna, this is Svetlana Petrov from block 6. Svetlana ... my wife, Donna.'

Donna nodded, dumbly, as she continued to stare, taking in the other woman's outlandish outfit. Svetlana glanced across at Donna but said nothing, quickly refocusing her angry stare on me, maintaining her defiant posture.

OK here goes. 'So what exactly is the problem?' I said, trying to sound placatory.

For the first time, I thought I detected a slight flicker of doubt in her heavily made-up eyes. 'Are you really saying you don't know?'

'I don't,' I said, spreading my hands.

'You didn't send him?' she said, suspicion still evident in her voice.

'Who? I don't know who you're talking about.'

'That muscle-bound brute with the spiky hair.'

Oh God! It's Bruce. What the hell has he been up to now?

'You mean Bruce from 5C?'

'That's him ... the one with the slutty girlfriend.'

Now this was a bit rich, I felt, coming from someone who had just marched into my home dressed like ... well, like a hooker. *Best not comment,* I thought.

'What has he done?' I sighed.

'He's been threatening my friends.'

'Oh ... look you'd better come and sit down and explain exactly what has happened.'

Her anger seemed to be subsiding a little as she accepted my invitation. I sat opposite her, which turned out to be a bit of a mistake because the triangle of shiny red satin which peeped at me from between her legs as her very short leather skirt rode up her thighs proved to be something of a distraction. Things hardly improved even when she crossed her legs, for her skirt was so short that her stocking tops were on full display.

With some difficulty I focused my gaze on her face. Even then, the swell of her breasts and the dark outline of her nipples beneath the see-through fabric of her top infiltrated my peripheral vision. I tried, with only limited success, to ignore the diversion. 'So what has happened?'

'A friend of mine was coming to see me this evening, but when he drove into the garage and got out of his car, that horrible man was waiting for him.'

Ah, so we have at least established that your 'friend' was male. No law against having male friends, though, I reminded myself.

'Waiting for him ... what in the garage? How would Bruce have even known that you had a visitor?'

'How would I know? He was just *there* waiting.' She tilted her head and blinked her long, black lashes. She certainly knew how to work her charms to best effect. Still, I suppose that was second nature in her line of work.

'Hmm ... and how did your ... friend ... get into the garage anyway? You assured me that it is not you who has been overriding the automatic closure mechanism.'

A shadow of confusion flitted briefly across her eyes, but she was wrong-footed only for a split second. 'I ... I lent him my remote control when I invited him over.'

'But surely, there would have been nowhere for him to park in the garage, if your own car was parked in your space.'

She uncrossed her legs, treating me to another flash of scarlet knickers, shifted position, and re-crossed her legs. My God, she was good at this; by the time I had refocused on her face she had her answer ready.

'Oh, the Austrian couple in 6A let me use their space when they're not here. Anyway,' she said, now sounding rather tetchy once more, 'the parking arrangements I make for my visitors are not important; the point is that that disgusting ape threatened my friend and chased him off, so that he didn't even come up to see me. And this is not the first time it has happened; the bastard is waging some sort of personal campaign against me and my friends.'

Oh, Bruce, I thought, *you're probably doing this with the best of intentions, but you're really not helping the situation.*

'You say you haven't put him up to this?'

'No, really, I haven't.'

'Well in that case,' she demanded, 'what are you going to do about it?' Her startling green eyes flashed and her chin jutted forward.

In spite of the fact that this woman was clearly operating a prostitution business within our community, and acting in a grossly antisocial manner to her neighbours, somehow *I* was now feeling like the guilty party here.

'Look, if what you say is true—'

'It *is* true. Are you calling me a liar?' The tone of her voice was becoming more strident by the second.

'No ... I didn't mean that. Look, I'll go and talk to Bruce and get his side of ...' *No, better rephrase that, unless I want to send her off the deep end again.* 'I'll ... find out why he's been doing this and try to resolve the situation.' *Oh, dear, that sounds like a bit of a woolly response, doesn't it?*

'You tell him to keep his nose out of my fucking business.'

Bit of an unfortunate turn of phrase, I thought, *since it is indeed your 'fucking business' which has brought all this about.*

She rose abruptly to her feet, treating me to one last glimpse of her satin-clad crotch, and smoothed down her skirt, which still barely concealed her stocking tops, even when standing.

'Goodbye Mrs Groves,' she said, with a toss of her wavy locks – it was the only remark she had addressed to Donna during the entire time she had been there – and strutted towards the door.

'Er ... goodnight then,' murmured Donna, looking somewhat dumbfounded.

As I followed Svetlana towards the door, surveying her long, slim legs and pert backside, it suddenly struck me that it probably wasn't the best idea for a woman – even an exponent of her chosen profession – to be walking alone, dressed so provocatively, after dark. I thought of summoning one of the security guards to give her a lift back to her apartment in the buggy, but swiftly rejected the idea: if it were Calvin, he'd be quite likely to suffer a cardiac arrest; if it were Sam, he'd probably offer to pimp for her.

'Er ... look, can I walk you back to your apartment?' I said, feeling extremely awkward, as I caught sight of Donna, who had now come through to the hallway. One of her eyebrows levitated as she heard my invitation.

Svetlana tilted her head and her angry expression was softened by a hint of a smile. 'Well I'm glad to see that there are still *some* gentlemen around here.'

I turned to Donna. 'Back soon,' I murmured. She responded with an almost-imperceptible shake of her head and a clearly audible tutting sound.

We walked side by side in almost total silence until we reached her apartment.

'Thank you,' said Svetlana, curtly. She bent down to retrieve a door key from under a plant pot on her terrace – I guessed that her outfit really didn't provide many places to accommodate even such a small object. 'You will make sure he stops his bullying, won't you?' she added.

'I'll talk to him as soon as possible,' I replied, noncommittally.

When I got home, Donna had finished clearing the dishes and was pouring two glasses of wine. She passed one to me as I stepped into the kitchen.

'So who's your new best friend then?' she said.

'Don't ask ... anyway, Paul's the one who's smitten by Svetlana's charms.'

'Oh yes?' she said. 'Well I didn't notice you exactly looking away as she put it all out on display there.'

I spread my hands. 'I'm a man ... what can I say?'

'Pervert!' she exclaimed, pressing an accusing forefinger to my chest, but she couldn't avoid laughing as she did so.

Chapter 38

The following morning, I went over to see Bruce. When he opened the door he was wearing only a pair of swimming shorts; he made an even more imposing figure than usual. His heavily-tattooed bull neck merged into broad shoulders and firmly muscled upper arms of impressive girth, also adorned with ornate tattoos. The deep barrel chest topped a firmly toned 'six-pack' torso. His enormous, sinewy thighs were criss-crossed with bulging veins that resembled a road map. Even though I knew him well by now, his physical presence was a little intimidating.

His momentarily surprised expression quickly gave way to that familiar smile, revealing his dazzling-white row of tombstones. 'Roy ... good to see you mate!' He clasped my hand in a vicelike grip, squeezing until it hurt, and shaking it vigorously. 'Come on in and have a beer. Me and Tracy were just catching some rays out on the terrace.' Judging by the mahogany tone of his skin he had already caught plenty.

I glanced at my watch. 'It's only eleven, Bruce ... a bit early for me.'

'Nah ... it's never too early in sunny Spain.'

'Well, OK then ... just the one. Look, I've got something I need to—'

He slapped an enormous hand onto my shoulder and practically pulled me through the door. 'Go on through ... I'll get you a beer. Tracy'll be pleased to see you.'

And she was. As I stepped out onto the terrace she jumped up from her sunbed and squealed with delight. 'Roy, what a nice surprise!' She seemed completely unconcerned that she was clad only in a skimpy pair of bikini briefs as she rushed over to me, her impressive breasts bouncing in what I have to admit was a rather fetching manner. She flung her arms around my neck and kissed me on both cheeks. 'Come and sit down. Is Bruce getting you a drink?' I nodded, smiling as I sat down. 'This,' she said, picking up her own drink – a bright pink concoction with what looked like virtually a complete fruit salad perched on the rim of the glass – 'is his own invention. He calls it "Perfect Pussy".' She dissolved into giggles.

Bruce reappeared, clutching two bottles of beer, handing me one before sitting down. 'Cheers!' he said, clinking his bottle with mine. He glanced at Tracy. 'Babe,' he said, indicating, with a nod of his head, her state of undress.

She looked down, and suddenly clapped a hand over her mouth, laughing. 'Oh, I'm not really dressed for entertaining, am I?'

Bruce picked up her bikini top from where it lay on the table and tossed it to her. She passed it behind her back, fastening it at the front, before swivelling it around, taking each breast in turn in her hand and nestling it into place. Finally, she slipped the straps over her shoulders and completed the manoeuvre by cupping both hands under her breasts and wriggling slightly from side to side to settle them into a comfortable position. 'There ... now I'm decent,' she declared.

'Thing is,' said Bruce, 'Tracy's practically always got her boobs out when the sun's shining and we're out here ... I think she just forgets about them.' She giggled, placing her hand to her mouth. 'She has got a cracking pair though, hasn't she?'

If I hadn't already become used to Bruce and Tracy's uniquely-unselfconscious manner, I could have been really quite embarrassed by such a question, but as it was I just said, 'She certainly has ... best around here by far.'

'Oooh, thank you, Roy,' she cooed. 'Mind you, they weren't always like this you know' – I didn't for a moment imagine they were – 'I had them done about three years ago by this really good surgeon in Marbella. He ...'

'Babe,' interrupted Bruce, laughing, 'I don't think Roy has come over to hear about your boob job.' She looked a little disappointed.

I smiled at her, 'Perhaps another time. I am really interested, but I've got something I need to discuss with Bruce right now.'

'So what's up?' said Bruce, taking a swig from his beer and wiping his upper lip with the back of his hand.

'Should we talk in private?' I said, feeling distinctly uncomfortable.

'Nah ... me and Tracy ain't got no secrets ... fire away.'

OK, well here goes then. 'I had a visit from Svetlana Petrov last night.'

'The hooker? What did she want?'

'She says you've been threatening her "friends" ... by which I assume she really means her clients.'

'Oh that,' he laughed. 'I've just been trying to help out your friend Robert – the Kraut – by gently persuading some of her customers that they might like to reconsider their options.'

'Bruce, tell me truthfully, have you been threatening them with violence?'

'Violence?' He looked positively wounded by such a suggestion. 'No, of course not ... what do you take me for?' I have to admit that that was a question for which I had no ready answer, but fortunately he did not wait for one. 'I simply pointed out to them that they were on CCTV: that the registration numbers of their cars were being recorded as well as photographs of their faces. I just asked them to consider what their wives might think.'

Hmm ... I thought, *that'd probably do it.*

'But no threats of violence?' I said.

'No, honest,' he confirmed. 'I wouldn't want to do any harm to innocent punters who just want a bit of spice that they probably don't get at home. Now if they had a hot babe like Tracy here to go home to' – she preened – 'they wouldn't need to go to no hooker. It's just that we don't want that stuff going on in a nice residential community like ours, do we?'

Before I could respond, Tracy stepped in, her voice unusually strident. 'No, we don't ... we have standards to keep up here. That Russian bitch is a slut and we don't want her here. My Bruce is doing you a favour.'

I had to smile, both at Tracy's indignant response, and her reference to Svetlana as a 'slut', neatly mirroring the other woman's opinion of her.

As I regarded Bruce's innocent-looking expression, I just knew that he was telling me the truth: that Svetlana had deliberately misrepresented the nature of his intervention in order to try to get me on her side. Nevertheless, I had to persuade Bruce – even though he was undoubtedly acting with the best of intentions – to desist from his one-man vigilante campaign.

'Bruce,' I said, 'I appreciate that you are just trying to help here ... and we all want to get rid of this wretched woman, but it really has to be done in the proper way. What happens if she gets her minders back here again to come and surprise you when you don't have your friends around to back you up?'

'I'm not scared of them fookers,' he said, his jaw firmly set. 'I could take two or three of them single-handed ... fat, soft Russian bastards.'

'Yes,' chipped in Tracy, 'my Bruce is top man when it comes to a fight.'

'Thanks, babe,' he responded, shooting her a smile.

Oh dear, this isn't going well. 'Look, I don't doubt you can handle yourself in a fight, but that's not really the point.' His brow creased in a puzzled frown as he apparently grappled to grasp how this could *not* be the point. 'I just can't have a vigilante campaign within our community.'

'A vigi-what?' he said.

'I can't have any of us just taking the law into our own hands; I can't have visitors intimidated; I can't have brawling on the premises; we have to do this by the book. Do you understand?'

His expression reminded me of a huge, overgrown, sad-eyed puppy. 'You want me to back off?'

'Yes,' I sighed, 'I want you to back off. I know you're really trying to help, but I worry that this approach could just cause the whole situation to escalate.'

'If you say so,' he said, obviously disconsolate.

'I do,' I said. 'We'll just carry on collecting CCTV evidence, recording incidents in the book and eventually we'll get rid of her through the proper channels.'

He fixed me with an unusually intense stare. 'I'll do what you say, Roy, but I don't think you appreciate just how these bastards operate. The only thing they understand is someone who pushes back harder than they do.'

Was he right? I wasn't sure, but I couldn't condone his approach. I drained the last of my beer and rose from my chair. 'I should go now ... thanks for the drink.'

Tracy stood up and put her arms around my neck, kissing me on both cheeks. 'My Bruce really is only trying to help you know.'

'I know,' I replied.

'Anyway,' she said, 'it was lovely to see you ... you should come over more often. Next time I can tell you all about my boob job. Actually I'm thinking about going back to the same guy to go a bit bigger; what do you think?'

She stood back and thrust her chest forward, her expression enquiring.

'I think you look perfect just as you are,' I said.

'Aww, you're so sweet,' she said, and then, turning to Bruce, 'isn't he babe?'

'He's just telling you what I'm always telling you.'

She rushed over and flung her arms around his neck as he gathered her up and lifted her clean off the ground with just one arm.

'And you're sweet too,' she cooed.

'Bye then,' I said, not wanting to intrude any further.

***

'How did you get on with Bruce?' enquired Donna, when I got home.

'Oh, OK I guess. According to him he didn't threaten anyone ... at least not with physical violence. He's just been making her customers – potential customers, that is – aware that they and their cars are being caught on camera. Unsurprisingly, many of them are not at all keen on that prospect.'

'I'll bet,' she said, smiling.

'Anyway, I've told him he really has to stay out of it now ... and he seems to have accepted that.'

'His heart's in the right place you know. He's only trying to help.'

Why does everyone keep telling me that? 'I know, but if her minders come back again, things could get really nasty.'

'I suppose so,' she said. 'Anyway, Marysa phoned while you were out.'

My heart sank; calls from Marysa rarely bore glad tidings. 'What did she want?'

'Apparently Dr Ramani has paid.'

What with the whole issue of Bruce and Svetlana, I had clean forgotten that the auction of Ramani's apartment was due to take place that very day. 'She has?' I said, astonished.

'Uh huh ... apparently she finally paid up just two hours before the auction was due to take place.'

'Unbelievable,' I gasped. 'My God, she's a stubborn bitch ... leaving it to the very last minute like that.'

'And do you want to know something else?' said Donna, smiling.

'What's that?'

'She's being fined an additional five thousand euros, to compensate the auction house for wasting their time.'

'Yes!' I exclaimed, jumping to my feet and punching the air with glee.

'I thought you'd like that,' said Donna, in a gigantic feat of understatement.

In the one-step-forward, one-step backward world of horizontal living, this was very definitely a step forward.

Chapter 39

A week or so after hearing the news about Dr Ramani's eventual climb-down, I received another piece of good news. Our court case against the developer – claiming one hundred and twenty thousand euros towards the cost of constructing a new retaining wall – was finally to be heard on 27th May: just three weeks away. I was delighted that, after years of delay, this matter was finally to come to the crunch. I had to admit, though, that I was anxious about the outcome. Although it seemed to me that our case was rock solid – unlike the bloody wall, which had collapsed like a house of cards at the first sniff of serious rain – I still retained, in my mind's eye, the image of Alfredo González handing over that fat, brown envelope to the court surveyor.

My ruminations about the court case were interrupted by the trilling of the phone. The half-American, half-German accent was immediately recognisable. I braced myself for the inevitable broadside which was surely to come.

'Oh, hello Robert. How are things going with your troublesome neighbour?' I thought it best to confront the subject head-on rather than beat about the proverbial bush.

'Wonderful!' he exclaimed. This really wasn't the reply I had expected.

'Er ... wonderful? What exactly do you mean?'

'She's gone.'

'Gone? What do you mean, gone?'

'I mean she's gone ... she's moved out.'

'Moved out?' I realised that I was beginning to sound like a particularly dull-witted parrot.

'Yes. She gave me the most foul-mouthed torrent of abuse just before she left, but that's it now ... she's gone.'

'But ... why ... er ... what happened to ... I mean did she say why?'

'It seems that the plan you and Bruce put together has worked brilliantly. The way he kept warning off her clients just meant that she was no longer making enough money to satisfy her bosses … or her own extravagant lifestyle. And when they sent her minders round for a third time …'

'A third time?' I spluttered. *I really have to stop doing this parrot thing.*

'Yes … didn't Bruce tell you that they'd been back?'

'Well no,' I admitted.

'Oh yes … just a couple of days ago. He was on his own this time, but he still sent them off with their tails between their legs.'

Oh, Bruce, didn't I warn you that this might happen?

'So she's actually gone?' I said, no doubt sounding even denser than I was actually feeling at that moment.

'Yes,' he repeated '… gone.' *Right, I think I've finally got that now.* 'I guess they concluded it was just too much trouble to keep the bitch operating from this location and decided to find another apartment somewhere else for her.'

'Anyway,' he continued, 'I just wanted to say thank you for the way that you and Bruce have sorted this issue out. I think you are doing a fantastic job as president and if there is anything ... anything at all ... I can do to help you, just let me know.'

'I … er, yes I will. Thanks Robert.'

'What was that all about?' enquired Donna, as I replaced the handset on its base, blinking stupidly as I struggled to process what I had just been told.

I spent the next ten minutes relating the story to her.

'You see?' she said, 'I told you Bruce had our best interests at heart.'

'I know,' I conceded, 'but it's just the way he goes about things. I mean we could have got involved in a full scale war with the local mafia over this.'

'Well we didn't, though, did we? I think you should go over and see Bruce to thank him for what he has done.'

'What are you … head of his fan club or something?'

She tossed her head, dismissively. 'I just think he's a very well-meaning man … and actually quite charming, in his own way.'

Right ... that's me told then.

***

'Roy … good to see you. Ouch!'

Bruce winced as he tried to smile. His left eye was completely closed and an ugly, purple bruise covered his cheek. His upper lip was split, encrusted in dried blood. As he extended his hand, I could see that his wrist was strapped with surgical binding.

'Christ, Bruce … you look even uglier than usual,' I said, as I shook his hand. In spite of the injury to his wrist he practically crushed my hand in his enormous paw.

'Ha ha! Ouch!' He stood to one side and ushered me into his apartment.

Tracy jumped up from the sofa and rushed towards me, squealing with delight. Her skirt finished a good foot or so above her knees, but at least she had her boobs covered this time. She flung her arms around my neck and planted a kiss on each of my cheeks.

'Lovely to see you, Roy,' she cooed. 'Have you heard about what happened? My Bruce was sooo brave.'

'Well, sort of,' I replied, disentangling myself from her enthusiastic embrace. 'Robert called me; I gather you had another visit from Svetlana's minders.'

'Yeah,' said Bruce, 'two of the bastards … they caught me by surprise this time. Came right up here and just rang my doorbell, bold as brass. As soon as I opened the door they piled into me before I realised what was happening.'

'They came here … right to your own apartment?'

'Uh, huh … one of them smacked me in the face with some sort of cosh while the other went for my stomach with a knuckleduster. Anyway, as soon as I got my bearings I caught the big guy square on the nose with a right hook. It hurt my wrist like hell – he held it up to display the strapping – but I heard his nose go splat, and he went down like a sack of potatoes … blood everywhere there was. Look at the state of our sheepskin rug.' He indicated the crumpled, crimson-stained heap alongside the front door.

'Oh, Christ, Bruce, you—'

He interrupted me. 'And Tracy was just brilliant, weren't you babe? Tell Roy what you did.'

She preened. 'I grabbed one of Bruce's golf clubs; he always keeps them there' – she indicated the set of clubs in a bag propped up in the hall – 'and whacked the other bastard over the back of the head.'

'She did a proper job on him too,' declared Bruce. 'Look at this.' He stepped into the kitchen for a moment and reappeared clutching the remains of the weapon in question. The shaft had snapped clean in half where it had evidently impacted upon the intruder's head.

'Ouch,' I said, 'I'll bet that hurt.'

'Fat bastard squealed like a pig and ran for the door holding his head with both hands,' said Tracy, beaming proudly.

'Yeah … beaten up by a girl!' added Bruce. 'But Tracy's not just any girl,' he said, placing a protective arm around her shoulders, 'she's special.' She tilted her head upwards, smiling into Bruce's battered face. 'Anyway I gave the other fooker – who was still curled up on the floor, whining – a good kicking for ruining our rug, before he finally crawled out of the door.'

'I … I really don't know what to say,' I stammered … and I didn't. Everything Bruce – and Tracy – had done was in direct contravention of what I had asked, and yet … well they had, in the end, resolved a problem which could have dragged on for months or years had it been tackled my way.

'You don't need to say nothing, Roy. I'm just glad that the bitch has finally gone.'

'Well, yes … so am I,' I admitted. 'I guess thanks are in order.'

'Aw, it was nothing,' said Bruce.

'Look,' I said, 'Donna's asked me to invite you both over to have dinner with us one evening.'

'She's a diamond, that wife of yours,' said Bruce, 'and pretty hot too, for an older bird.' His face began to crack into a smile, but he quickly suppressed the gesture, wincing painfully.

'Bruuuce!' cried Tracy, punching him on the upper arm, 'you can't say that about Roy's wife.'

'Oh, sorry … I meant it as a compliment.'

And I'm sure he really did. It was just impossible to take offence at the sometimes-indelicate comments that this likeable rogue often came out with.

'I'll tell her what you said,' I replied, smiling, 'I'm sure she'll take it in the sprit intended.'

'Nooo …' squealed Tracy, 'you can't tell her that!'

'Alright then … I won't,' I chuckled. 'Anyway, could you make next Saturday?'

'For Donna,' declared Bruce, 'I'll clear my diary of all other commitments.' Tracy punched him on the arm again.

As I turned to leave, Bruce placed a restraining hand on my shoulder. 'Before you go, Roy, I've got something to ask you.'

'You have? What's that?'

'It's ... well ... me and Tracy ... we've ... well, what we're planning ... it's well—'

'Oh, for Goodness' sake, Bruce,' interjected Tracy, 'tell him.' She held her left hand in front of my face, spreading her fingers to display an impressively large diamond on the third finger.

Bruce still appeared to be dumbstruck so Tracy continued. 'We're getting married!'

'Married?' I repeated, dumbly. 'I ... well, congratulations!'

'Well, ask him then,' prompted Tracy digging Bruce in the ribs with her elbow.'

He finally found his voice. 'We'd ... well, we like you to be Best Man.'

Chapter 40

Donna, Kate, and Angelique had gone out for a ladies' lunch together. It was remarkable how well the three women got on together considering the diversity in their ages, backgrounds, and nationalities but, for whatever reason, they really did seem to gel. Paul and I took the opportunity to go for a beer and a *bocadillo* at *La Esquina de Pedro* – a little bar just a short walk from the urbanisation – and take stock of the latest status of community matters.

The court case against Alfredo González and his duplicitous brother had finally been heard, and the decision had gone in our favour. That was the good news. The bad news was that we had been awarded just fifty-three thousand euros – the exact sum which the court surveyor had come up with: well short of the one hundred and twenty thousand claimed, and a country mile away from the likely actual cost of construction, which was now looking as though it could easily top two hundred and fifty thousand. My mind went back once more to the image of Alfredo handing over that fat, brown envelope to the court surveyor. I was rapidly becoming very much wiser as to the way things were done in Spain.

The chances of our being able to refund to owners any of the money they had contributed to the project now looked very slim. Indeed, it was touch and go whether we would even have enough to complete the job without seeking yet another contribution from owners. Furthermore, although the González brothers had been ordered by the court to pay the sum awarded, no money had yet been forthcoming, even though more than two weeks had elapsed since the judgement.

The construction of the wall itself was now running very late. A further, unseasonal bout of heavy rain, together with the inevitable, unexpected snags which tend to beset any construction project, had combined to put the project some eight weeks behind schedule. I was now fully expecting the original completion timescale of three months to stretch to something like double that time. At least we should be able to claw back some of the escalating costs by invoking the penalty clauses in the contract.

Still, amid all the doom and gloom, we had made a few small steps forward: Dr Ramani had finally paid up, as indeed, had most of the other debtors, and – mostly due to Bruce's efforts – we had rid the urbanisation of the beautiful, but extremely antisocial prostitute, Svetlana Petrov.

On the latter subject, Paul was a touch ambivalent. 'It's a shame that situation turned so ugly. I'm sure that, with a bit of patient diplomacy, we could have resolved most of the issues.' He took a sip of his beer, setting down his glass and gazing wistfully across the little square.

'For Christ's sake Paul,' I said, exasperated, 'she's a *hooker*; she brought her minders in to beat up her neighbour. How the hell can you negotiate with someone like that?'

'I suppose you're right,' he murmured, cradling his chin between forefinger and thumb and stroking the stubble there, 'but you have to admit she seemed quite cooperative when we went to see her ... and she is rather—'

I cut him off. 'Paul, she was playing us, pure and simple. She's got the looks, the figure, and the guile to wrap most men around her little finger ... especially you, it has to be said.'

'Well, that's a little unfair, I must say.' He sounded quite wounded. 'I didn't exactly notice you ...' His voice tailed off as he broke eye contact and he gazed over my shoulder at something behind me.

'What?' I said. 'What is it?'

He didn't reply, but indicated – by simultaneously dipping his head and raising his eyes – that I should take a look for myself. I swivelled around in my chair to see Alfredo González and his brother settling themselves down just a few tables away. A surge of anger boiled within me, and seconds later, almost without conscious intent, I found myself striding towards their table.

Alfredo's surprised expression quickly gave way to a supercilious, ingratiating smile. 'Why, Mr Groves ... what a surprise. Won't you take a seat?' He indicated one of the two spare seats at the table.

I did so, but wasted no time on pleasantries. 'It seems that our dispute – or at least part of it – has now been resolved by the court. The award of fifty-three thousand euros is, in my view, woefully inadequate, but nevertheless, that is the court's decision.'

'Indeed it is,' he said, nodding sagely.

'So why haven't you paid it?' I demanded. I really wasn't in the mood for subtlety of approach.

He pursed his lips, tilting his head to one side as though giving some thought as to how to frame his answer. Before that answer came, the waiter came over to that table.

'*¿Para beber?*' he asked.

'*Una botella de vino tinto de la casa, por favor,*' replied Alfredo, switching smoothly from his excellent English to his native tongue.

'*¿Tres copas?*' enquired the waiter.

'Will you join us for a glass of wine?' said Alfredo, turning towards me.

'No thank you,' I replied, tersely.

'*Pues ... solo dos copas,*' said Alfredo. The waiter nodded and withdrew smartly; I had the distinct impression that he had sensed the simmering tension.

'So why haven't you paid the money awarded by the court?' I repeated.

'Because,' he said, fixing me with an icy stare, 'I intend to appeal the court's decision.'

'Appeal?' I gasped. 'But the award is less than half of what we claimed, and less than a quarter of what the job is actually going to cost.'

He shrugged. 'It was your decision to go for such a ridiculously over-engineered structure. I offered you a perfectly good solution which could have been implemented without the need to involve the courts at all.'

'Perfectly good?' I spluttered. 'Your "perfectly good" wall fell down as soon as we experienced heavy rain, wrecking a car in the process. It's only down to good luck that no-one was injured or killed.'

'Oh, please ... don't be so melodramatic.'

I clenched my fists in exasperation. 'Look, you know full well that the sticking-plaster repair which you proposed was never going to hold back that weight of earth. You also know full well that the cost of a proper retaining wall is going to be way more than the fifty-three thousand which you cooked up with the court surveyor.' *Damn!* I hadn't intended to put it quite so bluntly, but the words, once uttered, could not be withdrawn.

Alfredo's dark eyes narrowed and his chin took on a determined set. 'If you are suggesting that I would bribe a court-appointed expert, then that is a very serious accusation.'

I wasn't going to give him the satisfaction of hearing me repeat the word 'bribe'. 'Look, I am not going to sit here arguing the toss with you over what is, or isn't an appropriate technical solution. The court has determined that fifty-three thousand is the sum you have to pay, so why can't you just accept that decision and pay up with good grace?'

'Because,' he growled, 'I only accept responsibility for repairing the small section of the wall which failed. I accept no responsibility for funding unnecessary improvements to the rest of the wall.'

That was it: my barely-contained anger bubbled over. I rose to my feet, leaning forward and jabbing the air with my forefinger. 'You, sir, are a disgrace to your profession, and I will fight you every step of the way on this.' He recoiled, his chair scraping noisily on the ground as he pushed it back, involuntarily.

Within seconds, he too rose to his feet. 'Do what you like,' he snarled, his lip curling downward at one corner. 'You will find that I don't roll over easily.'

'Why, you—' I felt a firm grasp on my shoulders, pulling me backwards.

'Leave it Roy,' came Paul's commanding tone. 'It's a waste of time trying to reason with him.'

With some difficulty, I managed to regain control, and allowed myself to be guided gently back to our own table.

'Come on, let's get out of here,' said Paul, flinging a fifty euro note down on the table alongside our half-eaten *bocadillos*, and weighting it down with an ashtray.

***

An hour, and three cans of beer later, I was feeling somewhat mellower, as we sat in Paul's lounge discussing the implications of Alfredo's latest move.

'Do you think the bastard really expects to get out of paying altogether?' I mused.

'I doubt it,' said Paul. 'The way I see it is this: he probably realised from the outset that he had no chance of actually winning the case, so his strategy is to try to minimise the amount he has to pay, and to delay that payment for as long as possible. He starts by bribing the court surveyor to undervalue the cost of repairs – and hence the amount he is ordered to pay – and then appeals the decision of the court in order to spin the whole thing out for as long as he possibly can.'

'Hmm … you're probably right, but what I don't get is that by the time he's paid whatever it cost to buy off the surveyor, and racked up yet more legal costs associated with the appeal procedure, he'll probably end up paying almost as much as if he'd just played it straight in the first place. Why's he persisting with this crap?'

Paul pursed his lips and inclined his head, pausing a moment before answering. 'I think Marysa was probably right when she suggested that the whole thing has now become personal for Alfredo. You've seen what he's like – the archetypal Spanish macho male for whom backing down is unthinkable.'

Paul was dead right, I knew he was, but before I could reply, my mobile trilled in my pocket.

'Oh, hi Marysa … tell me you've got some good news for a change.'

'I'm afraid not.'

Now there's a surprise.

'OK,' I sighed, 'so what's up then?'

'I gather you had a meeting with the developer earlier today.'

'Well, hardly a meeting; Paul and I bumped into him by accident while having lunch. Have you heard that the bastard is planning to appeal the court decision?'

'Yes, I just got a call from his lawyer.'

'His lawyer … why would his lawyer be phoning you directly? Surely the appeal process will be handled between his lawyer and ours?'

'It will, but he wasn't phoning to discuss the appeal process; he says that you threatened his client.'

'Threatened him? But that's ridiculous … I just tried to reason with him and get him to pay what the court ordered him to pay.'

'He says he has witnesses that you threatened to punch him in the face.'

'That's absurd,' I spluttered. 'Who are these so-called "witnesses"?'

'His brother, the architect—'

'His bloody brother is as crooked as he is,' I protested, cutting her off before she could complete her sentence. 'Who else?'

'The bar owner … one Pedro Gomez Ruiz.'

'Well, I wouldn't be surprised if bloody González slipped him a backhander to support his story,' I fumed.

'More than likely,' agreed Marysa, her voice characteristically emotionless. 'Anyway, the lawyer says that his client has agreed to overlook the incident on this occasion, on condition that you desist from any further direct contact. All further communication is to be lawyer to lawyer. He says that if you fail to comply with this instruction, he will have no option but to involve the police.'

Un-fucking-believable! I was silent for several long seconds, stunned by the sheer audacity of the Spaniard.

When I eventually found my voice, I was surprised to find that my anger had largely subsided. This was a game: not the type of game which I liked to play, but which I now realised I had to learn.

'You know that this is all a crock of shit, don't you,' I said. I had, long since, stopped making any concessions to the fact that English was not Marysa's first language, and I knew that my colloquial turn of phrase would not be lost on her.

'Of course it is,' she agreed. 'He's just trying to wind you up and muddy the waters surrounding the real case.'

Wind me up? Muddy the waters? Now who's fluently producing English colloquialisms? I had to smile, in spite of my less-than-cheerful mood.

'In any event,' she continued, you'd be well advised to stay out of his way and just let the legal process take its course.'

'However long that might take,' I added, ruefully.

Chapter 41

Donna and I had just finished a light lunch out on our terrace and were relaxing with our coffees. The October sunshine was still very warm in the middle of the day

'Seems almost too good to be true,' I mused, setting down my cup and settling back into my chair.

'What does?' enquired Donna.

'Well it's over a week now since my run-in with Alfredo González and since then everything's been so ... well, quiet.'

She inclined her head, giving an enquiring frown. 'What do you mean?'

'Well, I've heard nothing further from González; there's been no comeback from Svetlana Petrov, or her heavies; and even Dr Ramani seems to have gone quiet now. It's almost as if some sort of normality has settled over the place.'

Donna laughed. 'And what's more, it looks as though the new wall is almost complete now.'

'True, although it's touch and go whether we'll have enough cash to make the final payment for it. I'll really need to push the builder hard on penalty clauses.'

'Hmm ... well you've got plenty of ammunition on that point.' She paused for a few moments, looking thoughtful. 'You know there's someone else who seems to have gone unusually quiet just recently.'

'Uh-huh?'

'Julia.'

She was right: we hadn't heard a sound from Julia or her corpulent canine companion for almost a week. This was unprecedented. 'Well, now you come to mention it ...'

'Do you think she's alright?'

Now Julia's welfare wasn't exactly top of my agenda, but I had to admit that it did seem very strange that things were so quiet down there. Maybe she had had a heart attack and her body lay decomposing on the floor with her faithful dog lying alongside her, itself now surviving only on its generous fat reserves. It wasn't a particularly appealing image.

'Well, it does make you wonder,' I said. 'Do you think I should go down and check whether she's OK.

'It might be an idea. I know she's not our favourite person but, well, she's still our neighbour.'

I nodded, sighing heavily. 'I'll go down right now, but if all I get is a mouthful of abuse ...'

'Go on then. I'll clear up.'

As I approached Julia's apartment it was immediately obvious that something was wrong: the front door was open and the window alongside had been smashed. I was instantly on the alert.

I had no idea what I would find inside the apartment, but instinctively felt the need for something which could serve as a weapon if necessary. My eyes settled on the stone Buddha which I had previously used to bang on the door on the night of Julia's party; I picked it up and hefted it in my hand, shifting its position until I had a firm grip. I stepped forward and pushed the door a little further open, edging cautiously through it, my heart hammering furiously. The first thing that struck me was an overpowering, noxious smell. I tiptoed forward – Buddha at the ready – towards the lounge.

The sight which met my eyes was one of utter chaos. Most of the furniture had been upturned, there was spray paint all over the walls, and the glass patio door had been smashed. In the centre of the floor was a huge pile of excrement – evidently the source of the all-pervasive smell which filled the apartment. It looked too large to have been deposited by Julia's dog, even though I knew, from past experience, that the animal was capable of producing a surprisingly large volume of the stuff. In any event, it was dried and congealed, as though it had been there for some days.

I looked around, anxiously, for any sign that an intruder might still be lurking, but found none; this wanton destruction seemed to have been inflicted some time ago. My racing heartbeat began to settle a little, and I set down my improvised weapon.

How could this have happened without Donna and I hearing something? I could only suppose that it must have happened while we were out. But then, surely another neighbour would have heard something? Even as the thought crossed my mind, I was reminded of just how determined were some of the residents to turn a blind eye – or, in this case, ear – to anything which didn't directly affect them.

But what had happened to Julia? A swift search of the apartment revealed that there was no sign of her, or her dog. Had she been kidnapped? Unlikely, I thought – somewhat uncharitably, I suppose – that anyone would pay much of a ransom. Maybe she had disturbed the intruders, been murdered, and the body removed. Christ, this was serious: I decided to go straight back to my own apartment and call the police.

***

Both of the police officers spoke English, one of them virtually perfectly. I was constantly surprised by how many people in positions of authority in the area spoke such good English but, given that foreigners actually outnumbered native Spaniards in this part of Spain, and English had become the common-denominator language in the area, I suppose it was more or less part of the job.

After briefly surveying the scene of destruction, neither of them had any desire to linger in Julia's apartment a moment longer than necessary. As we stepped outside the front door to escape the nauseating stench, one of the policemen removed the handkerchief he had been holding over his nose and mouth, and gratefully sucked in a lungful of fresh air. His colleague – the one who spoke excellent English – was evidently made of sterner stuff; he merely wrinkled his nose before beginning to question me.

'So,' he began, 'how did you discover that this apartment had been wrecked?'

'Well, I live just upstairs in the next block, and normally, I frequently see – and hear – the comings and goings of my neighbour who lives here. Things seemed to have been very quiet for around a week, so I decided to come down this afternoon and see if she was alright.'

'A week,' he repeated, his brow creasing as he stroked his chin. 'But do you know when the damage was actually done?'

'No ... as I said, things have been unusually quiet for about a week, but I couldn't say when this actually happened.'

'You didn't hear anything? Sounds of breaking glass, crashing and banging?'

'No. Maybe we were out when it happened ... I don't know.'

He stared into my eyes for a second or two, before pausing to scribble a few notes in his book.

After perhaps twenty seconds, he resumed the questioning. 'I assume you know the identity of the person who lives here?'

'Yes. Her name is Julia Petchnik.'

He jotted down the name.

'Not a Spanish citizen then, judging by the name?'

'I don't think so ... Eastern European I believe.'

'A friend of yours?'

A friend? Give me a break.

'No, just a neighbour – and to be honest, not a very nice neighbour.'

'Not nice?' said the policeman, inclining his head and narrowing his eyes. 'In what way?'

'She's noisy, antisocial, and rude,' I said – regretting that I had volunteered this opinion almost as soon as the words had left my mouth.

'But you were concerned enough about her to come and investigate when you hadn't seen or heard her for a few days?'

'Well, yes. I may not like her, but she's still my neighbour, and I wouldn't want to see anything happen to her.'

The policeman paused for a few seconds and made another brief note in his book.

'So is this' – he consulted his book – 'Julia Petchnik the registered owner of the property?'

'No, she rents it.'

'Do you know the identity of the landlord?'

Do I? I've been locked in battle with the bastard for well over a year.

'His name is Alfredo González. He's head of the development company which built this urbanisation; it's called *Hermanos González Promociónes.*

'You seem to know a great deal about the lady's landlord,' suggested the policeman. 'How is that?'

I sighed. 'I am president of this urbanisation. Alfredo González is responsible for some shoddy and dangerous building defects. Our community is involved in a long-running legal battle over these issues. As president, I'm pretty much in the front line in this dispute.'

'I see,' said the policeman, nodding thoughtfully. 'So would I be right in assuming that your relationship with this Alfredo González is not a particularly friendly one?'

'Yes you would,' I agreed, 'but I fail to see what that has to do with this incident.

He shrugged. 'I am just trying to gather as much background information as possible to help us with our enquiries.' He paused again for a few seconds. 'So is there anything else which you think might help us?'

I considered this question for a few seconds before replying. 'No, I don't think so. I believe I've told you everything I know.'

He nodded, and closed his notebook. 'Thank you, Mr Groves. You have been most helpful.' He glanced at his colleague, who had remained silent throughout the whole exchange. '*Vamonos.*'

Even with my limited Spanish, I knew this meant they were about to leave. 'Will you let me know what you find out?' I said.

'Of course,' he said with an insincere-looking smile, 'or you can call me on this number.' He passed me a card bearing the name 'Manuel Moreno'.

A few moments later, they were gone.

Just what *had* taken place in that apartment ... and more to the point, what had happened to Julia?

Chapter 42

Finally, the wall was finished!

The job had taken almost six months to complete – as opposed to the three months originally estimated – and the cost had escalated from the original quotation of two hundred and thirty-three thousand euros to an eye-watering three hundred and ten thousand, as various unforeseen costs had arisen during the course of the project. However, the saving grace was that the penalty clauses – which, according to my calculations, would claw back around fifty thousand euros – would offset much of the cost overrun.

Donna and I were due to travel to England in less than a week's time for the birth of our daughter's baby and I was anxious to tie up the final agreement about costs and penalty clauses before I left. Paul and I had therefore set up a meeting that morning with Julio Montoya, the head of the building contractor, and Alejandro Cuadrado, the architect whom we had employed to design the new wall. I had asked that Sergio also attend – since he had been instrumental in introducing us to both architect and builder – but he had declined, citing a prior engagement. Marysa said that she would come in his place. The meeting was to be held on-site in the security guards' office.

I had about an hour and a half spare before the meeting was due to start, and I wanted to use that time to follow up on another issue which was troubling me. It was now almost a week since the police had begun their investigation into the mysterious circumstances surrounding Julia's disappearance, and I had heard absolutely nothing. Seriously worried now, I decided to call the number on the card that the policeman had given me. The phone rang and rang, with no reply. I was about to hang up when Officer Manuel Moreno's voicemail finally cut in. I left a message saying I was concerned about Julia and would appreciate any information they could give me. About forty minutes later, Officer Moreno called me back.

When I asked if there was any news about Julia, his response was rather cryptic. 'The case is now closed.'

'Closed? So what happened?'

'We understand that your neighbour had not been paying her rent for some time, so your ... friend ... Alfredo González served an eviction notice on her.'

'Oh ... but how does that explain ... I mean who trashed the place ... and what has happened to Julia?'

'It seems that she did not wait for the eviction date, but decided to leave of her own accord. Before she left, though, she decided to smash the place up to let her landlord know what she thought of him.'

'She did all that herself? Including the spray paint on the walls and ...'

He seemed to have read my mind. 'And the shit on the floor,' he confirmed.

The image which popped up in my head was a distinctly disturbing one: Julia's corpulent frame squatting in the middle of the floor as she strained to deposit the maximum possible volume of excrement as a farewell message to Alfredo. Eeeuw! I shook my head in an effort to dismiss the unwelcome vision.

'So where is she now?'

'She is in police custody; she has been charged with causing criminal damage.'

'So this was just a dispute between Julia Petchnik and Alfredo González then? There was no third party involved?'

'So it seems,' agreed the policeman.

Couldn't have happened to two more deserving people, I thought.

'Well, thank you for the update,' I said. 'I guess you won't need to talk to me again, then?'

'No,' he confirmed. 'It is what I believe you English call an "open-and-shut case".'

'OK, thanks.'

He hung up.

I could hardly believe it: my arch-enemy, Alfredo González, had, for once, actually done me a favour. *I'll bet that stuck in his craw*, I mused. Furthermore, the obnoxious Julia had finally received her just rewards for her constantly antisocial behaviour.

So there it was again: in the strange Salsa-like dance which characterised horizontal living, one step backward followed by one – or in this case, two – steps forward.

***

It was the first time I had actually met Julio Montoya face-to-face, and I have to say I took an almost instant dislike to the man. His unkempt, shoulder-length black hair framed a slim, olive-toned face which was almost feminine in the delicacy of its features. His voice held a disturbingly-high timbre and his eyes darted this way and that, never actually making proper contact with mine, even when I was speaking directly to him. He certainly didn't match my stereotypical image of a Spanish builder. At least his English was good, so there was no need for lengthy and potentially ambiguity-inducing translation.

'So,' I said, once initial pleasantries had been dispensed with, 'I believe we have agreed all the additional costs, over and above your original quotation, but now we need to discuss the penalty clauses.'

'Of course,' he said, dipping his head deferentially.

Oh, I thought, *maybe we're not actually going to have a fight here, after all.* He seemed to be waiting for me to continue, so I proceeded to set out my case.

'The contract,' I began, 'sets out a completion timescale of thirteen weeks.'

I waited for some acknowledgement, agreement, or denial but, as none was forthcoming, I continued.

'Well, according to my diary notes, the actual time taken was twenty-five weeks: an overrun of twelve weeks.'

Still, Julio Montoya said nothing, but sat impassively, avoiding eye contact. I pressed on with my argument.

'The terms of the contract specify penalty payments of six hundred euros for each day's overrun. Twelve weeks equates to eighty-four days, which at six hundred euros per day comes to a total of fifty thousand four hundred euros.'

Silence reigned.

After several awkward seconds of silence, I prompted Montoya for a response. 'Do I take it that you agree with my calculations?'

Finally he raised his eyes to meet mine. Unusually for a Spaniard, his eyes, fringed by surprisingly long, curled lashes, were a quite vivid shade of blue.

'I'm afraid, Mr Groves, that there are a number of errors in your analysis.'

OK, here comes the fight after all, I thought, my previous optimism rapidly evaporating.

'So, enlighten me then.'

'Firstly,' he said, tapping the forefinger of his right hand against the palm of his left, 'the timescale originally specified for the project was ninety days, not thirteen weeks.'

'But it's the same thing isn't it?' I said, puzzled.

'Oh no,' he responded, 'it is standard practice in contracts of this nature to refer to working days only – Saturdays and Sundays don't count.'

I looked across at Alejandro Cuadrado, who had drawn up the contract on our behalf; he nodded, quickly averting his eyes from my gaze. Montoya continued setting out his argument.

'Ninety days therefore amounts to eighteen weeks, not thirteen.'

I was totally wrong-footed by this revelation, and more than a little annoyed that Alejandro, who knew full well what I was going to put forward at the meeting, had not warned me about it. My previous suspicions of collusion between the architect and the builder came flooding back. I wasn't going to fold just yet though.

'Even if what you say is correct – and by the way, I am not accepting that until I have had the contract checked by our lawyer – the project was still' – I made a swift mental calculation – 'seven weeks late.'

Montoya shook his head slowly, in the manner of someone trying to explain to a small child something which was clearly too complex for it to understand. 'You are forgetting about the exclusions for interruptions due to bad weather.'

I glanced at Alejandro, who nodded guiltily before turning away.

'So tell me about it,' I muttered.

'Well, as you are aware, there were two lengthy interruptions due to heavy rain, which together caused' – he glanced at the notebook which lay open on the table in front of him – 'five weeks, or thirty-five days, delay.'

'Hold on there,' interjected Paul, his powerful voice booming across the room. 'A minute ago there were five days in a week and now, when it suits you, there are seven. You can't have it both ways.'

'Ah,' said Montoya, his high-pitched voice contrasting sharply with Paul's baritone boom, 'the weather is no respecter of working days or weekends.'

'That is a preposterous argument,' protested Paul. 'If weekends are not to be counted as working days then how is rain at the weekend supposed to be interrupting work?'

Montoya shrugged, but did not proffer an answer. I had another point to make, though.

'Correct me if I'm wrong,' I said, 'but I believe it only actually rained for three days out of the five weeks you mention.'

Montoya spread his hand and raised his eyebrows. 'But that doesn't alter the fact that work was interrupted for a full five weeks.'

'But that,' I insisted, 'was because of *your* decision to spread a four-foot layer of earth over the entire site and *your* failure to protect it from the weather.'

Montoya maintained his infuriating posture, shoulders raised and head inclined to one side in a 'how many times do I need to explain this?' sort of gesture. 'Standard practice in the building industry,' he said, 'in order to protect the client's road surface.'

'Well it may be standard practice,' I snapped, 'but I'm damned if I'll accept it as an excuse to wriggle out of the penalty clauses.'

He completely ignored my last remark, evidently determined to complete setting out his argument. 'So,' he concluded, 'the total delay was seven weeks, or thirty-five days' – he had conveniently switched back to calculating on the basis of a five-day week when it suited his purpose – 'and, as I explained earlier, that thirty-five days is entirely accounted for by interruptions due to bad weather, so in fact the project was completed exactly according to the originally-quoted timescale.'

I was, quite literally, lost for words. The man's creativity and ingenuity in the interpretation of the contract was nothing short of breathtaking.

Paul, however was ready to step in. 'Your arguments are absurd – the simple fact is that the project took twice as long as you promised.'

Montoya shrugged again. 'I've explained my position: everything has been completed correctly according to the terms of the contract.'

Marysa and Alejandro had hardly said a word during the entire exchange, which irritated me considerably. 'Marysa? Alejandro? Do either of you have anything to add to this ridiculous debate?'

Alejandro looked away, guiltily, shaking his head.

'No,' said Marysa, her expression unchanging, 'not at this stage.'

I looked back across the table at Julio Montoya. 'Then I suggest we adjourn this meeting for now. I intend to have the contract carefully examined by our lawyer and I will arrange a further meeting once I have his opinion.'

'As you wish,' said Montoya, his expression untroubled.

Smug bastard, I thought, but in spite of his arrogant stance I had at least one ace in my hand: so far, we had paid only fifty percent of the originally quoted two hundred and thirty three euros. The rest was to be paid upon satisfactory completion of the job.

'I should inform you,' I said 'that until this matter is resolved we will be making no further payments, so it is in your interest, as well as ours, to negotiate in good faith.'

That seemed to shake him out of his smug, self-satisfied frame of mind – at last I could detect a flare of anger in those feminine, blue eyes. When he replied, his voice had elevated another couple of semitones in pitch.

'I am warning you, Mr Groves, it would not be wise to pick a fight with me. I have completed my side of our contract and I expect you to complete yours. If not, there will be severe consequences.'

'Consequences?' I repeated. 'That sounds rather like a threat.'

In barely a second, the blaze in his eyes was gone as he regained control.

'No threat,' he said, smiling unpleasantly, 'just a reminder that I expect both parties to honour their commitments.'

I had, by now, had more than enough of this unproductive verbal sparring, I closed the folder in front of me and pushed my chair back, getting ready to stand up and signal clearly that the meeting was over. 'I'll be in touch again once—'

There was a firm rapping on the door of the office. Paul was nearest the door and stood up to open it. Two policemen stood outside. They wore the uniforms of the *Policía Nacional*, the national police force, rather than the local police. This was more than a little concerning, as this branch of the police normally only got involved in crimes of a serious nature. Surely this couldn't have anything to do with Julia's situation could it? After all, Officer Moreno had told me, that very morning, that it was an "open-and-shut case". I was immediately on edge.

'May we come in?' said the taller of the two men, in excellent, barely-accented English.

Looking at the stern expressions on the men's faces, and the bulky handguns at their sides, I didn't think it would be a terribly good idea to refuse such a request. 'Of course,' I said, ushering them forward. 'What can we do for you?'

'We would like to speak with Mr Roy Groves.'

Oh, oh! I don't like the sound of this. What the fuck am I supposed to have done?

'That's me,' I said. 'What seems to be the problem?'

The tall man withdrew from his pocket a photograph and handed it to me. 'Do you recognise this man, Mr Groves?'

There was no mistaking the dark, brooding eyes staring out from the swarthy complexion. 'Well, yes ...' I replied, haltingly, 'that is Alfredo González. He is head of the development company which built this urbanization.'

'When did you last see him?'

'Er ... well, about six or eight weeks ago I suppose, when Paul and I bumped into him at Pedro's bar just down the road.' I glanced at Paul, who nodded in confirmation of my estimate.

'And you haven't seen him again since then?' persisted the policeman.

'No, I haven't ... look, what's this all about?' I said, puzzled.

'He's been murdered.'

Chapter 43

'Murdered?' I repeated, shocked, 'but why … I mean who would …?'

'We'd like you to accompany us to the police station to answer a few questions.'

'But why? How can I possibly help you?'

'We'd just like to ask you a few questions,' he repeated.

This was happening too fast; I couldn't take it all in. Finally it dawned on me. 'You surely don't think that … that I had anything to do with this?'

Neither policeman actually answered my question. 'Please … it will be far better if we can continue this conversation at the police station.'

'Well, yes … if that's what you want, but I can't imagine that there's any way I can help with this.'

'Please come this way,' said the policemen, lightly clutching my upper arm and leading me towards the door.

'Do you want me to come with you?' said Paul.

The policeman didn't give me a chance to answer. 'That will not be necessary,' he said, holding up his hand, palm-outwards, in a restraining gesture.

'It's OK, Paul,' I said, 'I'm sure this is just some sort of misunderstanding.'

'Do you want me to let Donna know where you've gone?'

'Yes … thanks.'

'OK ... give me a call if you need me.'

***

The room was unwelcoming and dingy, walls and ceiling sharing the same yellowish-brown tone. The sole source of natural light was from a single window set high in the wall, through which a shaft of sunlight picked out the millions of dust particles floating in its path. The meagre illumination supplied by this window was supplemented by a small desk lamp on the table in front of me.

I had been sitting alone for around a quarter of an hour, during which time my level of anxiety had been ratcheting up by the minute. Why would they have dragged me down here unless they suspected that I was involved in Alfredo's murder? But then why would they suspect that I had? Surely they couldn't have anything which might implicate me? Maybe they were just interviewing everyone who had had any sort of recent dealings with the man. Yes, that had to be it: just casting the net wide in the hope of turning something up. I'd probably just have to answer a few questions to clear up any misunderstanding about my relationship with the developer and I'd be out of there and on my way. As I worked through this rationalisation of the situation, I began to relax a little.

The door opened and two men entered the room. They were not the policemen who had brought me in but plain-clothes officers, clad in sombre business suits.

'Hello Mr Groves,' said the shorter of the two men, as he extended his hand. I shook it, without, it has to be said, much enthusiasm. 'I am *Inspector Jefe* Rafael Abascal, and my colleague here is *Inspector* Victor Chavez. The taller man nodded but said nothing, withdrawing to a chair in the corner of the room as his senior colleague sat down opposite me.

'Cigarette?' said Abascal, withdrawing a packet of cigarettes from his pocket and pulling one halfway out of the pack before offering it to me across the table.

I shook my head. 'No thanks ... I don't smoke.'

He shrugged and took the cigarette from the pack, placing it between his own lips before rummaging in his pocket for a lighter. He appeared to be in no hurry to ask me any questions as he tried, repeatedly, to coax a flame from the lighter, without success.

'Damned cheap rubbish,' he grumbled, turning to his colleague, holding the cigarette in the air. 'Victor ... would you mind?'

The other man stepped forward, producing from his pocket a proper, chrome-plated lighter – rather more impressive-looking than his boss's disposable affair. It lit on the first click.

'*Gracias.*'

'*De nada, Jefe.*' The tall man melted back into the shadows in the corner of the room.

Abascal took a deep draw, holding the smoke inside for several long seconds before sighing deeply as he expelled it in my direction. I coughed involuntarily as the acrid fumes enveloped my face.

'So sorry, Mr Groves,' he said, looking anything but.

Smoking was, in fact, banned by law in all public places in Spain which, in my opinion, was a blessed relief after experiencing the choking fug which used to pervade bars and restaurants before the new law was passed. Did a police station count as a public place? I wasn't entirely sure, but decided that to raise the issue there and then probably wasn't a terribly good idea. I said nothing, but attempted a weak smile as I struggled to suppress a further bout of coughing.

The wretched man still seemed in no hurry to actually start the interview, so I decided to prompt him. 'Your uniformed colleague explained to me that Alfredo González has been murdered. Shocking … absolutely shocking.'

He regarded me for several seconds with dark, unblinking eyes. 'Indeed,' was his eventual, cryptic response.

'I'll do anything I possibly can to assist you with your enquiries, but I really don't think I can be of much help. I hardly know the man … I mean *knew* him, of course.'

The detective eyed me in silence for a few more seconds before continuing. 'So what was your relationship with Alfredo González?'

'Well, I suppose you'd call it a business relationship. His company built our urbanisation, and there are some outstanding warranty issues to be resolved. As president of the community, I am dealing … I mean, I *was* dealing with him on these issues.'

'I understand you were in dispute with him over the question of a retaining wall.'

'Yes … the wall started to collapse and he refused to cover the matter under warranty.'

'So you took him to court.' It wasn't a question – the detective clearly knew exactly what was going on.

'Well it wasn't me who actually initiated the legal action – that was my predecessor, Jim Watkins – but yes, I picked up the matter when I took over from Jim.'

'Has the court case been heard yet?'

'Yes.'

'And what was the outcome?'

As if you don't already know, you smug bastard. 'We won the case; he was ordered to pay fifty-three thousand euros.'

'So you must have been quite pleased about that.'

'Not really – the actual cost of repairs has turned out to be around three hundred thousand.'

'Oh,' said the detective, raising an eyebrow in a pretty poor impression of a man who has learned something he didn't already know, 'so perhaps you were not very happy with him after all?'

'No, I wasn't ... particularly since I'm damned sure he bribed the court surveyor to undervalue the cost of repairs.'

Abascal took a deep draw of his cigarette, savouring the smoke for a few seconds before tilting his head upwards and expelling it in a long slow stream which curled lazily in the shaft of sunlight cast by the single window. At least it didn't go straight into my face this time. He extinguished the stub, grinding it into the ashtray in the centre of the table with a deliberate, exaggerated circular motion.

'That is a very serious allegation, Mr Groves ... particularly against a dead man who is unable to defend himself. Why did you not report this to the police?'

Oh, Christ, why didn't I keep my big mouth shut? 'I ... I don't know really. I suppose because I didn't have any actual evidence.'

'I see – so this was nothing more than a suspicion on your part.'

'Well no, not just a suspicion: I saw Alfredo hand the surveyor a brown envelope.'

'Oh ... an envelope. And what made you think this envelope contained money?'

'I ... well, it was just after the surveyor's visit, and under the circumstances, it seemed ... suspicious.'

'So, as I said a moment ago, the suggestion that money changed hands was really nothing more than a suspicion on your part.'

Stop digging, Roy. 'Yes,' I conceded, 'I suppose so.'

'I see,' said the detective, lighting another cigarette, drawing on it deeply before turning his head sideways to exhale. He laid the smouldering cigarette down in the ashtray, stroking his chin as he appeared to consider his next question. 'Even so, this suspicion must have made your feelings towards señor González even more antagonistic.'

'I wasn't antagonistic,' I protested. 'Yes, I was annoyed and irritated by his unprofessional approach, but I did my best to keep the relationship civil.'

'Of course,' he said, smiling unpleasantly. 'My poor English, you see.'

There's nothing wrong with your English – you chose your words deliberately to needle me.

Suddenly he changed tack completely. 'So, have you now received the fifty-three thousand euros ordered by the court?'

As if you don't already know.

'No, Alfredo refused to pay – he said he intended to appeal the court decision.'

'Oh dear, that must have upset you even more, I would think.'

Keep calm – just answer the questions – don't let the bastard get to you.

'Yes it did, but I never let my personal feelings interfere with the business relationship.'

'Oh, so you agree that you felt a *personal* antipathy towards this man?'

'I didn't like him, no … but I always kept our business dealings on a professional level.'

The detective paused for a few moments as he leafed through the notes which lay on the table in front of him. He took another drag on his cigarette, holding onto the smoke for a few seconds, as he ground the stub in the ashtray, before expelling it in a long slow stream. He fixed me with a piercing stare.

'I understand that two of the local police visited you just a week ago.'

'Well yes, but that was nothing to do with—'

He raised his hand, cutting me off. 'I am aware of the nature of their visit.' *Well why are you fucking well raising it then?* 'According to their report, you told them that your relationship with señor González was distinctly unfriendly.'

I was getting really worried now. It seemed that this man was determined to find evidence that I had reason to do harm to González. I tried once more to defend my position.

'Look,' I said, 'I've already told you that I didn't like the man, but that was solely because of the underhand way he was approaching our legal dispute. I would never let my feelings towards him stop me from approaching our relationship in anything other than a professional manner.'

'Of course not,' he mused, sounding unconvinced. He paused for a second or two before continuing. 'Tell me … faced with a bill for three hundred thousand euros, and with not even the fifty-three thousand forthcoming from the González brothers, how on earth have you been able to fund the construction of the new wall?'

'Well, we haven't actually paid the whole bill yet – some of the costs have not yet been agreed with the builder – but in answer to your question, I had to ask all the owners to contribute to an extraordinary additional budget to fund the works.'

'Ah, very interesting,' said the detective, nodding slowly, his brow furrowed in a frown. 'Is it not the case that señor González was himself owner of a number of apartments?'

'Yes, but I don't see—'

He didn't let me finish. 'So at least he has had to make *some* contribution towards the cost of building the new wall?'

'Well, no actually – he refused to pay his share and launched a court action against the community, contesting the legality of the vote to implement the supplementary budget.'

'Hmm … most unfortunate,' he said, 'and how did that make you feel?'

Don't let him rile you – just keep answering the questions.

'I was, as I'm sure you can imagine, unhappy about it, but I was content to let the legal process take its course.'

'However long that might take …'

'However long that might take,' I repeated, through gritted teeth.

'Where were you on Thursday 6th of November?'

'Last Thursday? I believe I was at home all day.'

'Can anyone corroborate that?'

'Well, yes … my wife Donna.'

'Your wife … anyone else? Someone independent?'

'I … er … I'm not sure. I'd need to retrace my movements that day to think whether anyone else saw me at home.'

He didn't respond directly to my answer, which admittedly did sound a bit weak, even though it was truthful. Instead he pushed back his chair and stood up, pacing over towards his colleague. The quick-fire exchange in Spanish which followed was way too fast for me to follow.

Eventually, he turned back towards me. 'You are free to go.'

'I can go now?'

'Yes, but we may need to talk to you again. I hope you don't have any travel plans in the immediate future?'

'Well, yes … I do. I'm going back to England in a few days' time. My daughter is about to give birth.'

He shook his head, and waved a forefinger slowly from side to side. 'You need to stay here in Spain until our investigation is complete.'

'But—'

'No "buts" I'm afraid – you must stay here. Do you have your passport with you?'

'Well no … it's at home.'

'Then I will send an officer to your home with you to collect it. We will look after it until our investigation is complete.'

It seemed I had no choice in the matter. I pushed my chair back, preparing to stand.

'Oh, one more thing,' he said. I sank back into my chair. 'I don't believe we discussed the actual method of the murder itself.' He seemed to be studying my face intently now, as though trying to judge my reaction.

'Well, no, but I don't really see how that's relevant to—'

My words stuck in my throat as he laid a photograph on the table. My gaze fixed first upon the bloody pit where the naked man's genitals should have been. My eyes travelled up to his face, where to my horror, a gory mess hung from his mouth dripping blood down his chest and stomach. His cheeks were unnaturally distended by the mass of tissue which had been forced into his mouth. His eyes bulged from their sockets in his death grimace. Only then did I register the rope around the man's neck.

I felt the bile rise uncontrollably in my throat, and a moment later I vomited violently, the stinking mess smothering the obscene photograph on the table and splattering the front of the detective's suit.

Chapter 44

By the following afternoon, the news about the murder was all round the urbanisation. There had been an item in 'Euronews Weekly' – an English-language newspaper distributed along the entire Costa del Sol, aimed primarily at British expats. More disconcertingly, everyone also seemed to be aware that I had been questioned by the police in connection with the murder. Quite how *that* bit of news had spread, I really didn't know. I guessed that someone must have seen me being carted off in a police car the previous day; the very efficient gossip-mill which operated in our community would then have done the rest.

Rafael Abascal had interviewed Donna that morning in our own home. She had confirmed to them that I had been at home all day on the Thursday on which they had estimated the time of the murder to be. Clearly, however, they didn't consider her testimony to be truly independent – not unreasonably, I grudgingly admitted.

I did, however, have some other witnesses to call upon: Paul and Angelique had both seen me at home that day. Paul confirmed that he had been up with us that morning for a coffee and a meeting about some community matters. Angelique had also backed me up, relating that we had had one of our chats across the terrace wall at around 3 p.m. None of this seemed to convince the police, though, that I was beyond suspicion. Evidently they considered it quite feasible that I could have had a meeting with Paul in the morning, then hunted down my quarry, cut off his balls, stuffed them in his mouth, and hung him by the neck – before returning home for a nice lunch, followed by a convivial chat out on the terrace with Angelique.

I must confess, by the way, to feeling a pang of protective jealousy when I saw the hungry leer which spread across Abascal's face when he first set eyes on Angelique. She was, by her own standards, quite modestly dressed, in a knee-length dress with only a hint of cleavage on view, but as I've already explained, she had a knack of looking pretty stunning whatever she wore. Abascal managed to spin out the interview with Angelique for almost a full hour.

After he had gone, Angelique assured me that, as well as confirming that I was at home that afternoon, she had volunteered a character reference, telling the detective what an upright fellow I was and that it was inconceivable that I would commit such a horrific crime. I doubted that she realised just *how* horrific: the gorier details had been omitted in the newspaper article, which simply reported that the developer had been found hanged, in circumstances which suggested murder rather than suicide. I didn't imagine that Abascal would have shared the details with her, and I certainly hadn't.

Anyway, the net upshot of all this activity was ... no change to my situation. They clearly didn't have any actual evidence to connect me with the murder, but I was evidently still considered to be a suspect. They didn't offer to hand my passport back to me.

Donna was distraught. 'How on earth can they possibly think you had anything to do with it?' she sobbed, dabbing her eyes with a tissue.

'I can only assume that they don't have any solid leads. They're probably questioning anyone who might have a possible motive.'

'But, who else are they questioning ... why pick on you?'

I spread my hands, helplessly. 'I don't know – they're hardly likely to tell me who else they're questioning. I'll bet you a pound to a penny, though, that there *will* be others. If his business dealings with us were anything to go by, he'll have had plenty of enemies.'

'I suppose so,' she said, screwing up the tissue and throwing it onto the table alongside the several others which already lay there, sniffing deeply as she sought to regain her composure. 'What are we going to do about our trip to England? We're supposed to be flying the day after tomorrow.'

'I need to stay here,' I said. 'I'm not sure whether they have the legal right to keep me here without arresting me or charging me with anything, but the last thing I want to do is piss them off by trying to defy them.'

'I know,' she said, now starting to sniffle anew, 'but I really don't know how Bea is going to cope, with Rick having to keep working.'

'Why don't you go on your own?' I said. 'I can stay here until this nonsense is cleared up, and then I'll come over to join you. You never know ... if they can cross me off their list within the next few days I might still be able to make it in time for the birth.'

'Are you sure?' she said. 'It's an awful time for me to be leaving you on your own.'

'I'll be fine,' I said, hugging her to me. 'This whole thing is just some godawful misunderstanding ... I'm sure they'll let me off the hook any day now.'

'Well, OK then, I'll go ... but you'll let me know straightaway if there are any developments, won't you?'

I kissed her full on the lips. 'Of course I will. Give Bea my love and tell her to try to hold the baby in until I can be there for the birth.'

Donna didn't laugh at my – admittedly rather forced – attempt at humour; she just hung on to me, her breath coming in short, sharp pulses. She knew me far too well to be fooled by my pitiful attempt to make light of a situation which, in truth, was pretty desperate.

Chapter 45

Seven days had elapsed since I'd dropped Donna off at the airport. Since then she'd called me every day to check whether there had been any further developments in the murder investigation – which there hadn't – and to give me an update on how Bea was doing. The baby was due any day now, but as Bea put it when I had spoken to her earlier, 'The only thing that's happening is that I'm looking more and more like a baby elephant every day.'

For my part, I was getting thoroughly pissed off with being left in limbo. It was quite obvious that the police had no evidence to connect me with the murder, and they hadn't questioned me any further, yet still they wanted me to stick around in case they did need to talk to me again. Marysa had suggested that I should avail myself of the services of the community's lawyer, an offer which I would certainly take up if the police saw fit to question me further.

And it wasn't just the police who viewed me with suspicion. I had noticed a strange change in the way that other residents in the urbanisation regarded me. When I would pass someone while walking down towards the mailbox, instead of a greeting me with a cheery 'Good morning', they would mumble something incomprehensible while avoiding eye contact. The only ones whose attitude towards me appeared unchanged were Paul, Kate, Bruce, Tracy, Neil, Marion, and Angelique. I guess it's under circumstances like this that you find out who your true friends are.

Another aspect of my enforced confinement which was really starting to grate was my diet. Sounds a trivial thing, I know, but I guess I had been spoiled by years of Donna's cooking: proper fresh food, prepared and cooked to perfection. Since she had returned to England the only decent meal I had enjoyed was one evening eating out in Marbella with Neil and Marion. Otherwise I had dined entirely on ready-meals and toasted sandwiches. Cooking, you see, was definitely not my *forte*. This situation was, unbeknown to me though, about to change for the better.

The doorbell rang. It was Angelique; she was casually dressed in jeans and T-shirt, but that didn't prevent her from looking just as arresting as usual. Her stretchy top clung closely to her body and her jeans looked as though they were painted on. Her hair tumbled over her shoulders in careless waves. In an instant, all of my worries seemed that bit less oppressive.

''Alo, Roy,' she said, her face breaking into a dazzling smile, 'can I come in for a moment?'

'Of course,' I said, stepping aside. She came in and greeted me with her customary three kisses on the cheeks.

'Lovely to see you, Angelique. Can I get you a coffee?'

'Zanks,' she said, 'but I won't stay just now ... I 'ave to run Miriam round to 'er friend's 'ouse. As it's Friday, she's going for a –'ow you say it – sleepover?'

'Yes, a sleepover,' I smiled. I couldn't help noticing how much Angelique's English had improved in the short time that I'd known her. The accent hadn't changed though, and it still had the power to turn my knees to jelly. 'So ... what can I do for you?'

'We are both on our own tonight I zink, no?'

'Well, yes ... I guess we are.' I felt a flutter in my stomach as I wondered where this conversation was going.

'I wondered if you would like to 'ave dinner with me?'

Would I like to have dinner with a beautiful woman, who also happened to be great company, or settle for another microwaved curry in front of the TV, dwelling on my current unhappy situation? I pondered this question for about two nanoseconds before arriving at a conclusion.

'I'd love to ... where would you like to go?'

'I zought I might cook for you rather than go out ... if zat's OK with you, of course.'

'Absolutely ... that would be lovely.'

'Do you like *Bouef Borguignon*?'

'One of my favourites,' I replied.

'Good,' she said, flashing a dazzling smile, ''Zen 'zat's what I will cook.' She gave me a quick peck on the cheek, before making to turn towards the front door. 'I must dash now.'

'OK ... er, what time should I come?'

'Oh ... about eight thirty?'

'OK … see you then … and thank you so much for such a lovely invitation.'

She flashed that captivating smile once more and then, with a swirl of her long, dark hair, she was gone.

***

As I contemplated what to wear, I felt rather like a nervous teenager preparing for his first date. Ridiculous for man in his fifties, I know, but there it was.

How about a suit? I only had one suit in Spain, as opposed to the dozens which were gathering dust in my wardrobe back in the UK – a legacy of my former life in business. As I held it up to myself in front the mirror, dangling a couple of possible ties in front of it I quickly rejected the idea: too formal for a meal *en casa*.

OK, well maybe go the other way and plump for a super-casual look. Shorts would be going *too* far … maybe some smart-ish jeans and a polo shirt. But then she might think I hadn't bothered to make much of an effort. Good God, I can't remember the last time I had vacillated so much over a simple thing like choosing what clothes to wear.

I eventually settled for a pair of pale beige trousers – proper ones with creases down the front, mind – and a pale blue formal-style shirt, but open-necked, without a tie. A pair of light brown loafers completed my 'smart casual' look.

It suddenly occurred to me, that in the fifteen minutes or so that I'd been deliberating over my choice of outfit for the evening, the matter of the murder investigation still hanging over my head had not actually crossed my mind once. This woman certainly had the ability to take my mind off other things.

As I stood in front of her door, clutching the bottle of champagne which I'd dashed out to buy that afternoon, I felt irrationally nervous. I made sure that my shirt was properly tucked in and rang the bell.

Well, if I'd gone for the 'smart casual' look, she'd chosen the 'sophisticated sexy' look. She wore an ankle-length dress in a shiny, rich purple fabric; it clung to every curve of her sumptuous figure. She had piled her luxuriant dark locks into a chic 'updo' which allowed her glittering diamond earrings to be displayed to best effect. It was the first time that I had really noticed just how long and slender was her neck. The V-shaped neckline of her dress displayed an enticing, but not too-flagrant amount of cleavage, in which a diamond pendant nestled. Her makeup was just that bit heavier than she usually wore, giving her a dark, sultry look.

''Alo Roy,' she said, smiling, 'come on in.'

My throat was suddenly dry as dust; I swallowed awkwardly, proffering the bottle I was holding. 'I thought you might like some champagne.'

'Oh, zank you … zat's lovely.' She took the bottle and set it down on the table just inside the door before treating me to her usual three-kiss greeting. I followed her into the kitchen as she took the bottle through. The aroma of the food gently simmering on the cooker was delicious.

'Mmm … that smells—'

My words were cut short by a vicious hissing sound behind me. I looked round to see the cat glaring at me with malevolent eyes, its back arched and its tail held stiffly erect. It was quickly joined by another … presumably the kitten which Miriam had decided to keep, though it was now fully-grown. Now while the mother might reasonably hold a grudge against me, since she clearly held me responsible for her near-death experience after plummeting from Angelique's terrace wall, I saw no reason for her offspring to hold me in such contempt. Nevertheless the younger cat took its cue from its mother and emulated her aggressive posture.

'Brigitte, Nicole,' scolded Angelique, 'don't be so rude to our guest.' She gathered them up, one in each arm; the duplicitous little creatures purred and nuzzled up to her, taunting me. 'I don't zink zey like you much,' she informed me, somewhat superfluously.

'Well, just as long as you do …' was my unbelievably clumsy reply.

'I'll put zem in ze spare bedroom,' she said, laughing.

As she settled the venomous beasts in the bedroom, I uncorked the champagne and poured two glasses. I took my first sip before she had even returned, in order to lubricate my parched throat.

'Zere … zey will be 'appy enough in zere for ze evening,' she declared, as she took the glass I offered her.

'Cheers,' I said clinking glasses with her.

'Chin chin,' she responded, taking her first sip. 'Let's go through to ze lounge.'

'But don't you need to keep an eye on the meal?'

'Oh, it can simmer on a low 'eat for a while.' She took my hand and led me into the lounge where she sat alongside me on the sofa. The waft of her perfume infiltrated my senses.

'So 'ow is it going wiz ze police?' she said, tilting her head slightly to one side and crossing her legs, smoothing the silky purple fabric over her thigh to remove the creases which had formed.

'No real change,' I replied. 'They clearly don't have any evidence or I'd have been arrested by now.'

'Well zat's good, at least,' she opined.

'I suppose so,' I responded, 'but equally clearly, I'm still considered a suspect. They still don't want me to travel.'

'And your grandchild is due any time now, no?'

'Yes ... it doesn't seem likely that I'll be able to get back for the birth.'

'Oh, Roy,' she said, placing her hand on top of mine – I felt a distinct *frisson* at her touch – ''ow can zey suspect you of such an 'orrible crime?'

I shrugged. 'I don't know ... I guess they are just following up on anyone who had some sort of dispute with the guy.'

'Well, try not to worry' – she squeezed my hand gently – 'I'm sure zey will soon realise it wasn't you.'

'Let's hope so,' I said, draining my glass.

'Let me top your drink up,' she said, taking my glass and rising to her feet.

Try as I might, I could not tear my eyes from her gently undulating rear end as she moved through to the kitchen. Was she actually exaggerating her walk a little for my benefit? *Don't be ridiculous.*

'I zink ze *Bouef Borguignon* will be ready in about twenty minutes,' she said, as she returned with two full glasses. 'If you'd like to sit up at ze table, I'll get ze starters.'

I did as she asked, and a minute or two later she emerged from the kitchen carrying two small plates. 'It is smoked salmon with a special salad I invented myself,' she said. 'I 'ope you like it.'

I did. It was a lovely, light appetiser with a tangy, lemony flavour – a perfect counterpoint to the richly-flavoured beef dish which was to follow.

'That was delicious,' I declared, patting my lips with the linen napkin she had provided.

She smiled. 'Oh, zank you … Jean-Claude always used to love zat starter.' Even as she mentioned her ex-husband's name, her smile faded and a shadow flitted across her eyes.

In the awkwardness of the moment I wasn't quite sure what to say. I settled for 'Well, it was lovely.' A bit lame, I know, but that was what came out.

'I zink ze main course will be ready now,' she said, pushing her chair back.

'Here, let me …' I said, gathering up the empty plates.

'Oh, zank you. If you take zose through to ze kitchen and top up our glasses, I will put some music on.'

As I was pouring the last of the champagne into our glasses, I heard the mellow strains of some smooth jazz start up in the lounge.

As I turned to take our glasses back through to the lounge, Angelique appeared in the kitchen doorway. 'It will take me a few minutes to prepare ze main course. Why don't you sit down and listen to ze music?'

'Isn't there anything I can do to help?' I said, feeling a bit superfluous.

'Well, yes … zank you,' she said, smiling. 'If I get ze plates out from ze oven where zey 'ave been warming, perhaps you can get ze saucepan off ze 'ob and serve ze meals onto zem. Ze saucepan is very 'eavy, and I don't want to spill anyzing on my dress.'

'Definitely not,' I said. 'You wouldn't want to spoil such a beautiful dress … it looks, well … you look fabulous in it.' *Oh Christ, did those words really just spill out of my mouth?* I tried to retrieve the situation. 'Sorry, I didn't mean to … well I was just trying to say—'

She rescued me from my predicament by stepping forward and planting a kiss on my cheek. 'Don't be embarrassed, Roy … it was a lovely compliment.' I still felt like a complete prat, but her response went a long way to mitigating my discomfiture. She flashed me a radiant smile before downing the remainder of her champagne in one long draw. 'Is zere any more?' she asked, holding forth her glass and tilting her head slightly, and peering at me from beneath long black lashes.

'I'm afraid not,' I laughed.

'Oh dear … well in zat case can you open a bottle of wine? Zere is a nice red Rioja over zere' – she pointed to a wine rack in the corner. 'I'll get ze plates while you do zat.'

The next hour or so flew by. Angelique, quite apart from being devastatingly attractive, was just so engaging to talk to, and be with. We talked about everything from Spanish culture, news, and television, to the eclectic mix of bizarre characters which made up our little community. Her laugh intoxicated me as much as the copious amount of alcohol I had consumed, and yet, in the brief lulls in our conversation, I sensed that there was something on her mind, something she was reluctant to share with me.

'Do you want some dessert?' she asked, pushing her chair back and standing up. 'I don't usually 'ave dessert myself ... I like to watch my figure you see.' She emphasised the point by running both hands down the glossy fabric of her dress, starting from a point just below her bust and gliding down over her slender waist and hips to the tops of her thighs.

Well, I liked to watch her figure too, but I didn't want my response to be a repeat of my clumsy and too-presumptuous effort earlier in the evening. I settled for 'I really don't think you have too much to worry about in that department, Angelique.' When the words came out, they still sounded a bit crass, but Angelique seemed to accept them gracefully.

'You are very kind, Roy, but I do 'ave to be careful, just ze same.'

I smiled. 'But in answer to your question, I couldn't eat another thing. It was absolutely delicious.'

'I'm glad you enjoyed it,' she said, smiling.

She bent forward as she made to collect up the plates, swaying very slightly as she did so.

'Here, let me do that,' I offered.

'Zank you ... while you do zat I will get us anozer drink' – she held up the empty wine bottle – 'we seem to 'ave finished zis bottle. Do you want a liqueur or somezing?'

'Well, a small brandy would be nice,' I said. In truth I had probably had more than enough to drink already, but I didn't want the evening to end just yet.

'Ah, yes, I 'ave some French cognac ... would zat be OK?'

'Perfect,' I smiled.

'And I will 'ave a Cointreau,' she said, turning and making her way, a little unsteadily, towards her cocktail cabinet.

When I had finished loading the dishwasher and returned to the lounge, Angelique was reclining on the sofa, her head back and eyes half-closed; the hand holding her glass was swaying slowly back and forth to the gentle rhythm of the music which played quietly in the background. As Angelique's legs were stretched out along the sofa I made for the armchair opposite.

At my approach, she opened her eyes and swung her legs round and her feet onto the floor. 'Come and sit 'ere,' she purred, patting the seat cushion alongside her. 'Your cognac is 'ere.' She slid the glass along the coffee table so that it was directly in front of me and then, quite without warning, reached up and pulled some clips from her hair, allowing her luxuriant locks to tumble free, shaking her head from side to side. The resultant cascade looked a little unruly, but somehow endowed her with a wild, reckless look, which I have to admit, stirred a pang of desire in me. 'Zere ... zat is much better,' she sighed, '... much more comfortable.'

She raised her glass toward me, and I obliged with a gentle clink of my own. 'Cheers,' I said.

'Santé,' she replied, taking a generous swallow of her drink.

Suddenly, her eyes took on a faraway look, and I sensed, once again, that peculiar feeling that something was bothering her. I took a sip of my brandy and set down the glass before venturing into unknown territory.

'Angelique ... is something troubling you?'

Her eyes took on a haunted look. 'Troubling me ... why?'

'It's just that a few times this evening you have looked ... well sort of sad and distant. I've had such a lovely evening ... I don't want to leave you feeling ... well, I wondered if it's something you might want to share.'

She looked me directly in the eyes, and the tears began to well up. 'It is Jean-Claude.'

'Your ex-husband? What has he done to upset you?'

She shook her head, causing her mass of unrestrained hair to flail wildly. 'No ... it's not zat he has done anyzing to upset me exactly' – she grabbed a paper napkin from the table and wiped her eyes – 'it's just zat ... well, 'e wants me back.' The look she gave me was one of confusion and desperation. 'Oh, Roy, I don't know what to do.'

Oh, Christ! The role of agony aunt – or, I suppose, uncle – really wasn't one I felt at ease with. Yet I felt such warmth and compassion towards Angelique that there was no way on earth that I could just change the subject or shy away.

'But, I thought that he had made a new life with someone else in England.'

'Apparently zey 'ave split up. 'E says 'e made a terrible mistake … 'e says 'e still loves me.'

'And do you believe him?'

'I don't know. We 'ad such a good life together until 'e decided to go off wiz zat … bitch.' She spat the last word with a venom I'd never seen her express before. 'Maybe it was all down to 'er … maybe 'e never really stopped loving me at all.'

'But Angelique, it takes two to do something like that … it can't *all* be her fault.'

'I know, but …' She broke down into floods of tears, flinging her arms around my neck. Now under any normal circumstances, I would relish the prospect of Angelique hugging me so tightly, but right there and then, I just felt compassion for her obvious distress and more than a little anger at this bastard, whom I'd never met, but who had caused this woman – a woman for whom I now cared deeply – such pain and suffering.

I held her like that for several seconds, before easing her away from me, cupping her cheeks with my hands and looking straight into her frightened eyes. 'He's put you through a lot Angelique … how do you feel about him now?'

She gave a slight shake of her head. 'I 'ate 'im for what 'e did, but … well, deep down, I zink perhaps I still love 'im.'

'Oh, Angelique … don't ask me to say what you should do, only your own heart can tell you that.'

She finally pulled back from me a little, wiping her tears once again, evidently trying to compose herself. 'Zere is somezing else I 'ave to consider.'

'What's that?'

'Miriam … she absolutely 'ates her father for what 'e did.'

I recalled the malice with which Miriam had spoken of her father when she and Angelique had first come round for dinner – it felt like a lifetime ago, now. But I thought back to my own daughters at Miriam's age: how they could be vehemently opposed to an idea or a person and yet, with time, would come around.

'Miriam has every reason to feel bitter about what happened, but children are very resilient. I think you have to make your decision based on your own feelings. With time, Miriam will come to accept whatever is best for you.'

'You zink so?' she said, her beautiful eyes widening, atop dark streaks of smudged makeup.

'I know so.' I said … and somehow I really did.

She flung her arms around my neck once more. 'Oh, Roy it's so good to 'ave someone to talk to about this … I 'ave been bottling it up for days.'

After some seconds we eased apart from each other. 'The only thing I would say,' I cautioned, 'is take your time … be sure of your feelings before you decide one way or the other.'

She nodded, still dabbing her eyes with the napkin. 'I'm sorry to 'ave spoiled our evening, Roy'

'You haven't … I've had a wonderful evening, and I'm glad you have opened up to me about what's been troubling you.' She managed a small smile, nodding weakly. 'I really think I should be going now, though.'

I sipped the last remains of my brandy and stood up. She followed suit and we made our way towards the front door. As I went to kiss her on the cheek, everything suddenly changed – it was as though someone had flipped an invisible switch. As her eyes locked onto mine I felt electricity crackle in the air. She slid her hands behind my neck and pulled me towards her, her lips finding mine and her tongue urgently exploring mine. As her breasts pressed warmly against me, desire sprang in my loins. She must have felt it, for she pressed her lower body firmly against mine, allowing her hands to slide down from behind my neck to grasp my buttocks and pull me to her. Without any conscious instruction on my part, my own hands did the same, sliding down over her firmly-toned rear and encouraging her.

'You don't 'ave to go, Roy,' she breathed, her voice deep and husky. 'You can stay wiz me tonight.'

I was in utter turmoil. Here I was – an average-looking guy in his fifties – being propositioned by one of the most beautiful women I had ever met, some twenty years my junior, offering to spend the night with me. This should not have been a tough call … but it was.

Every fibre of my body wanted her, and a voice inside me assailed my alcohol-weakened brain with any number of perfectly plausible reasons why no harm would be done.

You've always wanted to know what it would be like to couple with that fabulous body, haven't you? You've even fantasised about it, right? Maybe you even love her a little, don't you? Now's your chance; if you don't do it now, maybe there'll never be another opportunity. Donna is over a thousand miles away; she need never know; what she doesn't know can't hurt her can it?

She further weakened my already-fragile resolve by sliding her hand down my stomach and finding my erection, massaging it through the fabric of my trousers. She looked up at me, her eyes intense, and her glistening lips slightly parted. 'I can see you want me, Roy. Stay wiz me tonight; no-one will know.'

Go on, she wants you ... what harm can it do? Oh Christ, it would have been so, so easy to just melt into her arms and let the night take us wherever it might, and yet ...

With a superhuman effort, I took her shoulders in my hands and eased her gently away.

'I do want you, Angelique ... far more than you can probably imagine.'

'I zink I can imagine,' she said reaching forward to stroke the straining bulge in my trousers once more, 'but you ... you don't want to stay wiz me?' The look of hurt and confusion in her lovely face was almost too much to bear.

'Oh, Angelique, you are the loveliest, most sensual woman I could ever hope to meet. I am flattered beyond imagining that you could even be interested in someone like me.'

'But I am, Roy ... you are such a lovely man. I just—'

'Look,' I said gripping her shoulders a little more firmly, 'we are both a little drunk, and your emotions are all over the place just now. Ask yourself if this is really what you want.'

Her eyes closed for a moment and she sighed deeply. 'I *do* want you, Roy.'

'Maybe you do right now, but you may feel differently in the morning. Right now we have a lovely friendship, but if we do this, everything could change. I can think of nothing I would rather do right now than spend the night here with you, but if that were to destroy our friendship I ... well I couldn't bear that.'

'I ... don't know. I just feel so confused. Jean-Claude ... 'e wants me back ... 'e says he 'e still loves me. 'E treated me so badly, but you ... you 'ave always been so kind to me. And yet ...' Her voice tailed off.

'Shhh ...' I hugged her to me as she began, softly, to sob.

Strangely, the sexual tension which, just a few minutes ago, had crackled in the air had evaporated. My erection was starting to subside and all I felt was compassion for a lovely friend in distress.

'There's something else,' I continued. She wiped a tear from her eye with the back of her hand as she looked up at me, spreading a dark streak of makeup across her cheek. 'I can't do this to Donna.' She closed her eyes for a moment, dipping her head slightly. 'I haven't told you this before, but I did once have an affair, and it nearly broke our marriage, but Donna was so ... well ... oh, it's difficult to explain. But anyway, we got things back on track. She never deserved what I did to her, and I can't do it to her again.'

She managed a small smile. 'I understand, Roy. She need never know, but even if she didn't ...'

'Even if she never knew,' I confirmed.

We looked at each other in silence for several long seconds. It wasn't an awkward silence, just a moment of shared understanding and an acknowledgement of what could never be.

Angelique was first to break the silence. 'I guess it's goodnight zen,' she said, a rueful smile on her dark-streaked face.

'I guess it is,' I agreed.

She moved slowly towards me and put her hands around my neck, pulling me to her and burying her face in the crook of my neck. We clung together like that for several seconds, and then, as if by some hidden signal, we let go of each other at exactly the same moment.

Just a minute or two later, I was back in my own apartment, numb and confused, wondering just what the hell had happened that evening.

Chapter 46

I was dimly aware of soft chimes sounding in some faraway place, threatening to pierce the comforting cocoon of silence and blackness which enveloped me. *Go away*, said my subconscious mind ... and for a few seconds it did. But then it sounded again, soft and melodious, but insistent. Suddenly, a much harsher sound intruded – a furious hammering noise. Finally, I abandoned my efforts to shut out the intrusion, pulled the pillow away from head and blinked sleepily at the clock on the bedside table: 9.43 a.m.

That was much later than I would normally sleep in, but it was early, by Spanish standards, for anyone to come calling. In any case, who would be visiting me at that time on a Saturday morning? Could it be Angelique? Did she want to talk about what had happened – or rather, hadn't happened – last night? The doorbell sounded again, accompanied by another barrage of blows to the door. I groaned as I sat up, swung my legs over the side of the bed, and groped for my dressing gown, which was strewn across the bottom of the bed.

It wasn't Angelique.

'Heavy night?' enquired *Inspector Jefe* Abascal, eying me up and down, evidently taking in my dishevelled state. Behind him stood two uniformed officers.

'I ... er ... well yes, I suppose so. But, what ... what is this all about?'

'May we come in?'

I glanced from Abascal to each of the uniformed policemen in turn. One had his hand resting lightly on the butt of the gun which hung from his belt; I noted that he had flipped off the leather strap which normally held it securely in its holster. I decided that declining Abascal's request really wouldn't be a good idea.

'Well yes ... I suppose you'd better.' I ushered them in. 'So what is this all about?' I asked, for a second time.

The detective held up a sheet of paper. 'I have a warrant to search your property.'

'Search my property?' I repeated, dumbly. 'But why ... what are you looking for?'

He ignored my question. 'I suggest that you and I move out onto the terrace while my officers conduct their search.'

'But you haven't explained what—'

He cut me off, taking hold of my arm, gesturing toward the patio door with his free hand. 'Please ...' he insisted.

I noted one of the police officers resting his hand on the butt of his gun once more. Not wishing to provoke any of them, I stepped out onto the terrace, followed by Abascal. We sat down on the terrace sofas, locking eyes across the glass-topped coffee table.

The silent standoff continued for several seconds, eventually broken by Abascal. 'Do you have anything else to tell me regarding the death of señor González?'

'No,' I replied, puzzled. 'All I know about his death is what *you* have told *me*.'

He regarded me with dark, unblinking eyes for several seconds. 'Are you quite sure, Mr Groves? It would not be wise for you to keep anything from us.'

'Look,' I sighed, 'I have answered all your questions and told you everything I know. Why are you searching my apartment?' I glanced towards the patio door where one of the policemen could be seen pulling the cushions from my armchairs and dumping them unceremoniously on the floor. 'Please ... just tell me what you're looking for and if it's there I'll hand it to you,' I pleaded. 'There's no need to wreck the place.'

He ignored my entreaty. 'Just let them get on with their work.'

I exhaled heavily, exasperated. There was clearly no point in persisting, so I lapsed into silence.

After about ten minutes the detective withdrew his mobile phone and began tapping away at it, alternately frowning and smiling as he worked through whatever the hell he was doing. It was as if I wasn't even there. I stood up and began pacing up and down the terrace, becoming increasingly alarmed at the banging and crashing noises emanating from within the apartment.

Finally, after about half an hour, one of the policemen opened the patio door and addressed Abascal. '*Jefe, venga ... mire esto.*' His gloved hand held up a translucent green plastic bag; I couldn't make out what was inside.

Absacal rose to his feet and stepped towards the patio door. I made to follow, but was quickly stopped in my tracks.

'Please stay where you are Mr. Groves.'

Frustrated and annoyed, I slumped down onto the sofa.

A minute or two passed before Abascal reappeared. 'I think you had better come down to the station with us. There are certain items of new information and evidence which we need to discuss.'

A cold spear of dread shot through me. 'But what new information ... what evidence? I can't tell you any more than I already have.'

He didn't answer my question. 'Please, Mr Groves, you need to get dressed now.'

I had no idea where this was going, but it was starting to sound bloody serious now. I searched his face for clues, but his countenance was stony and impassive. I remembered Marysa's earlier offer.

'OK, if you are intending to question me further, I want to have a lawyer present.'

'As you wish,' he responded, showing no emotion. 'So make your phone call, and then get dressed please.'

He stood aside to allow me through the patio door. The sight which met my eyes as I stepped inside made my stomach lurch: cushions all over the floor; sofas upturned; drawers upside down, with contents strewn asunder; rugs flung aside. My hitherto beautiful apartment looked as though it had been hit by the proverbial bomb.

My simmering anger boiled over. 'I will hold you personally responsible for wrecking my home like this,' I hissed, 'and I'll expect every scrap of damage to be paid for.'

Abascal merely inclined his head and shrugged. 'I think that now, Mr Groves, you have bigger things to worry about than a bit of mess in your apartment.' His expression hardened. 'Now make your phone call and get dressed. You have ten minutes.'

***

I sat in the same dark, airless room where I had been interviewed previously. Alongside me sat the community lawyer, José Cabrera, a scrawny, bespectacled man, probably in his mid-fifties with an undisciplined mass of coarse, grey hair which bushed out over his ears and curled over his collar. His voice held an incongruously high timbre, but at least his command of English was good. Opposite sat Abascal, and lurking in the corner was his sidekick whose name I had already forgotten. The atmosphere now felt even more foreboding than it had on the previous occasion I had been there.

'When was the last time that you saw señor González alive?' said Abascal.

'I already told you ... it was a couple of months ago, when I bumped into him in that bar.'

Abascal leafed, unhurriedly, through some notes he had in front of him. 'That would be *La Esquina de Pedro* on 29th September?'

'Well, I don't know the exact date, but yes, probably around then.'

'And how would you say that meeting went?'

'Well it wasn't really a meeting, as such ... I just ran into him by chance.'

'And what did you discuss with him?'

'We discussed the dispute over the retaining wall. Look, I've already told you that he was refusing to pay us what the court had ordered.'

'Indeed,' said Abascal, stroking his chin, 'and also that he had refused to pay his contribution, as an apartment owner himself, to the cash-call levied on all owners to help pay for the new wall.'

'Yes, that too,' I agreed.

'You didn't mention that he had also taken legal action against the community, claiming twelve thousand euros damages for inconvenience to his tenants due to restricted access while the construction work was underway.'

'Didn't I? In all honesty I can't remember every detail of our conversation.'

He picked up a sheaf of papers. 'I have the transcript of our conversation here ... and no, you did not mention this point.'

'OK,' I conceded, 'then I suppose I didn't.'

Abascal pushed his chair back, placing both hands behind his neck and gazing up at the ceiling as though carefully considering his next question. At length he leaned forward again and placed his forearms on the table.

'And how would you describe the tone of your conversation with señor González?'

'The tone?'

'I mean was it friendly, aggressive, or what?'

'Well ... hardly "friendly".'

At this point the lawyer intervened. 'Inspector Abascal, I think we have established that there was a long-running dispute between señor González and the community of which my client is president, so it is hardly surprising that relations were not the most cordial, but I fail to see—'

Abascal held up his hand to silence the lawyer. 'Please, bear with me, and the relevance of my questions will become clear.' He turned his attention back to me. 'So how *would* you describe the nature of the discussion?'

I took a deep breath as I considered my response. 'Well, when he refused point blank to consider any form of compromise on his entrenched position, it's hardly surprising that things became a little ... fractious.'

'"Fractious"? Hmm ... you will have to help me with my English. Did you threaten him?'

'Threaten him? Absolutely not.'

The detective leafed through his papers once more, withdrawing one sheet which he held up in front of him. 'I have a sworn statement here from the deceased man's brother, testifying that you threatened his brother, both verbally and physically.'

'Well his brother is hardly an independent witness is he?' I spluttered.

'Indeed he is not,' chipped in the lawyer. 'I must protest—'

Abascal cut him off. 'Please, señor Cabrera, I must ask you to desist from interrupting.' He picked up another sheet of paper, brandishing it in front of him. 'This is another sworn statement, from the owner of the bar ... his testimony confirms that of the deceased man's brother.'

'Look,' I protested, 'this is not what it seems. I did *not* threaten him ... the discussion just got a little ... heated.'

'Heated,' repeated the detective, 'hmm ...'

'Please,' I pleaded, 'there is another witness: my neighbour Paul MacPhearson was present. He'll tell you what really happened.'

'But I understand that Mr MacPhearson was seated at another table, some distance away from where this conversation took place.'

'Well yes, a few yards away ... but he could see and hear perfectly well what went on ... and in any case, he came over eventually. You must talk to him to get an unbiased account of what happened.'

'Unbiased ...' he repeated. 'So your neighbour and friend is going to be "unbiased" whereas the owner of the bar, who had absolutely no involvement with your dispute, would not be?'

I glanced desperately at the lawyer, who seemed momentarily lost for words. Eventually he managed, 'I must insist that you consider the testimony of all witnesses.'

'I will, of course, interview Mr MacPhearson, but now I'd like to turn to another piece of evidence.' He took a sheet of paper from his stack, turned it through a hundred and eighty degrees and slid it across the table towards me. 'Do you recognise this?'

As I began to read, my heart sank.

To: Alfredo González
From: Roy Groves
Subject: Collapsed retaining wall

I have just been informed of your decision to launch legal action against the community in respect of inconvenience caused to your tenants during the construction of the new retaining wall ...

The detective interrupted my silent reading. 'Perhaps I could draw your attention to the section highlighted in yellow towards the end.'

I turned the sheet over to locate the part in question.

... I want you to be aware that you cannot employ such underhand tactics without incurring consequences, so let me make my position crystal clear. I have been elected to represent the community to the best of my ability, and therefore I am determined to fight you every step of the way with regard to this matter. I will do whatever is necessary to ensure that you pay what is due in respect of your corner-cutting, shoddy workmanship.

A wave of nausea swept over me. What the hell had I been thinking of?

'Well?' prompted Abascal.

'I ... was angry at the time. I just wanted him to realise that we weren't going to ...' My voice tailed off as I realised just how lame this sounded.

'So now I think we know what you meant by "consequences", don't we?' snarled Abascal, stabbing a forefinger down on the table. 'Roy Groves, I am arresting you on suspicion of the murder of Alfredo González. I must warn you—'

'This is outrageous,' protested the lawyer, every piece of so-called evidence you have presented here is circumstantial. You have absolutely no physical evidence to connect my client with this murder.'

The detective's face broke into a slow smile. 'Oh, but I do.' He motioned to his colleague who came over and laid a green plastic evidence bag on the table. Abascal donned a pair of thin, white rubber gloves and withdrew from the bag a coil of blue, polypropylene rope. 'This,' he declared, 'is exactly the same type of rope as that used to hang the victim. It was found in your client's apartment this morning.'

Oh fuck.

Chapter 47

My first thought was that the bastard had planted the rope in my apartment; I wouldn't have put it past him. But then it came back to me: it was the rope left behind by the men who had delivered our new bed, more than a year earlier.

Abascal was unmoved by my explanation; he actually congratulated me on my inventiveness in concocting such a preposterous story. I could have happily strangled the smug bastard right there and then ... but then I suppose I really *would* have been guilty of murder.

My lawyer pursued a rather more constructive course of action. 'This proves nothing,' he declared. 'I imagine rope exactly like that could be purchased at any do-it-yourself store. Anyone could have bought it.'

'I will, of course, check the general availability of this product,' replied the detective.

'And you should talk to the delivery company,' said the lawyer. 'They may be able to identify which of their employees delivered my client's bed. If so, these men will be able to confirm that they left the rope.'

Abascal said nothing; he just gazed disinterestedly back at the lawyer, softly drumming his fingers on the table.

'At the very least,' continued the lawyer, 'they should be able to confirm that they use this type of rope.'

'Thank you for your advice on how I should conduct my investigation,' retorted Abascal, his voice heavy with sarcasm.

That seemed to ruffle the lawyer's feathers considerably – he rose to his feet and began jabbing the air, his voice rising even higher in pitch. 'Unless you can produce some forensic evidence proving that this coil of rope was actually at the murder scene or that my client was at the murder scene, you have nothing.'

Abascal leaned forward and pressed the 'off' button of the recorder on the table. When he spoke his voice adopted a chilling tone. 'Then I will have to find such evidence, won't I?'

In spite of the lawyer's best efforts, they pressed ahead with arresting me. They took away my mobile phone, and indeed every other item I had with me, including wallet, money, and keys. I was to be allowed just one phone call to let someone know that I was in police custody. I decided to call Donna; the lawyer could take care of informing Marysa and Paul.

There was no answer at our UK home address or at our daughter's. I decided to try Donna's mobile.

'Roy?' Her voice was breathless and excited. 'Where on earth have you been? I've been trying to call you ... Bea's waters have broken.'

'They have ... is she OK?'

'Oh yes, I think so ... but the contractions are coming quite frequently now – we're on our way to the hospital. Rick's driving, and his Mum is looking after Jason.'

I heard what sounded like a cry of pain in the background, and then Donna's voice again – muffled this time. 'It's OK, Bea ... we're nearly there.'

'Donna ... Donna ... what's happening?' I cried.

She came back on the phone.

'It's OK, but ... look, I'll have to ring off for now; we're just arriving at the hospital. Talk to you later.'

'Donna, the reason I was calling was—' she had hung up.

As I tried to redial her number, the policeman standing at my side, took the handset from me. 'Sorry ... one call only.'

'But I didn't have a chance to—'

'One call only,' he said. His tone left no room for discussion on the subject. How the hell was I going to let her know now?

***

I had never seen the inside of a police cell before, and it was every bit as gloomy and depressing as I had imagined it might be. It was about six feet by eight, with walls, floor, and ceiling all painted a uniform, drab, grey colour. There was a single, iron-framed bed, whose 'mattress' was, in reality, more like a thin, hard gym mat; a small metal table with attached seat; a washbasin; and a toilet, whose stainless steel bowl had no separate seat. Everything was fixed to the walls of the cell save for a single enamelled steel mug. At least there was a window – albeit tiny and barred – allowing some natural light into the wretched place. I gazed up at this small source of comfort as I lay back with my hands interlaced behind the back of my neck.

I wasn't sure how long I'd been ensconced: they had taken my watch away from me. It felt like several hours since they had brought me a light lunch, consisting of some beef sandwiches and an apple. Since then, no-one had been to see me, either to question me, or let me know what was happening. I just hoped that Abascal would, as the lawyer had suggested, follow up with the delivery company to verify my account of how I had come to be in possession of the rope. Hopefully, he would also interview Paul to get his version of the events which had transpired at Pedro's bar all those weeks ago. Somehow, though, I didn't get the impression that the detective was terribly interested in finding evidence which might prove my innocence.

Had Donna been trying to contact me? What would she be thinking when she couldn't get in touch? I just hoped that perhaps she would call Paul and Kate ... or even Marysa, so that she would at least know that I hadn't been involved in an accident or something. Maybe one of them might even take the initiative and call Donna. But then how would she take the news that I was under arrest? It was just so infuriating not to *know* what was happening ... or be allowed any contact with the outside world.

I wondered about Bea's baby; surely it must have been born by now. Was it a boy or a girl? Had the birth gone smoothly? Was Bea OK? Would I ever even be allowed out to see the child?

I chided myself for harbouring such gloomy thoughts; surely even in the Spanish legal system – in which, it has to be said, I had very little faith – sanity would eventually prevail. They still had no hard evidence to connect me with Alfredo's murder, though Abascal's words 'Then I will have to find such evidence, won't I?' weighed heavily on my mind.

How on earth had things come to this? It was less than two years since I had taken on the role of president, thinking that I could, fairly easily, get the community's shambolic affairs under control, and that possibly my efforts might even be appreciated by my fellow residents. That starry-eyed vision seemed very distant now.

My melancholy reflections were interrupted by the metallic scraping noise of the small viewing hatch in the cell door being opened. An eye appeared momentarily at the hatch before the jangling of keys announced that someone was about to enter the cell.

At last! Perhaps someone is finally going to tell me something.

The policeman who entered the cell was carrying a tray. '*Su cena,*' he announced, setting the tray down on the table.

'Please,' I pleaded, swinging my legs over the side of the bed and sitting up, 'can someone tell me what is happening?'

'*Lo siento ... no hablo Inglés,*' he said, sounding somewhat apologetic.

I racked my brains for the correct words in Spanish.

'*¿Por favor, puede decirme que pasa?*'

'*Yo no se nada,*' he said, shrugging, as he pulled the door shut behind him. It was pretty clear that I wasn't going to get much information out of him.

Dinner was a pretty unappetising affair, consisting of what appeared to be some sort of dumplings in a thick, gloopy gravy. I ate it in miserable solitude, my mind ranging back and forth over a plethora of questions to which I had no answers. This was driving me mad – I had absolutely nothing to occupy my mind other than endlessly raking over my desperate situation. I needed something ... anything ... to distract me

When the policeman returned, about an hour later, to collect my tray, I tried to enlist his help. 'Do you have any books or magazines I could read?' I did my best impression of someone leafing through the pages of a book, but evidently my miming skills weren't up to scratch – he gave me the sort of puzzled, sympathetic look which he probably normally reserved for complete imbeciles.

I had another go at exercising my meagre grasp of Spanish. '*¿Er ... tiene libros ... o revistas ... en Inglés?*'

'*Ah,*' he said, understanding evidently dawning. He raised a forefinger to the side of his chin. '*Voy a ver.*'

Five minutes later, he returned, bearing two fairly well-thumbed paperbacks.

I accepted them gratefully. '*Muchas gracias, señor.*'

'*De nada,*' he said, giving a brief smile before pulling the door shut with a resounding clang.

I examined the two books he had brought me.

The first was entitled 'Grumpy Old Men Abroad'. The blurb on the back cover declared it was 'An hilarious romp through the trials and tribulations faced by British expats on Spain's famous Costas.'

I didn't really feel in the mood for reading about how bloody hilarious life in the local area was so I turned to the second volume: 'Falsely Accused'. I turned it over and began to read the notes on the back cover. 'Tony Barton is looking forward to his first proper holiday in years, but within days of arriving on the holiday island of Majorca he finds himself accused by the police of a murder he didn't commit. As the evidence against him stacks up, he contemplates the prospect of life imprisonment in a Spanish jail.'

Some bloody choice!

I weighed up the unappealing options for a couple of minutes and eventually plumped for the comedy. I wasn't much in the mood for mirth, but the prospect of reading about some poor soul in a situation spookily similar to my own was just too depressing to contemplate.

As I began to read about the joys of airport security, missed flights, and inedible airline food, my eyes became heavy. I realised then just how much the events of the last couple of days had drained me. I closed my eyes, just for a moment ...

Chapter 48

It was a small noise which roused me from my slumbers: a sort of soft, slapping sound. As I prised my eyelids open and turned on my side, I was momentarily disoriented by the unfamiliar surroundings but, in an instant, the reality of my predicament came flooding back. I realised that the noise which had woken me was the sound of the book falling to the floor. I'd have lost my place now, but as I hadn't even finished the first chapter, it hardly mattered.

I looked up to see a weak shaft of sunlight streaming through the small window, set high in the wall. I had slept through the entire night, lying fully clothed on top of the covers. I felt awful. With a groan, I levered myself off the bed and staggered over to the washbasin, where I filled the cup with water and downed it in one long swallow, refilling it and wandering back to sit on the bed. I could hear the distant noises of activity in the police station; evidently the normal daytime activities were resuming, though I still had no idea what time it was.

At length, the hatch in the door opened, closed a second or two later and, after some noisy jangling of keys, a policemen appeared. It was not the man who had attended me the previous day and, thankfully, this guy spoke very good English.

'You have been asleep for over twelve hours,' he announced.

'I have? What's the time?' I said, rising to my feet.

'It is almost 10 a.m.' he said, eying my creased and rumpled clothes. 'I imagine you might appreciate a shower.'

'I would ... I really would. Thank you.'

He took me through to a single shower room, passing me a towelling dressing robe before I stepped inside. 'Here, you can change into this. I will be waiting outside.'

A hot shower and a clean dressing gown made all the difference. My situation was still dire, but at least I felt human once more. When the policemen ushered me back into my cell he pointed out a clean set of pyjamas folded up on the bed.

'Thank you,' I said. 'You have been very kind, but ... well, no-one seems to be able to tell me what is happening. I've been locked up here for almost twenty-four hours now, but I haven't actually been charged with anything, and I just don't know what happens next.'

I thought I detected a glimmer of sympathy in the man's eyes. 'Look sir, I'm afraid I cannot tell you anything. The investigation is continuing and Chief Inspector Abascal will no doubt come and talk to you in due course.'

'But, how long can—'

'I am sorry sir, I cannot tell you any more.' He stepped hurriedly out of the room and slammed the door shut. The sound hung in the air for a surprisingly long time as the reverberation gradually died away.

And so my second day in police custody passed in much the same way as the first. I tried my best to immerse myself in the supposedly hilarious goings-on surrounding expat life in Spain, but somehow couldn't really engage. Every time I settled down to read, my mind would wander off and begin, once again, meandering down the murky labyrinth of gloomy possibilities which might await me.

I could scarcely believe how long a single day could seem.

***

I must have slept soundly that night, for it was not until I heard the sound of keys rattling outside my door that I came to. By the time that the man bearing my breakfast had entered the cell, however, I was wide awake.

'I want to see Inspector Abascal,' I demanded, almost before the policeman was through the door.

If I'd waited a second or so longer I'd have realised that the man carrying the tray was the guy who'd attended me on my first day. He looked at me uncomprehendingly. '*Lo siento ... no comprendo,*' came the reply.

I paused for a second or two as I groped for the correct words in Spanish. '*Quisiera hablar con Inspector Abascal.*' I hoped that was more or less right.

He stepped forward and set the tray down on the table. '*Veré lo que puedo hacer.*' I took that to mean that he'd pass on my request.

Well, if he had talked to Abascal, it had had precious little effect, for nothing whatsoever happened for the next hour or so. Eventually, I heard the familiar scraping sound of the hatch in the door being opened; the eye which appeared there gave little clue as to its owner.

It wasn't Abascal.

When the same policemen entered the cell, I tried once more. '*¿Por favor ... donde está Inspector Abascal?,*' I pleaded.

The man hurriedly collected my breakfast tray, avoiding eye contact. '*Lo siento ... el Inspector Jefe no está disponible en este momento.*'

He beat a hasty retreat while I was still struggling to translate his words.

Interminable hours passed as I tried, once again, without much success, to find some solace in the pages of my book. It was almost a relief when a sturdily-built, uniformed woman arrived with my lunch.

'*Por favor señora ... puede contarme algo?*' I ventured, hoping that I was asking more or less the right thing.

She scowled as she set down the tray. '*Cerdo Inglés,*' she hissed. I wasn't sure what that meant, but judging from her tone, I deduced that it probably wasn't complimentary. She withdrew without uttering another word.

I must have dozed off after my somewhat unappetising lunch, for the next thing I registered was the same abrasive woman arriving with my dinner – a plateful of tiny shellfish, the smell of which turned my stomach. After she left, I tentatively approached the dish, prodding its contents with the plastic fork which they had provided. I felt the bile rise in my throat. *No way.*

I shambled back to the bed and lay down. The light was fading now; I closed my eyes and began, once again raking over, in my mind, every aspect of my desperate situation. *When is this nightmare ever going to end?*

Chapter 49

I woke well before sunrise the following day. By now I'd had more than enough of the endless hours of enforced solitude with absolutely no information as to what the hell was going on. Just how long were they allowed to detain me without charge? I should have asked the lawyer before he departed but, at the time, it had never occurred to me to do so. The bastards had already kept me there for three whole days; enough was enough. By the time my breakfast arrived I'd had several hours to dwell on this question; now I was feeling in combative mood. When, finally, I heard the familiar scraping sound of the inspection hatch being opened, I was ready.

As the policeman stepped into the cell, I just about exploded. '*EXIJO ver Abascal. ¡AHORA MISMO!*' I yelled. I'm not sure if I got the Spanish quite right, but I certainly got my message across: the policeman beat a hasty retreat, slamming the door behind him, without even stopping to deliver my breakfast.

A couple of minutes later Abascal finally appeared, with the other policeman just behind him.

'At last!' I stormed, jumping to my feet. 'I want to know what the hell is going on here. You have kept me here for three days without charge, you have denied me any contact with the outside world, and you have given me absolutely no information about what is happening. I demand an explanation.'

The detective listened impassively to my rant. He waited until I paused for breath before responding.

'You are free to go,' he said.

'Free to go?' I repeated, dumbly, barely able to believe what I was hearing. But, why ... what's happened to change the situation?'

'Certain new evidence has come to light. We have arrested someone else on suspicion of the murder of señor González.'

The relief swept over me like a tsunami; I felt my legs begin to buckle and grabbed the edge of the washbasin for support. I could still barely process what I was hearing. 'But who ... I mean how did you—'

Abascal held up his hand, palm-outward to suppress my incoherent babbling. 'I cannot discuss the details of the case with you. Is it not sufficient for you to know that you are no longer under suspicion?'

That was enough; I didn't want to push my luck any further. 'Y-yes ... of course,' I stammered.

'My colleague will assist you in getting ready to leave. Your lawyer will be here in around half an hour; he has offered to drive you home.'

The other policeman stepped forward now. He was holding my clothes, stacked in as neat a pile as was possible considering their crumpled state.

'Thank you ... er, *gracias*,' I mumbled, as he passed them to me.

'Oh, one last thing ...' said Abascal, 'should your lawyer suggest to you that you might consider taking some sort of action against the police in connection with this ... misunderstanding, I would strongly advise against it.'

At that moment, nothing was further from my mind – all I wanted to do was get the hell out of there, and never speak to a Spanish policeman ever again. I nodded. 'I understand.'

'Good,' said the detective. He turned on his heel and was gone.

Just forty-five minutes later, I was on my way home.

'So what happened to make him change his mind?' I asked the lawyer.

'Well,' he said, 'I wish I could say it was due to my efforts on your behalf, but that is not the case. Abascal would not give me full details – understandably, as it is a live criminal investigation – but it seems the deceased's brother, and the bar owner, both retracted their statements. They confirmed that your encounter with González was merely a heated exchange, and that you did not, in fact, threaten him.'

'But why?' I asked, puzzled.

Cabrera shrugged, spreading his hands expansively, in the process taking both from the wheel and allowing the car to swerve alarmingly. 'Sorry,' he said as he grabbed the wheel and corrected the car's course. 'I have no idea why they changed their testimony, but I should imagine that *they* may now be in trouble with the police themselves, for initially submitting misleading statements. Anyway, their revised accounts now match closely that of your neighbour.'

'But I still don't see how that has helped them identify another suspect.'

'I'm coming to that. Even at the time of your arrest, Abascal really only had circumstantial evidence against you, and once those statements were invalidated, all he had was your email – which really proved nothing – and the rope.'

'Yes ... what about the rope?'

'Well, apparently he was unable to identify the men that delivered your bed.'

'I'll bet he didn't try all that hard,' I interjected.

'Well, maybe or maybe not, but it turns out that that particular type of rope is very widely available in this area, and indeed throughout the whole of Spain. Furthermore, his forensic investigation showed that the rope found at your apartment was from a different manufacturing batch to that found at the murder scene – more than one year older. Finally, they found no forensic evidence which placed either you or that coil of rope at the murder scene. In the end he just didn't have enough evidence to charge you.'

'Well, thank God for that,' I sighed. 'Although the bastard seemed so determined to nail me that I wouldn't have been surprised if he had fabricated some evidence. You saw the way he switched off that voice recorder.'

'Indeed I did,' said the lawyer, 'but you are exonerated now, and I would suggest that you would be well-advised to keep that suspicion to yourself.'

'Oh, don't worry,' I said, 'I will. I have absolutely no desire to tangle with that character again. Anyway, none of this explains how they managed to identify another suspect.'

'Well', continued the lawyer, 'It seems that once Inspector Abascal found that he didn't have enough evidence to charge you, he ordered a second autopsy of the body and a further sweep of the crime scene in an effort to find some hard physical evidence to connect you with the murder.'

'And I guess he didn't find anything?'

'Oh yes ... apparently he did. He would not give me precise details, but it seems they found some DNA evidence on the body, and also recovered an item from the crime scene which gave them a fingerprint. The DNA and the fingerprint both matched those of the same person … but it wasn´t you.'

'It's a shame the bastard wasn't so thorough to begin with … before he falsely accused me. Anyway, do you know who the new suspect is?'

'Oh, I understand he's head of a local building company. Apparently he's done a number of projects for the González brothers and I understand that there was bad blood between them, with a substantial amount of money in dispute. So … as well as the physical evidence against him, it's clear that he had a motive.'

I guess I shouldn't have been surprised to learn that there were some murky financial dealings in play here. God knows I'd seen enough by now to know that it's just the way business is done in Spain, and yet to see it culminate in murder still came as a shock.

I sat in silence for a few moments, digesting what I had been told, before asking, 'Do you know the name of the suspect?'

'Er … Montoya, I believe.'

'Montoya?' I gasped, 'not Julio Montoya?'

'Yes … that is the man. Why … do you know him?'

'Indeed I do … he is the one who built our new retaining wall.'

***

As I stepped through the door, Donna rushed over and flung her arms around my neck. 'Oh, Roy, thank God this nightmare is over.'

I enfolded her in a hug, savouring the sweet smell of her hair as she nuzzled my neck. 'I'm so sorry I couldn't let you know what was happening; they wouldn't let me make a phone call or anything.'

'I know … it's OK,' she said, stepping back to look me in the eyes and dropping her hands to grasp both of mine. 'Marysa called Paul as soon as she knew what had happened and he immediately called me. I got the first flight back out here that I could.'

I squeezed her hands gently. 'Anyway, it's over now. So do we have another grandchild now?'

'We do,' she said, beaming, 'another boy … they're calling him Matthew. Oh Roy, he's adorable.'

'And Bea … is she OK?'

'She's fine. Look, I'll tell you all about it soon, but first … you have some visitors.'

'Visitors?'

'Come on through,' she said, leading me by the hand.

In the lounge were Paul, Kate, Neil, Marion, Bruce, Tracey, Angelique, and most surprising of all, Jim Watkins.

'Welcome back,' boomed Bruce, stepping over and enveloping me in a lung-crushing bear hug.

Paul settled for a more restrained, but nevertheless warm handshake, as did Neil. Jim's handshake was somehow a little more restrained, but I was most appreciative that he was there at all. Kate and Marion each gave me a gentle hug, Tracy a far more vigorous one. Angelique was last to greet me; she gave me her customary three kisses, but something had changed: she broke eye contact too quickly and I felt distinctly awkward. It was, of course, the first time we had seen each other since very nearly falling into bed together a few days ago; we needed to talk about it, to confront what had happened, and get our warm friendship back on track. I hoped we would get the opportunity to do so very soon.

I looked around me; the lounge was back to its usual neat and tidy condition. I looked at Donna enquiringly. 'The mess made by those policemen ... '

'Everyone here' – she gave a wide sweep of her hand – 'helped me clear up. It would have taken me forever on my own.'

'I don't know what to say,' I murmured, a tear pricking the corner of my eye. 'Thanks so much.'

'Anyway,' said Donna, clapping her hands together, 'this calls for a glass of champagne.' She disappeared into the kitchen for a moment and returned with an ice bucket, the bottle already uncorked. Once everyone's glass had been charged and my safe return had been duly toasted, we all sat down.

'Right, said Paul, now tell us all about it ... no details spared.'

So, over the next half an hour or so, I related the whole horrible experience. When I got to the part about José González and the bar owner retracting their statements, Tracy squealed with delight, clapping her hands together.

'That's down to my Bruce' – she turned towards him – 'isn't it babe?'

'Aw, don't big it up, Trace ... I just had a little word, like,' he said.

An awful sinking feeling spread through my stomach. 'Bruce ... what did you do?'

'Aw, it was nothing really, I just paid the González brother and that weaselly little Pedro guy each a visit and asked them to reconsider what was in their statements.'

'Oh, Bruce ... you didn't threaten them did you? If Abascal finds out ...'

'Relax. I just leaned on them a bit, that's all ... just to make sure they were telling the truth.'

'But if they tell the police ...'

'They won't be telling no-one,' he said, tapping the side of his nose with his finger, his face breaking into that familiar, crooked smile.

I shook my head; the man was utterly incorrigible. 'Well if I'd known what you were planning I'd have said don't do it, but as it's turned out ... well, thanks.'

'Hey, what are friends for?' he laughed.

'The thing is,' I said, 'the fact that those two amended their statements in line with yours, Paul ... for which, by the way, I haven't yet had a chance to thank you' – Paul dipped his head in acknowledgement – 'may well have been the turning point in the investigation.'

'How so?' asked Paul.

I went on to explain how Abascal had been prompted by this turn of events to look harder for physical evidence, leading to the arrest of Julio Montoya.

'I never did like that sonofabitch,' declared Paul, 'but I didn't have him down as a potential murderer.'

'Me neither,' I agreed, 'but then I guess you never can tell.'

We all sat chatting for another hour or so, in the process consuming two more bottles of champagne, before Bruce stood up to signal that Donna and I needed some time alone.

He turned to Tracy. 'Come on babe, I expect Donna's dying to tell Roy all about the new baby.' Tracy stood up, wriggling her hips from side to side as she tried to smooth down her clingy micro-skirt, which, even after her best efforts, still displayed a vast expanse of thigh. 'Anyway,' he continued, giving Tracy a conspiratorial nudge, 'I expect they've got a bit of catching up to do in the old bedroom department, too.'

Her eyes widened and her mouth formed a large 'O'. 'Bruce!' she squealed. 'You can't say that.'

'Oh sorry,' he said, not looking at all sorry, 'but coming home to a tasty bird like Donna after a few days in the nick, well ...'

Tracy punched him, hard, on the shoulder; he seemed not to notice. Donna coloured up slightly but was clearly trying to stifle a laugh.

'Er, I think we had better be going too,' said Paul, dragging Kate to her feet.

'And us,' said Marion.

'Me too,' added Angelique. 'I am very glad you are 'ome safe, Roy.' She gave me a perfunctory kiss on the cheek.

'And I should be going too,' said Jim. 'I ... er, well, I'm glad it's all worked out OK in the end.'

Funny how these things go isn't it? One minute everyone's still there, chattering away, and then, once the first person makes a move to leave, it triggers a mass exodus.

'I'm sorry about Bruce,' I said to Donna as I shut the front door. 'He's just ... well, he's ... just Bruce.'

'Oh, I don't mind,' she said, unconsciously smoothing the side of her hair down with her hand. 'It's just his way of giving a compliment.'

'I suppose,' I said, laughing.

'Angelique was very quiet, though, wasn't she?' said Donna, giving a small, puzzled frown.

A dead weight descended in my gut. Did she suspect something?

'Er, was she? I hadn't really noticed,' I lied. 'Anyway,' I said, anxious to change the subject, 'these clothes are pretty rank. I need a long, hot bath and a change of clothes, and then you can tell me all about our new grandson.'

'Would you like me to join you?' she said, fluttering her eyelashes. 'I could scrub your back for you.'

Maybe Bruce had a point, after all.

Epilogue
Eight months later

Following Alfredo's brutal murder, his brother, José, had evidently lost the will to fight. He dropped the appeal against the court decision regarding the wall and paid the money which was due to us, including the cash-call which had been levied on all apartment owners but which Alfredo had previously refused to pay. Furthermore, he abandoned the court action which they had launched against us in respect of the obstruction caused while work was ongoing.

Julio Montoya, the builder, was charged with the murder of Alfredo González; the case was yet to be heard in court. With Julio facing a murder charge it fell to his brother, Ignacio, to take over the reins of his building company. Ignacio proved to be a very much more reasonable individual than his brother, and we negotiated with him a reasonable compromise on the disputed penalty clauses, which saw us receive some eighty percent of the discount which we had originally claimed.

All this went a long way towards restoring the community's financial health.

Sam, the security guard, was arrested by the police and charged with smuggling of drugs, tobacco, and alcohol; I had always had my suspicions about Sam but was never entirely sure. I don't believe Calvin was ever actively involved, but he must have known what was going on. Nevertheless, once Sam had gone, Calvin seemed to make a reasonable effort to step up to the plate. He would never be the best of security guards, but he was no longer terrified of confronting even the most minor incidents. We ended up hiring a replacement for Sam – who so far, seemed to be doing well – and giving Calvin another chance.

Angelique decided to move to England and go back to her ex-husband. Things had never been the same between us since that fateful night; somehow there never seemed to be an opportunity to talk about it and clear the air. I truly hoped that it would work out for her – and for Miriam – this time.

Paul and I decided that we had had enough. Since we had been elected, we had built the new wall, brought the acrimonious legal wrangle with the González brothers to a conclusion, and resolved a myriad other issues. Sure, there were still problems facing the community – there always would be – but things were in far better shape than when we had taken over. Nevertheless, after two years of constant battling, we both felt drained. We felt it was time to hand over the reins to others and finally have some time to enjoy our homes in the sun.

When I had sent out a newsletter, inviting applicants for the roles of president and vice president, the first person who had approached me was Joe Haven. Now he was undoubtedly well-qualified for the job of president but the story of his very public drunken row with the prostitute had apparently gone around the entire urbanisation and had rather damaged his credibility. He could not find anyone to stand with him as vice president.

We tried canvassing a few other owners who we felt might be suitable, but none were willing to put themselves forward for election. Just when we were about to give up and resign ourselves to having to serve for another year, a solution emerged from an unexpected quarter.

Robert Hultmann offered himself as a candidate for president, and, astonishingly, Bruce said he'd like to work with Robert as vice president. The owners' meeting, at which they were proposed for election, had been a lively affair, with a number of owners expressing doubts about this unlikely team, but when it was pointed out that no-one else seemed to be willing to volunteer, Robert and Bruce were duly elected.

They had been in their new roles for about six months now and, against many people's expectations, were doing a very good job. Weirdly, in spite of their very different personalities, they gelled perfectly as a team.

My ruminations were interrupted by Donna nudging me in the ribs. 'It's nearly time,' she whispered.

I looked up, shielding my eyes from the glare of the sun, glinting off the azure blue waters of the Mediterranean. The couple in front had their backs to me but only Bruce and Tracy could pull off a look like this on their wedding day. In spite of the sweltering heat, Bruce wore a closely-tailored, white, high-necked, Nero-style suit, the fabric stretched tightly across his massive shoulders. Tracy wore a very short, stretchy white skirt which clung closely to her shapely backside. Her tanned midriff was bare beneath a white crop-top encrusted with crystal highlights. Her white stilettoes had all but disappeared into the soft sand, but she valiantly kept them on anyway. Most endearingly 'Tracy' of all, was the white fascinator in her hair – a clear nod to the traditional white veil worn by brides throughout the ages at more conventional weddings.

'And now,' said the registrar, 'can I call upon the Best Man to come forward with the rings?'

I stood up and stepped forward, proffering the rings. Tracy treated me to a truly lovely smile while Bruce whispered, 'Thanks, mate.'

With my brief part in the ceremony accomplished, I returned to my seat, and to my reflections.

***

The sun was starting to sink behind the mountains now, and the guests were starting to drift away, but Bruce and Tracy were still circulating, laughing, handshaking, and kissing for all they were worth.

'What is it?' said Donna, squeezing my arm.

'What's what?'

'You've been miles away – what are you thinking about?'

'Oh, I don't know ... just thinking back over all the stuff that's happened during the last couple of years. I had no idea what I was taking on when I agreed to be president. And now ... well it feels almost like the end of an era. You know, in a funny sort of a way I'm almost starting to miss it. What am I going to do with my time now it's all over?'

'I know what you mean,' she said, laughing. 'You really couldn't make it up, could you? You know, you could write a book about it ...'

THE END

17615241R00201

Printed in Poland
by Amazon Fulfillment
Poland Sp. z o.o., Wrocław